THE NIGHT SEASON

Lost Tales from the Golden Age of Macabre

THE NIGHT SEASON

Lost Tales from the Golden Age of Macabre

EDITED AND WITH AN INTRODUCTION BY

DUANE PARSONS

WILDSIDE PRESS

This book is for Tara, Chloe and Ella.

Published by Wildside Press LLC.
www.wildsidebooks.com

CONTENTS

INTRODUCTION

No unseen hand guided me in the preparation of this small collection of stories, for the most part forgotten to literary history; although the spirits of the dead have made many a night full with their eerie tales, I was so shallow as to presume that anything they had to offer was a tale well-known to all, and long since deemed a classic; it was therefore rather a matter of good fortune's favor that led me to the deserted and generally neglected section of a library cellar where I chanced upon a fine collection of literary annuals from the 1840s. I will be forthright is saying that the greater part of the stories contained therein were indeed justly forgotten, but my attention yet quickly centered on a piece by an author I had never heard of: Henry Fothergill Chorely. It was "The Silent Man." I was much taken aback to find a story that might have been written by Poe or Hearn buried in such utter obscurity. Poe, in fact, I soon discovered, was an admirer of this now-unknown person and had once favorably reviewed his work. Why then was he so forgotten? The answer to that question was soon provided as a search of other stories by him revealed an author at times brilliant, at other times laughingly bad. He also wrote several novels and they too were of a decidedly uneven quality. Of these I will vouch only for "The Prodigy."

This led me not to any ready conclusion but rather to a still larger question: have we erred in considering the author as a hero of sorts? I recollected developing such sentiments regarding Ernest Hemingway during my youth, and expending unwarranted time in reading his complete works, many of which were not worthy of my time: "The Torrents of Spring," "The Green Hills of Africa," "Across the River and Into the Trees," and so on. It had thus become evident to me quite early in life that it is a mistake to assume that everything by a Great Author is indeed great literature. Now I was led to a comparable but somewhat different conjecture, a sort of mirror reflection of the first, one might say: if it may said that not everything by a author deemed great is great, then might the reverse not also hold true, and lead us to let fall into obscurity exceptionally fine writing, simply because the author only rarely—perhaps even only once—touched true greatness? What would happen if I reconfigured my favorite genre of literature—the macabre tales of the early 19th century—in terms of the writing, and not the writer? Was this single masterful tale by an otherwise mediocre writer really all that unique? Macabre had been a thriving genre for more than forty years; most of it consisted of short stories, of which the bulk that survives in our esteem is assigned to a mere handful of authors. What else was there, other than the stories of Poe, Hawthorne and a few others? What writers did they know, work with, and often admire?

I soon found myself poring through volume after volume of American and British literary journals of the period, and after two fruitful and fascinating years found I had amassed five full boxes of stories I felt worthy of being unearthed from this literary graveyard. The mass of material came to almost five hundred in number. It was indeed like robbing graves, to plunder these rich fields of forgotten genius. What follows is but a small selection of representative works, many by personal friends of Poe, and in a few cases by personal enemies. Some of the best pieces however were by authors for whom the tale included here was their only known foray into the macabre.

There is therefore a great variety to this selection, and it may be that the variety of style and subject is perhaps at times overwhelming, and that a multi-volume work is more in order than that which follows. And perhaps this is so; but such a consideration is dependent on how well this preliminary piece of literary archeology—grave-robbing, if you must!—is received. I conclude by casting a nocturnal glance about me, sensing in the shrouded corners a multiplicity of persons—a gathering of souls long gone from this particular level of human reality—all of whom now turn to me as their last hope for rescue from literary oblivion. I am honored to be their representative, in both deed and sentiment. If ever I should betroth a ghost it would surely be the elegant Emma Embury; and as to my old friend Mr. Chorely, he is always welcome as a guest in my home. As for the rest, time and space demand that I must bestow on them a collective expression of gratitude for their posthumous participation in this small endeavour of mine. I will simply bid them all a brief rest from these labors; and beg the reader's indulgence if I must speak for them all and say: enjoy these tales, and remember the hands that wrote them.

—Duane Parsons

THE SILENT MAN

BY HENRY FOTHERGILL CHORLEY

(1832)

There are periods in every man's life overcast with gloom and difficulty—when the day is full of trouble, and the dreams of the night of
disquiet; and when the pilgrim is ready to lie down with his burden and
die, because there is no hand to help him. Such a period in mine was
comprised in about fifteen months of the years 1793 and 1794, which I
spent in a large sea-port town in the north. I was then three and twenty;
and the concurrence of many perplexing and calamitous events cast upon
me on my entrance into life a load of care, from the pressure of which I
then thought it impossible that I should ever rise.

During the winter of 1793, I inhabited an ancient and deserted house
in the quieter part of town; its extensive suites of dim and decaying rooms
scantily furnished were not a residence calculated to restore a cheerful
tone to my spirits. The property had been suffered to fall to ruin; and
the conclusion of a long protracted law-suit was alone awaited, to level
the stately old mansion with the ground, and to dispose of the land on
which it stood for more profitable purposes. Behind it lay a melancholy
and weed-grown garden, shaded by large dingy elms and poplars; in the
centre of this was a stagnant fish-pond, flanked on one side by a ruinous
summer-house, on the other by the glassless frames of a conservatory.
Beyond this dismal spectacle was seen the taper spire of a church, and,
yet more dimly in the distance, cumbrous piles of warehouses, which
stood up in the busier parts of town; silent edifices of wealth and activity,
strangely contrasted with the desolation of the foreground.

I had sat, one night, poring over old papers, until the midnight chime
warned me up stairs to rest. I had chosen my sleeping room to the front; it
was small, but the better for that in a house where increase of space was
also increase of dreariness. The feet of my bed faced the window; and
close to my head was a door, which I could open and shut without rising.
For the further understanding of my scene, I must say that my room was
at the top of the principal staircase, which was lighted by an immense
Venetian window in the back of the house, the height of two stories.

On the night of which I speak, I suppose that I fell asleep soon after
I went to bed. I know that my dreams were of agony, for I woke with

a start, and found myself sitting upright, my forehead covered with a cold perspiration. As soon, however, as I became fully awake, I was surprised with an unusual appearance upon my glass which stood upon the table in the window. In the centre of its dark, oblong field there burned a small but intense spot of steady and living fire, irregular, but unchanging, in shape, and casting no glimmer on any surrounding object. In my first confusion, I was unable to reason upon what I saw; a second look convinced me that it must arise from the reflection of light through the keyhole of my chamber-door. At once it struck me that someone must be without; and, anxious to ascertain who it could be, and with what intent come thither, I sprang out of bed, and, after waiting an instant for sound or signal without, and hearing none, I threw the door open wide.

The sight which met my eye was sufficiently awful, though different from what my heated imagination had conjured up; being neither robber nor visitant of a more appalling character (for, be it known, my present residence was haunted). When I opened the door, a flood of light brighter than the blaze of noonday burst into the room, filling every remote corner, and showing every object without—the broken balustrade of the massy oak staircase, and the cobwebs on the large, round-headed window—with wonderful directness. The tops of the trees in the garden had caught the glow; the spire of the church seemed swathed in gold; and behind these, the cause of this illumination, a volume of brilliant, wreathing fire, overtopping the tallest buildings by a height equal to their own, rose silently into the sky, while above huge clouds of crimsoned smoke rolled heavily off in the north quarter of the heavens.

Every object in the immediate neighborhood of the scene of devastation was traced out with startling vividness: the groups of people on the tops of houses, sweeping to and fro, as small as pygmies; the ships in the river beyond were all clearly visible, and brought close to the eye. But to me the chief awe of this scene was its complete and unbroken silence. I was far too removed from it to hear the tumult in the streets, the hissing of the ascending flames, the cries of the helpless or the alarmed. The wind bore away in another direction the solemn toll of the fire-bell; and the whole scene, at that dead hour, wore the strange and awful guise of some show conjured up by a potent magician, it was so unlike any sight familiar to my previous experience.

After the silent gaze of a few instants, I dressed myself in haste; and, having called up my servant, and ordered him to sit up for me, I repaired as quickly as I could to that part of town where the conflagration was raging. It was nearly a mile from my house, but I needed no direction as to the precise spot, for crowds of awakened people were streaming thitherward from every quarter. Presently, as I advanced, their numbers became so dense as to make it a matter of some difficulty to proceed; and, long before I came within a stone's throw of the spot, all further progress was impossible. The building on fire was a huge distillery: and, as the stores of manufactured spirits were reached, one after the other, enormous jets of intense colorless flame burst perpendicularly upward—the night fortunately being still—while every instant the fall of some floor or chimney was succeeded by a flight of sparks; and the sullen roaring of triumphant element was heard in a deep undertone amid the shouts of the firemen and the murmurs of the vast concourse of spectators. To give a yet deeper interest to the scene, the two unhappy watchmen belonging in the premises had been seen to perish in the flames, the spread of which had been so rapid that all that could now be hoped for was to prevent their communicating with the surrounding streets. The fire had already destroyed a court of small houses in the immediate vicinity.

Anxious to approach as near as I possibly could, it occurred to me that I might perhaps effect my purpose through a quiet, narrow street, terminating only in a warehouse which stood almost immediately opposite to the burning pile. Through this there was a thoroughfare allowed by sufferance, and with all speed I made my way around thither, through a labyrinth of alleys, in my eagerness forgetting that this warehouse was enclosed in a court shut up by strong gates, which were not likely to be open during a time of such confusion. This I found to be the case: the building was an empty one, and seemed to be left to its fate; and I was turning away in disappointment, when my attention was arrested by the scene without, which was to me more impressive than any I had yet witnessed.

The street in question was one of those anomalies which are found in the densest hearts of large towns, being quiet, clean, and dull; and the houses, of antique fashion, had been obviously built for some class of people better than that by which they were now occupied. On the causeways and in the windows stood the scared inhabitants, looking upwards in silence; and every now and then some strong man appeared reeling under a load of bedding or furniture belonging to the poor families who had lived in the court close to the distillery, and, having been awakened to a sense of their danger only just in time to save their lives, had been able to rescue little of their property. It was a touching sight to examine one face after another and to read one strong prevailing emotion upon every countenance; and it was grievous to hear the wailings of the poor homeless creatures who had been kindly received in the different houses, many of whom had lost all that they were worth in the world, the hardily accumulated earnings of years.

Apart from these and close in the shadow of the courtyard wall at the end of the street, I presently discovered an old man sitting disconsolately on a pile of stones. He was neatly dressed, but bare-headed; and his white locks were long and few. Beside him was a large chest; and while everyone else seemed to have his counselor and comforter, this sufferer alone was neglected , if not shunned; and he looked as if rooted there in stupid despair, reckless as to what could now befall him, and neither soliciting nor receiving the assistance of anyone. There was a mixture of meekness and agony in his fixed gaze, and a listless indifference in his attitude that arrested my compassion at once; and I asked a respectable woman, who was standing on a step with a child in her arms, if she knew who he was, and why the same good offices that were extended to his neighbors were so pointedly withheld from him.

"Why, sir," she answered readily, "I should like to know who would dare to speak with him or offer him anything. He's unlucky."

"You mean that he is not in his right mind," said I.

"I do not know that," she replied, shaking her head oracularly. "He has lived in yonder court for these six and twenty years, and I do not think in that time he has said as many words to any of us—nobody but himself ever entered his house."

"What is his name?"

"He is called Graham, we believe," she said, "but we are not sure; no letters have come to him that we know of. He is well off in the world, for he does no work—and we are used to call him 'the Silent Man.' The children are afraid of him, though his custom was to go little abroad till it was dusk. He neither lends nor borrows, nor, so far as we have seen, goes to church."

"And what is to become of him now that his house is burned down? Is he to sit here in the cold all night? I will go—"

"Lord bless you, sir!" said the good dame, laying her hand upon my arm, "don't think of such a thing. Take care what you do; he will shift for himself somehow or other, I have no doubt." And when she saw that I was bent upon accosting this singular being, she turned away from me hastily, as if afraid to share in the peril which, as her speech implied, I should bring upon myself, by offering him any assistance.

But my resolution was taken. I went up to the subject of our discourse, and touched him lightly on the shoulder. It would seem that he had been in a reverie; for he started, and looked up suddenly, and I was anew struck by the singular cast of his face. "You seem cold, my friend," said I; "will you not come under shelter?" He made no answer, but shook his head.

"At least," persevered I, "you cannot intend to remain where you are—it will be your death. Will you come home with me for the night, if you have no further occasion to stay here? I cannot promise you good accommodation, but, at all events, warmth and shelter—or, do you wait for someone else to join you?"

He answered in a low voice, but it was the voice and with the accent of a gentleman, "No one."

"Well then," said I, "you had surely better accept my offer—or, can anything more be done for you here? Is this your property—" I hesitated as I spoke, for I imagined him to be stupefied by the extent of his calamity.

"Beside me," was his answer, pointing to the large chest.

"Then I beg you to make up your mind at once. It is far to go, it is true; but anything is better than staying here. Come—let me assist you to rise," said I, taking hold of his arm.

He arose mechanically, as though he only half comprehended my meaning. "I do not know," said he, in a bewildered manner, "but I suppose it is best. Thank you."

I could make little of these broken words, but the supposition that his intellects were disordered, or that he was depressed beyond the power of speech by the total want of sympathy which had been shown him. But the common duty of humanity was not to be misunderstood; and, after addressing to him one or two other questions, to which he seemed unable or unwilling to reply, I gave him my arm. He looked wistfully down upon the chest; it was large, but, upon attempting to raise it, I felt it to be so light that I almost thought it must be empty. So, without making any further difficulties, I took it under my other arm, and, covering his bare head with my hat, we walked away slowly through the wondering people, who gave way as we passed. I was in hopes that my companion was so much absorbed in his own feelings that he did not notice this new gesture of distrust.

I never felt so totally in the dark as to what I was doing at that moment. He could not or would not speak in answer to my further inquiries, but tottered on, leaning upon my arm. It was nearly an hour before we reached the old house; and he seemed on our arrival to be so much exhausted that I directed my servant to carry him upstairs and lay him upon my bed. I caused a fire to be lighted, and administered to him such cordials as were expedient, without any resistance on his part. The only sign of consciousness that he showed was suddenly rising up and looking round him; his eye lighted upon his chest, and then, as if he were satisfied that his treasure was safe, he sunk back, and in a few moments was quietly asleep.

For me sleep was out of the question. I sat by his bedside all night, wondering in what strange new adventure I had involved myself, and shaping a thousand conjectures as to what might happen next. My mysterious guest could hardly be a poor man, for his linen was beautifully fine, and he wore a delicate gold ring upon one of his attenuated fingers. He could—but it was useless; anything beyond the wildest castle-building was impossible. And, summoning a faithful physician and clergyman betimes in the morning, I detailed to them the chances which had burdened me with so singular an inmate. I introduced the physician into the old man's chamber; but to him as to myself was his behavior a riddle: he took no notice of what passed. The medical man pronounced it to be his judgement that the old man was suffering from exhaustion or abstinence, but that otherwise he had no symptom of disease upon him, and recommended me to allow him to lie still, and feed him as often as he would permit with nourishing food. The clergyman promised for our satisfaction to endeavor to collect some further particulars as to his history and habits in the neighborhood where he had resided; and they left me in as little comfortable state as may well be imagined.

I found no difficulty in following Dr. Richards' suggestions. The patient was passive, took whatever was offered to him, and seemed to doze almost all the day. I could not make up my mind to leave the house, and spent the greater part of my time in the stranger's chamber. Any attempt to engage him in conversation, or even to obtain an answer to a question, was in vain; and I can scarcely describe the strange uneasiness which I felt creeping over me when evening set in and my two friends had paid their unsatisfactory visit—I say unsatisfactory, because the physician was entirely at fault as to the state of the invalid, and the clergyman had been unable to discover anything beyond what I had heard on the previous evening. Either would have remained with me all night, but they were called to distant parts of the town by the imperative duties of their profession—and again I was left alone.

Some will, I am sure, comprehend the feeling of heart-sickness with which I took my seat by the fire. The night was wild and stormy, and I sat for two hours without speaking or moving. At length, to my great amazement, the current of my unpleasant thoughts was interrupted by the first spontaneous speech which my inexplicable guest had yet made. "Come hither," he said faintly.

I obeyed, and stood before his bedside, waiting for an instant to see whether he would speak again—but he was silent as before. I then said— "Can I do anything for you?"

"No," replied he promptly; "unless you will sit still, and listen to my story."

"Anything you wish," answered I eagerly, wondering what kind of communication I was about to hear.

"Well then," said he, raising himself up a little—"and yet I hardly know why even now I should recall the past. Yet I will once more before I go—and it may explain to you what you ought to know. You stepped forward to assist me when I was otherwise deserted, and I am not ungrateful. But I lose time; my tales is long, and I have far to go before midnight."

He paused; and I, taking advantage of the moment's silence, drew my chair close to his side; and, in the midst of a storm without, wilder than I have ever heard before or since, I listened to his story.

"I have no friend or relation in the world that I know of," said he. "I am the natural son of a nobleman—but he has long since been dead; and the title, with the estates, has passed to a distant branch of the family. From my cradle my fate was marked out to be a strange one. I was educated and pampered in my father's house till I was eighteen, without the remotest idea that I was not his legitimate heir. Then, when he married, the veil was torn off, the delusion dissipated, at a moment's warning. I was told of my origin, but not the name of my mother—and to this day I have no idea who she was. I fancied that she died in giving me birth—perhaps for her folly disowned by her relations, who scarcely ever heard of my existence. I was turned out of doors, with a caution that, if ever I ventured to appear in my father's presence again, or to bear his name, I should forfeit his favor towards me, which would otherwise be continued in the shape of a liberal annual allowance.

"I had always been on a delicate frame, with feeble spirits and an imaginative disposition, but with wilder thoughts and passions than ever I had dared to reveal. You may judge how such a message, coarsely delivered to me by my father's chaplain, a debauched old man, was likely to affect me. My father had never shown any love to me—but I loved, I depended upon, him. And now I remonstrated, I entreated, with all the eloquence of strong and indignant feelings. I begged for an interview with my unnatural parent; it was denied me, with words of opprobrium that are yet ringing in my ears. The curse of their bitterness has clung to me ever since. I left—I will not mention the name of my home—a being marked out for unhappiness—and felt, while I groaned under the load of my misery, that it was laid upon me for life.

"The world, however, was before me. I was well provided with money, young and handsome; and over the morbid sadness of my heart I threw so thick a mask of gaiety, that even I myself was at times deceived, and fancied that I was happy. I would not stay in England; but spent the next five years in exploring the continent. Italy, Germany, France, all became as homes to me. But I was alone: I had no friends, though many acquaintances; and when any one of these strove to approach nearer to the secrets of my heart than the common intercourse of society permits, he found himself repelled; and refrained from further endeavors, he scarcely knew why.

"I have no time to trace out the workings of feelings—I will only mention facts. When I was in Paris, in the year 17—, the talk of the circles was entirely of a celebrated Sybil, Madame de Villerac, a woman whose age, for she was known to be no longer young, had not impaired her wit and beauty. Her predictions were said to be astonishingly precise and correct; and she was consulted and believed in by the loftiest and wisest in the land, although there were some, of more scrupulous or timid spirits, who did not speak of her without a shudder. I was resolved to prove her skill. I was presented to her at a grand fete, given by the Spanish ambassador. She was certainly the most striking-looking woman I ever saw. I well remember her imposing appearance. She was seated at a card-table, dressed in rich black velvet, with one solitary feather waving across her brow. 'You can play at Ecarte,' said the Chevalier Fleuret to me, rising from his seat; and, after simply naming us to each other, he pointed to the vacant chair, and left us alone together. Before I had time to think, I was engaged in deep play with this extraordinary and commanding woman. But conversation presently stole in, and we slackened our attention to the game. She spoke with astonishing eloquence: our talk was of the world and its ways. Then I endeavored to lead it to topics of graver interest—the past and the future—and, half in badinage, half in earnest, I ventured to ask if there was really any virtue in cards to unravel the secrets of destiny. She smiled scornfully, and, looking me full in the face, asked me, in the most indifferent tone imaginable—'Shall I try?'

"Of course I answered in the affirmative.

"'Remember, then, Chevalier Graham,' replied she, 'that I am not answerable for what I shall find. Am I to tell you all the truth?'

"'All—every word.'

"'Once again I warn you—but I see it is thrown away. Here, then'— and I drew a card from her proffered handful. After some unintelligible ceremony, she spread them before her. For an instant she looked intensely serious—then, as if she were resolved to carry off the matter as a pleasantry—'Good and evil, as usual,' she said. "I am no prophetess to foretell unmingled fairy luck—what do you think of an heiress for a wife—if you are to die by her hand?'

"I half started up from my seat.

"'Now you look as much shocked,' said she, 'as if I were indeed an oracle. Nay, positively not a word more'—and as she spoke she fixed her eyes very pointedly on a remarkably handsome ruby ring which I wore.

"'I have been told,' said I, attempting to catch her tone, 'that the only way to confirm the good and undo the evil is to bind the Sybil in some charm. May it please you to wear this ring for me for seven years and a day, and then I shall hope to be safe—it is a talisman.'

"She took it carelessly, as a matter of course, and, placing it upon her finger, 'Come,' said she, 'we will join the company.'

* * * *

"Two years afterwards I was married to the most beautiful woman in Italy, after a week's acquaintance. I met her in Venice; and was completely dazzled by the fascinations, whether of personal beauty, or of the grace, wit, and elegance of her manners. She seemed, like myself, totally unconnected; but I asked no questions. I wore her chains; I laid myself at her feet, and was accepted. Known only as a passing stranger, I escaped all unmeaning congratulations; and, careless of the envy of unsuccessful rivals, I carried off my beautiful wife in triumph. I married her, literally, from the fancy of a moment. Nor did I discover, till some weeks after we were united, that I had fulfilled the first prediction, and that my wife was heiress to great wealth as well as the possessor of great beauty. 'I have kept this a secret,' said she, 'because I was resolved never to be wooed and won for my money.'

"This was plausible, but not true. On becoming gradually acquainted with Clementine's history, I found that she had in truth had few, if any, honorable suitors; and I was curious to discover what circumstances could have enabled me to distance all thousand of inamorati of Italy. Then she had accepted my devotions so readily, so eagerly! But my researches were in vain. There was a mystery about her not to be penetrated. I soon found that we were to be totally separate as far as the interests of the heart were concerned. What my wife's secret was I had not the remotest idea; but her love—I should have said her liking—for me waned daily. And erelong I felt a strange and indescribable distrust creeping over me, a sense that I was tied to one who might be said to have another existence, independent of aught that I knew. I foresaw that this state of things could not last, and went on, blindly, madly, to my own undoing.

"One evening, when we were sitting together, 'It is strange, my Clementina,' said I, 'that I do not yet know the name of your mother.' She had changed hers, I had been given to understand, in order to possess some property bequeathed to her upon that condition.

"'Do you think so?' she replied carelessly—and then, half rising from her couch and casting a piercing look upon me—'It is odd, too, that I forget the name of yours.'

"I was dumb, and changed the conversation. A few evenings after this, however, in passing through her dressing-room, when my wife had gone to a ball, I chanced to find her jewel-casket open. At the top of many ornaments lay a miniature. Good heaven!—and I recognized the original at once—the never-to-be-forgotten eye of pride, the stately brow, the rich, dark hair—and, to confirm my assurance, there were these words traced on the back—'Clementine de Villerac's last gift to her daughter'—and underneath, in a hand which I knew to be my wife's—'My mother died when I was seventeen'—so that I had married the daughter, the heiress, of that mysterious Sybil; while it was next to a certainty that others, knowing from whom she was descended, had been deterred from approaching her.

"I shut up my knowledge in my breast—but thenceforth my peace of mind was gone forever. Upon my gloomy and irritable temperament the possession of such a secret wrought me increasing agony. I struggled with the presentiments which it engendered: I tried reason—I tried religion, society, solitude, change of place, study—all would not do. And what was remarkable, during four years of conflict such as this, my wife never seemed to advert to what would have grieved and surprised any other woman. So long as she received her accustomed tribute of admiration, and we lived with the semblance of tolerable concord, she was content. I suppose that the privileges which a married woman enjoys were what she sought in accepting my hand, and, satisfied in the possession of these, she concerned herself no further.

"Each year widened this mutual estrangement of feeling. As Clementina's beauty waned—and it waned early—she seemed more covetous of homage, and to allow herself greater latitude of conduct than formerly, while the mantle of my spirit grew darker and darker day by day. The second part of my mother-in-law's prediction arose unceasingly to my recollection. We came to England; and here I perceived, with a sort of gloomy apathy, that Clementina's deviations from a correct demeanor became daily wider—that in fact she allowed the attentions of other men in an unsuitable degree. My own father was dead, having, on his death, left me a fortune equivalent to my former yearly income. I was still young, had unbroken health—and yet God knows how often I have stood at a window of our sumptuous house and envied the most miserable beggar, old, poverty-stricken, and diseased, that crawled past for his daily alms. I had lost what little relish I ever had for the common pleasures of life. Gaming was to me no excitement, music only a source of pain, and the mere animal enjoyment of bodily exercises a weariness. I resembled one of those unhappy beings of whom one has to read in the old records of superstition, who are bound by spells that they have no power to break, and whose lives are as a long and weary dream of dull misery.

"It was about this time, now thirty years ago, that the devotion of a certain Lord Mordown to my wife became so evident that I resolved to arouse myself while there was yet time. I remonstrated with her kindly, yet spiritedly; and she as usual made no answer. On the evening of the day when I mentioned this hateful subject to her, she repaired alone to a masquerade, where she met the nobleman in question. I learned in the course of the evening, no matter how, that it was necessary that I should take speedy measures in my own defense, if at all; and, revolving many plans in my mind, I sat, in an unwonted tumult of feeling, awaiting her return.

"She came home much earlier than usual. I ran to meet her, and handed her out of her carriage. I remarked an unusual paleness on her lip, an unusual tremor of hand. 'I am very ill,' she said, almost throwing herself into my arms. I led her upstairs in silence. She called her maid to undress her as speedily as she could. I suppose that the seeds of some malignant disease had been lying dormant in her constitution, and that the excitement and the heat of entertainment had suddenly riped them, for in another hour she was in a raging fever. I dismissed her attendants, resolving to watch her myself. She grew worse; and about two in the morning she was seized with violent delirium, and cried out for water.

"It was the work of some demon that the prediction never occurred to me so strongly as at that moment. Will you not turn me out from your shelter? I say that the horrid idea of contradicting my destiny possessed me—so that I sat still, and called for no help. Every servant slept in a different part of the house. I tell you I sat still, listening to her ravings, with unmoved ear and cool calculating brow. 'It will be daylight soon,' I said to myself, 'and the servants will be up, and will hear'—and the voice was urging me, close in mine ear, to break loose from the spell which had enchanted me for so long. I heard it say—'Thy fate is in thy power!' It tempted me again—I shuddered—a distant glimmer of dawn began to lighten the heavy sky—I went to my wife's bedside, and—it was the work of a moment—the next, she lay a corpse before me.

"From that hour I was mad. Days, months, years—but let me hasten to say what I most wish. When I was released from confinement as a convalescent, I bribed the sexton of the church in which she was buried to disinter for me the remains of my ill-starred Clementina. They have been beside me ever since as a penance, as a memorial. When I am gone, open yonder chest. You will find only a few bones and a little dust, which you will restore to consecrated ground, and writings which will put you in possession of a handsome fortune. I have nothing more..."

He stopped suddenly. I hastened to call for light, the candle having burnt out in the course of his story. I supposed that the narrator had failed from exhaustion: but, when my servant obeyed the summons and I approached the stranger's bed, I perceived he had expired.

THE STRANGE ORMONDS

BY LEITCH RITCHIE

(1833)

The above title will call up some curious, but indistinct recollections to the minds of many inhabitants of an extensive district in the north of England. The family, or rather the succession of individuals, who were known by no other designation than that of "the Strange Ormonds," were in their day and generation, the objects alternately of ridicule, suspicion, fear, and horror. The child still lives whose infancy was scarred by the ill-omened name; and the man of science can still remember the derisive curl of his lip, while it syllable the word;—but he will not dare to deny, that with derision there was at times mingled doubt, and that his eye, while it instinctively sought the recesses of his library, was lighted up for an instant with the same species of enthusiasm which guided the speculations of that singular race.

It is to accident that I am indebted for my knowledge of the little I do know on the subject. Dr. S—, of B—, was supposed to be the only person capable of un-riddling the mystery; but his obstinate silence, while it added fuel to the public curiosity, baffled it completely. That gentleman is now dead, and I see no good reason why I should conceal what he at length disclosed to me; indeed, I can assign no probable reason for his own secrecy, unless it were a fear of the world's ridicule. For my part, I have no feelings of the sort—and I profess myself to be in a state of a most unhappy ignorance on every subject not immediately connected with the Belles Lettres. Let it be remembered at the same time, that I only "say the tale as 'twas told to me." Dr. S—'s character, as a man of honor, will bear out it's truth with those who knew him; and those who did not, will, perhaps, be inclined to waive a part of their skepticism, on being informed, that the facts were communicated to me on the solemn and affecting occasion of the death of his only daughter, who had accompanied him in his interview with the last of the Ormonds, and whose early fate was usually attributed to that cause.

* * * *

The house occupied by the Ormands was situated about two miles from the small town of B—, at a short distance from the main road. As a tall building, it was distinguished only by its extreme irregularity, for whatever might have been its original form was entirely obscured by the various additions that had from that time been patched to it, apparently without view to a general plan. The odd shapes of these additions, constructed without the slightest regard to the usual arrangements of architecture, and the huddled appearance of the whole mass, gave it a very remarkable, though unsightly, aspect; and few travelers passed the road without inquiring whether they beheld a human dwelling, and if so, what were the names and avocations of its inhabitants.

The replies to such inquiries varied with the ages and dispositions of the informers—but in general they were dark and unsatisfactory. The house had been occupied, from a period as distant as the memory or traditions of the district extended, by a succession of individuals of the same name. An old female servant was the only inmate except for the proprietor, who himself lived in a peaceable seclusion for a length of time, varying from twenty to thirty years; and at his death, was instantaneously replaced by a successor, whose appearance was only known in the neighborhood by his attendance at church.

There was something singular even in this meagre outline; but when the picture was duly filled up with the suspicions and surmises of the narrator, it presented an appearance that made some smile—some shudder—and some cross themselves. It was averred that lights were seen in the house at all hours of the night; that smoke was detected issuing from many parts of the roof, besides its only legitimate channel, the chimney; and that strange noises were heard by the benighted hind, who had the misfortune to pass the place at an hour when all noises, except that of sleeping aloud, are deemed incongruous and equivocal. Besides these suspicious circumstances, the new heir was generally unlike his predecessor, and of an age too far advanced to admit the idea of his being the son of the latter; while his sudden avatar, independent, as it seemed, of the usual means and modes of traveling, was enough of itself to strike the observer with astonishment.

On these occasions—the death and accession of an Ormand—the whole countryside was in a state of ferment. In the more distant periods of society, when superstition held its sway over the higher as well as the lower classes, the popular excitation, encouraged by patrician wisdom, more than once threatened to annihilate the accursed race; and there is still in preservation a curious document, professing to be a petition to the government, for the removal of so pestilent a nest of sorcerers from a peaceable and religious neighborhood. Even the area of ground surrounding the house for a considerable space, felt the effects of its bad character; and a pond, or rather small lake in its vicinity known by the name of the Devil's Well, whose waters were as black as night from the shadow of the encompassing rocks,—and which, besides, lay under the imputation of being bottomless—was put under a ban, as the abode of denizens more unholy than trouts or perches. In later times a coroner's inquest was talked of, although I cannot find out upon what grounds, as the declining health of the Ormonds was perceived long before their demise. They attended church regularly; and for months before the mortal hour arrived, the process of decay was visible to every spectator. Although not one of them, in the calculation of human time, reached sixty years, the approaches of age were seen in distinct footsteps; week after week the hair grew whiter—the face more thin and sallow—and the step slower and feebler; then a Sunday would come without bringing its accustomed worshipper: then another would arrive, and present him tottering on his cane, and turning his drenched eyes in vain towards the symbols of his redemption; and on the next, a new face would be seen in the family pew of the Ormonds.

But time, which never deepens an impression, except in poetry—

'As streams their channels deeper wear—'

gradually softened the acerbity of public opinion, if it did not bring about an entire revolution. The calm deportment, unmeddling habits, and philosophic abstraction of Ormond, disarmed the suspicion of his neighbours, and almost won their respect. The shrewder part of the young, who were in want of a patron or legacy, moved their hats to him as he passed, or picked up his cane when he let it fall; overtures (always rejected, however), were made to him by the fathers upon the subject of neighbourly communication; and at last, spinsters, trembling on the very verge of forty, would begin to wonder whether the man were married. The more adventurous of the boys, in process of time, even sought the haunted well for the purpose of angling; and their mothers although shaking their heads at their sons' temerity, would not refuse to dress the spoil, and in some instances were even prevailed on to eat of the fish, which in their own time, had borne so equivocal a character.

Matters had assumed this placable aspect at the time my story refers to; but the Ormond of that period did not seem destined to enjoy long the benefit of his neighbour's moderation. His health began seriously to decline; and the appearance of old age fell with a spectred suddenness on its usual prey, a broken constitution. Week after week he dragged his emaciated form to the house of God; and very week, although lighter in itself, it was the heavier for him to drag; his eyes, formerly bright and burning, became dim and spiritless—his hand shook as it undid the clasp of the prayer-book—his voice was thin and broken, and his step feeble and unsteady: he was dying. In common cases the tongue of malice is mute, the finger of scorn dropped, and the frown of hatred relaxed in the presence of Death; but this was the precise period when the operation of all three,—and of fifty other base and foolish passions,—was commonly directed against the ill-fated representative of "The Strange Ormonds." Every forgotten story that superstition had imagined, and bigotry believed, was drawn up in dreadful array against him; and although among the better-informed classes, compassion for the forlorn and deserted condition of the dying man, might have been the more powerful feeling; yet the old leaven of evil predominated as usual in the feelings of the mass. Dr. S— had watched with medical curiosity and interest his singularly rapid decay; and being of the number of those whose curiosity was blended with compassion, he resolved, about the time when he thought the last sands of fate were almost run, to venture of a visit of mercy, and smooth, since he could not retard, his passage to the grave. "Come Emily," said he one day, pushing the decanter away from him, after dinner; "the poor old man must not die without somebody to wet his lips and smooth his pillow: the sight will do you no harm, and the lesson it conveys may do you good; besides, a woman never looks so well—not at the most splendid ball—not on her wedding day, all smiles and tears and blushes, as by the bedside of the sick or dying, ministering with a tender and skillful hand to their necessities, and whispering love and comfort to their souls." Miss S—'s heart and imagination were touched by the picture which her father had intentionally presented; and conquering the more easily her natural timidity, she threw her shawl over her shoulders and putting her arm within his, they sallied forth in a gloomy November afternoon, on a visit in which even curiosity looked amiable, being gracefully enveloped in the mantle of charity.

Having reached the narrow avenue leading to the house, choked up by a self-planted colony of weeds, which the infrequent footstep of man had been unable to subdue, they looked round on such a scene of neglect and desolation as only a newly discovered country could present, or an old one after the moral cycle had gone round, which returned it to second barbarism. Stumbling among heaps of stones and withered branches, and entangled in mazes of weeds and bushes, they at length reached the door, and knocked for admittance. They waited for some time in silence, and almost in darkness, but no sound answered their demand: it seemed as if it were already the house of the dead; and the chill breath of evening, as it sighed through the wilderness around, although it broke the silence, added to the sepulchral horror of the scene.

The noise of a door opening was now heard at some distance in the interior of the building, and a sound followed, resembling the hissing of a cauldron when it boils. The visitors knocked again, and in a few seconds a window was raised, and the old female domestic inquired, in a sharp and cracked voice, what was their business. Dr. S— replied by the usual question—"Is your master at home?"

"My master at home!" shrieked the sybil, in a tone of the utmost astonishment; "you are the first one that has asked that question in my time; and were it only from curiosity to see what you are like, I would almost be tempted to take the trouble of opening the door—and what should hinder, if it likes me? If the house of the Ormonds could ever be without a master, this is surely the interregnum." But as she ran on mumbling in this manner, with all the garrulity of age, an expression of malice crossed her withered features, and reverting to the question,—

"Home!" he demanded urgently—"is Ormond home?" She in sharper tone—"No, not yet, but he is fast posting—he has reached his threshold—his hand is on the latch—and, by my sooth, a hot and hearty welcome he will get!" Dr. S—, somewhat shocked by an allusion he could not misunderstand, ordered her in a peremptory tone to open the door, adding, that understanding her master was unwell, he had called, as a neighbor and a medical man, to offer his assistance.

He had no sooner spoken the words, than the door suddenly and noiselessly opened, and a man, who had apparently been listening to the dialogue, seizing hold of the visitor's arm, literally dragged him into the house. "If you be a medical man," said he, 'come in, in the name of heaven! Save his life," he continued; "save his life but for one hour, and I will make you rich. Rich!" he added with emphasis, pressing the arm he still held with a skeleton grip, as he repeated the argument *ad hominem*. Miss S— followed them up the narrow staircase, and in another minute, the whole party was in the invalid's room.

A single glance was sufficient to convince them that assistance came too late. Ormond was sitting in an armchair, his head reclining on the back, his hands hanging lifeless by his sides, his eyes fixed and glazed, and his shrunk face covered with the waxy hue of death. Their conductor was apparently a much younger man, probably not more than thirty-five; he was tall and well-formed, but stooped much: his dress consisted of a jacket and trousers, the former without sleeves, and his bony arms were naked to the shoulders. And the circumstance of his face and hands being daubed with soot, might have given him the appearance of some inferior Vulcan of a smithy, had it not been for a redeeming expression of mental superiority in his countenance, indicated chiefly by a very commanding forehead, and remarkably bright and searching eyes.

He stood for some moments in the middle of the room, gazing on the strangers with a bewildered air, like one altogether unused to the presence of his kind. The graceful and feminine form of the young lady seemed in particular to attract his admiration, and when she had drawn off her glove, he touched her hand, as one would examine a bauble, leaving on the fair skin the marks of his own sooty fingers, while his eyes became radiant with almost boyish delight. Starting suddenly, however, he turned away, and approached the chair of the invalid, where Dr. S—, assisted by the old woman, was engaged in the few offices of kindness which his situation required or admitted of.

"Make haste!" said the dying man, with a feeble gesture of impatience, as he recognized his apprentice.

"It is impossible," replied the other; "you *must* live for at least half an hour! But I will go and try again."

"Then I *will* live!" said Ormond; but a rattling noise in his throat interrupted his words, and gave the lie to his assertion.

"Is it fair," he continued with renewed energy, 'that after a whole lifetime of labor, I should be half an hour late for my reward?"

"Hush, master dear!" said the comforting beldame, in a low, hypocritical whine. "Remember that a better man than you—aye, the beginner of you all—was three centuries too soon for his reward; be thankful for the length you have gone, and die in peace."

"Hag!" said Ormond, with the feeble fury of the dying; "I tell you I will not die; no, not till I please—not till it wills me to let forth the spirit!" Then, in the frenzy which sometimes precedes dissolution, he imagined Dr. S— to be, in real and palpable presence, that inevitable enemy, whom he dreaded and defied; and springing from his chair with the last effort of departing life, he grappled at his throat. "I will not die!" he shrieked: "You have no power; do you not know me? I am Ormond—the foe of Death, destined before the foundations of the world, to trample on and subdue him!" Then, feeling his strength departing, his defiance was changed into supplication, and he implored piteously the grace of one half hour.

At this instant a rushing noise was heard without, and the apprentice burst into the room, his long dark hair floating back over his forehead, his frame filled with an elasticity which gave his motion the appearance of flying; and a whole bonfire of triumph in his eyes. "Oh, save me!" cried the old man, as the hand of death relaxed his hold. "Die!" said the apprentice-heir, throwing him back violently into the seat—and with a deep suspiration Ormond yielded up the ghost.

Surprised and shocked at this extraordinary scene, Dr. S— and his daughter looked on in silence, and almost in consternation. The apprentice had already left the apartment, and the old woman, lifting up her master's body, laid it on a table in the middle of the room, and without removing the dress, employed herself busily in closing the eyes and stretching the limbs, which gradually stiffened into the rigidity of death. She then lighted a number of candles, which were in sconces around the room, till it became as clear as day. The apprentice—or rather, the new Ormond—now reappeared, carrying a salver, apparently of massive gold, supporting a covered goblet of the same metal, and a large syringe. His appearance was the same as before, and joy and triumph still burned in his eyes.

On uncovering the goblet, a thick black vapor escaped, and a sweet but faint smell was perceived. Having filled the syringe, he raised the head of the corpse and injected the contents of the instrument into its mouth; and having repeated this operation three times, he then bathed the eyes with the same liquid.

Some minutes ensued, during which no sound or motion was heard in the room, save the trembling of the operator, whose whole frame was shaken in the intensity of expectation. At length he clasped his hands and uttered a cry of joy. The wax-like hue of death disappeared from the face of the corpse, and the glow of life returned; the wrinkles of care were smoothed, and the furrows of time filled up; the white lips became red, and the grey hair black; and, as if by enchantment, the countenance of the dead was once more the home of youth and manly beauty! Is it the breath of life which inflates the chest? Is it an act of the living will that raises the hand—unveils the eye—and opens the lips? God knows. The hand drops, the eye closes, and the lips are again sealed—and forever.

A dark vapor was perceived rising from the body, which instantaneously assumed the discolored appearance which sometimes attends death by poison; in another moment; in another moment a small blue light was observed issuing from the mouth and nostrils, and speedily the whole corpse was in flames.

Miss S—, at this dreadful spectacle, rendered more appalling by the motion of the cracking skin and shrinking sinews which gave an appearance of life to the burning body, fainted into the arms of her father, who, as he carried her out of the house, heard the despairing shriek of the new Ormond at this conclusion to his hard apprenticeship, and the transmitted labors of three hundred years; and the sound seemed like a death-cry smothered in the blood of the victims. In a few minutes the whole house was on fire, and the neighbors crowded to the spot. The flames were seen of different colors in different parts of the building; and small quantities of combustible material successively exploded as the fire reached them, like the minute guns of a wreck at sea. A human form was seen flitting from place to place amidst the conflagration, not to save, but to destroy;

and when all was consumed, it was observed moving with supernatural swiftness towards the rocks which overhung the Devil's Well.

This was conjectured to be the last of the Ormonds; and the next morning every search that humanity could suggest was made for him; the rocks were examined—the woods—the glens; the lake, at length, was dragged—and all in vain—

> *Days flowed days—moons rolled on moons away*
> *But Conrad comes not—came not since that day.*

THE MYSTERIOUS WEDDING:
A DANISH STORY

BY HEINRICH STEFFANS

(1847)

In the north-west of Zealand stretches a small fertile peninsula, studded with hamlets, and connected with the mainland by a narrow strip of waste ground. Beyond the only town which this little peninsula possesses, the land runs out into the gloomy Cattegat, and presents an awfully wild and sterile appearance. The living sands have here obliterated every trace of vegetation; and the hurricanes which blow from all points of the ocean are constantly operating a change on the fluctuating surface of the desert, whose hills of sand rise and fall with a motion as incessant as that of the waves which roll around them. In traveling through this country, I spent upwards of an hour in this district, and never shall I forget the impression which the scene made upon my mind.

While riding along through the desolate region, a thunderstorm rose over the ocean towards the north—the waves roared—the clouds scudded along in gloomy masses before the wind—the sky grew every instant more dark, "menacing earth and sea"—the sand began to move in increasing volumes under my horse's feet, a whirlwind arose and filled the atmosphere with dust, the traces of the path became invisible—while air, earth, and ocean seemed mingled and blended together, every object being involved in a cloud of dust and vapor. I could not discern the slightest trace of life or vegetation around the dismal scene—the storm roared above me—the waves of the sea lashed mournfully against the shore—the thunder rolled in the distance—and scarcely could the lurid lightning-flash pierce the heavy cloud of sand which whirled around me. My danger became evident and extreme; but a sudden shower of rain laid the sand, and enabled me to push my way to the little town. The storm I had just encountered was a horrid mingling of all elements. An earthquake has been described as the sigh which troubled nature heaves from the depth of her bosom; perhaps not more fancifully might this chaotic tempest have typified the confusion of a widely distracted mind, to which pleasure and even hope itself have been long strangers—the cheerless desert of the past revealing only remorse and grief—the voice of conscience threatened like the thunder, and her awful anticipations casting a lurid light over the gloomy spirit—till at last the long-sealed-up sources of tears open away for their floods, and bury the anguish of the distracted soul beneath their waves.

In this desolate country there existed in former times a village called Roerwig, about a mile distant from the shore. The moving sands have now buried the village; and the descendants of its inhabitants—mostly shepherds and fishermen—have moved their cottages close to the shore. A single solitary building, situated upon a hill, yet rears its head above the cheerless shifting desert. This building—and the village church—was the scene of the following mysterious transaction:

In an early year of the last century, the venerable cure of Roerwig was one night seated in his study, absorbed in pious meditations. His house lay at the extremity of the village, and the simple manners of the inhabitants were so little tinged with distrust, that bolts and locks were unknown among them, and every door remained open and unguarded.

The lamp burned gloomily, and the sullen silence of the midnight hour was only interrupted by the rushing noise of the sea, on whose waves the pale moon shone reflected, when the cure heard the door below opened, and the next moment the sound of men's steps on the stair. He was anticipating a call to administer the last offices of religion to some parishioners on the point of death, when two foreigners, wrapped up in white cloaks, entered the room. One of them, approaching, addressed him with politeness: "Sir you will have the goodness to follow us instantly. You must perform a marriage ceremony; the bride and bridegroom are already waiting your arrival at the church. And this sum,"—here the stranger held out a purse full of gold—"will sufficiently recompense you for your trouble, and the alarm our sudden demand has given you."

The cure stared in mute terror upon the strangers, who seemed to carry something fearful, almost ghastly, in their looks, and the demand was repeated in an earnest and authoritative tone. When the old man had recovered from his surprise, he began mildly to represent that his duty did not allow him to celebrate so solemn a rite without some knowledge of the parties, and the intervention of those formalities required by law. The other stranger here-upon stepped forward in a menacing attitude; "Sir," said he, "you have your choice; follow us and take the sum we now offer you—or remain, and this bullet goes through your head." Whilst speaking, he leveled his pistol at the forehead of the venerable man, and coolly waited his answer; whereupon the cure rose, dressed himself, and informed his visitants—who had hitherto spoken Danish, but with a foreign accent—that he was ready to accompany them.

The mysterious stranger now proceeded silently through the village, followed by the clergyman. It was a dark autumn night, the moon having set; but when they emerged from the village, the old man perceived with terror and astonishment, that the distant church was all illumined. Meanwhile his companions, wrapped up in their white cloaks, strode hastily on before them through the barren plain. On reaching the church they bound up his eyes; he then heard a side door open with a well-known creaking noise, and felt himself violently pushed into a crowd of people whose murmuring he heard all around him, while close beside him some persons carried on a conversation in a language unknown to him, but which he thought was Russian. As he stood helpless and blindfolded, he felt himself seized by a man's hand, and drawn violently through the crowd. At last the bandage was removed from his eyes, and he found himself standing with one of the two strangers before the altar. A row of large tapers, in magnificent silver candlesticks, adorned the altar, and the church itself was splendidly lighted by a profusion of candles. The deepest silence now reigned through the whole building, though the side passages and all the seats were crowded to excess; but the middle passage was quite clear, and he perceived in it a newly dug grave, with the stone which had covered it leaning against a bench. Around him were only male figures, but on one of the distant benches he thought he perceived a female form. The terrible silence lasted for some minutes, during which not a motion could be detected in the vast assembly. Thus when the mind is bent on deeds of darkness, a silent gloomy brooding of soul often precedes the commission of the horrid action.

At last a man, whose magnificent dress distinguished him from all the rest, and bespoke his elevated rank, rose and walked hastily up to the altar; as he passed along, his steps resounded through the building, and every eye was turned upon him; he appeared to be of middle stature, with broad shoulders and strong limbs—his gait was commanding, his complexion of a yellowish brown, and his hair raven black—his features were severe, and his lips compressed as if in wrath—a bold aquiline nose heightened the haughty appearance of his countenance, and dark shaggy brows lowered over his fiery eyes. He wore a green coat, with broad gold braids, and a brilliant star. The bride, who also approached, and kneeled beside him at the altar, was magnificently dressed. A sky blue rose, richly trimmed with silver, enveloped her slender limbs and floated in large folds over her graceful form—a diadem sparkling with diamonds, adorned her fair hair—the utmost loveliness and beauty might be traced in her features, although despair now expressed itself in them—her cheeks were pale as those of a corpse—her features unanimated—her lips were blanched, her eyes dimmed—and her arms hung motionless at her side as she kneeled before the altar; terror seemed to have wrapped her consciousness as well as her vital powers in deep lethargy.

The cure now discovered near him an old ugly hag, in a parti-colored dress, with a blood-red turban on her head, who stood gazing with an expression of malignant fury on the kneeling bride; and behind the bridegroom, he noticed a man of gigantic size and a gloomy appearance, whose eyes were fixed immovably on the ground.

Horror-struck by the scene before him, the priest stood mute for some time, till a thrilling look from the bridegroom reminded him of the ceremony he had come hither to perform. But the uncertainty whether the couple he was about to marry understood his language, afforded him a fresh source of uneasiness. He ventured, however, to ask the bridegroom for his name and that of his bride! "Neander and Feodora," was the answer returned in a rough voice.

The priest now began to read the ritual in faltering accents, frequently stopping to repeat the words, without however either the bride or bridegroom appearing to observe his confusion, which confirmed him in the conjecture that his language was almost unknown to either of them. On putting the question, "Neander, wilt thou have this woman for thy wedded wife?" he doubted he would receive any answer; but to his astonishment, the bridegroom answered in the affirmative with a loud and almost screaming voice, which rung throughout the church, while deep sighs were heard from every quarter of the building, and a silent quivering like the reflection of distant lightning, threw a transitory motion over the deathly pale features of the bride. When the priest turned to her with the interrogatory: "Feodora, wilt thou have this man for thy wedded husband?" the lifeless form before him seemed to awake, a deep convulsive throb of terror trembled on her cheeks—her pale lips quivered—a passing gleam of fire shone in her eye—her breast heaved—a violent gush of tears flooded the brilliance of her eyes, and the "yes" was pronounced like the scream of anguish uttered by a dying person, and seemed to find a deep echo in the sounds of grief which burst from the surrounding multitude. The bride then sank into the arms of the horrid old hag, and after some minutes had passed in awful silence, the pale corpse-like female kneeled again, as if in a deep trance, and the ceremony was finished. The bridegroom now rose and led away the trembling bride, followed by the tall man and old woman; and two strangers then appeared again, and having bound the priest's eyes, drew him with violence through the crowd, and pushed him out at the door, which they bolted from within.

For some minutes the old man stood endeavoring to recollect himself, and uncertain whether the horrid scene, with all the ghastly attendant circumstances, might not have been a dream; but when he had torn the bandage from his eyes, and saw the illuminated church before him, and heard the murmuring of the crowd, he was forced to believe its reality. To learn the issue, he hid himself in the corner of the building, and while listening there he heard the murmuring within grow louder and louder—then it seemed as if a fierce altercation arose, in which he thought he could recognize the rough voice of the bridegroom commanding silence—a long pause followed—a shot fell—the shriek of a female voice was heard, which was succeeded by another pause—then followed a sound of pickaxes, which lasted about a quarter of an hour, after which the candles were extinguished, the door was flung open, and a multitude of persons rushed out of the church, and ran toward the sea.

The old priest now arose from his hiding place, and hastened back to the village, where he awoke his neighbors and friends, and related to them his incredible and marvelous adventure; but everything which had hitherto fallen out among those simple people, had been so calm and tranquil, so much measured by the laws of daily routine, that they were seized with a very different alarm; they believed that some unfortunate accident had deranged the intellects of their beloved pastor, and it was not without difficulty that he prevailed on some of them to follow him to the church, provided with picks and spades.

Meanwhile the morning had dawned, the sun arose, and as the priest and his companions ascended the hill toward the church, they saw a man-of-war standing off from the shore under full sail toward the north. So surprising a sight in this remote district, made his companions already hesitate to reject his story as improbable and still more were they inclined to listen to him when they saw that the side door of the church had been violently burst open. They entered, full of expectation, and the priest showed them the grave which he had seen opened in the night time; it was evident that the stone had been lifted up and replaced again. They therefore put their implements in motion, and soon came to a new and richly adorned coffin, in which lay the murdered bride—a bullet had pierced her right breast to the heart—the magnificent diadem which she had worn at the altar, no longer adorned her brows, but the distracted expression of deep grief had vanished from her countenance, and a heavenly calm seemed spread over her features. The old man threw himself down on his knees near the coffin, and wept and prayed aloud for the soul of the dead, while mute astonishment and horror seized his companions.

The clergyman found himself obliged to make this event instantly known, with all its circumstances, to his superior, the Bishop of Zealand; meanwhile, until he got further instructions from Copenhagen, he bound all his friends to secrecy by an oath. Shortly afterward a person of high rank suddenly arrived from the capital; he inquired into all the circumstances, visited the grave, commended the silence which had been hitherto observed, and stated that the whole event must remain forever a secret, threatening, at the same time, with a severe punishment any person who should dare to speak of it.

At the death of the priest, a writing was found in the parochial register narrating this event; some believed that it might have some secret connexion with the violent political changes which occurred in Russia, after the death of Catherine and Peter I; but to resolve the deep riddle of this mysterious affair will ever be a difficult, if not impossible task.

THE BURIAL BY FIRE

BY LOUISA MEDINA HAMBLIN

(1838)

"Will you not walk this gloomy evening? Come, the air is as soft as balm, and the sunset on the sea will be beautiful. The afternoon worship is over, and all the villagers are out in their Sunday clothes adoring their creator in his works. Come, my own Mary, and enjoy the beauty of the evening."

It was on a summer's Sabbath, in the beautiful neighborhood of Hastings, that William Lindsay spoke thus to Mary Stuart, a fair young girl who was his promised wife, when success in his toilsome profession might give sanction to the union. He was an artist of much talent but little celebrity, and she was the orphan child of a British officer. Her mother and herself lived in quiet contentment on the small pension allowed to the widow of a captain of Infantry. Their ways were simple—their wants were few—from their little, they had still a little to spare to such as needed, and they felt themselves

"Passing rich on forty pounds a year."

If the want of wealth ever caused a sigh in the gentle bosom of Mary, it was when she beheld her William debarred from the foreign treasures of art which he panted to behold, or when she heard her prudent mother prophesy a long lapse of years ere they might venture to unite their earthly fate together. Mary had received a tolerable education, and her mind was naturally poetic, her thoughts were fraught with natural beauty and often untutored language would flow in rich and melodious eloquence; she was never of a buoyant temper: a placid calmness, a softened serenity which was not sadness, was her usual mood, and the very style of her features harmonized with this shadowed feeling. Her cheek was very fair, but when a chance excitement called the eloquent blood into it, the color was rather the blush of hectic than the crimson of health; her hair was a pale brown but perfectly straight, and without any of those sunlight hues which sometimes wander through chestnut tresses—in a word, Mary was more a lovely twilight than a brilliant day. Captain Stuart had died of decline, not as they fondly believed a constitutional malady, but brought on by over-exertion and exposure; still, when William would notice the translucent fairness of his Mary's cheek, and mark the languid softness of her eye, a terrible fear would come across his heart, to be as instantly banished by the certainty of her perfect health.

She arose in answer to his invitation to walk and, with a gentle smile, passed her arm through his and strolled up the hill which bounded their dwelling. William had truly said that the evening was beautiful—not a breath of air was stirring, but the atmosphere was soft and redolent of perfume. The rays of the declining sun, slanting from the west, tessellated the heavens with chequers of gold and lengthened the shadows upon the earth—not a ripple stirred the mighty ocean, the vast expanse of blue water lying unruffled as a lake, without a sound save when the receding tide carried with it the pebbles from the beach with a lulled and dreamy sound. The lowing of the cattle in the distant pastures and the chirping of the nimble grasshoppers joined to an occasional twittering from the inhabitants of the trees, all contributed to produce that feeling of repose which the night always induces. Almost insensibly, the lovers turned away from the groups of merry villagers, and directed their course to the village churchyard. Of all spots on earth, that containing the "short and simple annals of the poor," is to a reflective mind most interesting, and that of Hastings is peculiarly so. From its mild and sheltered situation, its advantages of country joined to those of sea bathing, Hastings is recommended by the faculty to consumptive patients, and many a marble slab in the churchyard records the early exit of creatures in the spring and matin of their days, who have sought for health and found a grave. On one which this simple inscription,

"EMILY MARKHAM—AGED NINETEEN,"

Mary sat down, and pulling a few wild flowers, strewed them reverentially on the grave.

"William," at last she said, "burial is a frightful thing."

"Death is, do you mean, my Mary?" answered he; "for after death, on this earth feeling is no more."

"Are you assured of that?" asked Mary solemnly. "Does that conviction bear an *if*? Oh, God! To be shut down, away from light and warmth, to be straightened here, rigid, immoveable and stiff—to rot by scarce perceptible degrees, to have the flesh which in life we guard so carefully, mangled and gnawed by crawling vermin—nay, in our very selves to engender the foul life of corruption! It is too horrible!"

"Dearest Mary, this is a morbid feeling and a false fear. Our Creator made man in mercy, and could it be possible that the dead suffered by burial, it would long have been made manifest to the living. Now, for my part, this scene is one to me of rest and comfort—in this sacred spot the dead slumber in peace, the flowers grow here as sweet, and those graceful willows bend down their branches as if appointed by the Spirit of Holiness to guard the dead. And see—the evening star looks out upon this tranquil spot like a good angel calmly keeping

'Watch o'er them till their souls should waken.'"

Mary shuddered and shook her head. Alarmed to see her so depressed, William fondly urged her to return home.

"William, dear William, I am well—fear nothing for me, but oh! My beloved, my heart quails at the thought of burial. I do not fear to die— thanks be to heaven I have no fear of death; but the grave—the grave to me is overwhelmingly horrible. Oh, dear William! Would that we lived in ancient Rome, where the mortal remains were consigned to the funeral pyre! Surely we have decreased in civilization to relinquish the burial by fire for the internment underground. Fire is a glorious element, free, mighty and immaterial as the soul! Fire is a purifier, and separates the grosser clay from its immortal spirit—fire even ascends to heaven—it is a type and emblem of the human soul, it is tangible to the senses only while it has earthly food, when the poor material is consumed, the invisible and unknown spirit passes away from human sight or knowledge, and returns to Him, the master of the elements! Would that my burial might be by fire!"

"Your thoughts and wishes are strange, dear Mary; the survivor's heart would be more wrung to see the loved remains consumed by fire. When buried, they retain at least a knowledge that it is there, they can visit the spot and in memory recall its inhabitant."

"Aye, William—*but as what?*" she asked, with a strange look of excessive horror: "As what? A livid and loathsome mass of rottenness! A decaying, revolting, putrifying corruption, from which every sense recoils in loathing! Let the fondest love pursue in fancy the buried dead— the lips they kissed are foul with decay—the breath that used to part them is changed to the stench of rottenness—the fair bosom on which lay the loving head is alive indeed, for the long, slimy grave worms are feeding on it—the eyes, oh, God! Dare imagination picture that eye once beaming with the soul of love, now glowing with the unnatural fire of putrefaction?"

"No more, no more, dear Mary!" exclaimed William, alarmed at the excitement of her fancy on such a theme: "your mother will be waiting for us."

"Yet hear me out dearest; and oh, William, promise—promise me, that if God takes me from you, you will never lay me in the damp, cold ground to rot!—Think, oh, think how pure, how beautiful is the idea of resolving back each portion of our humanity into its native element! And then, how delightedly may fond affection weep over the consecrated ashes! The pure, inoffensive remains of all that was loved and lovely— while fancy dwells with rapture on the bright thought that the undying soul, the immortal mind, has mounted to its *first essence* on wings of ethereal flame! Come, let us go home. I shudder to tread this rank, rich soil, instinct with human corruption."

* * * *

From this time it appeared that the health of Mary Stuart suffered under some secret excitement; at times, indeed, her cheerfulness would return, and the awful phantom that haunted her be put to flight by the voice of love; but too soon again the gloom returned over her soul, and by slow but sure degrees undermined her health and life. No words can picture the grief which wrung the honest heart of her lover, argument and caresses he tried in vain, and at last, believing that the coil lay in her body not her mind, he applied in despair to a friendly physician of eminence who resided in the neighborhood. Happy it is for science when such a man as Doctor John Burton is its professor; learned without pedantry; humane without ostentation; firm without brutality, he joined the skill of the best physicians to the feelings of the kindest of men; he saw Mary Stuart and at once pronounced her case to be *monomania*—that sort of "perilous stuff which weighs upon the heart," and for which drugs have no healing and medical science no cure.

"You must take her from here," he said gently but firmly to her mother. "She is of a morbid temperament, and the close retirement of her life together with the vicinity of the churchyard has aided a predisposition to nervous excitement. She must have a change of scene."

"Alas, sir!" replied the mother, in tears, "I have not the power, my means are scanty—this little cottage is allowed us rent-free by the landlord, who was a dear friend of my husband—a single journey and moth's residence in a strange city would consume all we have to live on for a year."

Doctor Burton was not one of those Sir Oracles who content themselves by saying, "this must be done," without endeavoring to point out the way how; he smiled benevolently and took the widow's hand—

"Mrs. Stuart, I venture to predict a certain cure, if you will follow a pleasant and easy prescription, for your daughter; you must marry her at once to William Lindsay. Nothing so sure to chase ideas of death as the blushes of a bride."

"Oh! Doctor! They are poor enough now—if they marry and have a family, the expenses of the children—"

"Will be better to bear than losing the only one you have!" interrupted the Doctor, gravely; "my dear, madam, Mr. Lindsay is very clever in his profession—he has industry and good will to work; but as long as your daughter's illness distracts his mind, he can never be himself. He has friends, and the young couple will do well, I doubt not; but of this be sure," he continued with solemn decision, as she was about to speak— "of this be sure—on my reputation as a physician, I affirm, that if Miss Stuart continues in this situation much longer, her reason or her life will pay the penalty."

And without allowing the querulous old lady time to answer, he left her to ponder on his words. Great was the joy of Lindsay at this advice, and as the wise physician had truly prophesied, the startling proposal of immediate marriage, produced a reaction in the mind of Mary and very soon evinced its beneficial effects. Resolved not to do things by halves, the excellent doctor employed Lindsay professionally in copying specimens of morbid anatomy, and invited Mary to pass a few weeks with his wife and daughters and to consult them concerning her future arrangements. Oh! How much happiness can be conferred by a few kind words and actions of those whose fortune or skill raises them above their ordinary fellow-creatures! How little studious of their own enjoyment are such as never buy the dear delight of giving pleasure! What epicurean delight—what fashionable luxury—what expensive purchase ever conferred the soul-felt rapture called forth by unhoped-for benediction? What public fame or loud-mouthed huzzas—what sugared praise or subtle flattery—ever gave the heart the self-content derived from beholding the bliss itself has created? The truth of this too-little-considered fact was essentially proved by the pleased Doctor Burton and his amiable wife, as they watched the mantling blush which came over and anon like a bright bird of passage over Mary's faded features, as they saw the honest tear of gratitude glisten on William's manly cheek, or heard the murmured blessing from the relieved mother who felt that her widowed age would not now be robbed of it's only comfort.

Cheerily passes the time when the heart is at ease. The few weeks previous to the wedding day of Mary glided by as if the footfall of June only fell upon flowers. Each of the Miss Burtons presented the expected bride with a bridal dress, and if their graceful simplicity could not add to her beauty, they certainly contributed to her honest pride and pleasure. The cake was made, the love knots twisted, the ring was bought and two days only intervened between the happy day, when one evening as the family of Doctor Burton were sitting cheerfully conversing, the sound of carriage-wheels stopped at the door, and a heavy lumbering noise sounded in the hall.

"Oh, my father is arrived!" exclaimed Ellen Burton, rising rapidly.

"What sort of luggage are they bringing in, in the name of wonder?" said her sister.

"Let us go and see," said Ellen.

Mary stopped her; and, with a cheek as white as chalk, said, tremulously, "they tread like men who bear a heavy burden; they whisper, too, beneath their voices; there is a scent of camphor spreading through the house. *It is a corpse they are bring in!*"

"You dream, dear Mary—come, let us go and meet this dreaded luggage; my life upon it, its terror will vanish when encountered."

With gentle but steady grasp she raised the trembling Mary, and would have let her out, but was stayed by the entrance of her father. He looked pale and somewhat excited, and hurriedly evaded their questions. Suddenly he heard a hard, suppressed breathing, and looking round, beheld Mary gazing at him with wild and rigid stare; her blue lips apart, and her clenched hands pressed forcibly upon her breast. All his presence of mind at once returned, and, advancing to her with composure, he said— "What, Miss Stuart, and have my luckless glass vials and electronic machinery startled you also? For shame, young ladies, I thought you were all better soldiers!"

"It is William!" hissed poor Mary, never for a moment relaxing her distended gaze; "it is Lindsay's corpse!"

"Mary, my dear child! For God's sake do not thus torture yourself; Lindsay is well; but to see you thus, might well make him otherwise. What! You do not believe me? Then come in yourself, William, and convince this obstinate heretic to happiness."

He went to the door of his private surgery and called out Lindsay, who instantly flew to his beloved girl. The instant Mary beheld him, she uttered a frantic shriek, and fell in his arms, exclaiming, "Not dead! Not yet doomed to the dreadful grave! William—my William!"

A burst of tears relieved her o'ercharged heart, and the benevolent Doctor, smiling on her, said—

"Now, infidel, I have thee on the hip!"

In spite of this relief, the evening passed heavily; there seemed to be an indescribable something weighing on William's heart. Mary was exhausted from over-excitement, and the Doctor appeared to listen uneasily to every sound. Mrs. Burton and the ladies retired early, and Ellen left Mary, as she believed, in a sweet and fast sleep. The mystery existing in the surgery was soon explained to William. A certain man had died in one of the London hospitals of a disease which baffled the skill of the physicians. His relations obstinately refused his body for dissection, and with extreme peril and difficulty, a select committee, of which Dr. Burton was the president, had contrived to steal it from the grave. Fearing, however, lest the loss might be discovered and search made, the Doctor had boxed up the body and brought it down to his own private surgery, where, besides having time to examine minutely, he had the advantage of William's skill as a draughtsman to copy any peculiar appearance the system may present. It was the first time Lindsay had ever witnessed the process of dissection; and as the body had been many days in the grave, and was in an advanced state of decomposition, the trial to his nerves and senses was such, that he devoutly hoped it might be the last. He had for some time slept in a small room adjoining the surgery, and now, for the free circulation of air, left the intermediate door open. Towards the dead of night, his frightful occupation was interrupted by the sound of a footstep. He paused, looked round, called the Doctor by name, and then, seeing nothing, sat once more down to his awful task. All was as still as the grave which was thus robbed of its ghastly tenant; when, suddenly, a loud, long scream smote on his ear, more resembling the prolonged yell of a wild Indian, or the frantic howl of a maniac, than any natural cry of terror. He sprung up, and saw standing by him the figure of his Mary—if, as such, he might recognize the distorted face and writhing form that stood before him, glaring on the blackened corpse.

To his dying day Doctor Burton would never relate without shuddering, the scene he saw when William's appalling cries brought him to his aid. Erect as if fashioned of stone, with bloodshot eyeballs and livid features, with hair standing out stiffened with horror, and lips drawn up from the set teeth through which the blood was slowly trickling—there she stood, glaring on the reality of the very phantom which so long had haunted her; and Lindsay, palsied with horror, could only wind his arms around her stiffened figure, and rend the air with cries for help. The moment he entered, Dr. Burton threw a cloak over the corpse, and, as if with the loss of that object, there vanished the unnatural strength with which she had looked on it. Mary fell senseless to the ground. She was bled and carried to bed without giving any token of recollection, and with bitter fears they watched her all night; towards morning she seemed to sleep, and when wakened it was with no remembrance of the frightful events of the night previous. She would have risen, and seemed astonished to find herself so weak; but her manner was calm as usual, and she made no allusion at all to the previous day. William and the ladies rejoiced in deep thankfulness for what they considered almost a miracle of deliverance, but Doctor Burton, though he would not dash their joy, feared much for the stability of that reason which the terrible shock had on one subject completely annihilated. Mary however slowly recovered, and about two weeks after the originally appointed day, Lindsay led her proudly from the church, his wife; and the anxious Doctor was perhaps the only one who noticed that, on returning from it through the churchyard, she smiled and muttered to herself, as she looked on the grave, words of which he could only hear these, "*I shall never make one amongst ye!*"

Many months after their marriage passed in tranquility, and peace seemed once more to have built her nest in the heart of Mary. Her health, it was true, was delicate; but the frightful monomania which had hitherto poisoned her happiness seemed to slumber, and her benevolent friend and physician *hoped* it was lulled to rest forever. Blest with the wife he loved, Lindsay gave his time and attention to his profession with a devotion which ensured success: and having removed after his marriage to London, that populous city served not only to increase his employment, but wholly to divert the attention of his wife. And soon, to crown his joy, Mary proved likely to be a mother. As this trying time approached, although her frame was weak, her mind was unusually buoyant. No fears appeared to perplex her, and her sole wish was to meet her confinement in the little cottage of her mother at Hastings, which request William granted, rather contrary to the advice of Doctor Burton. Here, constantly attended by the good doctor and his wife, she met her trial with unflinching fortitude, and endured severe and protracted agonies with the courage of a heroine and the patience of a martyr. After three days of doubt and danger, a child was born to the alarmed husband, and about a week after, he and Dr. Burton returned to London, where both where engaged on matters of pressing emergence. The infant sickened shortly after, not of any violent disease, but wasting daily from some unknown cause, fading so gradually that Mrs. Burton hesitated to recall her husband from his important occupations in the metropolis until it was too late. The little sufferer's cry became weaker and more weak, its tiny limbs wasted, until, like a lamp that goes out for want of oil, the light of his little life sunk, and his baby breath was yielded in his mother's arms.

A mother's grief for her first-born child: who shall describe? Her long burthen and her bitter pain are as nothing when she looks in the infant eyes of her blessing; watching and weariness are unfelt, while hope still shines in her baby's smile; the voice of despair is unheard while its low cry still speaks her a mother; but when this is hushed forever—when the bright eyes and innocent smile are quenched by death—then hopeless and bereaved she sinks at once to the depths of lethargy. If this be so of all woman-kind, what additional woe must have fallen to the lot of hapless Mary? She, to whom death had been a dream of horror, an incubus of fear, was now doomed to witness it first in the person of her precious babe; on its loved limbs to mark the rigid impress—on its miniature features the cold seal of the conqueror; yet, to the wonder of it all, her sorrow rather seemed patient and resigned, than noisy or frantic. She resigned her breathless burthen to the arms of her weeping mother, and took from Mrs. Burton a strong opiate; after which, she was unresistingly undressed and put to bed. A messenger had been sent post-haste to London for Lindsay the same hour that his baby expired, and they hoped that if Mary could be kept calm until his arrival, the sight of him would prove her best consolation. While she slept, they shrouded the little pale corpse in muslin and lace, and laying it out on pillows strewed the whole with flowers. It was not until the midday following that the poor mother awakened, and at once asked leave to see her child.

"Do not deny me, dear friend," she said in a low, resigned tone, "I well know that he is dead, that no tears of mine can call back the breath which I felt pass away on my lips; yet let me see the precious one for whom I suffered, I sorrowed so much."

"Wait, dear Mary, until William comes; he will be here tonight, and then you shall see the babe."

"Tonight!" she repeated thoughtfully; "will Lindsay be here tonight?"

"We hope so, love," said her mother; "in the meantime, for all our sakes, keep tranquil."

"And am I not tranquil, mother?" she asked, raising herself on her arm and looking piteously in her mother's eyes; "have I not lost my own, my prized, my beautiful boy; and do I weep or wail? Ah! tears nor moans awake not the dead; yet I would that I could weep; my brain is hot, but my eyes are dry. Let me once more see my child, the blessed thing which came to reward my pains a thousand fold—once—I shall never ask it again."

She looked so pale and woebegone that they could no longer refuse her entreaty; and, supported by both, she was led to the chamber of death and looked long on the dead infant. It seemed that some memories of the past troubled her mind, for she murmured, "How beautiful he looks! Can this be death? No livid hues, no loathsome sores revolt the heart! Perhaps he only sleeps, and by and by will waken? You will tell his father when he comes how sweet he sleeps."

She stooped and kissed the cheek, and seemed revolted by its coldness.

"Ah! the ice-bolt has indeed stricken my child! Nothing but death was ever cold as this! He has left his mother's bosom for the grave—*the grave!*"

She said no more, and was partially led back to bed, where the remaining effects of the opiate soon buried her senses again to sleep. Finding her so composed, Mrs. Burton, who had not been home for days, took the opportunity to leave her for a few hours, while her poor mother, who took the post of watcher by her bed, fell from exhaustion into a profound slumber.

It was the dead of night when the poor, old woman was awakened by a stifling smoke, and starting up she dimly perceived by the obscured light, that the bed by which she had slept instead of watched, was empty! Tottering with fear and rage, confused and scarce awake, the bewildered woman followed the first instinct of self-preservation, and hurried down the stairs and out of the cottage door. Recalled to sense by the free air, she looked up and saw the flames bursting from the casements of the upper rooms. A recollection of her ill-fated daughter then thronged upon her brain, and over-powered her feeble strength. With cries of impotent terror, she tottered a few paces and fell senseless to the earth, just as a post chaise, driving furiously, appeared in sight on the brow of the hill. Then it stopped and Lindsay, who probably feared that the sound of his carriage might startle his Mary, sprung out to be greeted with—oh, sight of horror! the cottage which contained her, bursting into flames. He rushed madly down the hill, followed scarcely less rapidly by Dr. Burton, and came in front of the blazing building in time to hear a maniac laugh which rung to the silent sky, and to see—merciful God!—the form of his wretched wife standing at the casement, holding in one arm the body of her dead infant and with the other wildly brandishing a blazing billet of wood! There she stood one moment, her white dress already on fire, her beautiful face and flowing hair distinctly visible by the eddying flames, looking like the spirit of fire presiding over her native element. The next instant and the light material of the cottage gave way, and with a single crash, roof, walls, and floors fell in, burying her in the bursting volume of fire, from which the words still seemed to sound—

"No grave for us, my child! no grave for us!"

The terrible catastrophe was too clearly understood. The madness of the ill-fated Mary on one theme which had only slumbered, was aroused in full force by the sight of death, but with the cunning peculiar to monomania, she had concealed her purpose until she was unwatched, then with her own desperate hand, she had seized a brand from the chimney and like a second Mynha, fired her own funeral pyre. Her first, last, and strongest wish was awfully granted, for her no grave was dug—no earth closed over her mortal clay—the woe-worn spirit passed in madness to its maker and its earthly tenement found a burial by fire.

THE VAMPYRE

BY ELIZABETH ELLET

(1849)

About a century ago, there might have been seen, in a remote part of Scotland, the ruins of a castle, which once belonged to the baronial race Davenat. It stood on a hill of no considerable elevation: but the massive and ancient trees that had escaped the sacrilegious axe, and the clinging ivy, which protected the roofless walls, gave it a venerable aspect. The peasantry told wild stories of the ancient lords of that domain—the family had long been extinct—and of their heroic deeds at home and abroad. When the ruins themselves were levelled to make way for a modern edifice, the superstitious tales connected therewith were gradually dropped, and at length passed from the minds of men; yet one may not be deemed unworthy of preservation.

On a beautiful afternoon in spring, two figures might have been seen on the terrace that overlooked the smooth, sloping lawn in front of the castle. The one was an elderly man, in deep mourning—no other, in short, than the lord of the mansion, Sir Aubrey Davenat, who, since the death of his wife many years before, had worn the sombre dress which was but an emblem of the gloom in his heart.

The Baron was highly respected by his neighbors and acquaintances—few of whom enjoyed his intimacy. He was brave, and generous almost to a fault; and so scrupulous was his regard for truth—so rigidly was his word kept, even when the fulfillment of a promise involved pain or trouble to himself—that his simple assertion was more implicitly relied on than the oath of another. Withal, there was a sternness about him, amounting, at times, to severity. He showed little indulgence towards faults of which he himself was incapable, and those who knew him best stood most in awe of him.

Although Sir Aubrey manifested, by his uniform melancholy, how fondly he clung to the memory of his departed wife, he never made the least allusion to her in conversation. Yet, that his heart was not dead to affection, appeared from his devoted love for his only child—Malvine—the living image of her lost mother.

The other person on the terrace was this cherished daughter. She had just completed her seventeenth year, and was celebrated through all the adjoining districts for her rare and luxuriant beauty. Unconscious of the admiration she commanded, Malvine loved best to cheer the solitude of her only surviving parent, and seemed to feel interest in none but him.

Yes—there was one other with whom she had grown from childhood, whom she loved as a brother, and who was, in truth, of blood kindred to her own, though not of close consanguinity. Edgar was the orphan son of a cousin—twice removed—of Sir Aubrey. Left destitute by the death of both of his parents, he had been taken into his kinsman's house, and brought up with the same care and tenderness he would have bestowed upon his own son.

Three years before, Edgar had been sent to the continent on his travels, by his kind foster-father. His return was now expected—it had been announced—and it was in the hope of greeting the young cavalier that the father and daughter stood waiting for so long, looking down the broad road that swept around the hill at the foot of the castle.

A light cloud of dust floated above the tall old oaks on the roadside, and the plume of a horseman might be seen at intervals through the foliage.

"He comes!" cried Malvine, turning, with a happy smile, to her father, on whose face was a cheerful expression rarely seen.

The traveller skirted and ascended the hill: the bell at the castle gate sounded, and in a few moments Edgar was folded in the embrace of his noble kinsman.

Less impetuous was the greeting exchanged between the young man and the fair girl, whom he left a child and found now in the bloom of blushing womanhood. The luxuriance of blond hair, that once floated free, was confined by the ribbon worn by Scottish maidens of that day, save one light, neglected ringlet, that fell down her neck almost to the waist; the deep blue eyes that had formerly the wild, unshrinking, though soft boldness of the young fawn, now shot timid glances from their veil of shadowy lashes, or were bent modestly to the ground; the fair cheeks wore an added tint of rose, and the lips a smile that had less of sportiveness, and more of feeling. The charm of gracious youth encircled her as with a sacred spell, forbidding familiar approach.

But as Edgar, with a new-born respect, clasped the hand of his fair cousin, the feeling that sprung to life in his bosom was far warmer than the affection of his boyhood. Admiration—called forth by her surpassing loveliness—was ripening quickly into love.

It was not long ere the secret of his heart was revealed to him; and the rapturous thought came also, that the beautiful girl did not regard him with indifference, and might soon learn to love him. Who else had she, but himself, as companion in her walks, her studies, her gentle tastes? Who else could accompany her as she played the harp, and sang the wild songs of her country? Who else would ride by her side through the forest and bring her flowers, and train her hawks, and read to her tales of ancient lore?

"But whither trends all this?" was the stern question asked by the young man's conscience. "Shall I lift my eyes to the daughter and sole heir of Davenat? Shall I aspire to her hand?—I, who can cal nothing mine own?—who owe even my sword to her father's bounty?"

Painfully did the youth brood over these queries; and he answered them as became a man of truth and honor. He resolved to ask permission of his foster-father to go forth again into the world.

This resolution was immediately acted upon. Sir Aubrey listened in surprise to the request, looked earnestly on his young protégé, and asked with mild gravity—what had happened to make him to escape so soon from the house and company of his kinsman.

This inquiry implied a suspicion of ingratitude, or weariness of so lonely a home; and the thought pierced Edgar's heart. It was better to disclose all his feelings. Better that Sir Aubrey should know and condemn his presumption, than believe him capable of a base forgetfulness of the benefits he had received.

The tale was soon told. The Baron said, at its conclusion—

"Thou know'st, Edgar, I have always loved thee as a son; and were it not that my word is pledged elsewhere, I would myself place my daughter's hand in thine. Thy lineage is unstained and noble as my own; and thy poverty would not render thee unworthy of Malvine. Thou know'st how long and obstinate has been the feud between our race and the Lords of Marsden, whose domain borders on mine. Lord George—the proudest of all the descendants of that haughty line—sent on his deathbed to entreat my presence. I went—I entered his castle as a foe, deeming that he wished to see me on some matter of business. He offered me his hand and spoke words of reconciliation. He besought me to bestow my daughter on his younger brother, Ruthven, the last representative of the family. Thus the name would be preserved from extinction—for his brother had sworn he would wed no other—and our possessions would be united.

"I had heard naught but good of young Ruthven, who shortly before had set out on his travels. The Marsdens were of a proud, powerful and renowned race. I pledged the hand of Malvine; and from that day she has considered herself the betrothed of the young lord. I learned but the other day from the castellan, that he is expected soon to return home. He will then wed my daughter."

Edgar looked down for some moments in gloomy silence. At last, with a sudden effort, he said—

"Then I must depart—noble kinsman! Tomorrow—today—"

"Not so!" cried the Baron. "Thy duty, Edgar, is to be a man! Flee not from danger, like a weak, faint-hearted churl! Take the knowledge to thy heart, that she whom thou lovest is happy—her troth being plighted to another; and respect her innocence and truth! She loves thee as a brother: crush down thine ill-fated passion, and be to her a brother, indeed!"

"What do you ask?" faltered Edgar.

"Not more than thou canst accomplish, my true-hearted friend!" answered Sir Aubrey. "Will you deny me this one boon?"

"No!" said the young man; and though the conflict of his soul was evident, so also was the victory he obtained, when, with the dignity of virtuous resolution, he pressed the hand of his benefactor.

After this, Edgar continued to be the joy of the household, though he spent little time alone with Malvine. In the evening circle, he would entertain them with anecdotes of his foreign travel, and the strange countries he had visited. One night, when a storm raved without, and the quiet circle was formed, as usual, in the antique hall, through the crevices of which rushed the wind, flaring the candles, and chilling those who felt it, Malvine observed that Edgar was less cheerful than usual, and that his looks were bent in abstraction upon the ground.

"What aileth my good cousin?" she said, playfully, at length. "You were so merry and full of tales erewhile! Why now are you so grave and silent? 'Tis but ill weather for the season, but there are warm hearts and glowing fires within doors."

The young man passed his hand across his brow.

"I pray your pardon," he replied, "that I thus forget myself in gloomy recollections, but the storm conjured up such. It was on such a night, in Italy, that I met with one of those whose like I pray unto Heaven I may never more see!"

"Ha!" exclaimed the Baron, "another adventure! Let us have it, boy! Come, we need some wild tale to enliven this dreary evening!" And Malvine joined her entreaty that he would relate the occurrence.

After a few preliminaries, Edgar proceeded.

"I left Rome when the sickly season was at its height, for an excursion among the mountains of Albania. One day, while riding through a romantic valley, I chanced to overtake a young cavalier whom, at the first glance, I decided to be a countryman of my own.

"I was not mistaken; he was a Scot, of noble birth. We soon became acquainted and as generally happens with those of the same country in a foreign land, warm friends.

"Sir Arthur Dumbrin—that was his name—told me he had lived three years in Italy, and had some weeks before arrived in Rome from Naples. He had lingered there too long; the malaria had planted in his system the seeds of fever, of which he lay for many days ill at Albano. From this illness he had just recovered. This circumstance explained what had at first startled me, producing even a feeling akin to fear—his singular and excessive paleness. His features were fine and well-marked—but his complexion was the hue of death; and there was a look of coldness, or rather of vacancy, in his large black eyes, that sometimes inclined me to believe his mind unsettled by his recent suffering. He invited me to visit him at Albano, where he had just purchased a villa; and called upon me the following day at my lodgings.

"I resided at that time with an elderly woman, of much excellence of character, who had a daughter—Nazarena—of singular loveliness. In the bloom of fifteen, an unspoiled child of nature, the artless innocence that appeared in her face and manners, and in all her actions, was irresistibly engaging. She looked upon all she met as good and true, because she judged others by her own heart, and she thought evil of none. With this cheerful kindliness of disposition, I was surprised to see her shrink back suddenly, with evident and instinctive aversion and terror, when she saw my friend and countryman for the first time. As was natural, I asked the reason of this involuntary repulsion.

"'His *eyes!*' she exclaimed; 'those terrible eyes! I do not like your friend.'

"Donna Ursula, her mother, also confessed to me that the strange, cold look—the *soulless* look, as she called it—of the Baron, filled her with a secret dread whenever she saw him.

"It was not long, however, before they became quite accustomed to the corpse-like paleness of my friend, and he won greatly upon their regard when some time afterwards, at the imminent hazard of his life, he rescued me from robbers, who fell upon me while I was riding over the mountain. I had given myself up for lost, after ineffectual resistance, when Arthur suddenly sprang from behind a rock, and drawing his weapon, soon put the robbers to flight. From this day, both Ursula and her daughter treated him with confidence; and he occasionally bantered me by saying he had turned me out of my place in the heart of the charming Nazarena.

"I had never cherished any feeling stronger than friendship for the sweet girl; and could readily forgive the preference she now showed to my friend. But I feared for her; the more so as I was not pleased with the Baron's demeanor towards her or the principles he avowed. The regard I felt for him, however, and gratitude towards the preserver of my life, prevented me from expressing my displeasure openly. I was silent, though I knew his views with regard to women were unbecoming a nobleman and a Scot! Bitterly have I since rued that unworthy silence.

"To be brief—the fair Nazarena fled from the house of her mother. Vain was the search of the wretched parent the next day for her lost child; and heart-rending was the question—'Who was the betrayer?' Alas! I knew but too well—yet dared not name him!

"After three days, some peasants discovered the corpse of a female in the neighboring wood. It was Nazarena. On the neck of the helpless girl was a small puncture, scarcely visible indeed; but there was otherwise no wound on the body. A fine stiletto lay on the ground near her. I shuddered with horror when her eyes fell on this instrument of death. I knew it instantly: it was the weapon Arthur wore constantly about his person. I communicated my knowledge to the authorities; officers were dispatched to arrest the criminal; but he had disappeared. I have never heard aught of him."

"Heaven guard you, young man!" exclaimed the aged nurse of Malvine; "your friend was a Vampyre!"

"A Vampyre!" repeated Edgar, "and what is that, I pray?"

"Holy Maria!" cried the nurse, lifting up both her hands; "the man is a Scot, and knows not what a Vampyre is!"

"P'shaw! Nursery fables!" cried Sir Aubrey, half vexed, half laughing.

"A Vampyre," continued the old woman, forgetting respect in her interest, "is a dead person, who, on account of his sins, can find no repose in the grave, but is bound to the service of witches and sorcerers. Every year, on Walpurgis night, he is forced to attend the Witches' Sabbath, and swear a fearful oath to deliver to them a guiltless victim before the month is at an end. He marks out some tender maiden or tender youth as his victim, whom he kills and sucks the blood. If he fails to fulfill the oath, he falls himself a prey—and the witches deliver him to Satan as his forever and ever!"

"Strange," Edgar muttered. "It was in May that the terrible event occurred of which I spoke."

"Yes—yes!" cried the nurse eagerly; "I am not so mistaken!" And turning to her young mistress she besought her to sing the legend of the Vampyre which she had once learned of a wandering harper.

Malvine was ever ready to gratify her favorite attendant, who had been, in truth, a mother to her; and when her harp was brought, sang after a prelude—

THE LEGEND

I.

Mother—behold
   The pale man there—
   With haughty air,
And look so cold!
"—Child—child beware
   The pale man there!
   Turn thee away
   Or thou'rt his prey!
Ah! Many a maiden, young and fair,
Hath fallen his victim, in the snare!
   Hath drunken death
   From his poisonous breath:
   List—list, my child! A Vampyre he!
Heaven keep his demon glance from thee!"

II.

What, mother, doth the pale man there?
With look so full of dark despair?
"Child, child! Those fearful glances shun:
Foul deeds of evil hath he done!
   Such is his doom!
Though long since dead,
He cannot rest within the tomb!
   Forth he has fled,
      to wander round—
A living corpse o'er hallowed ground!
From house to house he takes his way,
A fair bride seeking for his prey:
His chosen bride was lost for aye!"

III.

He smiles on me—
The pale man—see!
And kind his look, those sad and wild!
—"Still look'st there!—alas, my child!
　　Haste—haste—the danger fly—
The mother's warning is in vain;
The pale man's spells the maid enchain;
　　At midnight, fast she flies
　　By the light of those fierce eyes—
Now she herself—so runs the tale—
Wanders o'er earth, a Vampyre pale.

* * * *

The following day was spent by Edgar hunting in the forest. His mind was disquieted; not by the struggle to overcome his unhappy love; for so hopeless he deemed it, that no room was left for conflict. But the wild stories of the nurse strangely affected him. Could it then be so? Was it true, that the man he had once loved as a friend, whom he now saw execrated as the betrayer of innocence, was that fearful being she had described? He was inclined to reject so monstrous a belief—though nurtured in the faith of those marvelous tales, long since exploded in the light of civilization and reason.

He met with no success in the sport, but continued to wander on, till the shades of twilight began to fall upon the forest. Then he returned, listlessly, on the way homeward. Suddenly a wild animal, which he took for a doe, bounded from the shelter of some bushes near him, and shot away. Edgar followed the game, now losing sight of her, now catching a glimpse as she sprang through the dense foliage, darting among the branches like an arrow in flight. At length he was forced to give up the pursuit, exhausted with running and clambering. He was in a wild part of the forest, surrounded as it seemed with rocks, the tall bare peaks of which were touched with silver by the moon, just then appearing above the horizon.

Edgar was endeavoring to find the shortest way to the castle, when he was startled by the sound of a man's voice, as if groaning in pain, and entreating help. Following the sound, he saw a man lying on the ground, and weltering in his blood. The sufferer perceived him, as it appeared, for he redoubled his cries for assistance.

Edgar raised him from the ground, and tried to staunch the blood that still flowed freely from a deep wound in the breast. His humane efforts were in part successful; the wounded man drew a deep breath, opened his eyes, and fixed them upon the youth.

Edgar stared back in sudden horror. "Arthur!" he exclaimed.

"Is it you, Edgar?" asked the sufferer, faintly. "Then all is well. I saved your life—you will not abandon me?"

"Nazarena!" murmured the young man, trembling with the feelings called up by this sudden meeting with one he deemed so fearfully guilty.

"Hush!" cried Arthur; "condemn me not till you know all. Aid me now!"

"Oh, that I could!" faltered Edgar.

"Mistake me not," said the wounded man, gloomily; "I know that my hours are numbered; my life is ebbing fast. I ask of you no leechcraft, for I fear not death! But swear to me, Edgar—by your own life, which you owe to me—by all that is dear to you on earth—by your soul's salvation—"

"What must I swear?" interrupted the young man.

"Swear," was the answer, "not to reveal to any mortal—to man or woman—aught that thou hast known me, or aught thou shalt know—before the first hour of the first day of the coming month! Swear it!"

"Strange!" muttered Edgar, while a cold thrill pervaded his whole frame. But the hands of the dying man grasped both of his—the eyes, glassed with approaching death, were fastened on him—the hollow voice again spoke imploringly—"Swear!"

"Be it so!" answered the youth, and he repeated the words of the oath.

"Yet one more boon!" said Arthur, after a pause, while his strength was fast sinking. "Bear me to the summit of yonder rock, and place me so that the moonlight will shine upon my face."

"Ha!" exclaimed Edgar, "what means this strange—thou art not—surely—"

"Hold!" cried Arthur, his eyes flashing suddenly, though the next moment a dimness came over them. Feebly raising his hand he pointed towards the rock.

Trembling, the young man lifted the expiring Baron, and bore him to the spot pointed out. But once spoke he after being placed there— "Remember the oath!" Then a quick convulsion passed over his features—he breathed gaspingly—and the next instant lay cold and motionless at the feet of his companion.

Filled with emotion he could neither control nor account for, Edgar hastened from the spot, and with all speed out of the wood. The moon rose higher, pouring a light more vivid, like a mantle of snow, upon the stark rock where lay the corpse. It seemed as if her silvery beams were concentrated upon the still form and upturned face. As the orb rose to her meridian, life returned by slow degrees to the upheaving breast. Arthur opened his eyes, and rose to his feet in full strength once more.

"Ha-ha!" he shouted in wild exultation—while in the darkness beneath his feet gleamed unearthly phantom faces—"who will slay the *dead*?"

* * * *

When Edgar arrived at the castle, pale, breathless, and exhausted, he heard news little calculated to revive his spirits. A messenger had announced the return of his fair cousins' affianced husband from abroad; and bore his greeting, which he intended to offer in person. Sir Aubrey himself, with looks of pleasure, announced this intelligence to him, and talked of the preparations he intended making for the reception of his son-in-law. But if this information, and the scene he had witnessed so lately, caused the young man a sleepless night, how was it next day with him, when the old Castellan, who had lodged in the small village two miles distant, brought to him the startling news he had learned there! The daughter of Baron Leslie, a rich noble who lived in an adjoining district, had fled from her home with a strange man, and had been found murdered in the wood. Her father, with his neighbors and servants, who discovered the hapless girl, found also the murderer, sitting by the body, from which, horrible to relate, he had just sucked the blood! He was a Vampyre! The bereaved father himself struck down the foe, while the others bore away the corpse of his victim.

"Then he was killed," said Edgar faintly.

"Ah, sir!" cried the Castellan, "though slain one hour, he will walk abroad the next, ever intent on his foul deeds. No! the only hope is that he may fail to do the will of the witches who hold him in their service! Then his power on earth will be at an end."

It would be vain to attempt a description of the effect of such rumors as these upon the sensitive mind of Edgar—associated, as they were, with what he himself had seen. His gloom and despondency were observed by his kinsman, who attributed them, unfortunately, to a different cause.

* * * *

Three weeks passed before another messenger announced that Lord Ruthven would be on the succeeding day at the castle. He came accordingly. Sir Aubrey himself received him with a warm welcome, and introduced him to his young kinsman. The first look Edgar cast upon him was like a death pang, curdling the blood in his heart. Lord Ruthven and Arthur were the same persons!

In the midst of his anguish and horror Edgar perceived that Malvine, at first sight of her lover, shuddered and shrank back, with the same instinctive aversion that had been shown by the ill-fated Nazarena. But she regained her self-possession by an effort, and spoke cordially to the man she had consented to receive as her husband.

The most fearful apprehensions that had reached the soul of Edgar fell short of the reality! Following Ruthven to the windows, to which he had turned at a pause in the conversation, Edgar whispered in his ear—

"Traitor! —Accursed! What dost thou here! Begone—"

The young lord turned, and gazed on him with looks of surprise.

"I know thee well!" said the agitated youth. "Begone, or—"

"What meaneth this?" asked Sir Aubrey, coming forward.

"This young man," answered Lord Ruthven, with a smile, "seems to mistake me for someone whose company pleases him not."

"Edgar!" repeated the Baron in displeasure, "is it thus thy word is kept?"

"Oh, you know not," cried the young man in agony, "you know not *whom* you have received—"

"*Thine oath!*" hissed a voice close in his ear.

Ruthven's lips moved not. Edgar cast a fearful glance around him, groaned aloud, and covering his face with his hands, rushed from the hall.

"Pardon the discourtesy of my kinsman," said the Baron to Lord Ruthven. "It is but too easy to see the cause of his wild behavior. He cherishes a passion for my daughter, which, till now he has seemed to combat successfully. But he shall not be permitted to disturb our happiness. If he lacks firmness to control his feelings, he shall leave the castle till your marriage is concluded."

Ruthven bowed with a smile of assent; and they proceeded to discourse of other matters. They were interrupted by the blast of a trumpet without; and after a few moments, a messenger from the capital was announced.

He brought the sovereign's commands to the young lord—that he should immediately repair to his presence, as he wished to entrust him with dispatches to the monarch of England. Especial haste was enjoined.

Lord Ruthven hastily glanced at the credentials of the messenger, and handed them to the Baron.

"You will perceive, my lord," he said, "that I cannot decline so imperative a duty as that of obedience to the king's command. I am especially disturbed thereby, and must grieve sincerely, unless"—and his countenance brightened—"you consent that the marriage shall take place tonight. All minor matters are already settled between us; why should not the coming day find your daughter the bride of Ruthven?"

"There is no reason, in good truth," answered Aubrey.

"You pardon the boldness of my petition?" cried the noble. "Win the consent of the beauteous Malvine, and I will presently ride to my castle—give the necessary orders for the journey on the morrow—and return at nightfall to claim my bride!"

The Baron made no opposition to this arrangement; and his will was law to his fair daughter. His word was pledged for both. Ruthven took leave for the brief period of his intended absence, after entreating his friend to present on his part a brilliant ring to his betrothed.

Lord Ruthven passed hastily through the great gallery, on his way to the court of the castle, where his horse stood already saddled. A wild-looking figure, with pale and haggard face, stood in his way.

"One word!" he said, imploringly.

Ruthven answered him not, but beckoning haughtily, turned and led the way to his chamber. They were alone.

Edgar threw himself at the feet of his companion.

"Yield thy prey for once!" he cried in agony—"Spare the innocent blood! Have mercy—have mercy!"

"Bid the rolling earth may stay her course!" muttered the mysterious stranger, a gloomy frown gathering on his brow. "Reverse the doom pronounced and I will thank thee on bended knee! Faugh! How frail a thing is human will!"

"Then it shall be done!" shrieked Edgar, springing to his feet in desperation. "The oath shall be broken! Happen what may to me, my beloved must be saved! What worse than her death, can befall me?"

"Would'st know?" again hissed the voice in his ear—"Thou shalt confess with horror that it is worse a thousand-fold!"

The eyes of the youth were fastened, as by a spell, on those of the fearful being who stood before him.

"Know it—then!" whispered the serpent-like voice; "go—if thou wilt—betray me!—load thy soul with the guilt of perjury—win my bride for my own! My doom will be upon thee! Years—years may pass—but the curse will be fulfilled! In pangs unutterable shalt thou render up thy soul! Thou shalt hear the dread sentence—*no mercy for the perjured*! Then—wandering in the darkness—thou shalt re-enter thine house of clay, and roam the earth a living corpse—condemned by a doom it cannot resist—to feed on the blood dearest to thee! Steeped in horror, sleepless, unspeakable, thou shalt prey, one after another, on thy household victims—wife—son—daughter—hear their frenzied supplications—see their last agonies—drain, compelled, though shuddering, the last drop that warms their hearts! Still driven by the inevitable fate, thou shalt wander forth—appalling, shunned by all—still seeking new victims—enacting new horrors—till, thy stay on earth expired, thou shalt descend to the abyss, and see the very fiends shrink from thee, as one more foul and accursed than they! Ha! Thou tremblest! Thy frame stiffens with affright! 'Tis *mine own* history I have told! Go—break thy oath—and be—like me!"

As Ruthven strode from the apartment, the appalled youth sank lifeless upon the floor.

* * * *

It was late in the evening: all the servants in the castle were busied in preparations for the approaching nuptials. A magnificent banquet was set out in the great hall; and the castle chapel was sumptuously decorated and brilliantly illuminated.

With unspeakable anguish Edgar heard of the hasty bridal that was to take place, and marked the stir of preparation. Unable, at length, to bear the anguish of his fearful secret, he summoned one of the attendants of his cousin, and demanded an instant interview. The servant went to her apartment, and presently returned with the message that the Lady Malvine was in the hands of her tire-woman, and prayed her cousin to excuse her not seeing him.

"To her father—then!" muttered Edgar; and following the servant who bore his request for a word in private with the Baron, found him in the great hall. Sir Aubrey's brow darkened as he looked on his pale kinsman, and heard his petition that he should desist from the preparations for his daughter's wedding with a man destitute of honor or feeling—who had lured to destruction many innocent maidens, and committed many crimes—

"I never thought thee, Edgar," said Sir Aubrey, with severity—"so weak—so enslaved to thy mad passion—as to stoop to calumny against a brave man—which, in sooth, degrades only thyself! Deemed I not that grief had crazed thee—held I not sacred the honor of thy race and the peace of my household—kept I not my hospitality inviolable—truly I would acquaint Ruthven with thy false accusations."

"Alas!" cried the youth, "the truth will appear—too late! Yet"—and a blessed thought flashed on him—"the truth may be proven—if—under any pretense—the bridal may be delayed till the first hour after midnight—which is the beginning of the new month!"

"I shall *not* be delayed!" cried the father. "Aubrey Davenat has pledged his word—and it shall never be broken!"

"Then I will dare the worst to save her!" exclaimed the heart-stricken young man. "Know—that Ruthven is—"

"*Thine oath!*" hissed the voice once more in his ear. Edgar turned quickly, and saw the deathly visage of Ruthven close behind him. He strove to speak; the words died on his lips in incoherent murmurs—and he fell upon the ground in frightful convulsions.

"Poor boy!" said Ruthven, sympathizingly, "what ails him?"

"He raves!" answered the Baron, in displeasure; and calling some of his attendants, he bade them carry the young man to his own apartment, and keep him there for the night.

Ruthven apologized for his late arrival—for it was already mid-night—by saying that he had found at home letters of importance, which he was forced to answer immediately.

"I pray now," he concluded, "to give notice to my fair bride that I await her; and pardon my haste, for I would have her mine own before the next hour strikes."

The arrival of the bridegroom, and his impatience, was notified to the Lady Malvine; but there was some delay before she appeared. Sir Aubrey received and embraced her—bestowing his paternal benediction upon her fair young head. In her spotless bridal robes—the veil floating like a cloud over her slight form—pearls adorning the brow that rivalled their whiteness, she looked like an angel rather than a mortal maiden. Her cheek was pale, and there was something of pensiveness, if not of sadness, in her deep blue eyes; but it only imparted a new charm to her matchless beauty.

Her maidens stood around her; and at her right hand, Lord Ruthven, wearing a rich robe of purple velvet embroidered with gold; his belt and sword handle flashing with jewels. His countenance wore an unusual expression of exultation, mingled with impatient glances at the delay of those who composed the bridal procession.

At length, taking the hand of his bride, he led the way to the chapel.

Slowly and solemnly passed the procession, from the hall across the lighted gallery, to the sacred place. Clouds of incense floated above the altar—the organ's music swelled—and the choir sang a sacred melody as they entered. All was silent as they stood before the altar; and the priest in his snowy robes began the service.

What form is that, rushing forward with wildly torn hair, and blood-shot rolling eyes? What shriek of mortal anguish pierces the ears of all present? Edgar had escaped from his guards. With a loud cry of "Hold—hold!" he threw himself between the bride and the bridegroom, clasping Malvine's robe convulsively, as he sank at her feet.

The Baron, furious at the interruption, ordered the young man to be carried out forcibly. Ruthven dragged him from the altar's foot, whispering—"*Thine oath!*"—into his ear.

"Fiend! Accursed!" cried the youth, releasing himself from his hold by a desperate effort; "The innocent shall not be thy prey! Heaven will approve the breaking of such an oath! Know—know all of ye"—glancing wildly round the room—this being is"—

"Take the madman away!" thundered Sir Aubrey, in a rage.

Several of the attendants lay hold of Edgar. Struggling as if for his life, his eyes flashing, his hands stretched towards Ruthven, he repeated—"He is"—

The clock on the tower struck *one*.

"A *Vampyre!*" shouted the young man.

There was a gleam of lightning filling the chapel with a glare that eclipsed the torchlight, and a burst of thunder that shook the whole castle from its massive foundations. Many averred afterwards that the face of Lord Ruthven, livid and ghastly in that intense light—wore such a look of fierce despair as never was seen on mortal countenance before. When the thunder ceased, he had disappeared, and the bride lay in a swoon on the steps of the altar.

When the first stunning moment of consternation and horror had passed, the proud baron turned to embrace his young kinsman, whose warning had saved his daughter. But Edgar heard not his thanks. The agony, the terror he had suffered, had driven reason from her throne!

A year elapsed before the young man was restored to consciousness, but peace returned no more to his breast! He went to Rome, where he entered a convent of the strictest order, and in a few years was released by death from the melancholy that had made life a burden.

Malvine mourned sincerely for her friend and cousins' suffering, and wished also to become the inmate of a cloister; but the entreaties of her father prevailed with her to relinquish the thought of thus retiring from the world. After some time she was induced to listen to the suit of the *real* Lord of Marsden, who had arrived at his castle shortly after the tragic occurrences related. She had never cause to regret her marriage with him.

THE SLEEPLESS WOMAN

BY WILLIAM JERDAN

(1831)

CHAPTER I

"Blessed be he that invented sleep, for it covers a man all over like a mantle."

Sanch Panza, passim.

Heavily set in massive brass, whose rich and ingenious carving was tarnished and dull, a ponderous lamp swung from a ceiling blackened by its smoke. Everything in the room spoke of time, but of time that had known no change. Knights, whose armor was, at the latest, of two centuries back—ladies, in dresses from which their descendants started in dismay—looked out from the discolored tapestry; and the floor, dark with age, added to the gloom. Beside the hearth, whose fire, from the rain beating down the huge chimney, burned every moment dimmer, sat two old domestics. The man in a scarlet gown, and a belt, from which hung a heavy bunch of keys, was the seneschal; and opposite was his wife, in a brown silk dress, and a string of ebony beads, which she was busily employed in counting. Between them was a small antique oak table, where a flask and two bell-mouthed glasses appeared temptations which, it must be owned, somewhat interrupted the telling of the beads. In the centre of the chamber stood an immense hearse-like bed; the purple velvet curtains swept to the ground, and at each corner dropped a large plume of black ostrich-feathers. On this bed lay a withered old man, apparently in the last extremity of age, and very close upon the border of death. His spare form was hidden in an ample black robe, fastened round the waist with a white girdle, on which were graved strange characters in red; and on his breast was a white square, covered with stars and signs wrought in gold. The old man's face was ghastly pale, and rendered yet paler by the contrast of his black skull-cap, which was drawn down even to his gray and shagged eyebrows. But the features were restless; and the small keen eyes, though fast losing their brightness, were full of anxiety. The wind shook the tall narrow windows, and howled in the old trees of the avenue; at every fresh gust the baron's impatience seemed to increase— for what we are telling relates to the Baron de Launaye.

"'Tis a rough night," muttered he; "but Adolphe is as rough a rider— and a dangerous road; but I am the first De Launaye who ever drew bridle for that. And then my summons—it was sure to reach him; ay, though alone, in the midnight bower of the mistress whose name and his suspicion had never coupled together even in a dream—even though consciousness were drowned in the crimson flowing of the wine—though sleeping as men sleep after battle, pillowed on the body of their deadliest enemy—, or that of their nearest and dearest friend—my summons would be borne on his inmost soul. But will he come, at the bidding of his dying uncle?—will Adolphe, he, the only human being whom I ever loved—will he or will he not come?"

The question was answered even at the moment it was breathed. The horn of the castle-gate was blown impatiently—the fall of the drawbridge was heard—a moment's pause; and a light foot sprang up the oaken staircase with all the speed of haste and youth. The door opened and in rushed a young cavalier. The white plumes of his cap were drenched with wet—the diamond clasp that fastened them was dim with damp—but his bright auburn hair glistened with the raindrops. Hastily flinging his riding-cloak, heavy with moisture, to the ground, the stranger sprang to the bedside. A gleam of human love, of human joy, passed over the old man's face, as tenderly and gently his nephew asked for his tidings, and expressed such hopes as affection hopes when hope there is none.

"Child of my love," murmured the dying baron, "for whose sake only have I ever given one thought to the things of this earth, bear yet a moment with the feeble wretch who but a brief while will stand between you and the title of your ancestors and wealth. Many a prince of your mother's house would think his kingdom overpaid if purchased by its half. You are young—I never was—my heart, even in boyhood, was old with premature knowledge. You have that beauty the want of which has made my life a curse—you have that strength of body the want of which has paralyzed my strength of mind. I have doubted if happiness dwells on this evil earth—I will not doubt when I hope for yours. You will hear me called necromancer: out on the base fools who malign that which they understand not, and would bring down the lofty aim of science, the glorious dream of virtue, to their own level! You will hear me called miser: Adolphe, have you ever found me so?"

"My father—my more than father!" passionately exclaimed the young man, hiding his face on the pillow, as if ashamed of the violence of mortal grief, in the presence of one so soon to be immortal.

"Adolphe," continued his uncle, "you have heard, though not from me—for I sought not to weigh down your ardent mind with all that has pressed upon me with the burden of hopelessness, and long has the knowledge been mine—that the fetters of clay are too heavy for the spirit. Your young hand was fitter for the lance than the crucible; and the bridle-rein would have been ill-exchanged for the lettered scroll. But something I know of that future, into which even the sage can look but dimly. Adolphe, the only question I asked was for thee! Alas! The vanity of such wisdom! It has told of danger that menaces, but not of the skill that avoids. My child, evil came into the world with woman, and in her is bound up the evil of your destiny. Vain as the glance they throw on the polished steel of their mirror—false as the vow they make for the pleasure of breaking—inconstant as the wind, which changes from point to point, and for whose change no philosophy hath ever discovered a cause: shun them, Adolphe, as you would disloyalty to your king, flight from your enemy, or falsehood to your friend."

The old man's voice became inaudible, and his head sank on Adolphe's shoulder:—"Margharita, water—or, Jacques, give me the wine." The youth tried to pour a few drops into the baron's mouth. The dying man motioned back the glass, and looking in the cavalier's face with a strong expression of affection and anxiety, muttered something of "woman" and "danger"—"bright," "eyes," "bright," "beware"—these were his last broken words. He expired.

CHAPTER II

Contrary to the charitable expectations of his neighbors, the Baron de Launaye was buried with all the rites of the church; the holy water was sprinkled on the corpse, and the holy psalm was sung over the coffin. A marble tablet marked his grave; and there the moonlight slept as lovingly as it ever did on the sinless tomb of saint or martyr. The new Baron de Launaye lamented his uncle's death in a very singular manner, for he was his heir—and the young and the rich have not much time for regret. But Adolphe (he was remarkable from a child for his memory) could not forget the kindness—and more than kindness—the love that his uncle had lavished on the little orphan, who, noble and penniless at the age of five years, was left dependent on his bounty. However, sorrow cannot—indeed nothing in this world can—last forever. Adolphe's grief became first only sad; next, melancholy; thirdly, calm; and fourthly, settled down into a respectful remembrance, and a resolve to bear his uncle's last words in mind. Indeed, the muttered, vague, and uncertain prediction quite haunted him.

"I am sure," said he, in one of his many pondering moods, "I am sure my past experience confirms his words. I never got into a scrape but a woman was the cause. I had been in my outset at court, page to the Duke Forte d'Imhault, and gone with him on that splendid embassy to Russia, had he not been displeased with my awkwardness in fastening the duchess's sandal."

And he laughed as he said this: who in the world could ever guess why the loss of his appointment should make the young baron laugh!

"And then, who caused the duel between me and my Pylades, the Marquis de Lusignan, but that little jilt Mdll. Laure? However, my sword only grazed his arm: he wore an exquisite blue silk scarf, and we were better friends than ever. Oh, my uncle was right: women were born to be our torment."

Still was this conviction impressed on his mind like a duty. Yet he could not help thinking that a few bright eyes would light up the old hall better than the huge brazen lamps which now served to make darkness visible. From thinking of the pleasantness of such an illumination, he began to think of its difficulties; and the difficulties of the project soon referred only to the place. One thought suggests another; and from thinking how many obstacles opposed the introduction of bright eyes and sweet smiles into the castle, he arrived at the conclusion, how easily they were to be obtained in other parts.

To say the truth, Paris became daily more familiar to his mind's eye; and, as he justly observed, staying at the dull old castle could do his uncle no good, and he was quite sure it did himself none. Now, in spite of philanthropy, people are not very fond of doing good gratuitously; but, to be sure, such doctrines were not so much discussed in those days as in ours, though the practice was about the same. Sometimes he argued with himself, "It is well to be out of harm's way;"—and the prediction and a cold shudder came together. But we are ready enough to dare the danger we do not know: and though a few years of Parisian life had placed the nephew's early on a level with the uncle's late experience, touching the evil inherent in womanhood, nevertheless Adolphe supposed their bad qualities might be borne, at all events, better than the dullness of the Chateau de Launaye.

One day riding with his bridle on his horse's neck, mediating whether his next ride should not be direct to Paris, a most uncommon spectacle in that unfrequented part of the country attracted his attention. This was a large lumbering coach, drawn by six horses, whose rich harness and housings bore the crest in gold—a lynx rampant. A very natural curiosity (by-the-by, all curiosity is natural enough) made him look in at the window. Was there ever a face half so beautiful as that of the girl who, like himself, actuated by natural curiosity, looked out as he looked in? The black silk wimple was drawn over her head, but allowed a very red upper lip, an exquisite Grecian nose, and a most brilliant pair of eyes to be seen. Our young cavalier sat as if he had been stupefied. This is a very common effect of love at first. It goes off, however—so it did with Adolphe. His first act on recovering his senses was to gallop after the coach. He spurred on, and caught a second glance of the most radiant orbs that ever revolved in light. Large, soft, clear, and hazel, as those of a robin—they were bright and piercing as those of a falcon. Certainly de Launaye had never seen such eyes before, or at least none that ever took such an effect upon him.

He ate no dinner that day—walked by moonlight on the terrace—and the only thing which excited his attention was the seneschal's information, that the Marquise de Surville and her granddaughter were come to stay some months at their chateau.

"They could not have done that in the late baron's time—the Lord be good unto his soul!" And the old man forthwith commenced the history of some mysterious feud between the two families, in which the deceased Baron Godfred had finally remained victor.

To this tedious narrative of ancient enmities Adolphe was little inclined to listen. "A name and an estate are all our ancestors have a right to leave behind them. The saints preserve us from a legacy of their foes! Nothing could be worse—except their friends."

The next morning the baron arranged his suit of sable with unusual care, though it must be confessed he always took care enough.

"Pray Heaven the marquise may be of my way of thinking respecting the quarrels of our forefathers! Some old ladies have terrible memories," were Adolphe's uppermost ideas as he rode over the drawbridge at the Chateau de Surville, which had been promptly lowered to his summons;—their only neighbor, he had thought it but courteous to offer his personal respects. How much more cheerful did the saloon, with its hangings in sea-green silk, worked in gold, seem than his own hall, encumbered with the dusty trophies of his ancestors. To be sure, the young baron was not at that moment a very fair judge; for the first thing that met him on his entrance was a glance from the same pair of large bright eyes which had been haunting him for the last four-and-twenty hours.

The grandmother was as stern a looking old gentlewoman as ever had knights in armor for ancestors: still, her eyes, also bright, clear, and piercing, somewhat resembled those of her granddaughter. On the rest of her face time had wrought "strange disfeatures." She was silent; and, after the first compliments, resumed the volume she had been reading on the baron's appearance. It was a small book, bound in black velvet, with gold clasps, richly wrought. Adolphe took it for granted it was her breviary; and inwardly concluded how respectable is that piety in an old woman which leaves the young one under her charge quite at liberty! The visitor's whole attention was soon devoted to the oriel window where sat the beautiful Clotilde de Surville. The Baron de Launaye piqued himself on fastidious taste in women and horses: he had had some experience in both. But Clotilde was faultless. There she leaned, with the splendor of day full upon her face; it fell upon her pure complexion like joy upon the heart, and the sunbeams glittered amid the thick ringlets till every curl was edged with gold. Her dress alone seemed capable of improvement; but it is as well to leave something to the imagination, and there was ample food for Adolphe's, in picturing the change that would be wrought upon Clotilde by a Parisian milliner. "This comes," thought he, "of being brought up in an old German castle."

For very shame he at last rose; when, with a grim change of countenance, meant for a smile, the marquise asked him to stay for dinner. It is a remark not the less true for being old (though nowadays opinions are all on the change), that love-making is a thing "to hear, and not to tell." We shall therefore leave the progress of the wooing, and come to the denouement, which was the most proper possible, viz. marriage. Adolphe had been the most devoted of lovers, and Clotilde had given him a great deal of modest encouragement; that is, her bright eyes had often wandered in search of his, and the moment they had found them, had dropped to the ground; and whenever he entered the room, a blush had come into her cheek, like the light into the pearl, filling it with the sweet hues of the rose. Never did love-affair proceed more prosperously. The old seneschal was the only person who grumbled. He begged leave to remind the young baron that it was not showing proper respect to his ancestors not to take up their quarrels.

"But things are altered since the days when lances were attached to every legacy," returned Adolphe.

"We are altering everything nowadays," replied the old man; "I don't see, however, that we are a bit the better off."

"I, at all events, expect happiness," replied his master, "in this change in my condition."

"Ay, ay, so we all do before we are married: what we find after there is no use in saying, for two reasons; first, that you would not believe me; secondly, my wife might hear what I'm telling."

"Ah!" exclaims the young baron, "the caution that marriage teaches! If it were only for the prudence I should acquire, it would be worth my while to marry."

"Alas! Rashness never yet wanted a reason. My poor young master! The old marquise and her dark-eyed granddaughter have taken you in completely."

"Taken me in!" ejaculated de Launaye angrily; "why you old fool, were this a mere match of interest I might thank my stars for such a lucky chance. Young, beautiful, high-born, and rich, Clotilde has but to appear at court and ensure a much higher alliance than mine. What motive could they have?"

"I don't know; but when I don't know people's motives, I always suppose the worst," replied the obstinate Dominique.

"Charitable," laughed the master.

"And besides," resumed the seneschal, "the old marquise plagued her husband into the grave; and I dare say her granddaughter means to do as much for you."

"A novel reason, at all events, for taking a husband," said de Launaye, "in order that you may plague him to death afterward."

CHAPTER III

Well, the wedding-day arrived at last. De Launaye could have found some fault with his bride's costume, but for her face. There was a stiffness in the rigid white satin, and the ruff was at least two inches too high—indeed he did not see any necessity for the ruff at all; they had been quite out some years at Paris. However, he said nothing, remembering that a former hint on the subject of dress had not been so successful as its merits deserved. He had insinuated, and that in a compliment too, a little lowering of the ruff before, as a mere act of justice to the ivory throat, when Clotilde had rejoined, answering in a tone which before marriage was gentle reproof (a few months after it would have sounded like reproach), that she hoped "the Baron de Launaye would prefer propriety in his wife to display." The sense of the speech was forgotten in its sentiment; a very unusual occurrence by-the-by. However, the bride looked most beautiful; her clear, dark eyes swam in light—the liquid brilliancy of happiness—the brightness, but not the sadness of tears. The ceremony was over, the priest and the marquise had given their blessings; the latter also added some excellent advice, which was not listened to with all the attention it deserved. The young couple went to their own castle in a new and huge coach, every one of whose six horses wore white and silver favors. Neighbors they had none; but a grand feast was given to the domestics; and Dominique, at his master's express orders, broached a pipe of Bordeaux. "I can't make my vassals," said de Launaye, "as happy as myself; but I can make them drunk, and that is something towards it."

The day darkened into night; and here, according to all regular precedents in romance, hero and heroine ought to be left to themselves; but there never yet was a rule without an exception. However, to infringe upon established custom as little as possible, we will enter into no details of how pretty the bride looked in her nightcap, but proceed forthwith to the baron's first sleep. He dreamed that the sun suddenly shone into his chamber. Dazzled by the glare he awoke, and found the bright eyes of his bride gazing tenderly on his face. Weary as he was, still he remembered how uncourteous it would be to lie sleeping while she was so wide awake, and he forthwith roused himself as well as he could. Many persons say they can't sleep in an unfamiliar bed; perhaps this might be the case with his bride; and in new situations people should have all possible allowance made for them.

They rose early the following morning, the baroness bright-eyed and blooming as usual, the baron pale and abattu. They wandered through the castle; de Launaye told of his uncle's prediction.

"How careful I must be of you," said the bride, smiling; "I shall be quite jealous."

Night came, and again Adolphe was wakened from his first sleep by Clotilde's bright eyes. The third night arrived, and human nature could bear no more.

"Good God, my dearest!" exclaimed the husband, "do you never sleep?"

"Sleep!" replied Clotilde, opening her large bright eyes, till they were even twice their usual size and brightness. "Sleep! One of my noble race sleep! I never slept in my life."

"She never sleeps!" ejaculated the baron, sinking back on his pillow in horror and exhaustion.

It had been settled that the young couple should forthwith visit Paris—thither they at once proceeded. The beauty of the baroness produced a most marvelous sensation even in that city of sensations. Nothing was heard of for a week but the enchanting eyes of the baroness de Launaye. A diamond necklace of a new pattern was invented in her honor, and called aux beaux yeux de Clotilde.

"Those eyes," said a prince of the blood, whose taste in such matters had been cultivated by some years of continual practice, "those eyes of Mde. De Launaye will rob many of our gallants of their rest."

"Very true," briefly replied her husband.

Well, the baroness shone like a meteor in every scene, while the baron accompanied her, the spectre of his former self. Sallow, emaciated, everybody said he was going into a consumption. Still it was quite delightful to witness the devotedness of his wife—she could scarcely bear him a moment out of her sight.

At length they left Paris, accompanied by a gay party, for their chateau. But brilliant as were these quests, nothing distracted the baroness's attention from her husband, whose declining health became every hour more alarming. One day, however, the young Chevalier de Ronsarde—he, the conqueror of a thousand hearts—the besieger of a thousand more—whose conversation was that happy mixture of flattery and scandal which is the beau ideal of dialogue—engrossed Mde. De Launaye's attention; and her husband took the opportunity of slipping away unobserved. He hastened into a gloomy avenue—the cedars, black with time and age, met like night overhead, and far and dark did their shadows fall on the still and deep lake beside. Worn, haggard, with a timorous and hurried, yet light step, the young baron might have been taken for one of his own ancestors, permitted for a brief period to revisit his home on earth, but invested with the ghastliness and the gloom of the grave.

"She never sleeps!" exclaimed the miserable Adolphe—"she never sleeps! Day and night her large bright eyes eat like fire into my heart." He paused, and rested for support against the trunk of one of the old cedars. "Oh, my uncle, why did not your prophecy, when it warned me against danger, tell me distinctly in what the danger consisted? To have a wife who never sleeps! Dark and quiet lake, how I envy the stillness of your depths—the shadows which rest upon your waves!"

At this moment a breath of wind blew a branch aside—a sunbeam fell upon the baron's face; he took it for the eyes of his wife. Alas! his remedy lay temptingly before him—the still, the profound, the shadowy lake. De Launaye took one plunge—it was into eternity. Two days he was missing—the third his lifeless body floated on the heavy waters. The Baron de Launaye had committed suicide, and the bright-eyed baroness was left a disconsolate widow.

Such is the tale recorded in the annals of the house of de Launaye. Some believe it entirely, justly observing there is nothing too extraordinary to happen. Others (for there always will be people who affect to be wiser than their neighbors) say that the story is an ingenious allegory—and that the real secret of the Sleepless Lady was jealousy. Now, if a jealous wife can't drive a man out of his mind and into a lake, we do not know what can!

A PEEP AT DEATH

BY PETER VON GEIST

(1843)

I was standing one bright day on the banks of a small stream which ran near the village where I was staying, gazing alternately at the clear blue sky and at the quiet green valley that stretched away before me. Suddenly I heard the sharp crack of a rifle, and before I had time to think again, I felt the bullet like a ball of fire tearing its way to, and into, my heart. All control over my muscles was instantly lost, and I fell to the ground; perfectly conscious, but unable to prevent all sorts of motions in my limbs: caused, I supposed, by the blood rushing back to the seat of life. The tumult soon ceased, and I knew that I was dead. I found myself pent up, if I may so speak, confined within the narrowest limits. What particular part of the body I was imprisoned in, I was unable to determine; but to one part, and that apparently a very small one, almost a point, I *was* confined. I tried to project myself, as of wont, along my limbs; but the power was gone. The ground on which I lay felt like air; indeed I don't believe that I felt it at all. The connection between me and the body was in a measure dissevered, and I shuddered as the thought came upon me that this was *death*. My eyelids closed, but I was able to see and hear as distinctly as ever; nay, more distinctly; for I could see not only the faces and forms of others, but their hearts; and could read their thoughts, even though they were but half formed.

The fellow who shot me came running up, wild terror almost over-powering his senses. The shot was purely accidental. This gave me some comfort; it was so much sweeter to go out of the world thus, than to die by the hand of an enemy. Soon other came up, crying out with fright. It was natural that I should look at their hearts, since it was just as easy as to look at their faces, and moreover, was somewhat new to me: but I soon grew sick of it. It was an ungracious task, and I don't wonder now, though I did formerly, that the Rosicruscians were all misanthropes.

The men took me up softly, as though they feared to hurt me by any roughness, and conveyed me into the house. They laid me on a bed, covered me with a white cloth, and pronounced me a corpse; put on long faces, spoke in whispers, and sent for the coroner. How I longed to throw off the sheet, jump up, and kick them all out of the room! I felt able to do it: but when I tried, my arms and feet were mere bars of lead, and refused to obey the commands of the will. So I lay still, and tried to groan, but I couldn't. What next? thought I; ay, what next! A cold shiver crept through me as I thought of the future; so I looked back on the past, and then tried to groan again; but with no better success. Soon the coroner came in, took a pinch of snuff, and felt of my wrist. 'Quite dead!' said he, cooly. 'Death caused by a rifle-ball through the heart.' He was thinking about the price of stocks all the while, for I could see into his *soul*. 'Ah!' he continued, 'sad event; very sad; better notify his friends; it's unpleasant; the sooner, the better. I'll make out my report today.' And with this, the little coroner waddled out of the house.

Nearly three days I had lain thus, and now I was to be buried. I was arrayed throughout in very white linen. Decidedly unbecoming, thought I. Oh! I wish somebody would bore a hole in me, and let me out! I was getting tired: for the last thirty-six hours had been thirty-six years. Nobody *did* bore a hole in me, however, and I remained in.

They took me up gently and laid me in the coffin. I struggled, and fought, and remonstrated; but they didn't seem aware of any motion that I made, but went gravely on with what they were about; and into the coffin I went. The lid was nailed down, all but the head-piece: so I knew that my countenance was to be exposed once more to the gaze of admiring friends. 'Snug quarters these!' thought I; 'rather close but soft. I wish it hadn't this confounding smell of the grave!'

I went to church in state; listened to a very affecting sermon on the uncertainty of life; heard a dirge performed by the choir; and very well it was performed too. But the young lady that sang the solo! How I longed to bite her! I knew her voice. She sung altogether too well—too artist-like. I hated her for it; and thought how I should like to sing a solo over *her* coffin.

The exercises being over, all gathered round to look again on the face of the dead. The lid was thrown back, and the light of day streamed in upon me. It was the last time it would ever visit me. My bed grew cold as I thought of it! Many familiar, many strange faces peered down into mine: some curious, some sad, but the most merely grave.

'I say,' cried I to them, though they didn't seem to hear me; 'I say, fine sport this; *very* fine; quite an amusing spectacle, no doubt! But see here, my good friends,' said I, raising my voice, 'I protest against this whole proceeding. If I was dead, or anything of the kind, I shouldn't object in the least; but I am no more dead than you are! My position here is really uncomfortable. Just consider how *you* would like to be thrust into a box, and dropped down into a hole in the ground, out of sight; and all done so cooly and deliberately, for the sake of aggravation! I don't see what right you have to treat a fellow in this way! I wish somebody would let me out! Holla! you wretch!' said I to the man who came with his instruments to fasten me in; 'do you suppose I am a dog, to be buried alive? Give me a little fresh air; *do* for mercy's sake!'

But the carpenter didn't hear me. He took hold of the cloth and spread it over my face, preparatory to nailing down the lid. 'Old fellow!' I cried energetically, for the blackness of despair and horror was coming over my soul; 'none of that! I tell you now, I *won't* be buried!' But he seemed to think that I *would* be buried, and very composedly proceeded to shut me in. One little gleam of sunshine, and that vanishing like early mist, was all that remained to me forever. I made a terrible struggle; something gave way with a cracking noise, resembling the snapping of a lute-string; and I was free! I dashed head-foremost through the crevice between the side of the coffin and the descending lid, and jumped nimbly on the top of my late habitation.

'Ah, ha!' said I to the undertaker, as I shook my fist in his face; 'ah, ha! you thought to catch me napping, did you? I was a little too quick for you!' But he went on with solemn countenance to screw down the cover, and smooth the pall over the whole: totally unconscious that anything unusual had taken place. I looked up to the gallery, and there stood the identical young lady who had just performed the solo, in the dirge. I had kissed her that day week! 'Oh, ho!' my dear,' I exclaimed, 'hadn't you better have reserved your lugubrious croak for a more fitting occasion? I shall dance at *your* funeral yet!' The young lady, without heeding me, looked down at the coffin mournfully; that is, as mournfully as she could look, and at the same time adjust her curls, and cast stolen glances at a young physician in one of the boy-pews, whom I had supplanted in her affections. I was about making some violent remarks on her want of attention to me, and the extreme disrespect of the assembly generally, in not listening to my voice, when it occurred to me that after all I might be only a spirit, and then of course my voice could not be heard by mortal ears.

This train of reflection led me to consider my corporeal frame. But here was a puzzle; for although everything looked as it used to do, so much so that I would have sworn that I stood on the top of the coffin wholly alive and material, yet it was equally undeniable that I was at that very instant reposing under my feet. With regard to my dress, there was a still greater puzzle. What its material was I could not determine. It felt very light and loose, and almost intangible. I found too that the power of gravitation had but little effect upon me, so that I could rise or sink like a cloud in mid-ether. All these discoveries filled me with wonder; but in the midst of my philosophical meditations I was disturbed by the pall-bearers, who were preparing to remove their load from the church. The day was a fine one; a large procession was formed; the bell sent forth its single heavy notes, and we were on our way to the church-yard.

'I may as well see the show out,' thought I; so I sat down astride the coffin, folded my arms, and apostrophized my former self beneath: 'Pleasant companion! Has it at length come to this? a sudden, violent and everlasting parting! Excuse me for not shedding tears, for I can't, or I would in a moment. A delightful, profitable, though somewhat uncouth servant and associate hast thou been to me, in times past. Kind-hearted wast thou; a little given to pains and grievings of thine own, yet always ready to share mine, and obedient to my slightest wish. I will not cast in thy teeth thy slips and errors of foot, which have been many, and of tongue, which have been more. Forgive any unkind feelings or thoughts which I have entertained toward thee on that account. Forget me, old friend! for I shall soon do the same by thee. I will see thee buried, and then be off. You needn't feel pained at going away from the world: all things earthly must sooner or later have an end, and hence you are not alone in your misery.'

Hallo, you, Sir pall-bearer! don't stumble over every third stone you come to, for you break in upon a very delightful philosophical homily of mine. Your twitchings and jouncings disturb me excessively. 'If I might suggest, Sir,' said I to the minister, who was walking very slowly before me, 'I would beg you to consider that I am bare-headed; the season of the year is mid-summer, and the sun is near his meridian. However, proceed no faster than you deem advisable. Great dunce!' continued I, aside; 'I might as well talk to a post! My good friends!' added I, turning round so as to face the procession behind, 'my good friends, it would give me great pleasure on this melancholy and distressing occasion to make some remarks on the brevity of human enjoyment, interspersing a few thoughts on the Graham system of diet, and concluding with a beautiful and affecting acknowledgement of the honor you are doing me in escorting my coffin through the streets of your miserable little town. I see, however, that we are now entering the graveyard, and will forbear.'

Softly, gentleman bearers! set me down softly. So! my course is run, and my ride finished, is it? The grave opens its great mouth, and I must vacate my agreeable seat. 'By the mysteries of the grave! what's this, though?' said I to a companion, who by some magic stood at that instant beside me. 'Isn't this Hans Von Spiegel?' 'Indeed it is,' quoth he. 'But who is Hans Von Spiegel?' asks the reader. He was a fellow who died five years ago, from a fall which he got from horseback. He was an intimate friend of mine; a little wild, perhaps, but a very good fellow at heart, notwithstanding. Hans sidled up to me and regarded me with a friendly stare. 'Oh, ho!' says I. 'Ah, ha!' says he. 'How are you?' says I. 'Tolerable,' says he. 'You must think us,' he added, 'an ill-mannered sort of people, not to have come out and meet you; but the fact is, you died suddenly. If we had known that you had been coming, we should have contrived to receive you with becoming honor. However, I take upon myself the responsibility of welcome.'

'You congratulate me on my escape from the 'vale of tears,' I suppose,' said I. 'And *sighs*,' he added. 'And *sighs!*' thought I; 'what an expressive ejaculation!' Hans, be it known, asserted with his last breath that it was love and not the fall which killed him, although everybody knew to the contrary. He lived just long enough after the accident to exclaim at least a hundred and fifty times: 'Oh! Blumine! cruel Blumine! you have seen the death of me!'

'How do you employ yourselves in this land of spirits?' I asked, after a pause.

'I'm out of breath, just now,' he answered, 'having come pretty fast to see you: but I'll tell you more about our way of life directly.'

'Where shall we go first?' I asked.

'Nowhere till your body is buried!' answered he, rather indignantly.

'Just as you please,' said I, while the ghost of a blush struggled upward into my forehead.

The coffin was now lowered into the grave, and the sexton stood with his shovel in hand, while the minister blessed my remains. 'Old friend!' said I, looking into the grave, 'farewell! A pleasant sleep to you! But mind and be ready should I want you again. Farewell!'

At this Hans and I departed.

KILLCROP THE CHANGELING

BY RICHARD THOMPSON

(1828)

Before the city walls of London were generally removed, and when several portions of the embattled bulwark with its high towers were yet remaining, that part of the plain, old-fashioned road leading from barbican to the Bars by Faun's Alley was denominated Pickaxe Street; in which ominously sounding part of London there was an old house, long since destroyed, which had at a former period been inhabited by one Jonah Gumphion, an eminent undertaker, who displayed what he called the sign of "Both Ends," in two large wooden models of a cradle and a coffin, which swung above his door.

The house itself was built of brown bricks, but round the windows were rich borders of red ones; and some parts of the erection were garnished with white stone.

Jonah Gumphion died in debt at the conclusion of his lease; and the tenement which he occupied being part of a property then waiting an award of the Court of the Chancery in the cause of Clutch *versus* Readyclaw, neither party paid any regard to the state of the habitation, and thus it daily grew less worth disputing about. The windows, in which many of the panes were either lost or fractured, became darker and darker by time, and dust, and cobwebs; the tiled penthouse over the shop fell into decay; the shop windows were shut up, but the shutters were broken and mouldering away; the narrow door, covered with ten years' soil, looked as if it had not been unclosed for ages; and a cloud of obscurity hid the once white and richly traced fanlight which appeared above it.

About the time our story commences, the building presented this lamentable spectacle, and many and terrible were the reports concerning it; for the common people believe, that to shut up a house and leave it to decay, is as sure to generate fairies, goblins, and spirits in the deserted chambers, as the keeping in of a glass-house fire for an hundred years is to produce a Salamander in the ashes. Added to this argument, it was urged that the last occupant was one who was familiar with death; that he had received many a corpse into his dwelling; that it was very probable some of them had returned; and finally, that it was certainly so. All this had no trifling effect on the character of the building; and the haunted house of Pickaxe Street was so well known throughout the neighborhood, that everyone prophesied, that to whichever of the two contending parties the property should be decreed, they would find it of little or no value, since they could neither inhabit it themselves, nor would anyone else venture to lodge in it, though it were offered rent free.

The consideration of these points led the legal advisers of Messrs. Clutch and Readyclaw to persuade their clients conjointly to advertise for some bold and adventuresome person to reside in Mr. Gumphion's vacant residence, until their suit should be decided; to which, as it was but too evident that such a consummation was even yet at a very far period, they with some hesitation consented; and the following advertisement was accordingly inserted in the *Postman*:

> "This is to give notice, that if any person will undertake to lodge for a time in the dilapidated house known by the sign of 'Both Ends,' of late in the occupation of **Mr. Jonah Gumphion, Undertaker,** deceased, No. 107, **Pickaxe Street**, nigh unto the **Three Cups Inn**, he shall be found in all provisions and furniture, and rewarded for his trouble. It is not to be believed what many people say concerning this house, for such reports are idly raised by ignorant or interested individuals; but it is recommended that none apply but a bold and undaunted person, who will not be intimidated from his purpose in living there. More particulars may be known of **Mr. Zaccheus Demur**, Attorney in **Furnival's Inn**, or of **Mr. Moses Mortmain**, attorney of **New Inn**, Solicitors in the Cause of **Clutch** *against* **Readyclaw** in Chancery, for whom this offer is made."

The peace of Aix-le-Chapelle, which took place in October 1748, caused the crew of the "Devourer," a first-rate man-of-war, to be paid off. One of these disbanded veterans was an ancient and valiant mariner, called Noah Fluke. In the sea-fight off Toulon which took place four years previously, of which he was both an active and triumphant eye-witness, his faithful friend and superior officer, Lieutenant Hartwell, had died in his arms, whilst recommending his widow and infant son to his protection; and without consulting any other feeling than his grief for his patron's death, and the warmth which he felt about his heart when the request was made, Fluke readily engaged to become their friend.

"And, d'ye see," he would say, when relating the circumstance, "who so fitting as I, that had known him from the time he was as high as a handspike? And, somehow, methought he weighed his anchor more cheerily when I'd given him my hard hand in token of promise, like."

Fluke, when he returned to England, which was but for a very short period, found the lieutenant's widow so deeply affected by her loss, that it was evident that half his charges would soon be at an end. He gave her his best consolation in his power, although it was somewhat of the roughest; but to this he added his own prize-money, with whatever wealth he possessed, in the most delicate manner he was able, and then left her with an exhortation to "keep her helm hard up against sorrow," and the assurance that 'whilst Noah Fluke had his head above water, there was a pilot for her and her little one to the end of life's voyage."

When the honest-hearted sailor next came back, which was not until the "Devourer" was paid off, as already stated, he found that the lieutenant's widow had gone to her long home about a twelve-month previous, leaving her son in the care of the persons with whom she had resided, until Fluke should return to take the charge upon himself. A few lines, written but a short time before the dissolution of Matilda Hartwell, were presented to the old mariner, who wetted the paper through his tears, and then spent the rest of his grief and affection in embracing little Basil, who held his hand and received his rough caresses with all the delighted confidence of the most artless childhood. Though Fluke, during a long service at sea, had become possessed of some property, yet it was but very little to support himself and the son of his old officer. The widow had left nothing but her prayers and blessings for her child and his protector. The wars were over, and the means which had formerly filled the seaman's purse were no longer available; besides, some wounds, especially those of time, had greatly unfitted him for active employment; while his young companion had already, with the sweetest endearments, twined so about his heart, that he could not summon up courage to leave him. In truth, little Basil was a most engaging infant, or rather child, for he was of that age when the inability of infancy was lost in the expanding powers of childhood; and the weeping April of the earliest hours of life has passed over into the glad serene May of its opening years.

It was at this period, when old Fluke found his affection for his charge every day increasing, and when he was every day becoming more anxious concerning his future support, that the advertisement in the *Postman*, already mentioned, caught his attention; and in this manner he reflected upon it:

"Why, what have we here?—if any person will undertake to lodge—lapidated house—ay, why, what then?—plenty of people ready and willing—no fear, no fear—found in their rations—why, what are the lubbers spelling after? Oh! here's the breakers ahead, I see—not to be believed what many people say—no, by George! the world's full of lies—recommended none need apply but a bold and undaunted—I'm off, devil of a thing do I fear, man or hobgoblin! Mr. Zaccheus Demur. Here goes—Furnival's Inn, ahoy!"

Notwithstanding the frequent appearance of this advertisement, no person had as yet applied to either of the solicitors at all qualified to discharge the office of residing in the "Both Ends" of Pickaxe Street; and Mr. Demur, with considerable honesty, stated to Fluke all that had been invented and reported concerning it.

When the old sailor had calmly heard him out, he said, "Well, brother, all this may be true, and mayhap it aren't, to which last I incline; but, d'ye see, I've been at sea ever since I was as tall as a cook's kettle, and I was never afraid yet, though to be sure I've met with some devildoms in my time, for the old one's at work upon the waters as well as on the land. But all that's neither here nor there: I'll take watch in the old undertaker's cabin; and damme, but I'll keep a clear ship of everything, whether it has two legs or four!"

"Well but, Mr. Fluke," interrupted the lawyer, "the man for such a situation should be pious as well as brave; and excuse me if I offend, but you"—

"Avast heaving, Master Scrivener, I don't pretend to be a parson any more than my neighbors; but you don't know the heart of a sailor. Why, look ye, brother, a man that's always in danger a'rn't such a fool as to be one of your wicked ones; for, d'ye see me, the best ship may start a plank, and the fairest wind blow up to a storm. But, howsomever, I'll walk your deck in Pickaxe Street, as I said heretofore, if you'll enter me. As for anything of this world, I don't fear it a rope's end, for I'll give 'em as good as they bring, and so let 'em look to it; and as for anything from the other, d'ye mind me, why, the Great Commander of all is too good to let aught appear to hurt or disturb an old faithful sailor and his young innocent orphan."

The solicitor objected no further, but concluded the engagement with Fluke, who was to remove immediately to his new dwelling, which was furnished with as many inconveniences as could be hastily gotten together, though all of Mr. Gumphion's property which time had not destroyed was yet remaining in the apartments.

It might be supposed that young Basil Hartwell would have been much alarmed at the prospect of inhabiting so terrible an abode; but no! His mind seemed animated by a soul which was not of earth; a gentleness so angelic, that the old mariner would sometimes say an evil spirit could not remain where that blessed little one was; an innocence so pure and so lovely, that he seemed to represent what the children of men might have been had they been born in Paradise; and he placed so sincere a love and confidence upon his rough but almost doting foster-father, that he would not have feared to have ventured into the wildest dangers, provided it were by the side of old Noah Fluke. Added to all this, he was as beautiful a creature as lived under heaven: the fairest flaxen hair, light laughing blue eyes, and all those features which have been attributed to youthful loveliness, were to be found in Basil Hartwell.

Although Fluke, to use his own expression, was "captain, cook, and loblolly boy" in Pickaxe Street, yet the little Basil never complained of loneliness; indeed, an additional gladness of heart seemed to have taken possession of him since they had resided there. He would sing to his beloved protector all his little childish songs, or amuse himself with his infantile histories; and if perchance he were for a short time left alone, he would roam about the house, and through its ruined chambers, caroling the same stanzas, or sit laughing at the gay scenes which presented themselves to his youthful fancy. In his night visions, too, the child would express his joy aloud; for then he said that he conversed with a number of "pretty ladies dressed in bright green, who lived in a beautiful garden full of flowers and fountains." These personages, he added, would sometimes appear to him when he was alone in the daytime, and court him to go along with them; but that, whenever his father entered the room, they all went away, and he could not find them. Old Fluke knew not well what to make of this story; for as he was not versed in popular superstitions, he was not aware that fairies, when they fixed their attentions on a mortal, ever select the most lovely in feature and the most angelic in mind, whom they endeavor to allure to their society by exhibiting all the glittering but deceitful pleasures of their green island. Woe unto the unhappy wretch who is seduced by them! for false and fleeting as are all the enjoyments of this world, those of the fairy world are much more so; and the victim they have gained must for years remain a prisoner in its scenes of gaudy mockery , unless some undaunted friend have the firmness and bravery to attempt his rescue.

There was on the first floor of the house of Pickaxe Street a room of large dimensions, and grand but old-fashioned fittings-up, which, while in the possession of Mr. Gumphion, had been used as a state funeral apartment, and several of his richly-carved sconces were still hanging upon the walls. The cornice and lower sides of the room were formed of dark brown wainscot; but the greater part of it was covered with a light green paper, having a large pattern printed upon it in a flock of octogonal pieces of oak, and the ample curtains which hung mouldering round the darkened windows were of heavy green damask, of which also were formed the cushions of the antique mahogany chairs. As this apartment was much too large for the residence of Noah Fluke and Basil, it was abandoned to decay; but the door being unfastened, the child took particular delight in wandering into what he called the "pretty green room," and in contemplating its richness, although to anyone else it sent the cold chill to the heart which arises from viewing a desolate state-chamber.

It chanced that, one sunny morning in spring little Basil withdrew, singing merrily up to the green apartment, whence old Fluke, to his great surprise, still continued to hear the chant louder, and even in sweeter tones, than those of his foster-son. His surprise, however, was soon increased, and his fears greatly excited, when suddenly a heavy fall, succeeded by a loud and piercing shriek from Basil, sounded from the chamber. In his youngest and most active days Fluke never obeyed a command with such rapidity as he followed the cry of his young companion. Hastily seizing his cutlass, and striding up four stairs at a time, he rushed into the room, and beheld the form of his little friend stretched lifeless upon the floor.

Flinging down the weapon in an agony of terror, and kneeling upon one knee, he raised the body on the other; but what was his horror, to behold the beautiful features, which he had so loved to look upon, distorted by strong convulsions! Those bright azure eyes were become pale and glazed, and were staring wildly upon vacancy; the plump glowing cheeks were changed to a sallow hue, and had so much fallen in, that the mouth, drawn back and extended at the sides, pointed outward, like that of a fox, whilst it was also open with a malignant smile. Even the hair and form of little Basil were equally changed; for in place of the long flowing golden locks which hung around his head, the creature whom Fluke now beheld had coarse red hair, matted in streaming flakes; and the youthful symmetry of young Hartwell was exchanged for a tall and gaunt form, the joints of which were all out of proportion to the rest of the body.

When the old mariner had beheld all this, loud and vehement were his cries for his "own brave boy," and frequent were his execrations against the devils who had conveyed him away. The thing which he now saw filled him with horror; and so great was his disgust, that he would instantly have quitted the house and all his prospects of employment, had not the hope of recovering Basil induced him to remain. But terrible indeed was the society of that changeling with whom he now associated. It never spoke; but wherever Fluke turned, there it was before his eyes, grinning, mocking, and staring wildly upon him; and if perchance the old sailor gave vent to his fury and distress in words, and called the being beside him an imp, and elf-child, or whatever else rose in his mind, these grimaces became ten times more terrible and disgusting. When he had prepared his meals, all desire for which had left him, the changeling sat opposite to him, devouring everything that appeared upon the table, and then uttered strange and inarticulate sounds for more. In this terrific society passed the day and the following night, but the next morning

Fluke determined to carry his spectral companion to a celebrated German doctor, who kept the "Dragon Overthrown," in Barbican.

Friedrich von Drenschendrugger von Finischmann was a short stout figure, usually dressed in an old scarlet coat and waistcoat, which was ornamented with faded gold embroidery, and wore upon his head within doors a crimson velvet night-cap, which was exchanged when he visited for a very large white wig, lined with blue silk, and surmounted by a small cocked hat bound with gold. But it was his boots which were the greatest rarity, surpassing all modern fashions of Jockey, Wellington, Hessian, Blucher, or Masquerade: they were of broad dimensions, especially at the tops, where they were bound with narrow edging of silver plate; and in addition to all this splendor, the doctor also carried a long gold-headed amber cane, whilst out of his coat-pockets were usually seen the necks and labels of two large bottles of his own "Vitae Elixir of the Moon," which he introduced upon all occasions, and recommended for all diseases.

To this German Hippocrates, then, Fluke led his supernatural companion; and not a little surprise was expressed by Finischmann at the dreadful appearance of the changeling, and the recital of the mariner's story.

"Herrn den himmel!" ejaculated the doctor, "you shall take him out of mine house; it is eine Killcrop, like what I have seen in de castle of Baron von Bloosterbugle, at Karkhentooth, in mine old land. I will not let you stay; I shall be frightened out of my wits. Engel den meine! as I am an honest man and goot doctor, it is ein Wechselbald: dat is what you call ein Teufel kind, ein Kleinergest—I cannot tell you what it is. You shametrell, why does you not take way that klein fend? I tell you it is Killcrop der changeling, der Teufel of Pickaxe Street!"

"Why, ay, brother, I believe you're right," answered Fluke; "but I came to you for sailing orders, and here you're for sending me off to sea without them. Come, shut your mouth, and open your medicine chest, and give this Killcrop, as you call him, a spell of your craft."

"Der Teufel!" replied the German, starting back, "I does not make physics for geisters, and thors, and Killcrops; I does desire dat you will get you both out of mine house."

"And what am I to do with this hobgoblin?" returned Fluke.

"Whatever you likes," said the alarmed Von Finischmann, "only you shall take him out of my sight. Der himmel! I wonders when I was ever see anything so terrible. Bah! bah! I was forget your old man, as you call alte Bootsknecht; I shall tell you dat in eine gape, dat ist eine street of Little Briteine, you shall fint what you call ein Stern-denter, dat ist ein astrologer, and he shall tell you what to do."

"Thank ye, Mr. Doctor, thanky, I'll be in his wake with this flying Dutchman in the reefing of a foresail. But what does he call his ship, and who's captain, eh, brother?"

"Aha! Der nahm des mannes, as you call he is ist mun goot frent; her is call Tolemee Horoskope, and he was living at der Zeichem, as you was call a sign of der Globe and der Comet. Now I does desires dat you schall go, donner und blitzen! Der Teufel! Hagel!"

"Well, well," answered Fluke, "I'm off, so good morning t'ye, and many thanks for your advice; we shall speak ships again some time."

The sailor and his spectral companion, who had evinced a thousand goblin tricks during this conference, now departed for Little Britain, but great was the reluctance and opposition which the changeling exhibited to such a proceeding, and it was by main force only that Fluke dragged him into the astrologer's house. The moment that Horoscope beheld the creature, he raised his hand to Fluke, who was about to relate his story, and said—

"Old man, I know your desires, but speak not a word till I give you permission. Parable, lead this child into my study, and turn the key; and, dost there?—no prattling, if thou wouldst not have a legion let loose upon thee! Now, friend, thy story."

Fluke then related in his own peculiar manner all that has already been told, and concluded by entreating of the astrologer to point out some means whereby he should be relieved from his unearthly companion, and recover his young Basil. Horoscope stated in reply, that the boy had been seduced away by fairies, who had left in his place one of their own elf-children; and that there was but one way to be pursued for the reversing of the spell, which required considerable courage and perseverance.

"This day," said the astrologer, "is one of the four great divisions of the year, upon all of which men have power over fairies; and it is, moreover, the holy season of Our Lady's Annunciation. Thou must then immediately go to those dark and marshy fields which lie to the north-east of this place in Finsbury, and prepare thee a grave; in which at night-time thou must place the changeling, repeating such a spell as I shall give thee. All this must be done alone; and alone and in silence thou must watch through the night, with thy back towards the grave. If these ceremonies be faithfully performed, when the first rays of the sun shall cast thy shadow upon the ground, look upon the grave, and thy Basil shall be restored; but if the least point be omitted, another quarter of a year must pass ere this spell can be repeated. Go now, prepare the grave, and at night come hither for thy elf-child and the spell."

Fluke departed, after thanking the astrologer, and promising the strictest attention to his instructions. Having prepared the grave, he passed the remainder of the day in refreshing himself for his night's watching; and about the hour of nine he went to Horoscope's for his charge, taking with him a dark lanthorn and his cutlass.

The changeling and the old mariner were soon on the road to Finsbury Fields, which at the time of this history spread its marshy wildness on either side of what is now called the Pavement, leaving only a long lane, guarded with low hedges passing between them, though the place is now occupied by splendid shops and stately dwelling-houses. Fluke's first care was to lay the elf in the grave, and much was he surprised to find him passive, and comparatively gentle to what he had formerly seen him; and then, holding up the lanthorn to Horoscope's written instructions, he read over the changeling the following spell:

> "Receive, O earth! O virgin earth!
>   This elf within thy narrow bed;
> And raise to life with second birth,
>   That beauteous form so lately fled.
>
> Throughout the night, throughout the night,
>   Mine eyes shall watch, mine heart shall grieve,
> But the first rays of golden light,
>   Those tears, those sorrows shall relieve.
>
> 'Tis done! in darkness works the spell,
>   No mortal sight thy work shall see;
> But morn shall prove it wrought full well,
>   And give my Basil back to me."

Having uttered these lines, Fluke wrapped himself in his watch-coat, unsheathed his cutlass, and then, turning his back to the grave, and to the east, sat down in much anxiety of mind upon a mound of earth. The night which followed was dark, fearful, and tempestuous; the lightning, and rain, and wind were continually in motion, and with the storm there seemed to mingle shouts from the grave; and sometimes he heard, or thought he heard, several voices, with singing and with laughter. Then again it would seem as if a procession passed him on horseback, with the bridle-bits and stirrups ringing loudly and merrily; but though the gloom of the midnight was too deep for discerning anything through it, the old mariner actually imagined that he saw a shadowy train ride by him, one of which bore something before him on his saddle-bow. When it had passed, a blaze of light seemed to burst out of the grave, followed by such strange sounds of mourning and shouting that the honest sailor could scarcely refrain from turning round to look upon it; but the remembrance of Horoscope's words made him resist the temptation.

Towards morning a deep sleep fell upon him, from which he awoke not till the sun's beams cast his shadow on the ground before him. He rose in a moment, and rushing to the spot where the grave was, he found instead of it a small mound of the most beautiful green turf, with little Basil Hartwell lying upon it asleep, and as lovely as when he was conveyed to Fairyland. Words cannot express Fluke's joy as he clasped the boy to his bosom, and departed. The same morning also, to increase his happiness, and set all his future fears at rest, the payment of a very large sum of prize, which had long been litigated, put an end to his continuing a resident in the "Both Ends" of Pickaxe Street.

CARL BLUVEN AND THE STRANGE MARINER

BY HENRY DAVID INGLIS

(1833)

On that wild part of the coast of Norway that stretches between Bergen and Stavenger, there once lived a fisherman called Carl Bluven. Carl was one of the poorest of all the fisherman who dwelt on that shore. He had scarcely the means of buying materials wherewith to mend his net, which was scarcely in a condition to hold the fish in it; still less so was he is a condition to make himself master of a new boat, which he stood greatly in need of; for it was so battered and worn, that while other fishermen adventured out into the open sea, Carl was obliged to content himself with picking up what he could among the rocks and creeks that lay along the coast.

Notwithstanding his poverty, Carl was on the eve of marriage. His bride was a daughter of a woodcutter in the neighboring forest, who contrived, partly with his hatchet, and partly with his gun, to eke out his livelihood; so that the match was pretty equal on both sides. But Carl was in a sad dilemma on one account; he had nothing to present to the minister on his marriage—not a keg of butter, nor a pot of sausages, nor a quarter of a sheep, nay not even a barrel of dried fish; and as he had been accustomed to boast to his father-in-law of his thriving trade, he knew not in what way to keep up appearances. In short, the evening before his wedding day arrived, and Carl was still unprovided.

So dejected had Carl been all day, that he had never stirred out of his hut; and it was approaching nightfall. The wind had risen, and the hollow bellowing of the waves, as they rolled in among the huge caverned rocks, sounded dismally in Carl's ear, for he knew he dared not launch his leaky boat in such a sea; and yet, if he caught no fish, there would be nothing for supper when he should bring his wife home. Carl rose, clapped his hat on his head, with the air of a man who is resolved to do something, and walked out upon the shore. Nothing could be more dismal than the prospect around Carl's hut; no more desolate and dreary home than Carl's could a man bring his bride to. Great black round-headed rocks, partly covered with seaweed, were thickly strewn along the coast for many miles; these, when the tide was back, were left dry, and when it flowed, their dark heads, now seen, now hidden, as the broad-backed waves rolled over them, seemed like the tumbling monsters of the deep.

When Carl left his hut, the rising tide had half-covered the rocks; and the waves, rushing through the narrow channels, broke in terrific violence on the shore, leaving a wide, restless bed of foam, as they retreated down the sloping beach. The sun, too, was just disappearing beneath the waves, and threw a bright and almost unnatural blaze upon the desolate coast. Carl wandered along, uncertain what to do. He might as well have swamped his boat at once, as have drawn it out of the creek where it lay secure; so, after wading in and out among the channels, in the hope of picking up some fish that might not have been able to find their way back with the wave that had thrown them on shore, he at length sat down upon a shelving rock, and looked out upon the sea, towards the great whirlpool called the Maelstroom, of which so many fearful things were recorded.

"What riches are buried there," said Carl to himself half aloud. "Let me see—within my time, six great ships have been sucked down; and if the world be, as they say, thousands of years old, what a mine of wealth must be at the bottom of the Maelstroom be! What casks of butter and hams—to say nothing of gold and silver—and here am I, Carl Bluven, to be married tomorrow, and not a keg for the minister. If I had but one cask from the bottom of the Maelstroom, I would"—but Carl did not finish the sentence. Like all fisherman of that coast, Carl had his superstitions and his beliefs; and he looked round him rather uneasily, for he well knew that all in the Maelstroom belonged to Kahlbrannar, the tall old mariner of the whirlpool; and after having had the hardihood to entertain so bold a wish, Carl felt more uncomfortable than he cared to own; and seeing the night gathering in, and the tide rising to his feet, while the spray dashed in his face, he was just about to return to his solitary hut, when a high crested wave, rushing through the channel beside him, bore a cask along with it, and threw it among the great stones that lay beneath the rocks.

As parts of wrecks had often been thrown upon this dangerous shore, Carl was not greatly surprised; and circumstances having allayed the superstitious fears that were beginning to rise, he had soon his hands upon the cask, getting it out from among the rocks in the best way he was able; till, having reached the sand, he rolled it easily up to the door of his dwelling; and having shut to the door, and lighted his lamp, he fell to work in opening the cask to see what it contained. It proved the very thing he

Next morning betimes, Carl Bluven was on his way to his wedding, rolling the cask before him with the larger half of the butter in it for his marriage fee. With such a present as this, Carl was well received by the minister, as well as by his father-in-law, and by Uldewalls the bride, who, with her crown upon her head, the Norwegian emblem of purity, became the wife of the fisherman; and he, after spending a day or two in feasting with his new relations, returned with Uldewalls to his hut on the sea shore, carrying back with him a reasonable supply of sausages and brandiwine, and Gammel Orsk cheese, and such like dainties, as the dowry of his wife.

For some little time all went well with Carl. What with the provisions he had brought home, and the remains of his butter, the new married couple did not fare amiss; even though the fisherman rarely drew a net; for Carl wished to enjoy his honeymoon, and not be wading and splashing among the sea-green waves, when he might be looking into the blue eyes of Uldewalls. At length, however, the sausage pots stood empty, and even the Gammel Orsk cheese was reduced to a shell: as for the butter, Carl and his wife had found it so good, that the cask had been empty long since.

Carl left his hut, taking his net and his oars over his shoulders, leaving Uldewalls picking cloudberries; and unmooring his boat, paddled out of the creek, and began throwing his nets; but not a fish could he take: still he continued to try his fortune, in an out among the creeks, til the sun set, and dusk began to creep over the shore. The tide had retired, so that Carl's boat was left dry a long way within water-mark, and he had to walk a dreary mile or more, over the shingle and sand, among the black dripping rocks that lay between him and his own dwelling. But there was no help for it: so, mooring his boat the best way he could, he turned towards the coast, in somewhat of a dejected mood, at his want of success.

As Carl turned away, he noticed at a little distance, close to the water, a small boat, that well he knew belonged to no fisherman of that coast; it was the very least boat he had ever seen, such as no seaman of Bergenhuus could keep afloat on such a sea; and the build of it, too, was the queerest he had ever beheld. But Carl, seeing from the solitary light that shone in the window of his hut, that Uldewalls expected him, kept his direct course homeward, resolved next day to return and examine the boat, which he had no doubt, had been thrown ashore from some foreign wreck. But Carl had soon still greater cause for wonder: raising his eyes from the pools of water, in which he hoped to find some floundering fish, he observed a tall figure advancing from the shore, in the direction of the little boat he had seen, and nearly in the same line which he was pursuing. Now Carl was no coward; yet he would rather have avoided this rencontre. He knew well that no fisherman would walk out among the rocks towards the sea, at the fall of night, and, besides, Carl knew all the fishermen within six leagues; and this was none of them; but he disdained to turn out of his way, which ,indeed, he could only have done by wading through some deep channels that lay on either side of him; and so he continued to walk straight on, his wonder, however, and perhaps his uneasiness, every moment increasing, as the lessening distance showed him more distinctly a face he was sure he had never seen on that coast, and which was of that singular character, which involuntarily raised in the mind of Carl certain uncomfortable sensations.

"A dreary night this, Carl Bluven," said the strange mariner to our fisherman, "and likely for a storm."

"I hope not," said Carl, not a little surprised that he should be addressed by his name; "I hope not, for the sake of the ships and the poor mariners."

"You hope not," said the other, with an ugly sneer; "and who, I wonder, likes better than Carl Bluven to roll a cast-a-way cask to his cabin door?"

"Why," returned Carl, apologetically, and still more suspicious of his company, from the knowledge he displayed, "what Providence kindly sends, 'tis not for a poor fisherman to refuse."

"You liked the butter I sent you, then!" said the strange mariner.

"You sent me!" said Carl.

But Carl's rejoinder remained without further explanation. "Ah ha!" said the tall mariner, pointing out to sea in the direction of the Maelstroom, "she bears right upon it—the *Frou,* of Drontheim, deeply laden. We'll meet again, Carl Bluven." And without further parley, the tall strange mariner brushed past Carl, and strode hastily towards the sea. Carl remained for some time rooted to the spot, looking after him through the deepening dusk, which, however, just enabled Carl to see him reach the little boat, and push off through the surf—but farther he was unable to follow him.

As Carl walked towards his own house, as fast as the huge stones and pools of back-water would permit him, he felt next thing to sure, that the tall mariner he had encountered was no other than Kahlbranner; and a feeling of satisfaction entered his heart, that he had made so important and useful an acquaintance, who not only could, but had already shown, his willingness to do him a kindness; and just as Carl had come to this conclusion, he reached the water-mark opposite to his own house, and, at the same time, his foot struck against a cask, lying high and dry, on the very spot where the other cask had drifted. Carl guessed where it came from; and was right merry at so reasonable a present; and rolling the cask to his own door, he was soon busy staving it, and drawing out, one after another, some of the choicest white puddings, and dried hams, that ever left the harbor of Bergen. "Here's to Kahlbrannar's health," said Carl, after supper, taking his cup of corn brandy in his hand, and offering to hobernob (ed.: to toast) with his wife. But Uldewalls shook her head, and refused to hobernob, or to drink, and Carl fancied, and no doubt it was but fancy, that he heard a strange laugh outside the hut, and that as he raised his eyes, he saw the face of the tall mariner draw back from the window. Carl, however, tossed off his cup; feeling rather proud of the friendship of Kahlbranner.

* * * *

Carl Bluven had a singular dream that night. He thought, that, looking out of the door of his hut, he saw the little boat he had noticed that evening, lying beyond the rocks at low tide, and that he walked out to examine it; and being curious to know whether he could steer so very small a boat, he stepped into it; and leaning forward, hoisted the little sail at the bow, the only one it had; and when he turned round to take the helm, he saw the tall mariner sitting as a steersman. Away shot the boat, Carl, nothing daunted at the company he was in, or the frailty of the vessel, for the helmsman steered with wonderful dexterity, and the boat flew along like a sea-bird skimming the waves. Not a word was spoken, till after a little while, the steersman, pointing forward, said, "There she is, as I told you, the *Frou,* of Drontheim, bearing right upon the Maelstroom, as my name is Kahlbranner; she'll be down to the bottom before us." Carl now looked out ahead, and saw a fearful sight: the sea, a league across, was like a boiling cauldron, whirling round and round and round, and gradually, as it were, shelving down to the centre, where there appeared a huge hole, round which the water wheeled with an awful swirl, strong enough to suck in all the fleets that ever sailed the seas. A gallant three-masted ship was within the whirlpool; she no longer answered the helm, but flew round and round the cauldron, gradually nearing the centre, which she soon reached, and, stern foremost, rushed down the gulph, that swallowed her up. But notwithstanding the terrors of the Maelstroom, and the horror of this spectacle, Carl did not yet awake from his dream. The little boat, piloted by the tall mariner, flew directly across the whirlpool to its centre—down, down, down they sunk; and the next moment Carl found himself walking with his companion on the ribbed sea-sand at the bottom of the Maelstroom. What a sight met the eyes of Carl! Mountains of wealth; piles of all that ships have carried, or nations trafficked in from the beginning of time; wrecks of a thousand vessels, great and small, scattered here and there, and the white bones of the mariners, thicker strewn than gravestones in a churchyard. But what mainly attracted the eye of Carl, was the gold and the silver that lay about as plentiful as pebble-stones; all bright and fresh, though ever so old; for Carl could read upon some of the coins which he picked up the name of Cluff Kyrre, the first king of Norway.

"Now," said Kahlbranner, after Carl had feasted his eyes awhile upon all he saw, "what would you give, Carl Bluven, to be master of all this?"

"Faith," said Carl, "it's of little use lying here; but, save and except the silver and gold, that which has lain in the salt water so long can be worth little."

"There you're wrong," said Kahlbranner, taking up a large pebble stone, and beating out the end of a cask, out of which rolled as fine fresh sausages as ever were beaten, grated, and mixed by any *Frou* of Bergenhuus; "just taste them, friend; and, besides, have ye forgotten the casks I sent?"

Carl tasted, and found them much to his liking. "You know," said he, "I am but a poor fisherman; you ask me what I would give for all I see here; and you know I have nothing to give."

"There you're wrong again," said Kahlbranner; "sit down upon that chest of gold, friend, and listen to what I am going to propose. You shall be the richest butter-merchant, and ham-merchant, and spirit-merchant, in all Bergenhuus, and have more gold and silver in your coffers than King Christian has in his treasury; and in return you shall marry your daughter to my son."

Carl having no daughter, and not knowing whether he might ever have one, tempted by the things about him, and the prospects set before him, and half thinking the offer a jest, said, "a bargain be it, then;" at the same time grasping the hand of the tall mariner; and just as he thought he had pronounced these words, he fancied that the water in which he had up to this time breathed as freely as if he had been on shore, began to choke him; and so, gasping for breath, while Kahlbrannar's laugh rung in his ears, Carl awoke, and found himself lying beside Uldewalls.

Carl told Uldewalls all that he had dreamed; how that he had walked with the strange mariner at the bottom of the Maelstroom, and seen all the wealth, and gold and silver; and of the offer Kahlbranner had made, and how that he thought he had closed a bargain with him.

"Thank God, Carl, it is but a dream!" said Uldewalls, throwing her milk-white arms about his neck: "have nothing to do with the tall mariner, as he is called; no good will come of the connection;" and it was this morning, for the first time, that Carl learned his prospect of being by-and-bye made a father. Carl thought more of his dream than he cared to tell his wife; he could not help fancying that all he had seen in his dream was real; and having already had substantial proof of Kahlbranner's good disposition towards him, he saw nothing incredible in the idea, that he might become all that riches could make him.

* * * *

It was the morning after this, that Carl, awakening just at daybreak, sprung out of bed, and telling Uldewalls that he was going to draw a net that morning, left his hut, and walked towards the rocks. Perhaps he had dreamed the same dream that had visited him the night before; or perhaps he could not dismiss his old dream from his mind; or it might be, that he really intended trying his fortune with his nets that morning. It is certain, however, that Carl left his hut in the early twilight; and that Uldewalls, feeling uneasy in her mind, rose and looked out through the small window, and saw her husband, in the grey of the morning, walk out among the black rocks (for the tide was back); and, although her eye was unable to follow all his turnings out and in among the channels, she could see him afterwards standing close to the low water line, and another of taller stature standing by him. Uldewalls' eyes filled with tears; and when she wiped away the dimness, she could perceive neither her husband nor his companion.

Carl, however, was not long absent; a terrific storm soon after arose, and in the midst of it he arrived, rolling a huge cask up to the door.

"It is singular," said Uldewalls, "that fortune should so often throw prizes in your way, Carl: for my part, I would rather eat some fish of your own catching, than the stores of poor shipwrecked mariners." But Carl laughed, and jested, and drank, and feasted, and was right merry; and swore that fishing was a poor trade; and that he thought of leaving it, and setting up for merchant in Bergen. Uldewalls thought he was making merry in his cups, and that he only jested; but she was mistaken. Next day Carl told her he was discontented with his manner of living—that he was resolved to be a rich man, and that the very next morning they should depart for Bergen. Uldewalls was not sorry to leave the neighborhood, for more reason than one; and besides, being a dutiful wife, she offered no opposition to her husband's will.

The same evening Carl walked out along the coast for the last time, that he might consider all that had passed, and all that was to come; and as he slowly paced along, he thus summed up the advantages of his agreement:—"It's a good bargain I've made anyhow," said he; "I may never have a daughter at all; and if I have, 'tis seventeen or eighteen good years before Kalhbranner can say aught about the matter; and long before that time, who knows what may happen, or what plan I may hit upon to slide out of my bargain." But Carl little knew with whom he had to deal, or he would scarcely have talked about sliding out of his bargain.

Well, next morning saw Carl and Uldewalls on their way to Bergen. Uldewalls proposed that they should take their provisions with them, and such little articles as they possessed; but Carl said there was no occasion

for such strict economy, as he had a well-stored warehouse, and everything comfortable at Bergen; and though Uldewalls wondered at all her
husband told her, she resolved to say nothing more about it just then; and
so Carl and his wife followed the path through the skirts of the forest,
sometimes diving into the deep solitudes of the old pines, and sometimes
emerging upon the sea-shore, till towards night they reached the side of
a great Fiord that ran many, many leagues inland; and Uldewalls looked
up in her husband's face, as if to ask how they were to get over. But Carl
pointed to a small creek just before them, where lay the very least boat,
and the queerest shape, that Uldewalls had ever seen: and Carl helped
her into it, and paddled her over. Uldewalls wished her husband to moor
the boat, that the owner might find it again; but Carl, with a significant
look, said, "Trust him for finding it;" and so the boat drifted down the
Fiord towards the sea; and Carl and his wife pursuing their journey, arrived the same afternoon at Bergen.

Carl led Uldewalls to a good house, facing the harbor, where, as he
had said, everything was prepared for their reception. A neighbor who
lived hard by brought the key, telling them that a good fire was lighted,
for a tall gentleman who engaged the house, had ordered everything to
be got ready that evening; and adding,—"The quantity of goods brought
into the warehouse this day, is the wonder of all Bergen: they've been
carried in as fast as boats could land them, and boatmen carry them; and
the boatmen, they say, were all as alike to each other, as one cask they
carried was to another."

Never, indeed, was a warehouse better stored than Carl Bluven's;
casks of butter, casks of rein-deer hams, casks of foreign spirits, jars of
grated meat, and jars of potted fish, all ready for sale or for export, were
piled in rows one above another; and besides all that, there a granary
filled with as fine Dantzic corn as ever was seen in Bergen market. Carl
drove all before him; and as everything that he sold was paid for in gold
counted down, he was soon looked upon as the most considerable merchant, and the most monied man in Bergenhuus. It is true, indeed, that
Carl had detractors. Some wondered where he came from; and other,
where he had got his money; and to all who did business with Carl, it
was a matter of surprise, that all his payments were made in old coin, or
strange coin, and not in the current money of the country. But prosperity
always raises up enemies, and there are whisperers in Bergen, as well as
elsewhere. And Carl's gold was good gold, and none the worse for its
age; and his payments were punctual; and so he soon rose above these
calumnies.

To Uldewalla all this was a mighty agreeable change; in place of being a poor fisherman's wife, clad in the course stuff of Stavenger, she

was the *frou* of the richest merchant in Bergenhaus; with her silks from France, and her muslins from England, and her furs, the richest that could be bought in the Hamburg market. And in good time Uldewalla became the mother of a girl so beautiful, that she was the admiration of her parents, and the wonder of all Bergen. About the time of this event, a cloud might be seen upon Carl's brow; but it wore off; and he was as fond and as happy a father as any in all Bergenhuss; and as Uldewalla never gave him but this one, he was the prouder of the one he had.

Well might anyone be proud of the little Carintha. The purest of hearts was mirrored in the most beautiful of all faces. But there was a seriousness in the depth of her large mild blue eyes, that was remarked by all who looked upon her; and in her gentle and courteous speech, there was a sadness, that never failed to reach the hearts of those upon whose ears her accents fell. And Carintha grew into greater beauty, and more and more won the affection of all who knew her; and at length she reached the verge of womanhood, and grew lovelier still, every day disclosing new charms, or adding another grace to those that had accompanied her from infancy.

* * * *

For the first fifteen years after Carintha was born, Carl was not only a thriving, but a right merry merchant. His dealings grew more and more extensive; and in respect of wealth, he distanced all competition. Carl enjoyed himself also: he had his five meals every day; sour black bread was never seen in his house; he had his wheaten bread and his dainty rye bread, sprinkled with caraway seeds; and his soup with spiced balls in it; and his white puddings, and his black puddings, and his coffee, ay, and his wine and his cognac; and he hobernobbed with his neighbors; and sung *Gamle Norge,* and, in short, enjoyed himself as the first merchant in Bergen might. But as Carintha grew up, Carl grew less merry; and when she had passed her sixteenth summer, and when Uldewalla, some little time after this, spoke to her husband about settling Carintha in the world, anyone, to have looked at Carl's face at that time, would have seen that something extraordinary was passing within.

It was about a year after this, that the son of the governor of Bergenhuus, Hamel Von Storgelven, cast his eyes upon Carintha, and became enamoured of her. She, on her part, did not rebuke his advances, except with that maidenly timidity that is becoming; and all Bergen said that there would be a wedding. The governor liked the marriage, though Carinthia was not a Froken (young lady of quality); calculating upon the wealth that would pass into his family: and as for Carl Bluven, rich as he was, he was elated at the thoughts of so high a connection; for Carintha having now passed her seventeenth year, and having heard nothing of a certain person, he began to treat all that had once passed as an old story; and seeing his money bags around him, and his warehouse full of goods—(goods as well as money all new and current—for he had long ago parted with his first stock, in the way of trade)—there was nothing to remind him of his hut on the seacoast, and what had happened there, and nothing but might well breed confidence in any man; so that when sitting in his substantial house, with his substantial dinner before him, and his substantial townsmen around him, he would have thought little matter of tossing a glass of corn brandy in Kahlbranner's face, if that individual had made so free as to intrude upon him. But the fancied security of the merchant was soon to be disturbed.

It was now the day before that upon which Carintha was to espouse Hamel Von Storgelven. The affair engrossed all Bergen; for Carl Bergen was chief magistrate of the city, and never before were such preparations witnessed in Bergenhuus. Carl, above all, was in high spirits; for although the bargain he had once made would sometimes intrude upon his thoughts, he had taught himself the habit of getting quickly rid of the recollection; and, indeed, the multifarious business of the chief magistrate, and first merchant in Bergen, left him little leisure for entertaining the remembrance of old stories.

It was a fine sunshiny day—the day, as has been said, before the celebration of Carintha's nuptials—and Carl Bluven was standing on the quay with the other merchants, looking at the cheerful sight of the ships passing in and out, and the bales of goods landing, and chatting about city matters, and trade, and such-like topics—everyone paying to Carl Bluven the deference that was due to one who was on the eve of being allied to the governor—when suddenly all eyes were directed towards the harbor; Carl's eyes followed the rest, and sure enough he saw something that might well create wonder in others, and something more in him.

"Where does it come from?" said one.

"What a singular build!" said another.

"Never was such a boat seen in Bergen harbor," said a third.

"And look at the helmsman," said a fourth; "he's taller than the mast."

The seamen who were aboard the ships, hurried to the sides of their vessels, and looked down as the small boat glided by with the tall mariner at the helm; the porters laid down their burdens, and stared with wondering eyes; even the children gave over their play, to look at the strange boat and the strange helmsman. As for Carl, he said nothing, but remained standing with the group of merchants. Meanwhile, the boat touched the landing place, and the tall mariner stepped out and ascended the steps that led to the quay. There was something in his appearance that nobody liked; everyone made way and stood back; and he, with a singular sneer in his face, walked directly up to Carl Bluven, who had not fallen back like the rest, but manfully stood his ground, and was, therefore, a little apart from his companions. No one could distinctly hear what passed between the tall old strange mariner and the chief magistrate, though it may well be believed that the conference created a small wonder; it was evident, however, that angry words passed between the two; the countenance of the mariner grew darker and darker; Carl's grew flushed and angry; and the bystanders thought things were about to proceed to extremities, when the mariner, darting a menacing scowl at his companion, turned away, and descended into his boat, which he paddled out of the harbor, while everyone looked after it, and asked of his neighbor the same question as before, "Where does it come from?" But no other than Carl Bluven could have answered that question.

"I served him right!" said the chief magistrate, as he walked homewards: "fulfill my bargain, indeed! No, no; if he was such a simpleton as to fill my warehouse with good and my coffers with cash, upon a mere promise, I'm not such a fool as to keep it. Let me but keep on dry land, and I may snap my fingers at him; and by the ghost of King Kyrre, if I catch him again on the quay of Bergen, I'll clap him in the city gaol."

So spoke the chief magistrate; and to do Carl Bluven justice, he had no small liking to his daughter Carintha; and if even he had no prospect of so high an alliance, he would never have entertained the thought of decoying his child into the power of Kahlbranner. He now, however, knew the worst. His promise could not bind Carintha in any way, who would be secure even against treachery, so soon as the wedding ring was placed upon her finger. But the mariner had told him, as plainly as words could, that having consented to her marriage to another, he had no mercy to expect; and bade him remember the white bones he had seen lying at the bottom of the Maelstroom.

It was Carintha's marriage day; and a beautiful bride she went forth; her eyes were blue, and deep, and lustrous as the heavens that looked down upon her; her smile was like an earl sunbeam upon one of her own sweet valleys; her blush, like the evening rose-tint upon her snowy mountains; her bosom, tranquil and yet gently heaving, like the summer sea that girded her shores. Carintha went forth to her nuptials, having first recommended herself to God, who took her into his keeping; and the ring was placed upon her finger, and she was wed; and from that moment, the danger that hung over her from her birth being forever gone by, the seriousness that all used to remark passed away forever from her countenance and from her speech.

There is little doubt that if Carl Bluven had kept his promise to the strange mariner, and decoyed Carintha into his power, God would have saved the child, and punished the unnatural father, by delivering him early into the hands of him with whom he had made so sinful a bargain. But, although it was wicked in Carl to make such a bargain, it would have been more wicked still to fulfill it; and Carl's refusal to do this, as well as the good use he made of his money, and the creditable way in which he discharged the duties of chief magistrate, had, no doubt, the effect of weakening the power of Kahlbranner over him, and of, therefore, preventing the success of the many stratagems resorted to for getting Carl into his power. And so for more than twenty years after the marriage of Carintha, Carl Bluven continued to enjoy his prosperity, and to exercise, at due intervals, the office of chief magistrate: and he saw his grandchildren grow up around him; and at length buried his wife Uldwalla. But the penalty of the rash promise had yet to be paid.

It chanced that Carl Bluven—who, by-the-by, was now Carl Von Bluven, having long ago received that dignity—was bidden to a feast at the house of a rich citizen, who lived just on the opposite side of the harbor. Although it was nearly half a league round the head of the harbor and across the drawbridge, Carl walked round, rather than trust himself across in a boat; a conveyance which, ever since his interview on the quay, he had studiously avoided. It was a great feast; many bowls of bishop (a kind of mulled wine) were emptied, and many a national song roared in chorus; so that Carl, as well as the rest of the guests, began to feel the effects of their potations. In the midst of their conviviality, and when it was nearly approached midnight, the merriment was suddenly interrupted by the hollow beat of the alarm drum; and all hastily arising and running to the window which looked out upon the harbor, Carl saw that his warehouse was in flames. Carl was not yet tired of being a rich man, and so with only some hasty expressions of dismay, he hurried from the banquet and ran at full speed towards the harbor. It was, as has been said, half a league round by the drawbridge: the merchant saw his well-stored warehouse within a stone's throw of him, burning away, and—the fumes of wine were in his head—without further thought, he leaped into a boat that lay just below, and pushed across.

Scarcely had Carl Bluven done this, when he recollected his danger. Paddle as he would, the boat made no way: what exertions the merchant made, and what were his thoughts, no one can tell. Some seamen were awoken by loud cries for help; and some, who jumped out of their hammocks, told how they saw a boat drifting out of the harbor.

Two or three days after this event, the *Tellemarke,* free trader, arrived in Bergen from Iceland, and reported, "that but for a strong northerly breeze, she would have been sucked into the Maelstroom; that a little before sunset, when within two leagues of the whirlpool, a small boat was seen drifting, empty; and that soon after another, the smallest and strangest built boat that ever was seen passed close under their bows, to windward, paddling in the direction of the Maelstroom; that two mariners were in it; he at the helm of an exceedingly tall stature, and singular countenance; that the other cried out for help; upon which the ship lay to, and manned a boat with four rowers; but that with all their exertions they were unable to gain upon the little boat, which was worked by a single paddle; and that the boatmen, fearing they might be drawn into the whirlpool, returned to the ship; and that, just at sunset, they could descry the small boat, by the help of their glasses, steering right across the Maelstroom, as if it had been a small pond." Of all which extraordinary facts, the master of the *Tellemarke* made a deposition before the chief magistrate who filled the chair after Carl Bluven had disappeared in so miraculous a manner.

THE PREDICTION

BY GEORGE HENRY BORROW

(1826)

'Let's talk of graves.'—Shakespeare

On the south-west coast of the principality of Wales stands a romantic little village, inhabited chiefly by the poorer class of people, consisting of small farmers and oyster dredgers, whose estates are the wide ocean, and whose ploughs are the small craft, in which they glide over its interminable fields in search of the treasures which they wring from its bosom; it is built on the very top of a hill, commanding on the one side, a view of an immense bay, and on the other, of the peaceful green fields and valleys, cultivated by the greater number of its quiet inhabitants. The approach to it from the nearest town was by a road which branched away into lanes and wooded walks, and from the sea by a beautiful little bay, running up far into the land; both sides of which, and indeed all the rest of the coast, were guarded by craggy and gigantic rocks, some of them hollowed into caverns, into which none of the inhabitants, from motives of superstition, had ever dared to penetrate. There were, at the period of which we are about to treat, no better sort of inhabitants in the little village just described, none of those so emphatically distinguished as 'quality' by the country people; they had neither parson, lawyer, nor doctor among them, and of course there was a tolerable equality amongst the residents. The farmer, who followed his own plough in the spring, singing the sweet wild national chant of the season, and bound up with his own hands his sheaves in the autumn, was not richer, greater, nor finer than he who, bare-legged on the strand, gathered in the hoar weed for the farmer in the spring, or dared the wild winds of autumn and the wrath of the winter in his little boat, to earn with his dredging net a yet harder subsistence for his family. Distinctions were unknown in the village; every man was the equal of his neighbor.

But, though rank and its polished distinctions were strange in the village of N—, the superiority of talent was felt and acknowledged almost without a pause or a murmur. There was one who was as a king amongst them, by the mere force of a mightier spirit than those with whom he sojourned had been accustomed to feel among them: he was a dark and moody, a stranger, evidently of a higher order than those around him, who had but a few months before, without any apparent object, settled among them: he was poor, but had no occupation—he lived frugally, but quite alone—and his sole enjoyments were to read during the day, and wander out unaccompanied into the fields or by the beach during the night. Sometimes indeed he would relieve a suffering child or rheumatic old man by medicinal herbs, reprove idleness and drunkenness in the youth, and predict to all the good and evil consequences of their conduct; and his success in some cases, his foresight in others, and his wisdom in all, won for him a high reputation among the cottagers, to which his taciturn habits contributed not a little, for, with the vulgar as with the educated, no talker was ever seriously taken for a conjurer, though a silent man is often decided to be a wise one.

There was but one person in N— at all disposed to rebel against the despotic sovereignty which Rhys Meredith was silently establishing over the quiet village, and that was precisely the person most likely to effect a revolution; she was a beautiful maiden, the glory and boast of the village, who had been the favorite of, and to a certain degree educated by, the late lady of the lord of the manor; but she had died, and her pupil, with a full consciousness of her intellectual superiority, had returned to her native village, where she determined to have an empire of her own, which no rival could dispute: she laughed at the maidens who listened to the predictions of Rhys, and she refused her smiles to the youths who consulted him upon their affairs and their prospects; and as the beautiful Ruth was generally beloved, the silent Rhys was soon in danger of being abandoned by all save doting men and paralytic women, and feeling himself an outcast in the village of N—.

But to be such was not the object of Meredith; he was an idle man, and the gifts of the villagers contributed to spare him from exertion; he knew, too, that in another point of view this ascendancy was necessary to his purposes; and as he had failed to establish it by wisdom and benevolence, he determined to try the effect of fear. The character of the people with whom he sojourned was admirably calculated to assist his projects; his predictions were now uttered more clearly, and his threats denounced in sterner tones and stronger and plainer words; and when he predicted that old Morgan Williams, who had been stricken with palsy, would die at the turn of the tide, three days from that on which he spoke, and that the light little boat of gay Griffy Morris, which sailed from the bay in a bright winter's morning, should never again make the shore; and the man died, and the storm arose, even as he had said; men's hearts died within them, and they bowed down before his words, as if he had been their general fate and the individual destiny of each.

Ruth's rosy lip grew pale for a moment as she heard of these things; in the next her spirit returned, and 'I will make him tell my fortune,' she said, as she went with a party of laughers to search out and deride the conjurer. He was alone when they broke in upon him, and their mockeries goaded his spirits; but his anger was deep, not loud; and while burning with wrath, he yet could calmly consider the means of vengeance: he knew the master spirit with which he had to contend; it was no ordinary mind, and would have smiled at ordinary terrors. To have threatened her with sickness, misfortune, or death, would have been to call forth the energies of that lofty spirit, and prepare it to endure, and it would have gloried in manifesting its powers of endurance; he must humble it therefore by debasement; he must ruin its confidence in itself; and to this end he resolved to threaten her with crime. His resolution was taken and effected, his credit was at stake; he must daunt his enemy, or surrender to her power: he foretold sorrows and joys to the listening throng, not according to his passion, but according to his judgement, and he drew a blush upon the cheek of one, by revealing a secret which Ruth herself, and another, alone knew, and which prepared the former to doubt of her own judgement, as it related to this extraordinary man.

Ruth was the last who approached to hear the secret of her destiny. The wizard paused as he looked upon her—opened his book—shut it—paused—and again looked sadly and fearfully upon her; she tried to smile, but felt startled, she knew not why; the bright inquiring glance of her dark eye could not change the purpose of her enemy. Her smile could not melt, nor even temper, the hardness of his deep-seated malice: he again looked sternly upon her brow, and then coldly wrung out the slow soul-withering words, 'Maiden, thou art doomed to be a murder!'

From that hour Rhys Meredith became the destiny of Ruth Tudor. At first she spurned at his prediction, and alternately cursed and laughed at him for the malice of his falsehood: but when she found that none laughed with her, that men looked upon her with suspicious eyes, women shrunk from her society, and children shrieked in her presence, she felt that these were signs of truth, and her high spirit no longer struggled against the conviction; a change came over her mind when she had known how horrid it was to be alone. Abhorring the prophet, she yet clung to his footsteps, and while she sat by his side, felt as if he alone could avert that evil destiny which he alone had foreseen. With him only was she seen to smile; elsewhere, sad, silent, stern, it seemed as if she were ever occupied in nerving her mind for that which she had to do, and her beauty, already of the majestic cast, grew absolutely awful, as her perfect features assumed an expression which might have belonged to the angel of vengeance or death.

But there were moments when her naturally strong spirit, not yet wholly subdued, struggled against her conviction, and endeavored to find modes of averting her fate: it was in one of these, perhaps, that she gave her hand to a wooer, from a distant part of the country, a sailor, who either had not hear, or did not regard the prediction of Rhys, upon condition that he should remove her far from her native village to the home of his family and friends, for she sometimes felt as if the decree which had gone forth against her could not be fulfilled except upon the spot where she had heard it, and that her heart would be lighter if men's eyes would again look upon her in kindliness, and she no longer sat beneath the glare of those who knew so well the secret of her soul. Thus thinking, she quitted N— with her husband; and the tormentor, who had poisoned her repose, soon after her departure, left the village as secretly and as suddenly as he had entered it.

But, though Ruth could depart from his corporeal presence, and look upon his cruel visage no more, yet the eye of her soul was fixed upon his shadow, and his airy form, the creation of her sorrow, still sat by her side; the blight that he had breathed upon her peace had withered her heart, and it was in vain that she sought to forget or banish the recollection from her brain. Men and women smiles upon her as before in the days of her joy, the friends of her husband welcomed her to their bosoms, but they could give no peace to her heart: she shrunk from their friendship, she shivered equally at their neglect, she dreaded any cause that might lead to that which, it had been said, she must do; nightly she sat alone and thought, and dwelt upon the characters of those around her, and shuddered that in some she violence and selfishness enough to cause injury, which she might be supposed to resent to blood. Then she wept bitter tears and thought of her native village, whose inhabitants were so mild, and whose previous knowledge of her hapless destiny might induce them to avoid all that might hasten its completion, and sighed to think she had ever left it in the mistaken hope of finding peace elsewhere. Again, her sick fancy would ponder upon the modes of murder, and wonder how her victim would fall. Against the use of actual violence she had disabled herself; she had never struck a blow, her small hand would have suffered injury in the attempt; she understood not the usage of firearms, she was ignorant of what were poisons, and a knife she never allowed herself, even for the most necessary purposes: how then could she slay? At times she took comfort from thoughts like these, and at others, in the blackness of despair, she would cry, 'If it must be, oh let it come, and there miserable anticipations cease; then I shall, at least, destroy but one; now, in my incertitude, I am the murderer of many!'

Her husband went forth and returned upon the voyages which made up the avocation and felicity of his life, without noticing the deep-rooted sorrow of his wife; he was a common man, and of a common mind; his eye had not seen the awful beauty of her whom he had chosen; his spirit had not felt her power; and, if he had marked, he would not have understood her grief; so she ministered to him as a duty. She was a silent and obedient wife, but she saw him come home without joy, and witnessed his departure without regret; he had neither added to nor diminished her sorrow; but destiny had one solitary blessing in store for the victim of its decrees,—a child was born to the hapless Ruth, a lovely little girl soon slept upon her bosom, and, coming as it did, the one lone and lovely rosebud in her desolate garden, she welcomed it with a warmer joy and cherished it with a kindlier hope.

A few years went by unsoiled by the wretchedness which had marked the preceding; the joy of the mother softened the anguish of the condemned, and sometimes when she looked upon her daughter she ceased to despair: but destiny had not forgotten her claim, and soon her hand pressed heavily upon her victim; the giant ocean rolled over the body of her husband, poverty visited the cottage of the widow, and famine's gaunt figure was visible in the distance. Oppression came with these, for arrears of rent were demanded, and he who asked was brutal in his anger and harsh in his language to the sufferers. Ruth shuddered as she heard him speak, and trembled for him, and for herself; the unforgotten prophecy arose in her mind, and she preferred even witnesses to his brutality and her degradation, rather than encounter his anger and her own dark thoughts alone.

Thus goaded, she saw but one thing that could save her. She fled from her persecutors to the home of her youth, and, leading her little Rachel by the hand, threw herself into the arms of her kin: they received her with distant kindness, and assured her that she should not want: in this they kept their promise, but it was all they did for Ruth and her daughter; a miserable subsistence was given to them, and that was embittered by distrust, and the knowledge that it was yielded unwillingly.

Among the villagers, although she was no longer shunned as formerly, her story was not forgotten; if it had been, her terrific beauty, the awful flashing of her eyes, her large black curls hanging like thunderclouds over her stern and stately brow and marble throat, her majestic stature and solemn movements, would have recalled it to their recollections. She was a marked being, and all believed (though each would have pitied her had they not been afraid) that her evil destiny was not to be averted; she looked like one fated to do some wonderful deed. They saw she was not of them, and though they did not directly avoid her, yet they never threw themselves in her way, and thus the hapless Ruth had ample leisure to contemplate and grieve over her fate. One night she sat alone in her wretched hovel, and, with many bitter ruminations, was watching the happy sleep of her child, who slumbered tranquilly on their only bed: midnight had long passed, yet Ruth was not disposed to rest; she trimmed her dull light, and said mentally, 'Were I not poor, such a temptation might not assail me, riches would procure me deference; but poverty, or the wrongs it brings, may drive me to do this evil; were I above want it would be less likely to be. O my child, for thy sake would I avoid this doom more than mine own, for if it should bring death to me, what will it not hurl on thee?—infamy, agony, scorn.'

She wept aloud as she spoke, and scarcely seemed to notice the singularity (at that late hour) of someone without, attempting to open the door; she heard, but the circumstance made little impression; she knew that as yet her doom was unfulfilled, and that, therefore, no danger could reach her; she was no coward at any time, but now despair had made her brave; the door opened and a stranger entered, without either alarming or disturbing her, and it was not till he had stood face to face with Ruth, and she discovered his features to be those of Rhys Meredith, that she sprung up from her seat and gazed wildly and earnestly upon him.

Meredith gave her no time to question; 'Ruth Tudor,' said he, 'behold the cruelest of thy foes comes sueing to thy pity and mercy; I have embittered thy existence, and doomed thee to a terrible lot; what first was dictated by vengeance and malice became truth as I uttered it, for what I spoke I believed. Yet, take comfort, some of my predictions have failed, and why may not this be false? In my own fate I have ever been deceived; perhaps I may be equally so in thine; in the meantime have pity upon him who was thy enemy, but who, when his vengeance was uttered, instantly became thy friend. I was poor, and thy scorn might have robbed me of subsistence in danger, and thy contempt might have given me up. Beggared by many disastrous events, hunted by creditors, I fled from my wife and son because I could no longer bear to contemplate their suffering; I sought fortune always since we parted, and always she eluded my grasp until last night, when she rather tempted than smiled upon me. At an idle fair I met the steward of this estate drunk and stupid, but loaded with gold; he traveled towards home alone; I could not, did not wrestle with the fiend that possessed me, but hastened to overtake him in his lonely ride.—Start not! No hair of his head was harmed by me; of his gold I robbed him, but not of his life, though, had I been the greater villain, I should now be in less danger, since he saw and marked my person: three hundred pounds is the meed of my daring, and I must keep it now or die. Ruth, thou art too poor and forsaken, but thou art faithful and kind, and wilt not betray me to justice; save me, and I will not enjoy my riches alone; thou knowest all the caves in all the rocks, those hideous hiding-places, where no foot save thine has dared to tread; conceal me in these till the pursuit be past, and I will give thee one half of my wealth, and return with the other to gladden my wife and son.'

The hand of Ruth was already opened, and in imagination she grasped the wealth he promised; oppression and poverty had somewhat clouded the nobleness, but not the fierceness of her spirit. She saw that riches could save her from wrath, perhaps from blood, and, as the means to escape so mighty an evil, she was not scrupulous respecting a lesser: independently of this, she felt a great interest in the safety of Rhys; her own fate seemed to hang upon his; she hid the ruffian in the caves and supplied him with light and food.

There was a happiness now in the heart of Ruth—a joy in her thoughts as she sat all day long upon the deserted settle of her wretched fireside, to which they had for many years been strangers. Many times during the past years of her sorrow she had thought of Rhys, and longed to look upon his face and sit beneath his shadow, as one whose presence could preserve her from the evil fate which he himself had predicted. She had long since forgiven him his prophecy; she believed he had spoken truth, and this gave her a wild confidence in his power; a confidence that sometimes thought, 'if he can foreknow, can he not also avert?' She said mentally, without any reference to the temporal good he had promised her, 'I have a treasure in those caves; *he* is there; he who hath foreseen and may oppose my destiny; he hath shadowed my days with sorrow, and forbidden me, like ordinary beings, to hope: yet he is now in my power; his life is in my hands; he says so, yet I believe him not, for I cannot betray him if I would; were I to lead the officers of justice to the spot where he lies crouching, he would be invisible to their sight or to mine; or I should become speechless ere I should say, "Behold him." No, he cannot die by me!'

And she thought she would deserve his confidence, and support him in his suffering; she had concealed him in a deep dark cave, hewn far in the rock, to which she alone knew the entrance from the beach; there was another (if a huge aperture in the top of the rock might be so called), which, far from attempting to descend, the peasants and the seekers for the culprit had scarcely dared to look into, so perpendicular, dark, and uncertain was the hideous descent into what justly appeared to them a bottomless abyss; they passed over his head in their search through the fields above, and before the mouth of his den upon the beach below, yet they left him in safety, though in incertitude and fear.

It was less wonderful, the suspicious conduct of the villagers towards Ruth, than the calm prudence with which she conducted all the details relating to her secret; her poverty was well known, yet she daily procured a double portion of food, which was won by double labor; she toiled in the fields for the meed of oaten cake and potatoes, or she dashed out in a crazy boat on the wide ocean to win with the dredgers the spoils of the oyster beds that lie on its bosom; the daintier fare was for the unhappy guest, and daily did she wander amid the rocks, when the tides were retiring, for the shell-fish which they had flung among the fissures in their retreat, which she bore, exhausted with fatigue, to her home—and which her lovely child, now rising into womanhood, prepared for the luxurious meal; it was wonderful too, the settled prudence of the little maiden, who spoke nothing of the food which was borne from their frugal board: if she suspected the secret of her mother, she respected it too much to allow others to discover that she did so.

Many sad hours did Ruth pass in the robber's cave; and many times, by conversing with him upon the subject of her destiny, did she seek to alleviate the pangs its recollection cost her; but the result of such discussions were by no means favorable to her hopes; Rhys had acknowledged that his threat had originated in malice, and that he intended to alarm and subdue, but not to the extent that he had effected: 'I knew well,' said he, 'that disgrace alone would operate upon you as I wished, for I foresaw you would glory in the thought of nobly sustained misfortune; I meant to degrade you to the lowest; I meant to attribute to you what I now painfully experience to be the vilest of vices; I intended to tell you, you were destined to be a thief, but I could not utter the words I had arranged, and I was struck with horror at those I heard involuntarily proceeding from my lips; I would have recalled them but I could not; I would have said, "Maiden, I did but jest," but there was something that seemed to withhold my speech and press upon my soul, "so as thou hast said shall this thing be"—yet take comfort, my own fortunes have ever deceived me, and doubtlessly ever will, for I feel as if I should one day return to this cave and make it my final home.'

He spoke solemnly and wept,—but the awful eye of his companion was unmoved as she looked on in wonder and contempt at his grief. 'Thou knowest not how to endure,' said she to him, 'and as soon as night shall again fall upon our mountains, I will lead thee forth on thy escape; the danger of pursuit is now past; at midnight be ready for thy journey, leave the cave, and ascend the rocks by the path I showed thee, to the field in which its mouth is situated; wait me there a few moments, and I will bring thee a fleet horse, ready saddled for the journey, for which thy gold must pay, since I must declare to the owner that I have sold it at a distance, and for more than its rated value.'

That midnight came, and Meredith waited with trembling anxiety for the haughty step of Ruth; at length he saw her, she had ascended the rock, and, standing between rock and sky, and scarcely seeming to touch the earth, her dark locks and loose garments scattered by the wind, she looked like some giant spirit of the older time, preparing to ascend into the mighty black cloud which singly hung from the empyreum, and upon which already appeared to recline; Meredith beheld her and shuddered,—but she approached and he recovered his recollection.

'You must be speedy in your movements,' said she, 'when you leave me; your horse waits on the other side of this field, and I would have you hasten lest his neighings should betray your purpose. But before you depart, Rhys Meredith, there is an account to be settled between us: I have dared danger and privations for you; that the temptations of the poor may not assail me, give me my reward and go.'

Rhys pressed his leathern bag to his bosom, but answered nothing to the speech of Ruth: he seemed to be studying for some evasion, for he looked upon the ground, and there was trouble in the working of his lip. At length he said cautiously, 'I have it not with me; I buried it, lest it should betray me, in a field some miles distant; thither will I go, dig it up, and send it to thee from B—, which is, as thou knowest, my first destination.'

Ruth gave him one glance of her awful eye when he had spoken; she had detected his meanness, and smiled at his incapacity to deceive. 'What dost thou press to thy bosom so earnestly?' she demanded; 'surely thou art not the wise man I deemed thee, thus to defraud *my* claim: thy friend alone thou mightest cheat, and safely; but I have been made wretched by thee, guilty by thee, and thy life is in my power; I could, as thou knowest, easily raise the village, and win half thy wealth by giving thee up to justice; but I prefer reward from thy wisdom and gratitude; give, therefore, and be gone.'

But Rhys knew too well the value of the metal of sin to yield one half of it to Ruth; he tried many miserable shifts and lies, and at last, baffled by the calm penetration of his antagonist, boldly avowed his intention of keeping all the spoil he had won with so much hazard. Ruth looked at him with scorn: 'Keep thy gold,' she said; 'if it thus hardens hearts, I covet not its possession; but there is one thing you must do, and that ere thou stir one foot. I have supported thee with hard-earned industry, *that* I give thee; more proud, it should seem, in bestowing than I could be, from such as thee, in receiving: but the horse that is to bear thee hence tonight

I borrowed for a distant journey; I must return with it, or with its value; open thy bag, pay me for that, and go.'

But Rhys seemed afraid to open his bag in the presence of her he had wronged. Ruth understood his fears; but, scorning vindication of *her* principles, contented herself with entreating him to be honest. 'Be more just to thyself and me,' she persisted: 'the debt of gratitude I pardon thee; but, I beseech thee, leave me not to encounter the consequence of having stolen from my friend the animal which is his only means of subsistence: I pray thee, Rhys, not to condemn me to scorn.'

It was to no avail that Ruth humbled herself to entreaties; Meredith answered her not, and while she was yet speaking, cast sidelong looks towards the gate where the horse was waiting for his service, and seemed meditating, whether he should not dart from Ruth, and escape her entreaties and demands by dint of speed. Her stern eye detected his purpose; and, indignant at his baseness, and ashamed of her own degradation, she sprung suddenly towards him, and made a desperate clutch at the leathern bag, and tore it from the grasp of the deceiver. Meredith made an attempt to recover it, and a fierce struggle ensued, which drove them both back towards the yawning mouth of the cave from which he had just ascended to the world. On its very verge, on its very extreme edge, the demon who had so long rules his spirit now instigated him to mischief, and abandoned him to his natural brutality: he struck the unhappy Ruth a revengeful and tremendous blow. At that moment a horrible thought glanced like lightning through her soul; he was to her no longer what he had been; he was a robber, ruffian, liar; one whom to destroy was justice, and perhaps it was he—'Villain!' she cried, 'thou—thou didst predict that I was doomed to be a murderer! art thou—art thou destined to be the victim?' She flung him from her with terrific force, as he stood close to the abyss, and the next instant she heard him dash against its sides, as he was whirled headlong into the darkness.

It was an awful feeling, the next that passed over the soul of Ruth Tudor, as she stood alone in the pale sorrowful-looking moonlight, endeavoring to remember what had chanced. She gazed on the purse, on the chasm, wiped the drops of agony from her heated brow, and then, with a sudden pang of recollection, rushed down to the cavern. The light was still burning, as Rhys had left it, and served to show her the wretch extended helplessly beneath the chasm. Though his body was crushed, his bones splintered, and his blood was on the cavern's sides, he was yet living, and raised his head to look upon her as she darkened the narrow entrance in her passage: he glared upon her with the visage of a demon, and spoke like a fiend in pain. 'Me hast thou murdered!' he said, 'but I shall be avenged in all thy life to come. Deem not that thy doom is fulfilled, that the deed to which thou art fated is done: in my dying hour I know, I feel what is to come upon thee; thou art yet again to do a deed of blood!' "Liar!' shrieked the infuriated victim. 'Thou art yet doomed to be a murderer!' 'Thou art—and of—thine only child!' She rushed to him, but he was dead.

Ruth Tudor stood for a moment by the corpse blind, stupefied, deaf, and dumb; in the next she laughed aloud, till the cavern rang with her ghastly mirth, and many voices mingled with and answered it; but the noises scared and displeased her, and in an instant she became stupidly grave; she threw back her dark locks with an air of offended dignity, and walked forth majestically from the cave. She took the horse by his rein, and led him back to his stable: with the same unvarying calmness she entered her cottage, and listened to the quiet breathings of her sleeping child; she longed to approach her nearer, but some new and horrid fear restrained her and held back her anxious step: suddenly remembrance and reason returned, and she uttered a shriek so full of agony, so loud and shrill, that her daughter sprang from her bed, and threw herself into her arms.

It was in vain that the gentle Rachel supplicated her mother to find rest in sleep. 'Not here,' she muttered, 'it must not be here; the deep cave and the hard rock, these shall be my resting place; and the bedfellow, lo! now, he waits my coming.' Then she would cry aloud, clasp her Rachel to her beating heart, and as suddenly, in horror thrust her from it.

The next midnight beheld Ruth Tudor in the cave, seated upon a point of rock at the head of the corpse, her chin resting upon her hands, gazing earnestly upon the distorted face. Decay had already begun its work; and Ruth sat there watching the progress of mortality as if she intended that her stern eye should quicken and facilitate its operation. The next night also beheld her there, but the current of her thoughts had changed, and the dismal interval which had passed appeared to be forgotten. She stood with her basket of food: 'Wilt thou not eat?' she demanded; 'arise, strengthen thee for thy journey; eat, eat, thou sleeper; wilt thou never awaken? look, here is the meat thou lovest'; and as she raised his head and put the food to his lips, the frail remnant of mortality shattered at her touch, and again she knew that he was dead.

It was evident to all that a shadow and a change was over the senses of Ruth; till this period she had been only wretched, but now madness was mingled with grief. It was in no instance more apparent than in her conduct towards her beloved child: indulgent to all her wishes, ministering to all her wants with a liberal hand, till men wondered from whence she derived the means of indulgence, she yet seized every opportunity to send her from her presence. The gentle-hearted Rachel wept at her conduct, yet did not complain, for she believed it the effect of the disease that had for so many years been preying upon her soul. Her nights were passed in roaming abroad, her days in the solitude of her hut; and even this became painful when the step of her child broke upon it. At length she signified that a relative of her husband had died and left her wealth, and that it should enable her to dispose of herself as she had long wished; so leaving Rachel with her relatives in N——, she retired to a hut upon a lonely heath, where she was less wretched, because abandoned to her wretchedness.

In many of her ravings she had frequently spoken darkly of her crime, and her nightly visits to the cave; and more frequently still she addressed some unseen thing, which she asserted was forever at her side. But few heard these horrors, and those who did, called to mind the early prophecy, and deemed them the workings of insanity in a fierce and imaginative mind. So thought also the beloved Rachel, who hastened daily to embrace her mother, but not now alone as formerly; a youth of the village was her companion and protector, one who had offered her worth and love, and whose gentle offers were not rejected. Ruth, with a hurried gladness, gave her consent, and a blessing to her child; and it was remarked that she received her daughter more kindly, and detained her longer at the cottage when Evan was by her side, than when she went to the gloomy heath alone. Rachel herself soon made this observation, and as she could depend upon the honesty and prudence of him she loved, she felt less fear at his being a frequent witness of her mother's terrific ravings. Thus all that human consolation was capable to afford was offered to the sufferer by her sympathizing children.

But the delirium of Ruth Tudor appeared to increase with every nightly visit to the cave of secret blood; some hideous shadow seemed to follow her steps in the darkness, and sit by her side in the light. Sometimes she held strange parley with this creation of her frenzy, and at others smiled upon it in scornful silence; now, her language was in the tones of entreaty, pity, and forgiveness; anon, it was the burst of execration, curses, and scorn. To the gentle listeners her words were blasphemy; and, shuddering at her boldness, they deemed, in the simple holiness of their own hearts, that the evil one was besetting her, and that religion alone could banish him. Possessed by this idea, Evan one day suddenly interrupted her tremendous denunciations upon her fate, and him who, she said, stood over her to fulfill it, with imploring her to open the book which he held in his hand, and seek consolation from its words and its promises. She listened, and grew calm in a moment; with an awful smile she bade him open and read at the first place which should meet his eye:

'from that, the word of truth, as thou sayest, I shall know my fate; what is there written I will believe.' He opened the book, and read—

'Wither shall I go from thy spirit? or whither shall I flee from thy presence? If I ascend up into heaven, thou art there: if I make my bed in hell, behold thou art there; If I take the wings of the morning, and dwell in the uttermost parts of the sea; even there shall thy hand lead me, and thy right hand shall hold me.'

Ruth laid her hand upon the book: 'it is enough; its words are truth; it hath said there is no hope, and I find comfort in my despair: I have already spoken thus in the secrecy of my heart, and I know that he will be obeyed; the unnamed sin must be——' Evan knew not how to comfort, so he shut up his book and retired; and Rachel kissed the cheek of her mother, as she bade her a tender good-night. Another month and she was to be the bride of Evan, and she passed over the heath with a light step, for the thought of her bridal seemed to give joy to her mother. 'We shall all be happy then,' said the smiling girl, as the youth of her heart parted from her hand for the night; 'and heaven kindly grant that happiness may last.'

The time appointed for the marriage of Rachel Tudor and Evan Edwards had long passed away, and winter had set in with unusual sternness even on that stormy coast; when, during a land tempest, on a dark November afternoon, a stranger to the country, journeying on foot, lost his way in endeavoring to find a short route to his destination, over stubble fields and meadow lands, by following the footmarks of those who had preceded him. The stranger was a young man, of a bright eye and a hardy look, and he went on buffeting the elements, and buffeted by them, without a thought of weariness, or a single expression of impatience. Night descended upon him as he walked, and the snowstorm came down with unusual violence, as if to try the temper of his mind, a mind cultivated and enlightened, though cased in a frame accustomed to hardship, and veiled by a plain, nay, almost rustic interior. The thunder roared loudly above him, and the wind blowing tremendously, raised the new-fallen snow from the earth, which, mingling with the showers as they fell, raised a clatter about his head which bewildered and blinded the traveller, who, finding himself near some leafless brambles and a few clustered bushes of the mountain broom, took shelter under them to recover his senses, and reconnoiter his position. 'Of all these ingredients for a storm,' said he smilingly to himself, 'the lightning is the most endurable after all; for if it does not kill, it may at least cure, by lighting the way out of a labyrinth, and by its bright flashes I hope to discover where I am.' In this hope he was not mistaken: the brilliant and beautiful gleam showed him, when the snow shower had somewhat abated, every stunted bush and blade of grass for some miles, and something, about the distance of one, that looked like a white-washed cottage of some poor enclose of the miserable heath upon which he was now standing. Full of hope of a shelter from the storm, and lit onwards by the magnificent torch of heaven, the stranger trod cheerily forwards, and in less than half an hour, making full allowance for his retrograding between the flashed, arrived at his beacon the white cottage, which, from the low wall of loose limestone by which it was surrounded, he judged to be, as he had already imagined, the humble residence of some poor tenant of the manor. He opened the little gate, and was proceeding to knock at the door, when his steps were arrested by a singular and unexpected sound; it was a choral burst of many voices, singing slowly and solemnly that magnificent dirge of the Church of England, the 104th psalm. The stranger loved music and the sombrous melody of that fine air had an instant effect upon his feelings; he lingered in solemn and silent admiration till the majestic strain had ceased; he then knocked gently at the door, which was instantly and courteously opened to his inquiry.

On entering, he found himself in a cottage of a more respectable interior than from its outward appearance he had been led to expect: but he had little leisure or inclination for the survey of its effects, for his senses and imagination were immediately and entirely occupied by the scene which presented itself on his entrance. In the center of the room into which he had been so readily admitted, stood, on its trestles, an open coffin; lights were at its head and foot, and on each side sat many persons of both sexes, who appeared to be engaged in the customary of watching the corpse previous to its internment in the morning. There were many who appeared to the stranger to be watchers, but there were two, who, in his eye, bore the appearance of mourners, and they had faces of grief which spoke too plainly of the anguish that was mining within: one, at the foot of the coffin, was a pale youth just blooming into manhood, who covered his dewy eyes with the trembling fingers that ill-concealed the tears which trickled down his wan cheeks beneath: the other—; but why should we again describe that still unbowed and lofty form? The awful marble brow upon which the stranger gazed, was that of Ruth Tudor.

There was much whispering and quiet talk amongst the people while refreshments were handed amongst them; and so little curiosity was excited by the appearance of the traveller, that he naturally concluded that it must be no common loss that could deaden a feeling so intense in the bosoms of Welsh peasants: he was even checked for an attempt to question; but one man,—he who had given him admittance, and seemed to possess authority in the circle—told him he would answer his question when the guests should depart, but till then he must keep silence. The traveller endeavored to obey, and sat down in quiet contemplation of the figure who most interested his attention, and who sat at the coffin's head. Ruth Tudor spoke nothing, nor did she appear to heed aught of the business that was passing around her. Absorbed by reflection, her eyes were generally cast to the ground; but when they were raised, the traveller looked in vain for that expression of grief which had struck him so forcibly on his entrance; there was something wonderfully strange in the character of her perfect features: could he have found words for his thought, and might have been permitted the expression, he would have called it triumphant despair; so deeply agonized, so proudly stern, looked the mourner who sat by the dead.

The interest which the traveller took in the scene became more intense the longer he gazed upon its action; unable to resist the anxiety which had begun to prey upon his spirit, he arose and walked towards the coffin, with the purpose of contemplating its inhabitant: a sad explanation was given, by its appearance, of the grief and the anguish he had witnessed; a beautiful girl was reposing in the narrow house, with a face as calm and lovely as if she but slept a deep and refreshing sleep, and the morning sun would again smile upon her awakening: salt, the emblem of the immortal soul, was placed upon her breast; and, in her pale and perishing fingers, a branch of living flowers were struggling for life in the grasp of death, and diffusing their sweet odor of mortality. These images, so opposite, yet so alike, affected the spirit of the gazer, and he almost wept as he continued looking upon them, till he was aroused from his trance by the strange conduct of Ruth Tudor, who had caught a glimpse of his face as he bent in sorrow over the coffin. She sprung up from her seat, and darting at him a terrible glance of recognition, pointed down to the corpse, and then, with a hollow burst of frantic laughter, shouted—'Behold, thou liar!'

The startled stranger was relieved from the necessity of speaking by someone taking his arm and gently leading him to the farther end of the cottage: the eyes of Ruth followed him, and it was not until he had done violence to himself in turning from her to his conductor, that he could escape their singular fascination. When he did so, he beheld a venerable man, the pastor of a distant village, who had come that night to speak comfort to the mourners, and perform the last sad duty to the dead on the morrow. 'Be not alarmed at what you have witnessed, my young friend,' said he; 'these ravings are not uncommon: this unhappy woman, at an early period of her life, gave ear to the miserable superstitions of her country, and wretched pretender to wisdom predicted that she should become a shedder of blood: madness has been the inevitable consequence in an ardent spirit, and in its ravings she dreams she has committed one sin, and is still tempted to add to it another.'

'You may say what you please, parson,' said the old man who had given admittance to the stranger, and who now, after dismissing all the guests save the youth, joined the talkers, and seated himself on the settle by their side; 'you may say what you please about madness and superstition, but I know Ruth Tudor was a fated woman, and the deed that was to be I believe she has done: ay, ay, her madness is conscience; and if the deep sea and the jagged rocks could speak, they might tell us a tale of other things than that: but she is judged now; her only child is gone—her pretty Rachel. Poor Evan! he was her suitor: ah, he little thought two months ago, when he was preparing for a gay bridal, that her slight sickness would end thus: *he* does not deserve it; but for her—God forgive me if I do her wrong, but I think it is the hand of God, and it lies heavy, as it should.' And the grey-haired old man hobbled away, satisfied that in thus thinking he was showing his zeal for virtue.

"Alas, that so white a head should acknowledge so hard a heart!' said the pastor; 'Ruth is condemned, according to his system, for committing that which a mightier hand compelled her to do; how harsh and misjudging is age! But we must not speak so loud,' continued he; 'for see, the youth Evan is retiring for the night, and the miserable mother has thrown herself on the floor to sleep; the sole domestic is rocking on her stool, and therefore I will do the honors of this poor cottage to you. There is a chamber above this, containing the only bed in the hut; thither you may go and rest, for otherwise it will certainly be vacant tonight. I shall find a bed in the village; and even Evan sleeps near you with some of the guests in the barn. But, before I go, if my question is not unwelcome and intrusive, tell me who you are, and wither you are bound.'

'I was ever a subscriber to the old man's creed of fatalism,' said the stranger, smiling, 'and I believe I am more confirmed in it by the singular events of this day. My father was a man of a certain rank in society, but of selfish and disorderly habits. A course of extravagance and idleness was succeeded by difficulties and distress. Harassed by creditors, he was pained by their demands, and his selfishness was unable to endure the sufferings of his wife and children. Instead of exertion, he had recourse to flight, and left us to face the difficulties from which he shrunk. He was absent for years, while his family toiled and struggled with success. Suddenly we heard that he was concealed on this part of the coast; the cause which made that concealment necessary I forbear to mention; but he as suddenly disappeared from the eyes of men, though we never could trace him beyond this part of the country. I have always believed that I should one day find my father, and have lately, though with difficulty, prevailed upon my mother to allow me to make my inquiries in this neighborhood; but my search is at an end today,—I believe that I have found my father. Roaming along the beach, I penetrated into several of those dark caverns of the rocks, which might well, by their rugged aspects, deter the idle and timid from entering. Through the fissures of one I discovered, in the interior, a light. Surprised, I penetrated to its concealment, and discovered a man sleeping on the ground. I advanced to wake him, and found but a fleshless skeleton, cased in tattered and decaying garments. He had probably met his death by accident, for exactly over the corpse I observed, at a terrific distance, the daylight, as if streaming down from an aperture above. Thus the wretched man must have fallen, but how long since, or who had discovered his body and left the light which I beheld, I knew not, although I cannot help cherishing a strong conviction that it was the body of Rhys Meredith that I saw.'

'Who talks of Rhys Meredith,' said a stern voice near the coffin, 'and the cave where the outcast rots?' They turned quickly at the sound, and beheld Ruth Tudor standing up as if she had been intently listening to the story. 'It was I who spoke, dame,' said the stranger gently, 'and my speech was of my father, of Rhys Meredith; I am Owen his son.'

'Son! Owen Rhys!' said the bewildered Ruth, passing her hand over her forehead, as if to enable her to recover the combination of these names: 'and who art thou, that thus givest human ties to him who is no more of humanity? why speakest thou of living things as pertaining to the dead? Father! he is father to naught save sin, and murder is his only begotten!'

She advanced to the traveller as she spoke, and again caught a view of his face; again he saw the wild look of recognition, and an unearthly shriek followed the convulsive horror of her face. 'There! there!' she said, 'I knew it must be thyself; once before tonight have I beheld thee, yet what can thy coming bode? Back with thee, ruffian! for is not thy dark work done?'

'Let us leave her,' said the good pastor, 'to the care of her attendant; do not continue to meet her gaze; your presence may increase, but cannot allay her malady: go up to your bed and rest.'

He retired as he spoke; and Owen, in compliance with his wish, ascended the ruinous stair which led to his chamber, after he beheld Ruth Tudor quietly place herself in her seat at the open coffin's head. The room to which he mounted was not of the most cheering aspect, yet he felt that he had often slept soundly in a worse. It was a gloomy unfinished chamber, and the wind was whistling coldly and drearily through the uncovered rafters above his head. Like many of the cottages in that part of the country, it appeared to have grown old and ruinous before it had been finished; for the flooring was so crazy as scarcely to support the huge wooden bedstead, and in many instances the boards were entirely separated from each other, and the center, time, or the rot, had so completely devoured the larger half of one, that through the gaping aperture Owen had an entire command of the room and the party below, looking down immediately upon the coffin. Ruth was in the same attitude as when he had left her, and the servant girl was dozing by her side. Everything being perfectly tranquil, Owen threw himself upon his hard couch and endeavored to compose himself to rest for the night, but this had become a task, and one of no easy nature to surmount; his thoughts still wandered to the events of the day, and he felt there was some strange connection between the scene he had just witnessed, and the darker one of the secret cave. He was an imaginative man, and of a quick and feverish temperament, and he thought of Ruth Tudor's ravings, and the wretched skeleton of the rock, till he had worked out in his brain the chain of events that linked one consequence with the other: he grew restless and wretched, and amidst the tossings of impatient anxiety, fatigue overpowered him, and he sunk into a perturbed and heated sleep. His slumber was broken by dreams that might well be the shadows of his waking reveries. He was alone (as in reality) upon his humble bed, when imagination brought to his ear the sound of many voices again singing the slow and monotonous psalm; it was interrupted by the outcries of some unseen things who had attempted to enter his chamber, and amid yells of fear and execrations of anger, bade him 'Arise and save her.' In his sleep he attempted to spring up, but a horrid fear restrained him, a fear that he should be too late; then he crouched like a coward beneath his coverings, to hide from the reproaches of the spectre, while shouts of laughter and shrieks of agony were poured like a tempest around him: he sprung from his bed and awoke.

It was some moments ere he could recover recollection, or shake off the horror which had seized upon his soul. He listened, and with infinite satisfaction observed an unbroken silence throughout the house. He smiled at his own terrors, attributed them to the events of the day, or the presence of a corpse, and determined not to look down into the lower room till he should be summoned thither in the morning. He walked to the casement and looked abroad to the night; the clouds were many, black, and lowering, and the face of the sky looked angrily at the wind, and glared portentously upon the earth; the *sleet* was still falling; distant thunder announced the approach or departure of a storm, and Owen marked the clouds coming in afar towards him, laden with the rapid and destructive lightning: he shut the casement and returned towards his bed;

but the light from below attracted his eye, and he could not pass the aperture without taking one glance at the party.

They were in the same attitude in which he had left them; the servant was sleeping, but Ruth was earnestly gazing on the lower end of the room upon something, without the sight of Owen; his attention was next fixed upon the corpse, and he thought he had never seen any living thing so lovely; and so calm was the aspect of her last repose, that Meredith thought it more resembled a temporary suspension of the faculties than the eternal stupor of death: her features were pale, but not distorted, and there was none of the livid hue of death in her beautiful mouth and lips; but the flowers in her hand gave stronger demonstration of the presence of the power before whose potency their little strength was fading; drooping with a mortal sickness, they bowed down their heads in submission, as one by one they dropped from her pale and perishing fingers. Owen gazed till he thought he saw the grasp of her hand relax, and a convulsive smile pass over her cold and rigid features; he looked again; the eyelids shook and vibrated like the string of some fine-strung instrument; the hair rose, and the head-cloth moved: he started up ashamed: 'Does the madness of this woman affect all who would sleep beneath her roof?' said he; 'what is this that disturbs me—or am I yet in a dream? Hark! what is that?' It was the voice of Ruth; she had risen from her seat, and was standing near the coffin, apparently addressing someone who stood at the lower end of the room: 'To what purpose is thy coming now?' said she, in a low and melancholy voice, 'and at what dost thou laugh and gibe? lo! you; she is here, and the sin you know of, cannot be; how can I take the life which another hath already withdrawn? Go, go, hence to thy cave of night, for this is no place of safety for thee.' Her thoughts now took another turn; she seemed to hide one from the pursuit of others: 'Lie still! Lie still!' she whispered; 'put out thy light! so, so, they pass by and mark thee not; thou art safe; good-night, good-night! now will I home to sleep'; and she seated herself in her chair, as if composing her senses to rest.

Owen was again bewildered in the chaos of thought, but for this time he determined to subdue his imagination, and throwing himself upon his bed, again gave himself up to sleep; but the images of his former dreams still haunted him, and their hideous phantasms were more powerfully renewed; again he heard the solemn psalm of death, but unsung by mortals—it was pealed through earth up to high heaven, by myriads of the viewless and the mighty; again he heard the execrations of millions for some unremembered sin, and the wrath and the hatred of a world was rushing upon him: 'Come forth! come forth!' was the cry; and amid yells and howls they were darting upon him, when the pale form of the beautiful dead arose between them, and shielded him from their malice; but he heard her say aloud, 'It is time for this, that thou wilt not save me; arise, arise, and help!'

He sprung up as he was commanded; sleeping or waking he never knew; but he started from his bed to look down into the chamber, as he heard the voice of Ruth in terrific denunciation: he looked; she was standing, uttering yells of madness and rage, and close to her was a well-known form of appalling recollection—his father, as he had seen him last; he arose and darted to the door: 'I am mad,' said he; 'I am surely mad, or this is still a continuation of my dream.': he looked again; Ruth was still there, but alone.

But, though no visible form stood by the maniac, some fiend had entered her soul and mastered her mighty spirit; she had armed herself with an axe, and shouting, 'Liar, liar, hence!' was pursuing some imaginary foe to the darker side of the cottage. Owen strove hard to trace her motions, but as she had retreated under the space occupied by his bed, he could no longer see her, and his eyes involuntarily fastened themselves upon the coffin; there a new horror met them; the dead corpse had risen, and with wild and glaring eyes was watching the scene before her. Owen distrusted his senses till he heard the terrific voice of Ruth, as she marked the miracle he had witnessed: 'The fiend, the robber!' she yelled, 'it is he who hath entered the pure body of my child. Back to thy cave of blood, thou lost one! back to thine own dark hell!' Owen flew to the door; it was too late; he heard the shriek—the blow: he *fell* into the room, but only in time to hear the second blow, and see the cleft head of the hapless Rachel fall back upon its bloody pillow; his terrible cries brought in the sleepers from the barn, headed by the wretched Evan, and, for a time, the thunders of heaven were drowned in the clamorous grief of man. No one dared to approach the miserable Ruth, who now, in utter frenzy, strode around the room, brandishing, with diabolical grandeur, the bloody axe, and singing a wild song of triumph and joy. All fell back as she approached, and shrunk from the infernal majesty of her terrific form; and the thunders of heaven rolling above their heads, and the flashing of the fires of eternity in their eyes, were less terrible than the savage glare and desperate wrath of the maniac:—suddenly, the house rocked to its foundations; its inmates were blinded for a moment, and sunk, felled by a stunning blow, to the earth;—slowly each man recovered and arose, wondering he was yet alive;—all were unhurt save one. Ruth Tudor was on the earth, her blackened limbs prostrate beneath the coffin of her child, and her dead cheek resting on the rent and bloody axe;—it had been the destroyer of both.

THE STORY OF THE UNFINISHED PICTURE

BY CHARLES HOOTEN

(1847)

"Weigel was an intimate acquaintance of mine,—a good painter, and had commenced his career promisingly. Calculating on a fortune not yet made, and a reputation that still had to take root, although it put forth strongly, he married a handsome girl of poor and obscure parentage, and found himself involved in all the cares of a young family before he was three-and-twenty. Fortune almost seemed to abandon him from the very day of his wedding, and from hard experience he soon found that he had begun the world too soon. But he was ambitious to an excess, and frequently used to say to his acquaintants that he would willingly lay down his life, only to become an artist that the world would never forget. Nay, I have often heard him say he was in the nightly habit of invoking the aid, in prayers, of either good spirits or bad (he cared not which), whichever, if such existed, would come first to assist him in the attainment of a painter's success and immortality. 'What matters,' says he, 'even if a man *could* give away his immortality in the uncertain here-after, for a certain immortality here, though he should go so far as to do it? 'Twould be but as exchange of equivalents; or perhaps a gain on the side of earth which is real, positive, known; rather than on the chance of the future beyond death, which to our philosophy is unreal, not positive, and unknown. It may be darkness and nothingness,—I do not say it is, but it may be: and to barter away our title to it may be nothing more than parting with the shadow of a shadow—even the shade—for such this future may be, and nothing more,—cast forwards by the light of real life, and called in our ignorance another world. For my part,' he said, 'if there were good spirits, they would assist me; if bad they would accept my offers. Now I have often tempted both, but never seen either, and hence conclude them to be only the idle work of idle imaginations,—the future to be a blank, the present only a reality, in which the power to create an immortality is given us and which, if not exercised, we return to a state after life and being, as perfect in its nonentity to us, as is that in which we were, if we really were at all, before life and being commenced. Talk as you will, we really *know* no more of the life after, than of the life prior to, this. Of the latter nobody professes either dogmas or doctrine; for men never saw profit or advantage to be derived from the establishment of a spiritual world anterior to earth-life; while of the former, the religious of the world give us but assertion and opinion, not knowledge; for I hold nothing to be knowledge which is beyond the definition of philosophy. *Probability* it may be, but it is not knowledge.'

"Thus he used to think and talk, and every day getting poorer and poorer as the demands of his family increased, and his own unwearied exertions failed to meet with reward: a state of things, I fear, which went far to induce his peculiar belief. I have often seen him in a fearful burst of passionate excitement, when his wife and family and himself were in want of the most ordinary necessaries, cast some fine unsold picture into the fire, and swear most solemnly and deeply, that if there were a devil, and if he himself had a soul worth the devil's purchase, he would sell it him in bonds of fire and blood, if the price would but redeem their present misery, and find all that he most loved on earth in even as much food for their wants as God could find for the wild wolf or raven, without toil, without the chance of an immortality to risk, and without heart or intellect to feel privation as he felt it, even should it come upon them. He would then turn suddenly to me and exclaim, "Now Zeittler, if these idle tales were true, why does this Evil One not come? Why not take me at my word? for he must know that in this I am no liar."

"At that time he occupied two small rooms on the upper story of a large old house in Heidelburg, the door of the outer one of which opened upon a common staircase and passage, in which he usually paced up and down with a large pipe in his mouth during several hours in the gloom of an evening, for the sake of fresher air and exercise, and perhaps also to dissipate, if possible, his miserable reflections. He also used to do the same at any time of the night when he could not sleep. He would rise in the dark from the side of his sleeping wife and child, fill his huge meerschaum pipe, light a tinder to fire his tobacco, and then stalk backwards and forwards in the blind passage with steps as noiseless as a ghost, and exactly as confident, calm, and un-apprehensive as though in the summer sunshine of a public road. I do not say there was anything to be frightened at, but my imagination would never allow me exactly to fancy his particular taste in that respect."

At this part of his story Zeittler charged his audience to mark particularly that he was not giving them opinions nor speculations.

"I am speaking of facts and results," said he, "of things I have seen and heard, and therefore known; make of them what you can or will.

"One morning I walked into his chambers just to chat about the news of the day—for there had been a terrible storm in the night, and a church-spire rent from top to bottom by the lightning—when I found

intently engaged upon a new picture, a fact which somewhat sur-
?d me by the waywardness of temper it displayed, as he had thrown
uυ√n his pencils in vexation the afternoon before, and vowed never to
touch them again, but buy a spade, and go and earn his bread like Cain,
by the sweat of his brow.

"'Ah, Weigel,' said I, 'how is this? At it once more, as I knew you
would be before another sun went round.'

"'Yes,' he replied, 'I took good advice last night.'

"I told him I was glad to hear of it, for the arts would have had reason
to deplore his wild resolution of yesterday, if he had adhered to it. I then
asked him what friend had had the good fortune so to influence him?

"'Why,' he replied, 'you know how it thundered between twelve and
three o'clock? I could not sleep, so I got up, lit my pipe, and took my old
walk in the passage. Crash came the thunder-claps on the roof, and the
lightning flew about me like the blazes of a burning house. It might have
withered me to ashes for what I cared, since I neither hoped here nor
feared hereafter. I had nearly smoked my pipe out, when a man met me
in the passage, and as is usual with the people here, just inquired how I
was coming on. I told him my resolve, and added that I intended to keep
it. He said, as you say, that it would be a pity to see such a poetical soul
as mine reduced to the necessity of spending time in common labor that
any peasant huid might do as well or better, just for the sake of finding
food and shelter for myself and my family. I answered that that soul as
constituted had been my curse, and swore the devil might have it if it
were any use to him, providing I could but keep the bodies of those who
were dependent on me from starvation worse than that of the beasts. He
begged me not to speak rashly, but advised me to take heart and try once
more. Go to your easel tomorrow, said he, you will find a subject ready
in your own room. I will make a bargain with you. You shall work upon
it as long as you fancy you can improve upon it; if you finish it anytime
within one exact year—even a moment within—I will buy it of you at
a price that shall make your fortune, on condition that if you do not, at
the expiration of that time, you take leave of your family and walk away
into the forest with me when I call for you. Done! said I, a bargain! And
can you believe it, Zeitter, I fancied that I heard that word a bargain, a
bargain, a bargain, repeated by twenty different echoes? We shook hands
and parted. I filled my pipe again, and walked about till the storm was
over.'

"I then," continued Zeitter, "asked Weigel who the man was. He said
that he could not tell, as he never troubled himself to look particularly
where he came from or where he went. 'And the subject that you were to
find in your room? said I,' glancing upon his new, clear canvas—'is this

it?' 'That it is,' answered he, 'for though when I sat down I did not think what I was going to be about, yet half-unconsciously I began to draw that portrait. But the most odd thing about it is, that as I advanced with it, thinking I was sketching from fancy only, I happened to cast my eyes into the dark corner beside my easel, and there I saw the identical face looking through the gloom at me!'"

"Exactly so," remarked Stretcher,—"and you saw it as well, no doubt?"

"Not so," answered Zeitter,—"but as I looked on my friend, I concluded that misery had made him mad."

"Pretty shrewd guess, that. Well, go on, old fellow. What sort of picture was it?"

"There was nothing but a rude outline then, but afterwards, as it seemed to grow towards perfection under his hands, it struck the spectator at first view as the highest conceivable manly beauty of an ethereal nature—a picture of a being whose very outward form was spiritual, yet heightened by a still deeper expression of remoter spirituality that made the heart quail as though standing before the presence of a very angel. But as you continued to gaze, that feeling grew imperceptibly into one of fear, you knew not how or why; and then again, and at last, into a sense of utter dread and horror; for the beauty seemed to become spiritually sinful, and what appeared to be an angel to the sight sunk into the soul like the lightening presence of a demon. Never," continued Zeitter, "shall I get that picture from before my eyes; for against it even Raphael and Correggio were tame. After three months' incessant labor, I thought it was finished, for so it seemed to all eyes save Weigel's: but, on and on, he still worked as incessantly as before, for he said that the longer he went on, the more did his visionary model increase in beauty and expression, and finish:—the labor of a lifetime was before him—not of a year only; and even then he should drop into his grave and leave it an 'unfinished picture.' After six months' toil, he fell sick from anxiety and incessant application, but still persisted in his labor. He said that the work grew under his hands, for the farther he proceeded, the more he had to do: a year seemed now but as a day, and yet he had but six months left. Only six months to do all in, or to lose all. The consciousness of this pressed heavily upon him, and incited him to labor even when he almost required to be supported on a seat before his easel. At the end of three hundred and sixty days he was worn to a shadow, while the picture was brought up to such a wonderful pitch of perfection that *it* seemed the living palpable reality, and he, the workman, only such a dim animated shade as human art and earthly colors might produce. Together they looked like spirit creating matter;—the invisible making the visible,—the supernatural and visionary giving form, and bulk, and substance to sensitive material. But what struck me as most singular was, that during the whole of this time he had never once alluded again to the strange speculations which previously (as I described at the setting out) appeared to occupy so great a portion of his thoughts. He did so, at length, in the following manner:—

"'Look what I have done, Zeitter, my friend. Behold this picture. Will it make a man immortal? But it is well you cannot see the original. I *know* now that no man in this world may truly see him and live. That accursed, glorious, and yet hideous shadow! It has blasted me with poring upon. Night and day; day and night, alike. Dream and reality, light and darkness; all have been alike to me: still the same unchangeably, until my eyes know no other object than that everlasting one. His look has become a part of my existence, and if I do not make haste, make haste,— I have but five days and some odd hours left,—I feel that he will swallow me up, body and soul! But I will be diligent; I will escape him yet; five days are a long time; and if I am in the hands of the Evil One—if, say, all I have doubted be true, I'll finish in five days, five hours, and a half, and cheat the devil out of his prize at last.'

"I endeavored to persuade him that the picture was more than finished already,—that in plain truth the world possessed not such another; and that he had better so consider it himself, and lay his pallet down for the close of labor. But he could not be convinced that it was finished. 'Besides,' said he, '*he* has not yet come to purchase it, for the time is not yet up. One moment within the year, exactly, and he will be here. I know he will, for I feel him, as it were, even now creeping through my blood and along my bones,' and he shivered in agony as the pencils fell from his hands, and his whole form sunk almost as senseless as a corpse back in his antique chair.

"In spite of even the daily conclusions of my own senses, that nothing more within the reach of the most consummate art could possibly be done to heighten the picture,—what actually *was* done day after day, contradicted me, and showed again and again, that Weigel was right: it was yet unfinished, because a higher perfection seemed still attainable, though only because the eye constantly distinguished that he *did* attain it.

"Five days and five hours more were gone. The conclusion was at hand. Curious and anxious to know what it would be, I was alone by his side from the commencement of the last half hour until all was over. I know not how to describe it, for my own excitement was such, that the circumstances, impressions, and feelings of that time seemed to whirl through my brain confusedly and indistinct, like objects mingled together on the circumference of a revolving wheel. I knew a climax of some sort was at hand, and one all the more impressive and fearful, because though so close, it was inscrutable, though involving beyond doubt the fate of a man of a most gifted and rare genius. Weigel hung his watch upon the easel above his picture, while his eye, with painful regularity, and an expression of intensity, that seemed to dilate the pupil much beyond its ordinary size, while it partially closed the lids and drew down the brows closely and rigidly,—passed from the moving hands to the dark corner where his supernatural model was, and then to the picture:—only to return while touch was added to touch to the shadow again, to the picture, and then to the dial. His mouth was slightly opened in an indescribable expression of agony and fear, and whenever his pencil was not actually in contact with the palette or the painting, I observed it tremble in his grasp like a shivering reed.

"'Five minutes more!' at length he gasped; 'and the head grows more and more glorious, till this picture looks but a school-boy's sketch! Three minutes! I shall never have done, never! One minute!—Ah!—not one—not half a one! Zeitter, Zeitter!—my friend!' he shrieked; 'ah!—ah!—ah!—*the year is out,* and it is not done!'

"The palette and pencils fell from his hands to the floor, and his head sunk heavily upon his breast, as though bowed in death before the idol of his art. I flew to seize and support him, for he was apparently insensible. At that moment his wife and a strange man, whom I had never seen before, entered the room. The former wept and cried like a woman frantic; but the latter looked coldly on, and placing his finger on Weigel's breast merely said solemnly, 'He is better now.' At that voice and touch the artist raised himself up, as though suddenly re-animated, and looked seriously, but confidently and calmly, in the face of the stranger. Not a word passed between them; but the latter turned towards Weigel's wife, and told her that at a certain bank in the city, which he named, she would find payment for that picture to the amount of three thousand pounds.

"'It will at least,' said he, 'save you and your family from want for life; and that is all your husband cares for.'

"'All!—all!' said Weigel; 'and now for the forest!'

"So saying, he arose with the alacrity of a youth whose health and spirits has never broken; put on his cap, filled his pipe, as though nothing had happened, and kissed his wife and children, after having extorted a promise from them to be happy *until he came back again.*

"'I will see that they fulfil it!' murmured the stranger. 'Come!—the moon is up, and we must be there *by* midnight.'

"'May I not accompany you, Weigel?' I exclaimed.

"'No!—not as you value your life; and take heed, Zeitter, take heed also, that you never come to me.'

"Nevertheless, I felt impelled to go along with them, and followed until we entered the shadows of the forest. Two black horses, or creatures that bore their resemblance, stood in the road.

"'Mount!' cried the stranger, as he vaulted on to the back of one, and Weigel on the other; 'DARKNESS is mine, and RUIN thine! Away, away!'

"They swept the forest like a Winter's blast; bowing the trees as they passed, sweeping leaves away like a hurricane, and gathering a tempest of black hurrying clouds from the skies along the horizon towards which they fled. The moon sunk like an opaque scarlet fire, and the hair of my head stood up as I returned home in darkness. Need I say that Weigel never came back again?"

Here Herr Zeitter paused.

"And the picture,—did they take that too?" asked Sapio Green.

"The picture," replied Zeitter, "was sent for the next day by a strange old baron, who inhabited a castle hard by, and who said he had purchased it by commission. However that might be, his name was on the check for payment, and the bank discharged it out of his deposits. I anticipate your next question, but he was *not* the stranger; nor was anyone like him known in that quarter of the country. Up to this day, however, it is believed that a figure like Weigel may be seen on moonlight nights still working away with his shadowy pencils upon the 'Unfinished Picture,' as it hangs in distinguished state in a room appropriated (with reference to works of art) to it alone."

EULE: THE EMPEROR'S DWARF

BY JOHN RUTTER CHORLEY

(1838)

Before Spinola had burned Aix-la-Chapelle (in the seventeenth century), the old city had a wonderfully solemn and antiquated air. There was something in the place, even during its festival times, which reminded the stranger that he beheld the mausoleum of a great king. The grotesque buildings, and narrow, crooked streets, with the quaint costume and manners of the burghers, seemed yet to belong to the time of the Franks; and when the city was deserted by its summer guests, it was as somber and weariful a place as could be found in all Westphalia; as far, indeed, out of the world's way as Malspart the strong-hold, to which the old lay tells how Reynard the Fox betook himself, when he foreswore the life of a courtier, and turned hermit.

This was the reason which induced Master Albrecht to choose it for his residence when he withdrew from Heidelberg. A soldier out of employ, a wooer disappointed in love—and young enough to regard both of these misfortunes as something unjust and unusual—he fancied that life and its enjoyments concerned him no longer. There, was, indeed, some reason for surprise at the treatment he had met with from the counselor's fair daughter, Christine; as her heart betrayed no other preference, and he was such a suitor as maidens do not often repel. But he little knew the pains which his rivals had taken to poison her ear, nor how often, when he was beside her, the innocent girl had wished in her heart that the tales she had heard were untrue. But she did believe them, being herself too artless to suspect the plausible conspiracy against poor Albrecht. Thus, while she avoided his approach, and denied him all opportunity of expostulation, he could only ascribe to fixed aversion a reserve which her heart in secret gainsaid. He despaired, and departed.

On the night with which my anecdote should begin, there were few watchers in Aix-la-Chapelle more listless and sad at heart than Albrecht, as he sat alone, indulging himself with the self-torment so dear to the fancy-stricken. His lodging was in a large old house on the south side of the market-place, directly opposite to the bronze statue of Charlemagne. This was, in Catholic times, the property of the Cistercians; but the different suites of rooms—some rich and in good repair, others mean and ruinous—were now hired by various occupants. All had been quiet for some hours, and Albrecht was far gone in the pursuit of his own fancies, when a tap at the chamber door recalled him. His lamp was so nearly spent, that he could not discern the features of the visitor: it seemed to be a child, from the smallness of his stature.

"Whom do you seek?" inquired Albrecht.

He was answered in a voice strange, but not unpleasant, "My master, Wenzel, is near his end, and asks to see you."

"How? my poor philosopher! Stay, I will follow you on the instant!" But when he turned, after closing the door, the messenger was already gone.

He did not, however, want a guide to Wenzel's chamber; a poor apartment under the same roof, but in a wing of the building which had fallen into decay. Here Albrecht had found him, by accident, soon after arriving in Aix-la-Chapelle, living apparently on the slenderest means, and quite alone. In Heidelberg he had known him in different circumstances, attached to the suite of a Hungarian prince, over whom he appeared to exercise an entire influence, until the transaction occurred which drove him from Heidelberg. He was a man in the prime of life, of graceful manners and discreet speech, reputed to be deeply learned, and certainly gifted with the power of controlling all whom he approached in a singular degree: amongst others, Albrecht, so unlike himself, was at first attracted, and soon became attached to him. But Wenzel's position at the Palatine court grew suspected, and then dangerous. Rumors were circulated respecting his objects there; and, in those times, the bare report that he was an agent of the king of Spain was enough to render him odious. It was then that accusations charging him with unlawful practices, and ascribing the influence he had acquired to wicked means, found ready believers. Albrecht was one of the few whom these reports did not move; and to his assistance Wenzel owed his escape from an attempt, the authors of which were not discovered, to dispose of him by assassination. For some days he was sheltered by Albrecht, until means were found for his departure from Heidelberg privately. Thus again brought together by chance, both living as it were in banishment and misfortune, their former intimacy became closer in Aix-la-Chapelle. All offers of pecuniary assistance Wenzel had haughtily refused; but Albrecht found a singular pleasure in his company, and in listening to strange and eloquent discourse on subjects wholly foreign to his natural mood. The announcement of his danger took Albrecht by surprise; the day before, he had seen him apparently as well as usual. The possession of a servant, too, seemed a novelty; hitherto he had appeared unwilling as well as unable to maintain such an encumbrance.

Albrecht was struck with surprise, on entering Wenzel's chamber, to find him dressed in what seemed to be grave-clothes, and sitting upright on the miserable mattress with his eyes, which were still open, turned towards the door. A small but very bright lamp stood on a table at the bed's foot, which was covered on this occasion with a velvet cloth; a silver cup and a naked sword, the blade ornamented with Arabic letters in gold, were also placed upon it. Besides this, and a crazy wooden stool, there was no other furniture visible.

Wenzel's voice was as clear and strong as ever, as he greeted his friend.

"Welcome for the last time, Master Albrecht; I am glad you are here while the light is still burning."

Albrecht would have replied, but Wenzel interrupted him:

"Nay, I know what you would say. It is even so; and the minutes are few. Listen! Until now I have never thanked you. You have done well—meant kindly by me; I would offer some return."

"Indeed, Master Wenzel, you owe me no thanks!"

"Thanks!" he replied, "they are mere words. What would such profit you? I would make you a gift; take it, and do not fear to use what I have meant for your service. There is a trusty creature of mine; now he shall be yours: do not let him go while you need him. Dost hear, Eule?" And, as he spoke, there crept from behind the bed's head a little figure, with thin limbs, and a brown shriveled face, strongly featured, and lighted by a pair of large keen gray eyes; he came bowing to the side of the bed.

"Hearken, Eule; I give thee to Master Albrecht here; serve him until he has found what he requires." And, turning to Albrecht, Wenzel continued, "Do not quarrel with Eule; he is somewhat willful, but you will find him quick and wise." He had barely uttered the last word, when a deep sigh escaped him, and he fell at length on the bed. Albrecht hastened to his side, but the dwarf motioned him back. "It is of no use"—the voice was the same that had called at his door—"he has been two hours dead! See, the lamp is out—let us go." And Albrecht hurried from the room, hardly knowing, at the moment, what he did. Eule shut the door, and seemed to follow, as Albrecht went down the narrow stair.

Death is at all times a mystery; but, in this of Wenzel's, there was a strangeness which the solitary place and the dark hour rendered peculiarly startling. Albrecht had reached the door of his own chamber, still fancying he heard the shuffling step of the dwarf on his heels, before he turned round; then he looked behind him, but his follower was not there. In the morning, he prepared to take order for Wenzel's burial, as he knew there was no one beside to care for it; when he was told that there had been people busy in his chamber all the night. It seems they must have carried away the body, for the place was found utterly deserted and bare. As the deceased owed nothing to anyone, and had no wealth to excite the interest of strangers, his disappearance passed without questions; and Albrecht, after what he had witnessed, felt averse to search into the matter. He was, moreover, in that nerveless mood which follows a first disappointment, and, for a time, renders action of any kind distressing.

But, on the following night (it was the last of April, when it is still misty and cold in that region), the tap came again to Albrecht's chamber-door. "Come in," he said; for he was loathe to stir from the light of the stove. He had to repeat the permission twice again, before the dwarf entered.

"I am here to serve you," he said; "what must I do?" And the little grotesque thing came close to the side of his chair, dressed in a short red cloak and blue hose, with a peaked cap and feather in his hand, making a variety of queer obeisances. Albrecht felt inclined alternately to shudder and to laugh.

"Where have you been, Eule?" he said, at length; "and what has been done with poor Master Wenzel?"

"I have been sleeping in the belfry. With the dead I have no business. Give me some better employment than answering idle questions. It is not my way."

"I need no service," said Albrecht, who felt disturbed at the strange looks and manner of the dwarf. The creature had squatted itself cross-legged with its back to the fire, and peered into Albrecht's face, with a look of familiar cunning.

"Go to, master," he said, "you are afraid of a strange face. You may know me better; remember what *he* told you—'quick and wise.'"

"You served Wenzel long?" said Albrecht; "I never saw you with him." The dwarf grinned. "May be, I do not appear much by day. Why, did you fancy me a menial, like one of your snorting sots in the ante-chamber yonder?"

"What then can you do, and why do you come hither?"

"More questions! I do not come unbidden. Do? I can read thought—and prosper them. Somewhat of the past I know, too. Shall I remind you of the words you spoke last Nicholas' eve in the porch of the Heiliger-kloster?"

Albrecht started: he remembered them well. But who could have heard them but Christine and himself? The dwarf rattled his withered legs, and laughed with a sound like a creaking wheel.

"Come," he said, "noble sir, I know more of that story, may be, than one or both. So quick, and headstrong, and blind!—you lovers are always running the wrong way. What if I show you a letter?"

The direct allusion to a subject of painful interest would at any other time have been received by Albrecht with anger and impatience. But the visit of the dwarf, in itself calculated to take the fancy by surprise, had found him in that mood of excitement, which no intense direction of the mind to any remote object of desire is apt to create. There is no state more prone than this to superstition; when the will, repulsed by realities, is fain to grasp at some hope or promise beyond them. In this temper of mind Albrecht readily connected Wenzel's singular legacy with some fulfillment of his dearest wish; and the intelligence professed by the dwarf awakened a host of vague expectations.

"I would give my life," he said, "to read her heart truly for one instant."

"The offer, Master Albrecht, is not very tempting to one like me," the dwarf replied, drily. "But my charge just now is not to bargain with you. What if I can serve you better than this?—stay, there are two conditions; come whither I bid you, and ask no vain questions."

At this instant a sound was heard, like the call of a trumpet at a distance. The dwarf sprang to his feet. "Fie on it," he said, "I shall be waited for! There are fine doings at the palace tonight. Will you come?"

"Befall what may," thought Albrecht, "I risk nothing; for what have I to lose? The game begins strangely; let me even see what will become of it!"

The natural recklessness of his character for the moment revived; and, taking his cap and sword, "Go on," he said, "I will follow you. But beware how you deal with me. I will have no quacksalver's tricks or mockery."

Eule scuttled down the staircase at a wonderful pace, chuckling and chattering like an ape; it was no easy matter to keep up with him. On passing out into the open space before his lodging, Albrecht was struck by the unusual spectacle of a concourse of people, at an hour when there was not wont to be a soul awake in the city. The lights, which were held at intervals over the heads of the crowd, allowed their dress and features to be partially seen; and these, also, were strange and surprising to Albrecht. There were men and women of all ages, in stiff dingy costumes; and before them, as if to keep the way clear, stood files of men at arms, with fierce hairy visages, and of unusual stature. As Albrecht passed nearer to them, the hue of their faces looked dead and sullen; and he perceived that the uncouth weapons in their hands were discolored with rust. They did not speak, but, as Albrecht followed his guide, nodded and pointed to each other, with such distorted motions, that he involuntarily turned his eyes away.

"A goodly company," said the dwarf, as he hurried along; "the Emperor's coming has brought them all out tonight. But now we are at the gate of the palace—follow me closely; I have a pass."

The entrance of the building (for it was the place, at least, of the old town-house) was quite changed to Albrecht's eye. It was lighted by many iron lamps; and at the doors, and along the staircase, were ranged attendants, as it seemed, of a certain rude splendor.

As Eule crossed the threshold, the first that stood before it, called out, in a shrill tone of voice, "Ho, there, make way for the Emperor's dwarf!" And the cry was repeated up the staircase, with such a strange accent, that Albrecht shivered, and would fain have held back. But the dwarf, turning round, whispered, "Come on; you will repent if you tarry."

So he went forward.

The door at the head of the staircase was thrown open as they advanced; and before them lay the entire extent of the hall, blazing with lights, and crowded with an assemblage of great strangeness and dignity. On either side of the apartment—and all of them—were grouped members of both sexes, of stately aspect, and clothed in rich, but singular, apparel. Albrecht was struck by the beauty of the women, and the profusion and fairness of their hair, which fell from the crown of the head in long ringlets. At the upper end of the room, a number of noble figures, surpassing all the rest in stature and manly beauty, were ranged on either side of a throne, which was occupied by one of august presence, seated and covered. The expression of his countenance, which might have been called fierce, was softened by arched eyebrows, which, as well as the ample beard that descended to his girdle, were of snowy whiteness. The impressiveness of the scene was rendered more striking by the silence of all; but a certain fixed gaze in the eyes, and a rigid calm in their features, gave a ghastly air to the company. The lights were strangely disposed from above, amongst the fretted quoins and pendants of the roof; and the grotesque heads which stared from the spring of the arches, and beneath the corbels, seemed, to Albrecht's hurried glance, as fully alive as the group below, shedding light from their eyes, and panting through their open jaws. To observe what has now been described was the work of a moment; in the next, Albrecht saw every eye turned upon his guide, and every face in the hall smiles: but this sign of welcome was more unearthly than the previous stillness. Then the stately figure on the throne raised his head, and beckoned the dwarf to come forward.

As Albrecht mechanically followed, Eule composedly whispered to him, "Take heed now—they are going to dance; do you as the rest, and do not fail to keep the hand of the partner I shall give you."

So the dwarf went up the room, and, as he drew near to the dias, Albrecht fell aside, where there was a vacant place beneath a pillar; none seeming to give heed to him. A smile came over the face of the grave personage, as Eule knelt before him; and, when the obeisance was completed, he rose, and, at a sign from his hand, a strange burst of music (if such wild sounds might be so called) was uttered from some unseen instruments above, and the multitude ordered themselves in pairs, each cavalier presenting his hand to a lady, and leading her forth. One of these—the least distinguished in beauty or apparel—was left alone; when Eule led Albrecht towards her, saying, "Wait, and when the next measure is begun, offer your hand."

In the mean while, the rest were all in motion, pacing to and fro with a grave solemnity, which seemed more like a procession than a dance. After a short pause, the Emperor himself uncovered, and approached the solitary lady, when Eule said to Albrecht, "Now is the time; take her hand, and grasp it firmly."

Hardly knowing what he did, Albrecht obeyed the instructions, and, bowing, seized the hand, which was not refused him. The instant he had done so, a look of fury distorted the monarch's countenance, and, to his consternation the lady's hand crumbled to dust in his grasp. The lights were at once quenched, and a confused uproar drowned the music. Eule was at his side: "Keep firm hold of my cloak," he said, "and make your best speed hence; but do not lose the ring."

Amidst the darkness and tumult, he hurried after his guide; doors were violently opened and flung together. In the bewilderment, his senses forsook him: he knew not how he reached home. When he woke on the following morning, feeble and feverish, in his own chamber, the recollections of the night were those of a delirious dream. He closed his eyes again, and slept heavily throughout the day.

The voice of the dwarf at his bedside made him wake with a start. It was evening.

"Have you got the ring?" he said.

Albrecht looked; and, behold, on his forefinger, a serpent, rudely chased, of pale gold, with eyes of fiery carbuncle. He shuddered: the wild spectacle of the past night had then been a real existence!

"I have done enough for you," said Eule; "you will find what virtue there is in that toy. It turned an emperor's head, and built a city; try if it cannot cure a froward girl. Will you wear it, and let me go?"

"Go, in God's name!" exclaimed Albrecht; "I will have no more part in these unnatural things." And many more disclaimers he would probably have uttered, but the dwarf had contrived to depart on the instant.

What passed in Albrecht's mind, after he was gone, there are now no means of knowing; but this is certain—that, on the following day, he left Aix-la-Chapelle—that he did not throw away the ring—and that, in three days afterwards, his rivals at the Palatine court were surprised by his reappearance at Heidelberg.

Their displeasure, it may be supposed, was, at least, equal to their surprise, at the marked change in Lady Christine's manner towards him; and when, after a few weeks, it was understood that the favored suitor was shortly to become her lord and master, it was openly asserted that such an instance of sudden caprice exceeded the ordinary license of a lady's will, and was, indeed, indecorous and unnatural. Nevertheless, the marriage took place.

They had been, for some years, furnishing matter of conversation to all the court idlers, by the unchanging attachment which seemed to unite them, when the circumstances of Albrecht's visit to Aix-la-Chapelle, in some way or other, transpired. Probably he had disclosed them, in a moment of confidence, to his lady; and she, of course, could not remain the sole possessor of so rare a secret. At once, the wonder seemed clearly explained; and the well-known legend of enchantment which belonged to a ring, whereby the Emperor Charlemagne was ensnared of old, was in everybody's mouth; and it is said, that many were the schemes laid (chiefly by female plotters) to obtain possession of Albrecht's jewel. But whether he had faith in its virtue or no, it is related that he never trusted it on any hand but his own. It may be doubted, perhaps, whether the success of his wooing, and his wedded happiness, could not be explained without a reference to magic—by the discovery of slanders, and the existence of a strong mutual affection. But these are inquiries beyond the province of the narrator, who can merely relate the story, as it is set forth in records of the time, leaving the explanation of dubious questions to wits more subtle than his own.

THE GREEN HUNTSMAN

BY JOSEPH HOLT INGRAHAM

(1841)

"IS IT A TRUE AND HONEST TALE, FAIR MASTER?"

"NAY - I VOUCH NOT. I GIVE IT THEE AS I HAD IT."

In the upper *faubourg* of New Orleans and conspicuous from the river on which it fronts, stands a vast, square mansion, gray and ruinous through neglect rather than time. A few old moss-stained oaks of a century's growth, rear their majestic heads above its rank lawn, and the hedges and walls that once enclosed it are broken down or utterly destroyed. Everywhere are the marks of its having been, in a better day, the abode of affluence and aristocratic pride. Lonely, in dilapidated grandeur, stately and imposing even in its ruin, it has for years attracted the eye of the curious stranger as he sailed past it. But vainly does the traveller seek to learn from those about him, the history of the spot. All that he can ascertain is, that it is called "The Haunted Villa."

Less than half a mile above this dilapidated edifice on the estate adjacent also stands a mansion, which is no less striking for its beauty, adorned as it is with verandahs, porticos, and latticed conservatories, and half-hid in the most luxuriant foliage, with well-appointed hedges of the rose-thorn interspersed with lemon, acacia and pomegranate trees enclosing a lawn of the softest green. It seems the abode of taste, refinement and graceful affluence—the home of domestic bliss and social happiness. Never two mansions or grounds presented stranger or more remarkable contrasts, made still more striking by their juxtaposition.

At the latter villa on the evening of our story, there was held a Christmas festival, of a gayer and more brilliant description than usual, for it was a bridal night also—and the bride and bridegroom with the joyous train mingled merrily in the holiday festivities. The bride! How shall her matchless beauty be given to the eye of the reader! She was on stately stature, and graceful as the swan in her movements. Her eyes were dark, and burning with the light of love. There was an unfathomable well of feeling in their dangerous depths, and though they could occasionally flash fire and sparkle, their usual aspect was soft and timid as the gazelle's. She was called Ephese, and men's eyes have seldom looked on a more beautiful woman, or a bridegroom's worshipping glance adorned a fairer bride. She was wedded the night of our story, in the gorgeous rooms of the mansion just described. The owner of this mansion was a French gentleman, and had been a widower for many years. He called Ephese his child. Some said she was his daughter, others that she was not. There was evidently a mystery about her. She was just eighteen the night of her bridal, which was as well both her birthday and wedding-day, a Christmas eve. The bridegroom was a rich young Creole of Orleans, handsome, chivalrous and well-born, and every way worthy to wear so bright a jewel as Ephese in his bosom.

It was a happy and merry night. All the youthful cavaliers for many leagues around were gathered there to grace the nuptials, and threescore maidens, with the dark eye and raven hair of that sunny clime, presented their rival-charms in the presence of the incomparable bride. In the wanton waltz and stately dance, amid never ceasing strains of ravishing music, and with the numerous scenes and changes of a bridal festival conjoined with a Christmas merry-making, the silvery hours flew swiftly on. Midnight at length approached, and the blushing bride, half-reluctant, half-consenting, was borne from the hall by a group of laughing virgins, to the nuptial chamber. At the instant the door closed behind her, the festive halls were strangely illuminated by a sudden light of a pale-green cast that outshone the brilliant candelabra in the rooms and threw over every face the ghastly pallor of death. At the same instant a loud, heavy, rumbling noise, like underground thunder, appalled every ear.

"Look! the Haunted Villa!" shouted several voices on the verandah.

In an instant the halls were deserted, and the verandah and lawn looking in the direction of the ruined mansion, were crowded with terrified gazers. Terrific spectacle! The whole interior of the ruin, towards which their eyes were turned, seemed to be on fire. Through every aperture of door and window and gaping crevice, the fire shone out as if from a furnace, with an intense glowing heat. Yet there ascended no smoke from it, nor could there be heard any sound of crackling flame. But what was most fearful was a tongue of green flame, which rising from the midst of the molten mass, flung itself, lapping and curling high into the air, like a serpent, and then contracted and coiled down upon the surface of the bed of fire, again to unfold and dart upward, and shed its baleful glare a wide league around. The most death-like silence pervaded the groups of banqueters as they looked upon this spectacle. To all the name of the Haunted Villa was familiar, and to every mind supernatural terror was associated with it. No one breathed. Expectation and alarm sat on every face. Gradually the intensity of the glowing interior lessened, and in a few minutes all became dark as before, save the tongue of flame which continued to curl and writhe above the central tower with fiercer strength. All at once it disappeared, like a lamp blown out, and in its place a small globe of green fire, that shone with a steady light, was alone visible upon the summit of the tower.

Awed and full of conjectures and trembling apprehensions, the company instantly broke up. In a few minutes, nearly all were on their way to their homes, anxious to place the widest distance between themselves and this spot of supernatural sounds and spectacles. Five or six young men alone remained in the deserted verandah. They were intimate friends of the bridegroom, who himself stood among them as they discoursed together on the event.

"Did you notice that it was just as the door closed behind the bride?" remarked Don Antonio Baradas, one of the group upon the colonnade.

"I did, signor," replied Eugene Brissot, with animation, "for my eye was following her departure, surrounded by her bridesmaids, and methought I had never seen woman so lovely, and I mourned so bright a star should set to every eye but Henride's."

"You all noticed it was just as she left the room, signors?" repeated young Don Antonio, looking round with a marked manner and speaking in a solemn tone.

"We did," all answered, "but has Ephese anything to do with—"

"Speak, Don Antonio! what evil threatens or is connected with my beloved bride?" demanded the young husband, earnestly grasping his friend's hand.

"Liston, signor," answered Don Antonio Baradas.

The young cavaliers, joined by one or two ladies, now grouped closer about the young Spaniard as he leaned gracefully against a column, his arms folded within his silk mantle across his breast. His attitude was striking and commanding. His age appeared not less than thirty, but care or deep and active thought had worn in his face strong lines, which, while they added to its intellect, took from his youth. He had been very handsome and was still striking for his manly appearance. His figure was tall and slender and finely shaped. His complexion was so dark as to approach a swarthy hue. His features were finely aquiline, and his large dark eyes beamed with the fire of intelligence. Sometimes there was in them a strangeness of expression terrible to look upon, while ere it could be commented upon by those who observed it, passed away, instantly followed by the sweetest smile human lips ever wore. With the early history of Don Antonio, none were acquainted. He had come to New

Orleans on a Christmas eve, eight years before, a traveller and as the heir of a noble Cuban family. After a sojourn of a few weeks, he gave out that he had become so much pleased with the city as to determine to abide there permanently. His lodgings were magnificently furnished, and in his horses and equipage, he rivalled the wealthiest Creoles. He soon found friends, and the halls of the oldest and best families of the land were thrown open to him. He was admired for his wit, accomplishments, and manly graces, and everywhere courted for his wealth. Thus for seven years had Don Antonio lived among the hospitable and refined Orleanois. During all this while it was remarked that he had never drank wine nor spoken to a woman—though the loveliest in the world were alluring him with their smiles. Between him and Henride Claviere, the bridegroom, there had existed a long and close intimacy. He had now been invited to wait on him as a groomsman, but had singularly and strangely to his friend, declined, saying he could be present only as a guest.

"Listen, signor," he said, in an impressive manner, as his friends gathered around him, their curiosity aroused by the tone and emphasis of his words. "It is twenty-one minutes yet to midnight! There will be full time 'till twelve for me to speak. Patience, Henride! thy bride hath not been gone ten minutes and thou must wait for the cathedral bell to toll midnight ere thou leave us."

"The Cathedral bell! It was never heard this distance," exclaimed several.

"It will be heard here tonight, as if swinging within the dome of this hall," he answered, in a deep voice that with his words made each heart weigh heavier in the bosom against which it audibly throbbed. "Yonder mansion, my friends, was built by a Castilian noble, in whose veins flowed the best blood of Spain. His wealth was inexhaustible. He possessed also boundless ambition, and never did human life stand between him and his object. His passions were evil and indulged at any sacrifice. He lived solitary in a lonely castle amid the most fertile and lovely region of Castile. There he associated only with his gold, which he kept in coffers in his vaults, and with his horse and black hounds, with which he used to hunt every Christmas eve, from sunset to sunrise, in company, it is said, with the free spirits of the air, with whom, riding like the wind, they traversed the kingdom in its breadth and length ere the dawn. And what think you be hunted my friends? A Castilian maid who should be both *perfectly beautiful and perfectly blind*!—for there is a tradition in Spain, that such a maiden shall become the mother of an Emperor who shall unite all the kingdoms of Europe into one Empire. But it was not for this he would possess this blind beauty. He was in person the ugliest and most hideous man in all Spain. Men looked upon him with disgust and women with fear. He wanted a wife and forsooth, one that was beautiful too, for next to his money and hounds he admired women. But no female could be found to marry him, so hideous was his visage, for all the gold in his coffers. He had heard of this tradition, and the idea of having a bride who should be perfectly beautiful and yet be blind, was highly gratifying to his vanity, for he could feast upon her charms while she would be ignorant of his ugliness."

"And why should he seek her by night?" demanded Don Antonio's listeners.

"It is said he had a talisman purchased by a mint of golden zecchino of Pius VI, by which he would be guided to the abode of such a maiden, who could be borne off, says the tradition, only at the midnight hour and while buried in deep sleep.

"At length, one Christmas eve, when this Castilian noble was thirty years of age, he sallied forth with hound and horse and horn to seek the blind and beautiful maiden for his bride. It was a few minutes before midnight, that the priests who were chanting prayers in a monastery in the Pyrenees valley, heard the unusual sound of huntsmen and the hoarse bay of hounds approaching in full cry. The sounds came nearer and nearer and the wide doors of the chapel were burst open, and this young Castilian noble rode in at top speed, followed by his pack, and galloped straight towards the altar. The horror-stricken priests seized the golden crucifix that stood upon it and held it up between the sacred place and the intruders, whom they believed to be the spirit of the "Wicked Huntsman" of the Pyrenees, and no mortal man.

"Without heeding the priests or their crucifix, Don Rolando Os-ormo—for that was his name—leaped from his coal-black steed and passed through a small wicket that led into the cloisters of the nunnery. With a rapid step he traversed the corridor and stopped before a cell, the door of which was closed. It flew open at his touch. On a low couch, her features faintly visible by a lamp burning beside it, slept a nun of the most perfect symmetry of limbs and features. Don Rolando knelt beside her and lifted the lamp so as to obtain a more perfect view of her face. It was transcendently lovely. He smiled with satisfaction, and lifting her in his arms, bore her forth into the corridor."

"How knew he that a maiden slept there?" asked one of the group.

"By the talisman on his whip, it is said."

"What was that, Don Antonio?"

"A lock of the Virgin Mary's hair braided in the snapper, says the legend. The pliant lash would straighten and point forward as he held it in his hand in the direction he should proceed. Its touch opened all barriers, and gave him ingress to the inmost closet of castle or cot. But the impious noble was soon to learn that he could not enter, even with such a talisman, a consecrated temple and bear off with impunity a bride of the church. His punishment, though long deferred, came. He returned into the chapel with his prize ere the terrified monks had recovered from their astonishment. Leaping upon his steed and followed by his hounds, he spurred down the echoing aisles again, and left the convent as the bell tolled midnight, the noise of his riding and the bay of his hounds breaking far and wide upon the stillness of the night, as he coursed homeward down the valley.

"Don Rolando soon reached his castle and laid his intended bride upon a gorgeous couch. Then sending for musicians, he placed them in a concealed alcove and bade them play the softest strains 'till she awoke."

"How was he certain that she was blind as well as beautiful, Don Antonio?" asked Eugene Brissot. "Methinks a lady's beauty lieth mostly in her eye."

"The tradition saith that the maiden in question is to be *perfectly beautiful* still *perfectly blind*. She must have, therefore, perfect eyes to the observer though useless to herself as instruments of vision."

"Poor lady," sighed the young cavalier.

"I prithee proceed with thy story, Signor Antonio," said the impatient bridegroom.

"It indeed becomes me to hasten, for the midnight hour is near at hand. Don Rolando having arrayed himself magnificently and perfumed himself with the costliest essences of Persia, stood concealed behind the curtains of her couch to witness her awaking. At length the music stole into her senses, and slowly she began to open her eyes and throw off the deep sleep that had weighed upon the fringed lids. Don Rolando watched her with the most intense interest. He trembled lest he should have been deceived—for, already he passionately loved her. She rose in her couch and gazed around. Her eyes were blue as heaven, large, liquid, and full of love and feeling. But whether they had vision he was unable to determine. He was about to show himself to make the trial, but restrained the impulse and remained still concealed, feeling assured that a few moments would decide it. She looked around her upon the damask hangings that on all sides enveloped her couch, but there was no individual object about her to arrest and fix the eye. She now threw back her golden hair from her forehead, as if perfectly awake, and gazed around with intelligent surprize, too visibly depicted on her features and in the enlargement of her dilating eye to be mistaken. Don Rolando's heart began to sink within him. She looked each moment more bewildered and alarmed.

"'Holy Virgin, where am I?' she cried at length, in a voice which alarm had made most sweetly touching. 'These silken hangings—this heavenly music—this gorgeous chamber—' for she had now put aside the curtains. 'Whither have I been borne in my sleep? It were Heaven, did not yonder lattice, with a view of the distant stars through, tell me I am yet on earth.'

"'She *sees*, and the talisman has played me false! Accursed be it and the head it grew upon!' muttered Don Rolando through his clenched teeth.

"He was about to rush forward and bury his dagger in her heart, for his vanity and pride would not allow him to permit her to see his features, inasmuch as he already loved her, and the thought of seeing her shudder at their ugliness was madness to him. He had rather slay her with his own hand. This he was about to do, when suddenly his arm was arrested by a light touch. He turned and beheld a low black figure, with a body no higher than his knees, with a prodigious head, in the brow of which was set a single eye of green flame like a shining emerald, and with hands and arms of supernatural length.

"'Avaunt, fiend!' he cried, starting back with horror and affright.

"'Fear me not, Don Rolando,' said the dwarf, in a hoarse low tone. 'I know thy disappointment, ha, ha, ha! She has eyes brighter than stars.'

"'By Heaven she hath! How know you my thoughts and purposes?' demanded he with surprize.

"'It matters not. I can aid thy purpose!'

"'How?'

"'Destroy her vision!'

"'*Thou*, hell-hound! would'st thou mar such glorious beauty? She shall die first by my own hand.'

"'I will not mar it. I will take away her sight nor lay hand upon her.'

"'Give me proof of it and thou shalt attempt it. I would give half my wealth could it be so. Give me proof.'

"The demon-dwarf fixed upon him his single eye for an instant with such a steady gaze, that Don Rolando's eyes were irresistibly riveted upon it as if fascinated. In vain he tried to take them off. They were no longer subservient to his will. The demon's eye grew larger and larger, brighter and brighter each moment, 'till the light of it became painfully intense, and seemed to Don Rolando's eyes to fill the whole space before him and to pervade the whole room. By degrees it then faded away, lessening and growing dimmer and dimmer until it left the place to his vision dark as midnight.

"'Where art thou, fiend, that thou hast charmed me thus and left me in darkness?'

"'Ha, ha, ha! Don Rolando, dost thou find thyself in darkness?' said the dwarf, speaking from the self-same spot where Don Rolando has last seen him.

"'Art thou here, demon? Who hath extinguished the lights?'

"'No lights are extinguished, Don Rolando. The darkness is in thine own vision. Thou art stone blind.'

"'Thou liest. Ho, lights, lights, knaves! bring lights!'

"'Thou mayest call for lights 'till they rival in brightness the sun, and thou shalt not see their brilliancy.'

"'Fiend, hast thou done this?'

"'With a single glance of my eye. I have given thee but the proof thou didst seek. Look upon me once more.'

"'I see thee not.'

"'Be patient and I will restore thy vision.' The demon then placed a finger upon each eyelid of Don Rolando, and pressing upon them asked him if he saw two golden rings.

"'I do,' answered Don Rolando.

"'Fix thy inward gaze upon them as steadily as but now you fixed your external gaze upon my eye.'

"'Don Rolando with an effort did so and by degrees the golden rings enlarged until he seemed to be in a universe of roseate light. The dwarf then removed his fingers and opened his eyes. All around him then seemed an atmosphere of pale light but no object was visible. Gradually the light assumed a delicate blue shade, and then a green color, and seemed to gather itself into a circle opposite to him. This circle gradually lessened in size and increased in brilliancy. He kept his eyes steadily upon it as if by a supernatural energy, until it diminished to a small orb. That orb was the *dwarf's eye*, whom he now beheld standing in his presence as before.

"'It is enough! Thou shalt make use of thy power,' said Don Rolando. 'She is on yonder couch.'

"'The terms are the souls of the children she may bring thee,' said the dwarf, without moving.

"Don Rolando started. He saw that his visitor was resolute. 'It is but a contingency at the best,' thought he. 'I consent,' he said hesitatingly.

"'Lay thy thumb and forefinger upon my eyelid and it shall be thy oath,' said the demon.

"Don Rolando did so. The dwarf then placed himself at the foot of the couch in shadow, so that his bright green eye alone was visible from it. It instantly arrested the maiden's eyes and her glance was fascinated. In a few moments her vision was forever darkened.

"The demon departed as suddenly as he had appeared, and Don Rolando stood by the couch of the blind maiden. He watched her motions. Her gaze was vacant and her hands moved like one who is in the dark.

"'Alas, alas! whither am I borne? To what fate am I doomed? A moment since all was bright and gorgeous, and now all is dark as midnight. *Ay de mi!* Hapless vestal!'

"'Nay, sweet lady,' said Don Rolando, in a gentle tone, for though his visage was hideous his voice was soft and harmonious; 'you are brought from the damp cells of a cloister to the halls of luxury and affluence—to a noble castle that waits to hail you as its mistress, and to a true knight's home, who is ready to lay his heart and honor at your feet.'

"Thus and in like manner spoke Don Rolando. His soothing voice and tender speech at length won her ear, and she listened to him with pleasure. But the story of his wooing and nuptials, and of her submission to her blindness, for which she could not account, and which, be it mentioned here, did nothing to mar her beauty, must be passed over. Years rolled by and Don Rolando had become the father of seven beautiful daughters, every one of whom had been born on a Christmas eve. He loved his lovely and sightless wife each succeeding year more and more. Blessings seemed to flow in upon him on every side. The only desire he now had, to complete his happiness, was for a son, that he might have him heir to his name and vast estates. But this wish he was never destined to see fulfilled.

"At length his eldest daughter reached her eighteenth year, and a neighboring noble who had won her heart was to lead her to the altar on her birthday eve. The bridal party were assembled, the rites were performed, and the hours of festivity flew on with joy and hope. The bride, who was scarcely less lovely than Henride's, was in the midst of a waltz, when the castle clock tolled twelve. Ere the last stroke had ceased vibrating upon the ears of the banqueters, there entered the hall a tall dark stranger, in a green velvet dress richly studded with emeralds. In his bonnet was a sable plume fastened by an emerald that glowed like fire, and at his belt was a hunting horn. His aspect was noble and his face intellectual. His entrance drew nearly all eyes upon him. But there was something about him that made Don Rolando's heart shrink with ominous foreboding. He strode across the hall to where Don Rolando was seated, and said in a low tone—

"'Don Rolando, I have come for thy daughter.'

"Don Rolando started back and looked him in the face for an instant, and then with a shriek fell backward into the arms of his attendants.

"Leaving him, the stranger then approached the bride as she yet circled in the waltz, for while in its giddy mazes she had not yet noticed his entrance. He stood near her and sought to catch her eye. He succeeded! Instantly she stopped as if paralyzed, and then, without turning her glance aside from his steady gaze, approached him. He receded from her as she did so, still keeping upon her his riveted gaze, which seemed to fascinate her like a serpent's, for as he moved across the hall she followed him as if irresistibly drawn solely by the power of his eye. He now took his way through the hall in the direction of the outer gate of the castle, steadily looking back towards her over his shoulder, while like a hound she continued to follow, step for step. All arrayed in her bridal robes and sparkling with jewels, with a face like death's and eyes supernaturally dilated, she went on after him, looking neither to the right nor to the left. Poor maiden—without once removing his glance from her terrified eyes, the stranger passed out into the hall, descended the marble steps to the court below and crossed the court to the outer gate; and through hall, corridor, and courtyard, the charmed bride followed him, keeping the same distance behind until she disappeared after him through the portal. Of the guests all were at first paralyzed, and followed them at a distance, the boldest, nor even the bridegroom himself, having power to attempt her rescue. Slowly behind her they followed, with silent amazement and horror, 'till the ill-fated bride had disappeared through the gate, when the spell that seemed to have bound all present was broken.

"'Ho! cavaliers and gentlemen! To the rescue!' was the universal cry.

"Ere they reached the gate they heard the receding footsteps of the horseman and the full cry of hounds as if a huntsman was scouring the country at the head of his pack. The sounds soon died away in a distant glen, and from that night forward nothing was ever heard of the bride that had been so strangely charmed away.

"The next day Don Rolando, who alone could unravel this mystery, sent ten thousand golden pistoles to the convent from whence he had abducted his wife nineteen years before, praying that masses might be nightly offered for his daughter's soul.

"Two years elapsed, and time, which heals all things, had in some degree thrown over this event its oblivious veil, when the second daughter, not less lovely than the eldest, attained her eighteenth year, and on her birth-night was led to the altar by a noble Arragonese cavalier. As before it was night of mirth and festivity. Alas, for it! When the clock struck twelve, the bride was just entering her bridal chamber. On the threshold she looked back to receive Don Rolando's blessing when her eye encountered the fixed glance of the swart stranger. With a shudder she turned back from the very threshold of the bridal chamber and followed him at a short distance behind, through hall, court and corridor, to the outer gate of the castle. Again were heard, a moment afterwards, the huntsman and his hounds coursing up the glen, again the cavaliers present, 'till now spellbound, rushed forth to the rescue. But never from that time forward was there intelligence of the fate of the second daughter of Don Rolando Osormo.

"By a strange fatality the bridal night was always on the birthday night, which happened ever on Christmas eve, the anniversary of the night on which Don Rolando committed the sacrilege of abducting the novice."

"Doubtless Holy Church had something to do with his terrible punishment in the loss of his daughters," said Eugene Brissot.

Don Antonio Baradas smiled coldly and significantly and without replying continued—

"That these nuptials should be suffered to take place a second and a third time, after such a horrible consummation of them, is no less strange, than that the parties should be so little affected by circumstances that ought to have made a lasting impression on every mind. It would seem that Don Rolando and his friends and his daughter's wooers, were, one and all afflicted with a judicial blindness. A third, fourth and a fifth bridal took place, with two years interval between each, with precisely the same results—the nightly appearance, at the stroke of twelve, of the dark stranger—the fascination of the bride—her submissive following, and disappearance, with the retiring sound of horse and hounds winding up the glen. What is most remarkable connected with this affair, was, that at each visit of the dark stranger, the sightless mother recovered her vision during the time he was present, but immediately lost it on his departure. At the loss of her fifth daughter she died of a broken heart for her bereavements.

"At length Don Rolando roused himself at this series of judgments, and resolved to avert the fate of his two remaining daughters, one of whom was sixteen and the other and youngest of all but six years of age. For this purpose he secretly left his castle and his native land, and came hither, as if the wide sea were a wall between justice and the adjudged. He built yonder solitary and gloomy mansion, and defended its portals with iron gates. He consecrated every stone with holy water, and in every threshold sunk a silver cross. The two years elapsed as before, and strange infatuation, he suffered his daughter to be led to the altar on her eighteenth birthday. A wealthy and high-born Creole had wooed and won her. Don Rolando gave his consent, believing the power he dreaded would not reach him here. He wished, too, with a resistless curiosity, to relieve his mind by the trial. He incurred the risk, and *sacrificed his daughter!*"

"Did the green stranger appear?" asked every voice.

"True to the hour and stroke of midnight. The bride followed him from the drawing rooms and across the lawn, and a moment afterwards the sound of horse and horn resounded all along the winding shore 'till lost in the dark cypress forests to the south. The guests fled from the fatal halls in terror. But none could afterwards tell the tale or describe the scene. A spell seemed to have been laid upon their memories. All was confused and indistinct when they could recall it, but the impression of a supernatural presence there on that night remained uneffaced. From that time the 'Haunted Villa' became the scene of mysteries no man could unravel. The morning after this supernatural event, M. Vergniaud, at present our noble host, was surprised at the entrance of Don Rolando leading in his youthful daughter, a beautiful child in her eighth year. To him Don Rolando consigned her, after telling him the strange story you have heard me relate. With him he left keys to coffers of gold in the vaults of his mansion, and then blessing his daughter, took his leave of her forever! He is now, as a rigid and holy monk, doing penance night and day in the monastery which he had so sacrilegiously violated. Where is M. Vergniaud? Methinks I have not seen him present among you."

A low groan arrested every ear. A figure lay upon the ground in a kneeling posture—it was M. Vergniaud. He had fainted there at the first sight of the spectacle the Haunted Villa had presented. Ephese had been to him as an own child. He felt that the curse had not departed from her race, and had fallen forward insensible, with a cry of mercy! mercy! for her on his lips. They lifted him up and laid him upon an ottoman. Those who assisted him were scarce more alive than himself. Don Antonio's tale had filled the soul of everyone that listened to it with horror. Henride Claviere, the bridegroom, stood before Don Antonio like a statue of stone, and all eyes were fixed upon the young Spaniard in silence. They expected something—they knew not what—but something that would harrow their senses and chill their blood. The connection of the fearful tale with the bride was too plain to be mistaken.

"Let us save her or die with her, good Don Antonio," cried Eugene Brissot.

"Hark! it is twelve o'clock!" they cried, in the deep voice of fearful expectation.

"It is the Cathedral bell! The saints preserve us!" fell from every pallid lip.

At the last stroke Don Antonio cast aside his silken cloak from his tall figure and stood before them the Green Huntsman—the Swart Stranger of his tale. Without a word he left them, and entering the drawing room from the verandah, crossed it to the door through which Ephese had gone with her bridesmaids. It opened ere he touched it. Passing on he traversed a suite of lighted rooms until he came to the door of the nuptial chamber. Disrobed of her rich bridal attire, Ephese was standing among her brides-maids in a *robe de chambre* and cap of snowy white, that made her look, if possible, still more lovely than ever. The door swung open and Don Antonio instantly fixed his eye upon hers and turned to leave the cham-ber. She clasped her hands together in agony, as if instinctively she knew her fate, and followed him. He did not keep his eyes upon her constantly, but strode forward without looking behind, as if satisfied she followed. Twice she stopped and stood still, wringing her hands supplicatingly. He had only to glance back over his shoulder, at such times, and she came crouching along close to his feet. Thus he led the ill-fated bride into the hall and forth upon the verandah. Here stood Henride—here stood Eu-gene Brissot and their friends. They beheld him advancing and saw him pass by close to the spot where they stood. They saw—oh, horror! oh, Heavenly pity! they saw too, the poor Ephese following him—now stop-ping and wringing her snowy hands as he took his eyes from her, now as he turned and fixed them upon hers crouching and moving on mourn-fully in his fatal footsteps. Yet they could move neither hand nor foot to save her. Henride's eyes followed his bride with a glassy stare, and the brave Eugene Brissot seemed divested of every vital function and sense save the single sense of horror. Thrice she tried to turn and look upon her husband, but each time his eye arrested the movement of her head and drew her still on after him. From the verandah they traversed the lawn, reached the gate and passed through it. The next moment was heard the galloping of horse, the sound of hounds, and those on the verandah dis-tinctly beheld the Green Huntsman riding like the wind in the direction of the Haunted Villa, bearing before him in his saddle the hapless victim bride. As he rode they saw his form change, (for he seemed to emit a hor-rid shining light that exhibited him as plainly as noonday to their vision) and assume the form of a hideous dwarf. On rode the demon and his victim, and on followed the pack of black hounds, baying in full cry. All at once the Haunted Villa became illuminated as before, with a red glare through window, portal and crevice, while again the writhing tongue of green flame lapped the air and shed a baleful light a league around.

The demon with his victim borne before him and followed by his whole sable pack, now turned into the lawn and rode towards the infernal mansion, at the wildest speed. Without pausing they all, rider, victim, horse and hound, dashed through the yawning portal and leaped into the midst of the glowing furnace. Shrieks and yells most piercing and appalling rent the air; the flames were suddenly extinguished, and in an instant darkness and terrible gloom shrouded the spot where a moment before seemed to yawn the sulphurous mouth of hell.

Such is the legend of the "Haunted Villa;" and such is the penalty of a parent's crime, which sooner or later Heaven will punish, even to making wicked spirits the instruments of its just vengeance.

A REVELATION OF A PREVIOUS LIFE

BY NATHANIEL PARKER WILLIS

(1843)

The death of a lady, in a foreign land, leaves me at liberty to narrate the circumstances which follow.

A few words of previous explanation, however.

I am inclined to believe, from conversations on the subject with many sensible persons, that there are few men who have not had, at different intervals in their lives, sudden emotions, currents of thought, affections of mind and body, which not only were wholly disconnected with the course of life thus interrupted, but seemed to belong to a wholly different being.

Perhaps I shall somewhere touch the reader's experience by describing rather minutely, and in the first person, some sensations of this kind not unusual to myself.

Walking in a crowded street, for example, in perfect health, with every faculty gaily alive, I suddenly lose the sense of neighborhood. I see—I hear—but I feel as if I had become invisible where I stand, and was at the same time present and visible elsewhere. I know everything that passes around me, but I seem disconnected, and (magnetically speaking) unlinked from the human beings near. If spoken to at such a moment, I answer with difficulty. The person who speaks seems to be addressing me from a world to which I no longer belong. At the same time, I have an irresistible inner consciousness of being present in another scene of everyday life—where there are streets and houses and people—where I am looked on without surprise as a familiar object—where I have cares, fears, objects to attain—a different scene altogether, and a different life, from the scene and life of which I was a moment before conscious. I have a dull ache at the back of my eye for the minute or two that this trance lasts, and then, slowly and reluctantly, my absent soul seems creeping back, the magnetic links of conscious neighborhood, one by one, re-attach, and I resume my ordinary life, but with an irrepressible feeling of sadness.

It is in vain that I try to fix these shadows as they recede. I have struggled a thousand times in vain to particularize and note down what

I saw in the strange city to which I was translated. The memory glides from my grasp with preternatural evasiveness.

In a book called "The Man of Two Lives," similar sensations to these are made the basis of the story. Indeed, till I saw that book, the fear of having my sanity suspected, sealed my lips on the subject.

I have still a reserve in my confession. I have been conscious, since boyhood, of a mental peculiarity which I fear to name while I doubt that it is possessed by others than myself—which I should not allude to now, but that it forms a strange link of identity between me and another being to be mentioned in this story.

I may say, also, without attaching any importance to it, except as it bears upon this same identity, that, of those things which I had no occasion to be taught, or which I did, as the common phrase is, by intuition, drawing was the easiest and most passionately followed of my boyish pursuits.

With these preliminaries, and probably some similar experience of his own, the reader may haply form a woof on which to embroider the following circumstances.

Traveling through Styria, some years since, I chanced to have, for a fellow-occupant of the coupe of a diligence, a very courteous and well-bred person, a gentleman of Gratz. As we rolled slowly along the banks of the Muer, approaching his native town, he very kindly invited me to remain with him a day or two, offering me, as an inducement, a presentation at the *soiree* of a certain lady of consequence, who was to receive on the night of our arrival, and at whose house I should see, some fair specimens of the beauty of Styria.

Accepted.

It was a lovely summer's night, when we strolled through the principal street, toward our gay destination, and as I draw upon my friend's arm to stop him while the military band of the fortress finished a delicious waltz, (they were playing in the public square), he pointed out to me the spacious balconies of the Countess's palace, whither we were going, crowded with the well-dressed company, listening silently to the same enchanting music. We entered, and after an interchange of compliments with the hostess, I availed myself of my friend's second introduction to take a stand in one of the balconies beside the person I was presented to, and under cover of her favor, to hear out the unfinished music of the band.

As the evening darkened, the lights gleamed out from the illuminated rooms more brightly, and most of the guests deserted the balconies and joined the gayer circles within. My companion in the balcony was a very quiet lady, and, like myself, she seemed subdued by the sweet harmonies we had listened to, and willing to remain within the shadow of the curtain. We were not alone there, however. A tall lady, of very stately presence, and with the remains of remarkable beauty, stood on the opposite side of the balcony, and she too, seemed to shrink from the glare within, and cling to the dewy darkness of the summer night.

After the cessation of the music, there was no longer an excuse for the intermittent conversation, and, starting a subject which afforded rather freer scope, I did my best to credit my friend's flattering introduction. I had discoursed away for half an hour very unreservedly before I discovered that, with her hand upon her side, in an attitude of repressed emotion, the tall lady was earnestly listening to me. A third person embarrasses even the most indifferent dialogue. The conversation languished, and my companion rose and took my arm for a promenade through the rooms.

Later in the evening, my friend came in search for me in the supper-room.

"*Mon ami!*" he said, "a great honor has fallen out of the sky for you. I am sent to bring you to the *beau reste* of the handsomest woman of Styria—Margaret, Baroness R—, whose chateau I pointed out to you in the gold of yesterday's sunset. She wishes to know you—*why* I cannot wholly divine—for it the first sign of ordinary feeling that she has given in twenty years. But she seems agitated, and sits alone in the Countess's boudoir. *Allons-y!*"

As we made our way through the crowd, he hastily sketched me an outline of the lady's history: "At seventeen taken from a convent for a forced marriage with the baron whose name she bears; at eighteen a widow, and, for the first time, in love—the subject of her passion a young artist of Vienna on his way to Italy. The artist died at her chateau—they were to have been married—she has ever since worn weeds for him. And the remainder you must imagine—for here we are!"

The baroness leaned with her elbow upon a small table of *ormolu*, and her position was so taken that I seated myself necessarily in a strong light, while her features were in shadow. Still, the light was sufficient to show me the expression of her countenance. She was a woman apparently about forty-five, of noble physiognomy, and a peculiar fullness of the eyelid—something like to which I thought I remembered to have seen in a portrait of a young girl, many years before. The resemblance troubled me somewhat.

"You will pardon me this freedom," said the Baroness with forced composure, "when I tell you, that—a friend—whom I have mourned for twenty-five years—seems present when you speak."

I was silent, for I knew not what to say. The Baroness shaded her eyes with her hand, and sat silent for a few moments, gazing at me.

"You are not like him in a single feature," she resumed, 'yet the expression of your face, strangely, very strangely, is the same. He was darker—slighter"—

"Of my age?" I inquired, to break my own silence. For there was something in her voice which gave me the sensation of a voice heard in a dream.

"Oh God! that voice! that voice!" she exclaimed wildly, burying her face in her hands, and giving way to a passionate burst of tears.

"Rudolph," she resumed, recovering herself with a strong effort, "Rudolph died with the promise on his lips that death should not divide us. And I have seen him! Not in dreams—not in reverie—not at times when my fancy could delude me. I have seen him suddenly before me in the street—in Vienna—here—at home at noonday—for minutes together, gazing on me. It is more in latter years that I have been visited by him; and a hope has latterly sprung into being in my heart—I know not how— that in person, palpable and breathing, I should again hold converse with him—fold him living to my bosom. Pardon me! You will think me mad!"

I might well pardon her; for, as she talked, a vague sense of familiarity with her voice, a memory, powerful, though indistinct, of having dwelt before on those majestic features, an impulse of tearful passion to rush to her embrace, well nigh overpowered me. She turned to me again.

"You are an artist?" she said, inquiringly.

"No, although intended for one, I believe, by nature."

"And you were born in the year —."

"I was!"

With a scream she added the day of my birth, and waiting an instant for my assent, dropped to the floor and clung convulsively and weeping to my knees.

"Rudolph! Rudolph!" she murmured faintly, as her long gray tresses fell over her shoulders, and her head dropped insensibly upon her breast.

Her cry had been heard, and several persons entered the room. I rushed out of doors. I had need to be in darkness and alone.

It was an hour after midnight when I re-entered my hotel. A chasseur stood sentry at the door of my apartment with a letter in his hand. He called me by name, gave me his missive, and disappeared. It was from the Baroness, and ran thus:

"You did not retire from me to sleep. This letter will find you waking. And I must write, for my heart and brain are overflowing.

"Shall I write to you as a stranger?—you whom I have strained so often to my bosom—you whom I have loved and still love with the utmost idolatry of mortal passion—you who have once given me the soul that, like a gem long lost, is found again, but in a newer casket! Mine still—for did we not swear to love forever!

"But I am taking counsel of my heart only. You may still be unconvinced. You may think that a few singular coincidences have driven me mad. You may think that, though born in the same hour that my Rudolph died, possessing the same voice, the same countenance, the same gifts—though by irresistible consciousness I *know* you to be *him*—my lost lover returned in another body to life—you may think the evidence incomplete—you may, perhaps, even now, be smiling in pity at my delusion. Indulge me one moment.

"The Rudolph Isenberg whom I lost, possessed a faculty of mind, which, if you are he, answers with the voice of an angel to my appeal. In that soul resided, and, wherever it be, must *now* reside, the singular power.

* * * *

(The reader must be content with my omission of this fragment of the letter. It contained a secret never before clothed in language—a secret that will die with me, unless betrayed by what indeed it may lead to—madness! As I saw it in writing—defined accurately and inevitably in the words of another—I felt as if the innermost chamber of my soul was suddenly laid open to the day—I abandoned doubt—I answered to the name by which she called me—I believed in the previous existence of my whole life, no less than these extraordinary circumstances, had furnished me with repeated evidence. But, to resume the letter.)

"And now that we know each other again—now that I can tell you by name, as in the past, and be sure that your innermost consciousness must reply—a new terror seizes me! Your soul comes back, youthfully and newly clad, while mine, though of unfading freshness and youthfulness within, shows to your eye the same outer garment grown dull with mourning and faded with the wear of time. Am I grown distasteful? Is it with the sight only of this new body that you look upon me? Rudolph!—spirit that was my devoted and passionate admirer! soul that was sworn to me forever!—am I—the same Margaret, re-found and recognized, grown repulsive? Oh God! What a bitter answer would this be to my prayers for your return to me!

"I will trust in Him to whose benign goodness smiles upon fidelity of love. I will prepare a fitter meeting for two who parted as lovers. You shall not see me again in the house of a stranger and in mourning attire. When this letter is written, I will depart at once for the scene of our love. I hear my horses already in the courtyard, and while you read this I am speeding swiftly home. The bridal dress you were secretly shown the day before death came between us, is still freshly kept. The room where we sat—the bowers of the stream—the walks where we projected our sweet promise of a future—they shall all be made ready. They shall be as they were! And I—oh, Rudolph, I shall be the same! My heart is not grown old, Rudolph! Believe me, I am unchanged in soul! And I will strive to be—I will strive to look—God help me to look and be as of yore!

"Farewell now! I leave horses and servants to wait on you til I send to bring you to me. Alas, for my delay! but we will pass this life and all other time together. We have seen that a vow of eternal union may be kept—that death cannot divide those who *will* to love forever! Farewell now!

Margaret."

Circumstances compelled me to read this letter with but one feeling, exquisite pain! Love lasts till death, but it is mortal! The affections, however intense and faithful, (I now knew,) are part of the perishable coil, forgotten in the grave. With the memory of this love of another life, haunting me through my youth, and keeping its vow of visitation, I had given the whole heart of my second youth to another. Affianced to her, waited for by her, bound to her by vows which death had not divided, I had but one course to pursue. I left Gratz in an hour, never to return.

* * * *

A few days since, I was walking alone in the crowded thoroughfare of the city where I live. Suddenly my sense of presence there fell off me. I walked on, but my inward sight absorbed all my consciousness. A room which was familiar to me shut me in, and a bed hung in mourning became apparent. In another instant a figure laid out in a winding sheet, and partially covered with a velvet pall, grew distinct through the dimness, and in the low laid head I recognized, what a presentiment had already betrayed to me, the features of Margaret, Baroness R—. It will be moths before I can see the announcement of her death. But she is dead.

MOODS OF THE MIND: THE OLD PORTRAIT

BY EMMA EMBURY

(1843)

I was amused and interested by a discussion which I heard a few days since, between two persons who were my near neighbors on board a New York ferry boat. They had been in close conversation when they entered the cabin, and as they did not lower their tones I soon discovered that the dapper, neatly-whiskered, dogmatic little man beside me was a young physician who had just been ground out by a new "sawbones" mill and was not yet sifted, if one might judge by the husks of learning which seemed mingled with the good grain. His companion, a modest, pale-faced, sickly-seeming German, evidently regarded him with much respect and listened to him as if there was no possible appeal from his opinions.

"Depend upon it, sir," said the doctor, "depend upon it there is a great deal of misconception about this matter; a person who dreams cannot be said to be asleep; (this was a startling proposition, by the way, to one who is an accomplished sleeper, and a most inveterate dreamer;) you may rely upon it that no person ever enjoys a quiet, natural, healthful sleep if his mental faculties are awake," he continued, tapping his little cane most determinedly against the toe of his boot.

"But," said the German timidly, "you surely do not mean to say that the habit of dreaming argues an unsound state of the physical system; there are persons who enjoy the most robust health and yet whose faculty for dreaming is almost an ideosyncracy."

"Impossible, my dear sir!" and the doctor compressed his lips with the air of a man who knows he is right; "the mental faculties slumber with the corporeal functions; the man who is under the influence of a profound, healthful sleep is, in a manner, dead to all impressions; unconsciousness, a total forgetfulness of every mental and bodily capacity, are necessary to the enjoyment of repose. No, sir; *slumber* may bring dreams, but *sleep* must be unbroken by the vagaries of the imagination; therefore a man is not asleep when he dreams."

This was uttered in such Johnsonian style, there was such a bridling up of the neck, such a peculiar pigeon-breasted swelling out of the speaker's person, as if he would have said:

> *"I am Sir Oracle, and when I ope*
> *My mouth, let no dog bark,"*

that his companion was silenced if not convinced. At this moment the boat touched the wharf and I soon lost sight of the interlocutors; but as I wended my way I could not help thinking how much cause I had to feel pity for myself, for, if the doctor's theory were true, from my childhood to the present hour I had *never slept.*

Right sorry should I be to believe any such material doctrine. Sad indeed would be my privation if compelled to relinquish my nocturnal wanderings in the fairy-land of dreams. Sure, when

> *"Darkness shows us realms of light*
> *We never saw by day."*

we may rejoice in the brightness and beauty of that spirit-life which we can never enter while the fetters of clay cling as closely as they do in our waking hours. Day has its cares and its toils, its anxieties and its doubts, its vexations and its sorrows; scarcely does a sun rise and set without the destruction of some fair scheme, the withering of some green hope. Amid the glare of sunshine we live and move and suffer; it brings us active, sentient life; but it is all external—the world claims us and the energies of the soul are all employed by, and for the service of, the perishing body. But when night closes around us—when the brow of Heaven is wearing its coronal of stars—when the far-sweeping breeze comes with lulling music to the ear wearied with the turmoil of the world, then is it not sweet to lie down on our couch of nightly rest, and with the accents of prayer upon our lips and thoughts of tenderness concentrating within our hearts like the honey-dew in the petals of the flower, to close the eyes of the body in calm slumber, while the mind awakens in unfettered vigor to tread the realms of space and range the glorious spirit-land of dreams? Strange that the mind has this power to roam at large! strange that it is thus privileged to annihilate time and space in its unchecked career! Yet methinks the only idea that a finite mind can form of infinitude is derived from this wonderful faculty, which enables us to condense a life into an hour.

> *"Sleep has its own world,*
> *And a wide realm of wild reality,*
> *And dreams in their development have breath,*
> *And tears, and torture, and the touch of joy;*
> *They leave a weight upon our waking thoughts,*
> *They take a weight from off our waking toils;*

They do divide our being; they become
A portion of ourselves as of our time,
And seem like heralds of eternity."

But there is another mood of mind far more wonderful than that which admits us through the ivory portal of dreams. There are moments when a peculiar retroversive vision is given to the soul; when, amid scenes which have never before met the bodily eye, a sudden consciousness of a pre-existence in which they were once familiar comes over the spirit. Who has not experienced that instant insensibility to mere outward impressions, while the soul was looking back through the vista of memory and beholding there precisely the same objects which were vainly addressing themselves to the external senses? Who has not paused in painful wonder at the discovery that the material things which surrounded him were but the tangible forms of some shadowy reminiscence? Who has not felt, at some especial moment, that the present was to him but a renewal of a bygone scene, and that his mind was wandering in a vague past, where all was dim, dark and troublous to the spirit?

The speculations into which my subject has unconsciously led me remind me of a singular instance of hallucination, or perhaps of clairvoyance—according as one chooses to determine—in the case of a personal friend, which occurred some years since.

Mrs. L— was one of the most quiet, gentle, womanly creatures that I have ever known. Intelligent and well-informed, without being positively intellectual in her tastes, her varied accomplishments gave her brilliancy in society, while her kindliness of heart made her a decided favorite with all who came near enough to share it. With just enough imagination to adorn but not to outshine her other qualities, with sufficient sentiment to give depth of tone to the lights and shades of her character, and destitute of a single strongly developed passion, she always appeared to me peculiarly happy in the possession of one of those unexcitable tempers which ever secure content.

"She was pensive more than melancholy
And serious more than pensive, and severe,
It may be, more than either;"

and had I been called to designate one who looked neither into the vague past nor the dim future, but found enjoyment in the tranquil present, I should have pointed to my pretty and agreeable friend.

An incident, trifling in itself, but leading to a singular development of character, showed me the folly of thus judging of another's nature, especially when we have never been admitted to the intimacy of friendship until after the door of the inner sanctuary of the soul was closed against earthly sympathies.

It happened one morning that I accompanied Mrs. L— to the rooms of a celebrated picture-dealer whom she wished to consult respecting the framing of a valuable painting she had recently received from Italy. The virtuoso was absent, but learning that he was expected to be at home in a short time, we determined to wait and in the meantime to amuse ourselves with the various articles of taste and fancy with which his apartments were filled. I had been for some time leaning over a scagliola table, absorbed in the study of some exquisite cameos, when an exclamation from my companion, who had been occupied with the pictures, aroused me from my abstraction. As I looked up I beheld her standing opposite a painting, but her close bonnet entirely concealed her face from me, and conjecturing that she had discovered something of superior merit I stepped up behind her to observe it also.

It was only a portrait of a man in the prime of life; an old portrait, for the surface was in some places cracked and broken, while the unframed canvas showed on its edges the discoloration as well as the rents of time. But never did I see a face to which the doubly significant word "fascinating," could be so exactly applied. The broad, high forehead was bare, while the long chestnut curls which fell back from its expanse were so mellowed into the background of the picture that the outline of the head was undefined and the charm of vagueness was thus given; as if the face was looking out from behind a curtain, or rather from the indistinct gloom of a chamber. The eyes were large, dark and dreamy, with that sad but not sorrowful drooping of the delicately cut lids, that downward bend of the outer corner, which ever denotes the world-sated rather than the wounded spirit. But the mouth was the most peculiar feature, for the upper lip was curled like a bow at its utmost tension, and rested with so slight a pressure upon the full softness of its fellow that one almost expected to see it expand with smiles at the beholder's gaze. The rounded and beardless cheek was almost too massive in its downward sweep, and the chin, though Napoleonesque in its outline, had that heaviness of finish which marks the influence of its animal nature; but the coloring of the face—its pale, clear, yet not effeminate hue—the dark, well defined brows arching over those superb eyes—the shadow flung upon the cheek by those fringed eyelids—the deep, rich color of the womanish mouth— the softness of the flesh-tints—and, above all, the almost serpent-like fascination of expression which pervaded the whole countenance, all combined to form a most remarkable and beautiful physiognomy. The costume was that of the time of George II, and a diamond star on the breast of the gold-embroidered coat bore witness to the rank of him whose pictured semblance was without a name to designate its claims to our respect. Beautiful was that face in its calm immobility—how gloriously beautiful must have been the flashings of the soul through such exquisite features, when that eye was lighted up with life and that lip was eloquent with passionate emotion! Yet even while my fancy conjured up the image of such a being, those instincts which in woman's heart are ever true, if the world have not checked their honest teachings, made me recoil from the creature of my imagination. Something in those delicate features, something in that sweet sadness of the eye and lip, something in the almost girlish hand which lay half hidden in its point-lace ruffle, seemed to speak of the voluptuary—of one who with the holy fires of intellect had kindled a flame on the altar of sensual and selfish indulgence.

But all these things were observed in much less time than is required for the description of them, and I was turning away with an expression of the mingled feeling that had been excited by the picture, when my attention was excited by the fixedness of Mrs. L—'s attitude. Changing my position so as to obtain a view of her face, I was startled by the extraordinary change which had taken place in her appearance. With her tall figure drawn up to its full height, yet shrinking back as if alarmed; her arms folded tightly upon her bosom and her hands grasping the drapery of her shawl, as if to veil herself from the eyes bent down upon her from the canvas, she stood entranced before the picture. Her face was ashy pale, her eyes dilated and vacant, her lips parted and almost livid in their hue, and her whole countenance bore the impress of intense horror. Alarmed at her appearance I addressed her, but without attracting her notice; I attempted to draw her away, but to my surprise I felt her arm as rigid as stone beneath my touch, while her whole attitude was that of one who is subjected to cataleptic influence.

Gradually the spell which bound her faculties seemed to disperse, and as she slowly and shudderingly turned from the picture she fell almost fainting into my arms.

"Let us go—quick—let us go;" she gasped, and terrified by her unusual agitation I hurried her into the carriage. During our ride she did not utter a word, but when we reached her door she exclaimed, "Do not leave me; I would not be alone just now;" and drawing her veil over her face she hurried up to her apartment. As soon as we were alone and safe from intruders, she flung herself upon a couch and a violent flood of tears seemed somewhat to relieve the dreadful tension of her nerves. It was long before she recovered from her excessive agitation, and all my attempts to soothe her were utterly useless until she had exhausted her excitement by indulgence; then, when her emotion had subsided into the deep calm which comes from utter feebleness of body, she unfolded to me one of the strangest moods of mind that it has ever been my fortune to discover.

"How long were we at Mr.—'s room this morning?" she asked.

"Perhaps a quarter of an hour," was my reply.

"And how long did I stand before that dreadful picture?"

"Not more than five minutes."

"And yet in that brief space the events of a whole life passed before me."

"Your thoughts must have traveled with a speed like that which transported Mahomet to the seventh heaven, and restored him to his couch, before the vessel of water which had been overturned in his ascent had lost one drop of its contents."

"Nay, this is no jest; it is to me sad and sober earnest. Let me tell you, E—, my ideas on the subject of pre-existence."

"My dear friend, you are nervous and excited; we had better not discuss such matters."

"You think me a little *egarte*—you mistake; my nerves have shaken, but my mind is perfectly unclouded. Ever since I have been able to look into my own nature I have been convinced that my present life is only the completion of an earthly probation which was begun long, long since."

"What do you mean? You are surely not in earnest."

"I never was more so in my life, and yet I scarcely know how to explain myself to you. There are persons who live and die with natures but half developed; circumstances call forth one set of feelings and faculties, while others are left dormant. Such I believe to be the case with the great proportion of men and especially of women in this world, and therefore it is that I have much charity for those who fall short of my standard of goodness, since there may be an infinite deal of latent virtue hidden in their hearts. But there are others among mankind who seem to have the use of only half their souls; not from want of development, but rather from exhaustion of the faculties. Among the latter class I rank myself. I am calm, cold, and passionless; never violently excited, never deeply depressed; kindly in my feelings and warm but not ardent in my affections. Yet do I often feel within me the faint stirrings of a wild and passionate nature; a throe of the spirit which tells, not of repressed emotion, but rather of half extinct capacity for suffering. In a word, I believe that *in a former state of existence I have outlived my passions.*

"You are surprised. I tell you my life is full of vague memories of a dark and troubled past. I am as one in a dream; the things which surround me in actual life are entirely distinct from the objects that are daily presented to my mental view as forming part of my existence. Often that strange, painful consciousness of some past scene precisely resembling the present comes over me. My very affections seem to me rather like old habitudes of feeling, and when I look upon my children or listen to their merry voices, a dreamy consciousness of having, years since, heard the same 'sweet discord' and gazed with a mother's pride upon creatures as fair and dear, makes me doubt my own identity.

"That which is vague is always terrible, and my thoughts have gone out fearfully into that dark, cloudy past, seeking vainly to comprehend the wild memories that so disturb my present tranquillity. But today—to-day—I have seen a vision which has satisfied my quest. I had wandered listlessly about Mr.—'s rooms this morning, thinking only of beguiling the time until his return, when my eye fell upon the old portrait. You saw the effect it produced, (and she shuddered at the recollection,) but you could not know why it thus overpowered me. Now listen and remember that I know well what I am saying; that I am perfectly calm and collected, and as sane in mind as yourself.

"As my look became fastened on that superb face a strain of low, unearthly music floated on the air, and suddenly I found myself in a gorgeous apartment, blazing with lights and filled with a gay company attired in the rich fashion of the olden time. A large mirror hung opposite me, and as I raised my eyes I saw reflected on its silvery surface the image of a young girl moving in the stately mazes of the minuet with a handsome and graceful partner. I saw the blush which mantled the maiden's cheek as her companion's deep, dark eyes rested upon her; I beheld the quivering of her lip as she timidly replied to the courtly flatteries which were rather breathed than uttered from that exquisite mouth; I marked the trembling of her hand as it touched his in the evolutions of the formal dance; the very beatings of her heart as it bounded against her jeweled bodice were visible to me. That maiden was myself; not a lineament was changed; it was myself, wearing the same freshness of tint and frankness of expression as in the youthful portrait which hangs in yonder recess, differing only in the costume, which was that in fashion a century ago; while he who was thus awakening me to a consciousness of passionate existence was the living semblance of that nameless picture.

"Again that strain of music sounded; a mist came before my eyes, and as it cleared away I saw a wide and beautiful landscape. There were gently swelling hills in the distance, enfolding as it were in their embrace one of those rich parks which are said to form so lovely a feature in English scenery. Broad oaks stretched their gnarled branches over the soft, green turf, and here and there an antlered deer was seen bounding across the lawn-like verdure. But in the foreground of the picture was a closely shaded walk where the boughs of the overarching trees had been carefully interlaced, so as to exclude every straggling ray of sunshine. A sweet and tender light, as soft as moonlight but far warmer in its glow, filled the place, and there in that secluded spot sat a maiden on a mossy bank. The graceful form of her partner in the dance was bending over her in the attitude of protecting tenderness, and as she lifted her face confidingly toward the eyes which seemed radiant with affection, as she met their glance, I again recognized my own features.

"Once more that faint melody swept by, again my eyes were darkened, and the next scene showed me the arrangements of a joyous bridal. A gay company were assembled in a small but beautiful chapel, and, as if power had been given to my mental vision to embrace all objects whether great or small, I could distinctly trace the rich carvings of the clustered pillars and the grotesque corbels of the groined roof, while the flickering tints which fell upon the snowy vestments of the bridal party, from the stained glass window behind the altar, added gorgeousness to the scene. As the newly wedded pair turned from the shrine, while merry friends pressed round them with looks of pride and joy, I beheld again the familiar face which twice before had met my view.

"But the vision faded, the figures vanished, and a cloud seemed to arise, in which only the noble face of the portrait was visible. Presently the cloud shifted, as if moved by a passing breeze, and my own face, pale, tearful and sad, looked out from its dim shadow. Again the cloud closed over the apparition, and thus, folding and unfolding, as we often see the edges of a thundercloud in the sky, it gave out alternate glimpses of the two faces as it altered its position and its form. But a change gradually came over the countenances of both; my own became faded and sorrowful, while the cold sneer upon those bright lips, the keen glitter of those soft eyes and an expression of bitter contempt in the scowl of that placid brow, converted its glorious beauty into the beauty of 'archangel ruined.'

"Again came that tone of music, but it was now dirge-like and mournful as it trembled upon my ear. The shadow passed away and I beheld a funeral bier. A rigid form lay extended upon it, and a child of some ten summers knelt beside the body, while her sunny curls mingled with the dark locks which lay so lifelessly on the brow of the dead. As the child raised her head to wipe away the gushing tears I beheld the face of the departed, and again did I recognize my own features. A feeling of irrepressible horror crept over me, but I was compelled to gaze, while slowly, and as if emerging from the darkness of the distant apartment, came out the shadowy face of that old portrait, as if bending over the cold lineaments of death.

"At this moment you spoke to me, but I could not answer; you touched me, but I was fixed and almost turned to stone; nor could I move until the fearful vision had entirely vanished, and then, exhausted and almost lifeless, I found myself resting in your arms, with that cold calm picture looking quietly down upon me from the wall."

Such was my friend's account of this most extraordinary fantasy, and without pretending to trace its source, or to explain the probable cause of such a mood of mind, I would only add that it was followed by a severe attack of brain fever. She recovered, however, and lived several years, but never again gave the slightest evidence of any tendency to the vague speculations of which she had spoken to me; though, as I afterward learned, she had vainly endeavored to purchase the old portrait, which had been sold, during her illness, to some unknown picture fancier. I pretend not to elucidate the mystery of her changeful vision, or to define my own belief in her fanciful creed of pre-existence. It is enough for me to know that our dreams, whether they be waking visions or nightly slumbering fantasies, often

> *"Pass like spirits of the past, and speak*
> *Like sybils of the future."*

A NIGHT ON THE ENCHANTED MOUNTAIN

BY CHARLES FENNO HOFFMAN

(1839)

There are few parts of our broad country, which, for beauty of scenery, amenity of climate, and, I might add, for the primitive and interesting character of the inhabitants, can compare with the mountainous region of eastern Tennessee.

It is a wild and romantic district, composed of rocks and broken hills, where the primeval forests overhang valleys watered by limpid streams whose meadowy banks are grazed by innumerable herds of cattle. The various mountain ridges, which at one point traverse the country almost in parallel lines, while at another they swoop off in vast curves, and describe a majestic amphitheatre, are all, more or less, connected with the Appalachian characterize the Alleganies. In some places, the transition from valley to highland is so gradual, that you are hardly aware of the undulations of the surface when passing over it. In others, the frowning heights rise in precipitous walls from the plains; while again their wooded and dome-like summits will heave upward from the broad meadows like enormous tumuli heaped upon their bosom.

The hills, also, are frequently seamed with deep and dark ravines, whose sheer sides, and dimly descried bottom, will make the eye swim as it tries to fathom them, while often they are pierced with cavernous galleries which lead miles under ground, and branch off into grottoes so spacious that an army might be marshalled within their yawning chambers.

Here, too, those remarkable conical cavities which are generally known by the name of "sink holes" in the western country, are thickly scattered over the surface, and so perfect in shape are many of them, that it is difficult to persuade the ruder residents that they are not the work of art, nor fashioned out as drinking bowls for the extinct monsters whose fossil remains are so abundant in this region. Indeed, the singular formation of the earth's surface, with the entire seclusion in which they live amid their pastoral valleys, must account for, and excuse many a less reasonable belief and superstition prevailing among those hospitable mountaineers. "The Enchanted Mountains," as one of the ranges we have been attempting to describe is called, are especially distinguished by the number of incredible traditions and wild superstitions connected with them. Those uncouth paintings along their cliffs, and the footprints of men and horses stamped in the solid rock upon the highest summits, as mentioned by Mr. Flint in his Geography of the Western Country, constitute but a small part of the material which they offer to an uneducated and imaginative people for the creation of strange fantasies. The singular echoes that tremble at times through these lonely glens, and the shifting forms, which, as the morning mist rises from the upland, may be seen stealing over the tops of the crags, and hiding themselves within their crevices, are alike accounted for by supernatural causes.

Having always been imbued with a certain love of the marvelous, and being one of the pious few, who, in this enlightened age of reality, nurse up a lingering superstition or two, I found myself, while loitering through this romantic district, and associating upon the most easy terms with its rural population, irresistibly imbibing a portion of the feeling and spirit which prevailed around me. The cavernous ravines and sounding aisles of the tall forest, had "airy tongues" for me, as well as for those who were more familiar with their whisperings. But as for the freakish beings, who were supposed to give them utterance as they pranked it away in the dim retreats around, I somehow or other could never obtain a fair sight of one of them. The forms that sometimes rose between my eyes and the mist-breathing cascade, or flitted across the shadowy glade at some sudden turn of my forest path, always managed to disappear behind some jutting rock, or make good their escape into some convenient thicket, before I could make out their lineaments, or even swear to their existence at all. My repeated disappointment in this way had begun to put me quite out of conceit of my quickness and accuracy of vision, when a new opportunity was given of testing them in the manner I am about to relate.

I happened one day to dine at a little inn situated at the mouth of a wooded gorge, where it lay tucked away so closely beneath the ponderous limbs of a large tulip tree, that the blue smoke from the kitchen fire alone betrayed its locality. My host proved to one of those talkative worthies, who, being supplied with but little information to exercise his tongue upon, make amends for the defects of education and circumstance by dwelling with exaggeration upon every trivial incident around him. Such people, in polished society, become the scandal mongers of the circle in which they move, while in more simple communities they are only the chroniclers of everything marvellous that had ever occurred in the neighborhood "within the memory of the oldest inhabitant." I had hardly placed myself at the dinner table, before my garrulous entertainer began to display his retentive facilities by giving me the exact year and day upon which every chicken with two heads, or calf with five legs, had been born throughout the whole country around. Then followed the most minute particulars about a murder or two which had been perpetrated within the last twenty years; and after this I was drilled into the exact situation and bearings of a haunted house which I should probably see the next day by pursuing the road I was then traveling; finally, I was inducted into all the arcana of a remarkable cavern in the vicinity—where are moon-elf or water-sprite had taken up her residence, to the great annoyance of everyone except my landlord's buxom daughter, who was said to be upon the most enviable terms with the freakish lady of the grotto. The animated and really eloquent description which mine host gave of this cavern, made me readily overlook the puerile credulity with which he would up his account of its peculiarities. It interested me, indeed, so much, that I determined to stable my horse for the night, and proceed at once to explore the place. A fresh and blooming girl, with the laughing eye and free step of a mountaineer, volunteered to be my guide on the occasion, hinting, at the same time, while she gave me a mischievous look at her father, that I would find it difficult to procure a cicerone other than herself in the neighborhood. She then directed me how to find the principal entrance to the cave, where she promised to join me soon after.

A rough scramble in the hills soon brought me to the place of meeting, and entering the first chamber of the cavern, I stretched myself upon a rocky ledge which leaned over a brook that meandered through the place, and, lulled by the dash of a distant waterfall, surrendered myself to a thousand musing fancies. Fatigue, or possibly too liberal a devotion to the good things which had been placed before me at table, caused me soon to be overtaken by sleep. My slumbers, however, were broken and uneasy, and after repeatedly opening my eyes to look with some impatience at my watch, as I tossed upon my stony couch, I abandoned the idea of a nap entirely, while momentarily expecting that my guide would make her appearance, and contented myself with gazing listlessly upon the streamlet which rippled over its pebbled bed beneath me. I must have remained for some time in this vacant mood, when my idle musings were interrupted by a new source of interest presenting itself.

A slight rustling near disturbed me, and turning round as I opened my eyes, a female figure in a drapery of snowy whiteness appeared to flit before them, and retire behind a tall cascade immediately in front of me. The uncertain light of the place, with the spray of the waterfall, which partially impeded my view of the farther part of the cavern made me at first doubt the evidence of my senses; but gradually a distinct form was perceptible amid the mist, apparently moving slowly from me, and beckoning the while to follow. The height of the figure struck me immediately as being about the same as that of the frank daughter of my landlord; and, though the proportions seemed more slender, I had no doubt, upon recalling her arch expression of countenance while her father was relating to me the wild superstitions of the cavern, that a ready solution of one of its mysteries at least was at hand. Some woman's whim, I had no doubt, prompted the girl to get up a little diversion at my expense, and sent her thither to put the freak in execution. I had been told that there were a dozen outlets to the cavern, and presumed that I was now to be involved in its labyrinths for the purpose of seeing in what part of the mountain I might subsequently make my exit. He is no true lover of a pair of bright eyes who will mar the jest of a pretty woman. The lady beckoned, and I followed.

I had some difficulty in scaling the precipice, over which tumbled the waterfall, but after slipping once or twice upon the wet ledges of rock which supplied a treacherous foot-hold, I at last gained the summit, and stood within a few yards of my whimsical conductor. She had paused upon the farthest side of the chamber into which the cavern here expanded. It was a vast and noble apartment. The lofty ceiling swelling almost into a perfect dome, save where a ragged aperture at the top admitted the noonday sun, whose rays, as they fell through the vines and wild flowers that embowered the orifice, were glinted back from a thousand sparry points and pillars around. The walls, indeed, were completely fretted with stalactites. In some places, small, and apparently freshly formed, they hung in fringed rows from the ceiling to the ground. In others they drooped so heavily as to knit the glistening roof to the marble floor beneath it, or rose in slender pyramids from the floor itself, until they appeared to sustain the vault above.

The motion of the air created by the cascade gave a delightful coolness to this apartment, while the murmur of the falling water was echoed back from the vibrating columns with tones as rich and melodious as those which sweep from an Æolian harp. Never, methought, had I seen a spot so alluring. And yet, when I surveyed each charm of the grotto, I knew not whether I should be contented in any one part of it. Nothing, indeed, could be more inviting to tranquil enjoyment than the place where I then stood; but the clustering columns, with their interlacing screen work of woven spar, allured my eye into a hundred romantic aisles which I longed to explore; while the pendant wild flowers which luxuriated in the sunlight around the opening above, prompted me to scale the dangerous height, and try what pinnacle of the mountain I might gain by emerging from the cavern through the lofty aperture.

These reflections were abruptly terminated by an impatient gesture from my guide, and for the first time I caught a glimpse of her countenance as she glided by a deep pool in which it was reflected.

That glance had a singular, almost a preternatural effect upon me—the features were different, very different, from those I had expected to behold. They were not those of the new acquaintance whom I thought I was following, but the expression they wore was one so familiar to me in bygone years, that I started as if I had seen an apparition.

It was the look of one who had been long since dead—of one around whose name, when life was new, the whole tissue of my hopes and fears was woven—for whom all my aspirations after worldly honors had been breathed—in whom all my dreams of heaven had been wound up. She had mingled in purer hours with all the fond and home-loving fancies of boyhood—she had been the queen of each romantic vision of my youth; and, amid the worldly cares and selfish struggles of maturer life, the thought of her had lived separate and apart in my bosom, with no companion in its hallowed chamber save the religion I had learned at my mother's knee—save that hope of better things, which, once implanted by a mother's love, survives amid the storms and conflicts of the world—a beacon to warn us more often, alas! how far we have wandered from her teachings, than to guide us to the haven whither they were meant to lead. I had loved her, and I had lost her. How, it matters not. Perchance disease had reft her from me by some sudden blow, at the moment when possession made her dearest. Perchance I saw her fade in the arms of another, while I was banned and barred from ministering to a spirit that stole away to the grave with all I prized on earth. It boots not how I lost her. But he who has centered every thought and feeling in one object—whose morning hopes have for years gone forth to the same goal—whose evening reflections have for years come back to the same bourne—whose waking visions, and whose midnight dreams, have for years been haunted by the same image—whose schemes of toil and advancement have all tended to the same end—*He* knows what it is to have the pivot upon which every wheel of his heart hath turned, wrenched from its centre—to have the sun round which revolved every joy that lighted his bosom, plucked from its system.

Well, it was her face—as I live it was the soul-breathing features of Linda that now beamed before me—fresh as when in dawning womanhood they first caught my youthful fancy—resistless as when in their noontide blaze of beauty I poured out my whole adoring soul before them. There was that same appealing look of the large lustrous eyes—the same sunny and soul-melting smile, which, playing over a countenance thoughtful even to sadness, touched it with a beauty so radiant that the charm seemed borrowed from heaven itself. I could not but think it strange that such an image should be presented to my view in such a place; and yet, if I now rightly recollect my emotions, surprise was the least active among them. I cared not why or whence the apparition came—I thought not whether it were reality or a mocking resemblance—the phantasy of my own brain, or the shadowy creation of some supernatural power around me. I knew only that it was there—I knew only that the eyes in whose perilous light my soul had bathed herself to madness, beamed anew before me—that the lips whose lightest smile had often rapt me in elysium—that the brow whose holy light—But why should I thus attempt to paint what pencil never yet hath reached—why essay a portrait whose colors I have no where found, save in the heart where they are laid so deeply that death alone can dim them. Enough that the only human being to which my soul ever bowed in inferiority—enough that the idol to which it had knelt in adoration, now stood palpably before it. An hour agone, and I would have crossed the threshold of the grave itself to stand one moment in that presence—to gaze, if but for an instant, upon those features. What recked I now, then, how or whence they were conjured up? Had the Fiend himself stood night, I should have pressed nearer, and gazed, and followed as I did. The figure beckoned, and I went on.

The vaulted gateway was at first smooth and easily followed, but after passing through several of the cavernous chambers into which it ever and anon expanded, the route became more and more difficult; loose masses of rock encumbering the floor, or drooping in pendant crags from the roof, rendered the defiles between them both toilsome and hazardous. The light which fell through the opening behind us soon disappeared entirely, and it gave me a singular sinking of the spirits as we passed into deeper and deeper gloom, to hear the musical sounds which I have already noted in the grotto from which we first passed, dying away in the distance, and leaving the place at last to total silence. Long, indeed, after they had ceased to reach my ear with any distinctness, they would seem at times to swell along the winding vault, and break anew upon me at some turn in our devious route. So strangely, too, do the innumerable subtle echoes metamorphose each sound in such a place, that continually did I find myself mistaking the muttered reverberations for the sounds of a human voice. At one moment it seemed to be calling me back to the sparry grotto and bright sunshine behind me, while the very next it appeared with sudden and harsh intonation to warn me against proceeding further—anon then it would die away with a mournful cadence, a melancholy wailing, like the requiem of one who was beyond the reach of all earthly counsel or assistance. Again and again did I pause in my career to listen to this wild chanting, while my feelings would, for the moment, take their hue and complexion from the sources which thus bewildered my senses. I thought of my early dreams of fame and honor—of the singing hopes that lured me on my path, when one fatal image stepped between my soul and all its high endeavor—I thought of that bouyancy of spirit, once so irrepressible in its elasticity, that it seemed proof alike against time and sorrow, now sapped, wasted, and destroyed, by the frenzied pursuit of one object—I thought of the home which had so much to embellish and endear it, and which yet, with all its heart-cheering joys, had been neglected and left, like the sunlit grotto, to follow a shifting phantom through a heartless world—I thought of the reproachful voices around me, and the ceaseless upbraider in my own bosom, which told of time and talents wasted—of opportunities thrown away—of mental energies squandered—of heart, brain, and soul, consumed in a devotion deeper and more absorbing than Heaven itself exacts from its votaries—I thought—and I looked at the object for which I had lavished them all—I thought that my life must have been some hideous dream—some damned vision in which my fated soul was bound by imaginary ties to a being doomed to be its bane upon earth, and shut out at last from heaven. And I laughed in scornful glee as I twisted my bodily frame in the hope that at length I might wake from the long-enduring sleep. I caught a smile from the lips—I saw a beckon from the hand of the phantom, and I wished again to dream and to follow forever—I plunged into the abyss of darkness to which it pointed, and reckless of everything I might leave behind, followed where so ever it might marshall me.

A damp and chilling atmosphere now pervaded the place, and the clammy moisture stood thick upon my brow as I groped my way through a labyrinth of winding galleries which intersected each other so often, both obliquely and transversely, that the whole mountain seemed honeycombed. At one moment the steep and broken pathway led up acclivities almost impossible to scale; at another, the black edge of a precipice indicated our hazardous route along the brink of some unfathomed gulf; while again a savage torrent, roaring through the sinuous vault, left scarcely room enough for a foothold between the base of the wall and its furious tide. And still my guide kept on, and still I followed. Returning, indeed, had the thought occurred to me, were now impossible; for the pale light which seemed to hang around her person, emanating, as it were, from her white raiment, was all that engulfed me through these shadowy realms. But not for a moment now did I think of retracing my steps, or pausing in that wild pursuit—onward and still onward it led, while my spirit, once set upon its purpose, seemed to gather sterner determination from every difficulty it encountered, and kindle once more the chief attribute of my nature.

At length the chase seemed ended, as we approached one of those abrupt and startling turns common in these caverns, where the passage, suddenly veering to the right or left, leads you, as if by design, to the sheer edge of some gulph that is impassible. My strange companion seemed pausing for a moment upon the brink of the abyss. It was a moment to me of delirious joy, mingled with more than mortal agony; the object of my wild pursuit seemed at length within my grasp—a single bound, and my outstretched arms would have encircled her person—a single bound, nay, the least movement toward her, might only have precipitated the destruction upon whose brink she hovered. Her form seemed to flutter upon the very edge of that horrid precipice, as, gazing like one fascinated, over it, she stretched her hand backward toward me. It was like inviting me to perdition—and yet, forgive me, Heaven—to perish with her was my proudest hope, as I sprang to grasp it. But oh! God, what held I in that withering grasp? The ice of death seemed curdling in my veins as I touched those clammy and pulseless fingers—a strange and unhallowed light shot upward from the black abyss, and the features from which I *could* not take my eyes away were changed to those of a demon in that hideous glare. And now the hand that I had so longed to clasp, closed with remorseless pressure round my own, and drew me toward the yawning gulf—it tightened in its grasp, and I hovered still nearer to my horrid doom—it clenched yet more closely, and the frenzied shriek I gave ——*awoke* me.

A soft palm was gently pressed against my own—a pair of laughing blue eyes were bent archly upon me, and the fair locks which floated over her blooming cheeks revealed the joyous and romping damsel who had promised to act as my guide through the cavern. She had been prevented by some household cares from keeping her appointment until the approach of evening made it too late, and had taken it for granted that I had then returned to my lodgings at the inn. My absence from the breakfast table in the morning, however, had awakened some concern in the family, and induced her to seek me where we then met. The pressure of her hand in trying to awaken me, will partially account for the latter part of my hideous dream. The general tenor of it is easily traceable to the impression made upon my mind by the prevalent superstition connected with the cavern; but no metaphysical ingenuity of which I am master, can explain how one whose life has, with the exception of one dark shadow, been passed under such uniform sunny influences as mine, could, even in a dream, have conjured up such a train of wild and bitter fancies; much less how the fearful tissue could have been interwoven with the recollection of one whose gentle spirit, when on earth, could never have wounded the bosom that loved her, and whose memory, through the long, long years, that have elapsed since we parted, has ever been associated in my mind with all that was true and tender, generous, noble, and confiding.

If half be true, however, that is told concerning them, still more extravagant sallies of the imagination overtake persons of quite as easy and careless a disposition as myself, when venturing to pass a Night upon the Enchanted Mountains.

THE LIVING APPARITION

BY G.P.R. JAMES

(1846)

"I am of an Italian family," said my friend, "but my father and my grandfather were born in Germany; exceedingly good people in their way, but by no means very wealthy. My elder brother was being educated for a physician, and had just finished his course of study, when my father, having given me as good an education as he could in Nuremberg, thought it fit to send me to Hamburg, that I might pursue my studies there, and take advantage of any opportunity that might occur for advancing myself in life. My stock of all kinds was exceedingly small when I set out; my purse contained the closely-estimated expenses of my journey, and the allowance made for my maintenance during six months, which did not admit the slightest idea of luxury of any kind. I was grateful, however, for what was given, for I knew that my father could afford no more, and I had no hope of another 'heller' till my half year was out. I had my ordinary travelling dress, and my mother gave me six new shirts which she had spun with her own hands; besides these, my portmanteau contained one complete black suit, two pair of shoes, and a pair of silver buckles, which my father took off his own feet and bestowed them upon me with his benediction. My elder brother always loved me, and was kind to me; and when my going was first talked of, he regretted deeply that he had nothing to give me; but my little preparations occupied a fortnight, and during that time good luck befriended him and me, and he treated and killed his first patient. Thus he obtained the means of making me a sumptuous present for my journey, which consisted of a straight-cut blue mantle, with a square collar. Let me dwell upon the mantle, for it is important. It was in the Nuremberg fashion, which had gone out of vogue over all of Germany for at least thirty years, and when I first put it on, I felt very proud of it, thinking that I looked like one of the cavaliers in the great picture in the town hall. However, there was not another mantle like it in all Germany, except in Nuremberg—sky-blue, falling three inches below the knee, with a square-cut collar.

"I will pass over my journey to Hamburg, till my arrival in a little common inn, in the old part of town. Not having a penny to spare, I set out early the next morning to look out for a lodging, and saw several

that would have suited myself very well, but which did not suit my finances. At length, seeing the wife of a grocer standing at the door, with
a good-humored countenance, in a narrow and dark street, containing
some large, fine houses which had seen the splendors of former times, I
walked up to her, and asked if she could recommend a lodging to a young
man who was not over rich. After thinking for a moment, she pointed
over the way, to a house with a decorated front, which had become as
black as ink with age. The lower story was entirely occupied by an iron
warehouse; but she said that up above on the first floor I should find
Widow Gentner, who let one room, and who had, she believed, no lodger
at the time. I thanked her many times for her civility, and walking across
the street to the point she indicated, I looked up at the cornices and other
ornaments which were displayed upon the facade. Dirty they were, beyond all doubt. A pair of stone ladies with baskets in their hands, which
had probably been once as white as snow, now displayed long dripping
lines of black upon their garments; their noses had disappeared, but the
balls of the eyes were of the deepest brown, though above the center
appeared a white spot, which seemed to show the presence of a cataract.
The fruit in the baskets, however, consisted apparently of black cherries,
and a dingy cornucopia, which stood by the side of each, vomited forth
swarthy fruit and flowers of a very uninviting quality. I gazed in surprise
and admiration, and asked myself if it ever would be my fate to live in
so fine a mansion.

"Taking courage, however, I inquired at the ironmonger's which was
the door of Widow Gentner, and of the three which opened into the lower
part of the house, I was directed to the second. On the first floor I found
a tidy little maid, who introduced me to the presence of her mistress,
a quiet, dry old lady, who was seated in a room which had apparently
formed part of a magnificent saloon—I say formed part, for it was evident that the size of the chamber had been much curtailed. On the ceiling, which was the most magnificent stucco work I ever saw, appeared
various groups of angels and cherubs in high relief, as large as life, and
seated amid clouds and bunches of flowers as big as feather-beds. But
that ceiling betrayed the dismemberment of the room; for all along the
side where ran this wall behind the good lady were seen angels' legs
without the heads and bodies, baskets of flowers cut in two, and cherubs
with not above one-half of the members even, which sculptors have left
them. This was soon explained: the widow informed me that she had
divided her chamber into three, of which she reserved one for herself,
another for her little maid, and let the third, which had a staircase to itself
opening from the street. She had done so with a good wall, she said, to
support the platform, so that if I wanted to see the room she had to let,

I must go down again with her and mount the other stairs, as there was no door of communication. I admired her prudence, and accompanied her at once to a small room, arrived at by a small staircase with its own street-door; and there I found on the ceiling above my head the lost legs and wings of the angels on the other side, besides a very solid pair of cherubins of my own. It contained a little narrow bed, a table, a scanty proportion of chairs and other things necessary for the existence of a student; and though an unpleasant feeling of solitude crept over me as I thought of inhabiting an apartment so entirely cut off from all human proximity, yet as the widow's rent was small, I closed the bargain at once, and soon was installed in my new abode. The good lady was very kind and attentive, and did all she could to make me comfortable, inquiring, among other things, what letters of introduction I had in Hamburg. I had but one which I considered of any value, which was addressed, with many of those flourishes which you know are common among us, to Mr. S., a famous man in his day, both as a philosopher and literary man, and who was also a man of sense in the world, and what is more than all, of a kind and benevolent heart. I went to deliver it that very day, and met with a most kind and friendly reception from a good-looking old gentleman, of perhaps sixty-three or four, who at once made me feel myself at home with him, treating me with that parental which inspires both respect and confidence. He asked several questions about my journey, where I lodged, how I intended to employ my time, and last, what was the state of my finances. I told him all exactly as it was, and when I rose to depart, he laid his hand on my arm with the most benevolent air in the world, saying, 'You will dine with me tomorrow at twelve o'clock, and I shall expect to see you at dinner three days in the week as long as you stay. From eight to ten at night I am always at home, and whenever you have nothing else to do, come in and spend those hours with us.' I will not pretend to say I was not quite well aware that the place thus granted me at his dinner-table was offered from a knowledge of the limited state of my finances; but pride in my case was out of the question, and I was exceedingly grateful for the act of kindness, which saved me a considerable sum in my housekeeping, and enabled me to indulge in a few little luxuries which I could not otherwise have commanded.

"It was the autumn of the year when I arrived at Hamburg, but the time passed very pleasantly. All the day I was engaged in my studies; at twelve o'clock I dined, either at my own chambers or at worthy Mr. S.'s, and almost every evening was spent at his house, where he failed not to regale me, either with a cup of fine coffee, or sometimes as a great treat, with a cup of tea, according to your English mode. In short, I became his nightly guest, and as the evening grew dark and sometimes foggy, I bought a little lantern to light myself through the long and lonely streets which I had to pass from his house to my own. On these occasions, too, as the weather grew intensely cold, my blue cloak with the square collar proved a most serviceable friend, and every night at ten o'clock I might be seen in precisely the same attire, with my black suit, in great part covered by the azure mantle, and the small lantern in my hand, finding my way homeward to my solitary abode. Mr. S. lived in the fine new part of the town, where he had a handsome house, with two maidservants and his coachman, but the latter slept at the stables. I lived, as I have said before, in the old part of the town, well nigh a mile distant; thus, in coming and going, I got exercise at night, if I did not in the day, and I mark it particularly, that I used to enjoy my walk to his house and back, and used to look forward to it with pleasure during my hours of study, in order that you may see, that on the occasions of which I am about to speak, I was affected by no fantastical melancholy.

"At length, one night in the winter of 17—, after passing the evening at the house of Mr. S., where I had taken nothing but a cup of coffee and a slice of brown bread-and-butter, I took leave of my friend, put on my blue mantle with a square collar, lighted my lantern at the housemaid's candle, and having safely shut the glass, set out on my walk home. It was about a quarter past ten, and the night was clear and very dark; the sky, indeed, was full of stars, which looked peculiarly bright as I gazed up at them, between the tall houses, as if from the bottom of a well, and I felt a sort of exhilarating freshness in the air that raised my spirits rather than otherwise. I walked along to the end of the first street with a light step, turned into the second, and was just entering the third, when I saw a figure some thirty or forty paces before me, standing in a corner as if waiting for someone. Although the streets, in the good old days of Hamburg, were generally by that time of night quite deserted, yet there was nothing extraordinary in my meeting one or two persons as I went home, so that I took little or no notice of this figure, till I had advanced to within about twenty paces, when it turned itself full toward me, and at the same time the light of the lantern fell directly upon it. Guess my surprise when I saw a being, so exactly like myself, that I could have imagined I was looking in a glass. There were the black legs, the shoes and silver buckles, the blue mantle with the square-cut collar, and the little lantern with the handle at the back, held just as I held mine. I stopped suddenly, and rubbed my eyes with my left hand; but the figure immediately turned round and walked away before me. At the same time my heart beat violently, and a sort of strange dreamy sensation of horror came over me, like that which takes possession of one sometimes when laboring under the nightmare. An instant's reflection made me ashamed of what I felt, and saying to myself, 'I'll look a little closer at this gentleman,' I walked on, hurrying my pace. The figure, however, quickened its steps in the same proportion. I did not like to run, but I was always a quick walker, and I hastened as fast as ever I could; but to no effect: the figure, without the least apparent effort, kept always at the same distance, and every moment I felt the sort of superstitious dread which had taken possession of me, increasing, and struggling against the efforts of resolution. Resolution conquered, however, and determined to see who this was that was so like me, without showing him too plainly that I was chasing him, I stopped at a corner where a street wound round, and entered again the one that I was pursuing at some distance, and then taking to my heels, I ran as hard as I could to get before my friend in the blue mantle. When I entered the other street again, though I must have gained two or three minutes at least, instead of seeing the figure coming from the side where I had left it, there it was, walking on deliberately in the direction I usually followed toward my own house. We were now within three streets of Widow Gentner's, and though they were all of them narrow enough, I generally took those which were most open. There was lane, however, to the left, which, passing by the grocer's I have mentioned, cut off at least a quarter of the way, and as I was now overpowered by feelings I cannot describe, I resolved to take the shortest path, and run as hard as I could, in order to get home and shut myself in before the figure in the blue mantle reached the spot. Off I set then down the narrow lane like lightning, but when I came to the grocer's corner, my horror was complete, on beholding the lame figure walking along past the closed windows of the iron-shop, and I stopped with my heart beating as if it would have burst through my ribs. With eyes almost starting from my head and the light of the lantern turned full upon it, I gazed at its proceedings, when behold, it walked quietly up to my door, stopped, turned round toward the house, put the right hand in its pocket, and seemed feeling for my key. The key was produced, and stooping down, just as I should have done, after a little searching for the keyhole, the door was opened, the figure went in, and instantly the door closed again.

"If you had given me the empire of a world, I could not have made up my mind to go in after it, and setting off more like a madman than anything else, I returned to the house of Mr. S., with the intention of telling him what had occurred. The bell was answered quickly enough by the housemaid, who gazed at my wild and scared appearance with some surprise. She told me, however, that the old gentleman had gone to bed, and that she could not think of waking him on my account; and resolved not to go home, and yet not liking to walk the streets of Hamburg all night, I persuaded her with some difficulty to let me sit in the saloon till I could speak with Mr. S. in the morning. I will not detain you by describing how I passed the night; but when my friend came down the next day, I related to him all that had occurred, with many excuses for the liberty I had taken. He listened gravely, and his first question naturally was, if I were quite sure I had gone straight homeward, without entering any of those places where strong drinks were sold. I assured him most solemnly that the only thing that had entered my lips that night was the cup of coffee which I had taken at his house.

"'The maid can tell you,' I said, 'that I had not been absent more than three quarters of an hour when I returned.'

"'Well, my young friend,' he replied, 'I believe you fully; very strange things occasionally happen to us in life, and this seems one. However, we will have some breakfast, and then go and inquire into it.'

"After breakfast we set out and walked to my house, I pointing out by the way, all the different spots connected with my tale. When we reached the gloomy old mansion, with its decorated front, I was going direct to my door, but Mr. S. said, 'Stay, we will first talk to your landlady for a minute.' And we accordingly walked up to the rooms of Widow Gentner by the other door and the other staircase. The widow was very proud of the visit of so distinguished a person in the town as Mr. S., and answered his questions with due respect. The first was a very common one in that part of Germany, namely, whether she had slept well that night. She assured him she had, perfectly well; and he then proceeded with a somewhat impressive air, to inquire if nothing had occurred to disturb her, She then suddenly seemed to recollect herself, and answered: 'Now you mention it, I recollect I was awoke about eleven o'clock, I think, by a noise on the other side of the wall; but thinking that Mr. Z had thrown over his table, or something of that kind, I turned on the other side, and went to sleep again.'

"No further information being to be obtained, we descended to the street, and taking out my keys, I opened the door, and we went in. My heart beat a little as we mounted the stairs, but resolving not to show any want of courage, I boldly unlocked the room door and threw it open. The sight that presented itself made me pause on the threshold, for there on my bed, where I should have been lying at the very moment of its fall, was the whole ceiling of that part of the room, angels' legs, and cherubims' wings, flower-baskets, and everything, and so great was the weight and force with which it had come down, that it had broken the solid bedstead underneath it. As I do not suppose my head is composed of much more strong materials, it is probable that it would have been cracked as well as the bed, and I heartily thank God for my preservation. All my good old friend ventured to say, however, was, 'A most fortunate escape! Had you slept here last night, you would have been killed to a certainty.' Though a doctor of philosophy, he did not risk any speculations upon the strange apparition which I had beheld the night before; but invited me to take up my abode in his house till my room could be put in order, never afterward mentioning the appearance of my double; and I have only to add that from that time to this, now between fifty and sixty years, I have never seen myself again except in a looking-glass."

THE THREE SOULS

BY ALEXANDER CHATRIAN AND EMILE ERCKMANN

(1859)

In the year 1805 I was engaged in my sixth year of transcendental philosophy at Heidelberg. You understand the life of a university student; it is a grand life—the life of a great lord. He rises at noon, smokes his pipe, drinks two or three glasses of schnaps, and then, unbuttoning his coat to his chin, he places his little flat Prussian cap jauntily on his head, and quietly goes to listen for half an hour to the illustrious Professor Hasenkopf discuss on ideas *a priori a posteriori*. While listening to him he may yawn as much as he pleases, or even go to sleep if he likes.

The lecture over, he goes to a tavern; he stretches his legs under a table, and pretty waitresses run about with plates of sausages, slices of ham and large jugs of strong beer. he sings the air of the "Brigands" of Schiller, he drinks, he eats. He whistles to his dog Hector, and takes a walk, or perhaps some difficulty arises in the tavern, blows are exchanged, glasses are knocked over, and jugs fall to the ground. The watchman arrives, he seizes the students, and they pass a night in the station-house.

Thus pass away days, months, years.

In Heidelberg are to be seen princes, dukes and barons in embryo; there are also the sons of shoemakers, schoolmasters and honorable traders. The young noblemen form a band to themselves, but the rest mingle fraternally together.

I was then thirty-two years of age; my beard had commenced to turn gray; beer, pipes and sauerkraut began to decline in my esteem. I felt the necessity of change. With respect to Hasenkopf, the listening to so many lectures on discursive ideas and intuitive ideas, on apodietical truths and predicted truths, turned by head into a veritable *pot-pouri*. It seemed to me that the foundation of science was *ex nihilo nihili*. Often I exclaimed to myself, stretching out my arms,

"Kasper Zann, Kasper Zann! it is not wise to know too much; nature has no more illusions for you. You can say, in a voice of lamentation, with the prophet Jeremiah, *Vanitas vanitatum et omnia vanitas!*"

Such were my melancholy thoughts when, towards the end of the spring of the year 1805, a terrible event caused me to realize the fact that

I did not know everything, and that a philosophical career is not always strewn with roses.

Amongst my old comrades there was a certain Wolfgang Scharf, the most inflexible logician that I had ever met. Picture to yourself a little, dried-up man, with sunken eyes, white eyebrows, bushy red hair, hollow cheeks, ornamented with straggling whiskers, large shoulders and exceeding dilapidated clothes. To see him glide along the walls, with a loaf of bread under his arm, with his sparkling eyes and stooping shoulders, you would have said he resembled an old cat searching for his sweetheart. But Wolfgang thought of nothing but metaphysics. For five or six years he had lived on bread and water in a garret belonging to a disused butcher's establishment. No bottle of sparkling ale nor Rhine wine had ever calmed his ardor for science, no slice of ham had ever impaired the course of his sublime meditations. The poor wretch was, therefore, frightful to see. I say frightful, for in spite of his apparent marasmus, there was a force of cohesion in his bony structure terrible to contemplate. The muscles of his jaws and hands protruded, like clusters of iron; in addition to which he was cross-eyed.

This strange being, in the midst of his voluntary isolation, appeared to have preserved for me alone a portion of his sympathy. He came to see me from time to time, and gravely seated in my armchair, with his fingers moving convulsively, he would entertain me with his metaphysical lucubrations.

"Kaspar," said he to me one day, proceeding in the Socratic manner of argument, "Kaspar, what is the soul?"

Proud to display my erudition, I replied with dictatorial air:

"According to Thales, it is a kind of lodestone; according to Plato, a substance which moves of itself; according to Asclepiades, an excitation of the senses. Anaximander says that it is composed of earth and water; Empedocles, of blood; Hippocrates, a spirit diffused through the body; Zeno, the quintessence of the four elements; Xenocrates—"

"Yes, yes; but what do you believe the substance of the soul to be?"

"I, Wolfgang? I say, with Lactantius, that I know nothing. I am an Epicurian from nature. For, according to the Epicurians, all judgement comes from the senses, and as the soul does not come under my senses, I cannot judge of it."

"And yet, Kaspar, there a number of animals, such as insects, fishes, that live deprived of several senses. Who knows if we possess all? If there does not exist some of which we have no idea?"

"It is possible, but as it is a doubtful question, I refrain from giving an opinion."

"Do you believe, Kasper, that it is possible to know anything without having learned it?"

"No; all science proceeds from experience or study."

"But how is it, comrade, that little chickens, the moment they issue from the egg, begin to run and pick up their nourishment? How is it that they perceive the hawk in the midst of the clouds, and hide themselves under their mother's wing? Did they learn to recognize their enemy in the egg?"

"That is the effect of instinct, Wolfgang; all animals obey instinct."

"Then it appears that instinct consists in knowing what has never been learned?"

"Now you are asking too much," I cried. "How can I answer you?"

He smiled in a disdainful manner, and, throwing his worn-out cloak over his shoulders, left me without adding another word.

I looked upon him as a madman, but a madman of the most innocent kind; for who could imagine that a passion for metaphysics could be dangerous?

Such was the condition of affairs when the old cake-dealer, Catherine Wogel, suddenly disappeared. This good woman, with her tray suspended from her stork-like neck, would present herself at the taverns frequented by the students. She was a great favorite with the young men, and they would jest with her and she with them.

Her disappearance was remarked on the third day.

"What the deuce has become of Catherine?" said one of the students. "Can she be sick? It is very strange; she appeared so merry the last time she was here."

We learned that the police were in search of her. My own opinion was, that the poor old woman, overcome by *kirsch-wasser*, had fallen into the river.

But the next morning, as I was leaving the lecture-room of Hasenkopf, I met Wolfgang. The moment he saw me his eyes sparkled, and he said:

"I have been looking for you, Kaspar. I have been looking for you; the hour of triumph has come. You must follow me."

His appearance, his gestures, his pallor betrayed extreme agitation, and when he seized me by the arm, dragging me towards the Tanner's quarter, I could not help experiencing a feeling of undefinable fear, without having courage to resist.

The little street down which we proceeded was situated in the rear of the Munster, and was the very oldest part of Heidelberg. The square roofs, the wooden galleries, in which hung the clothes of the poor people who resided in the houses, the external staircases with worm-eaten steps, the thousand wan and curious faces, which, with half-open mouths, projected from the little windows and regarded with eager glances the strangers who were passing through their filthy quarter; the long poles reaching from one roof to the other, and loaded with bleeding skins, and the thick smoke which issued from the chimneys of every roof—all these things combined was like a resurrection of the middle ages to me, and, although the sky was clear, the long shadows cast by the sun on the decrepit walls added to my emotion by the strangeness of contrast.

There are moments when a man loses all presence of mind. I had not even the idea to ask Wolfgang where we were going.

After we had passed through this populous quarter, where misery reigned triumphant, we reached the, comparatively speaking, deserted Butcher's Quarter. Suddenly Wolfgang, whose cold and dry hand seemed riveted to my wrist, dragged me into a building which was destitute of windows.

"Go forward!" said he.

I followed a wall, at the end of which I found a staircase, so much dilapidated that it was with the greatest difficulty I could ascend. My comrade kept repeating to me, in an impatient voice:

"Higher! Higher!"

I stopped sometimes, almost frozen with fear, under the pretext of taking breath, and for the purpose of examining the nooks of this sombre dwelling, but in fact to deliberate if it were not time to escape.

At last we reached the foot of a ladder, the upper steps of which were lost in the darkness. I have often asked myself since, how I could be so imprudent as to ascend this ladder, without exacting the slightest explanation from my friend Wolfgang. It seems that madness is contagious.

I ascended then, he behind me. I reached the top, and my feet came in contact with a dusty floor. I looked around me, and found that I was in an immense garret, the roof of which contained three windows; on the left the gray wall of the gable reached the top of the roof. A small table, loaded with books and papers, stood in the middle of the loft. Above it was so dark that the beams supporting the roof could scarcely be distinguished. It was impossible to look out into the street, for the windows were ten or twelve feet from the floor.

At the first moment I did not notice a low door with a large vent-hole contrived in the gable-wall, breast high.

Wolfgang, without saying a word, pushed towards me a trunk, which served him for a chair, and then taking in both his hands a large pitcher of water he took a long drink, whilst I gazed on him as if I were in a dream.

"We are in the false roof of an old slaughter-house," said he, with a strange smile. "The council has voted funds to build another outside the city. I have been here five years without paying any rent. Not a soul has come to trouble my studies."

He sat down on a heap of firewood in a corner.

"Well," he continued, "let us proceed to business. Are you sure, Kaspar, that we have a soul?"

"Listen, Wolfgang," said I in a bad humor, "if you have led me here to talk metaphysics, you have done wrong. I had just left Hasenkopf's lecture, and was going to breakfast, when you intercepted me. I take my dose of abstract ideas every day—that is sufficient for me. Explain yourself clearly, then, or let me go to breakfast."

"You only like to eat, then?" said he in a hoarse voice. "Do you know that I have passed whole days without putting a bit into my mouth? And I have done this from love of science."

"Everyone to his taste; you live on syllogisms and preposterous theories. I love sausages and beer. I can't help it—my appetite is stronger than my love of science."

He became quite pale, his lips trembled, but conquering his anger, he said:

"Kaspar, since you will not answer my question, listen at least to my explanations. Man has need of admirers, and I wish you to admire me. I wish to confound you by the sublime discovery that I have made; I think it not too much to ask an hour's attention for ten years of conscientious study."

"Very well, go on, I will listen—but hurry."

His face twitched again and made me reflect. I repented having accompanied him, and I assumed a grave demeanor for the purpose of not irritating the maniac. My meditative face appeared to calm him a little, for after a few moments' silence he resumed:

"You are hungry—here, take my bread; and here is water—eat, drink, but listen."

"It is unnecessary, Wolfgang; I can listen very well without that."

He smiled bitterly, and continued:

"We have a soul—a thing admitted from the earliest ages. From plants to man, all living things have souls. Is it necessary for me to attend Hasenkopf's lectures six years to make you this reply—"All organized beings have at least one soul." But the more their organization is made more perfect, the more complicated it is, the more the souls multiply. It is this which distinguishes animated beings one from the other. A plant has only one soul, the vegetable soul. Its function is simple, unique; it has to imbibe nourishment from the air by means of its leaves, and from the earth by means of its roots. An animal has two souls—first, the vegetable soul, the functions of which are the same as in the plant, nutrition by means of the lungs and stomach; secondly, the animal soul, properly so-called, which has for its end sensibility, and the organ of which is the heart. Man, who sums up terrestrial creation, has three souls—the vegetable soul, the animal soul, the functions of which are exercised the same as in the brute, and the human soul, which has for its object reason and intelligence—its organ is the brain. The nearer animals approach man, the more perfect is their cerebral organization, the more they participate in this third soul—such as the dog, the elephant, the horse—but men of genius alone possess this soul in its fullest perfection."

Here Wolfgang paused a few moments, and fixed his glance on me.

"Well," said he, "what have you to reply?"

"That it is like any other theory, it wants proof."

A kind of frantic exultation seized Wolfgang at this reply. He jumped up with a bound, and crossing his hands in the air, cried:

"Yes, yes, proof was wanting. It is this that has rent my soul for ten years; it is this that has been the cause of so many vigils, so much moral suffering and privation. For it was on myself, Kaspar, that I first experimented. Fasting only forced on my mind the conviction of this sublime truth, without my being able to establish the proof. But at last it is discovered—the proof is made manifest! You shall hear the three souls manifest themselves—proclaim their own existence. You shall hear them!"

After this explosion of enthusiasm, which was announced with such energy that it made me shiver, he suddenly became cold again, and sitting down with his elbows resting on the table he resumed, pointing to the lofty gable-wall:

"The proof is there, behind that wall. I will show it you by-and-bye; but first of all, you must follow the progressive march of my ideas. You know the opinion of the ancients on the nature of souls. They admitted four united in man. *Caro*, the flesh, a mixture of earth and water, which is dissolved by death; *manes*, the phantom which hovers around the grave— its name comes from *manere*, to rest, to dwell; *umbra*, the shadow, more immaterial than the *manes*; and last of all, *spiritus*, the spirit—the immaterial substance which ascends to the gods. This classification appears to me to be just; the question was to decompose a human being, in order to establish the existence of three souls distinct from the flesh. Reason told me that every man before reaching his last development must have passed through the state of a plant and an animal, or in other words, that Pythagoras had a glimpse of the truth without being able to furnish the demonstration. Well, I determined to resolve this problem. It was necessary that I should successively extinguish in myself the three souls and then reanimate them. I had recourse to rigorous fasting. Unfortunately, the human soul must succumb first to allow the animal soul to act freely.

Hunger made me lose the faculty of observing the animal condition. By exhausting myself I made myself powerless to judge of the animal state. After a number of fruitless efforts on my own organization, I became convinced that there was but one means to attain the end I had in view. It was to act on another! But who would resign himself to this species of observation?"

Wolfgang paused. His lips became contracted, and in an abrupt tone he added:

"A subject was necessary to me at any price. I resolved to experiment *in anima vili!*"

I shivered, this man was then capable of anything.

"Do you understand?" said he.

"Very well! You required a victim."

"To decompose," he added coldly.

"And you have found one?"

"Yes; I have promised that you shall hear the three souls. It may perhaps be difficult now, but yesterday you might have heard them howl, roar, supplicate and grind their teeth by turns."

A cold shiver ran through me. Wolfgang, perfectly impassible, lighted a little lamp which he used for his night studies, and approached the vent-hole to the left.

"Look," said he, extending his arms in the darkness; "approach and look, and then listen!"

In spite of my baleful presentiments, in spite of the cold shiver of terror which agitated me, drawn there by the attraction of mystery, I gazed through the sombre opening. There, under the rays of the lamp, about fifteen feet below the surface of the floor, I saw a kind of pit, without any means of exit excepting that of the garret. I immediately comprehended that it was one of those holes into which butchers throw the skins of slaughtered animals, that they may become green before handing them over to the tanners. It appeared to me to be empty, and for some moments I could distinguish nothing.

"Look well," said Wolfgang to me in a low voice; "do you not see a bundle of rags heaped up in a corner? It is old Catherine Wogel, the cake-dealer, wh—"

He had not time to finish, for a piercing, savage cry, resembling the lugubrious mewing of a cat whose paw is crushed, was heard at the bottom of the pit. A wild-looking being rose up, and seemed to be trying to climb up the walls with her nails. And I, more dead than alive, my forehead covered with cold perspiration, drew back, exclaiming:

"Oh, it is horrible!"

"Did you hear?" said Wolfgang, his face lighted up with infernal joy. "Was not that the cry of a cat? The old woman before attaining the human condition was either a cat or a panther. Now the beast is awakened. Oh, hunger, hunger, and especially thirst, performs miracles!"

He was so absorbed by his discovery that he did not look at me. An abominable complacency and self-satisfaction could be traced to his look, in his attitude and in his smile.

The piercing cries of the poor old woman had ceased. The madman, having placed his lamp on the table, added in the form of a commentary:

"She has been without food for four days. I attracted her here under the pretext of selling her a little cask of *kirsch-wasser*. I made her descend into the pit, and then I shut her in. Intemperance is the cause of her ruin. She is expiating for her immoderate thirst. The first two days the human soul was in all its vigor. She supplicated me, she implored me, she proclaimed her innocence, saying that she had done nothing to me, and that I had no rights over her. Then rage took possession of her. She overwhelmed me with reproaches, calling me a monster and a wretch, etc. The third day, which was yesterday, a Wednesday, the human soul completely disappeared. The cat showed its claws—she commenced to mew and to growl. Fortunately, we are in a retired spot. Last night the inhabitants of the Tanner's quarter must have thought there was a real battle of cats—the cries were enough to make one tremble. Now do you know when the beast shall be exhausted what will be the result? The vegetable soul will have its turn; it is that which will perish last. It has already been remarked that the hair and nails of the dead grow in their graves; there is also formed in the interstices of the skull a sort of human moss, and which is considered as engendered by the animal juices of the brain. At last the vegetable soul itself retires. You see, Kaspar, that the proof of the three souls is complete."

These words struck my ears like the reasonings of a madman. I seemed to be a victim of the most horrible of nightmares. Catherine Wogel's cries had pierced me to the very marrow of my bones. I no longer recognized myself—I seemed to have lost my senses. But, suddenly awakening out of this moral stupor, indignation exerted its sway. I rose up. I seized the maniac by the throat and dragged him towards the entrance of the loft.

"Wretch!" said I, "who gave you permission to raise your hand against one of your fellow-creatures—against one of God's creatures, for the purpose of satisfying your infamous curiosity? I will myself deliver you up to justice!"

He was so surprised at my aggression—his acts had appeared to him so natural, that he at first made no resistance, and allowed me to drag him towards the ladder without making me any reply. But, suddenly, turning with all the suppleness of a wild beast, he, in turn, seized me by the throat, his eyes shooting fire, his lips foaming. His hands, powerful as steel, lifted me from the ground and nailed me to the wall, while with the other he pushed back the bolt of the door which opened into the pit. Fully comprehending his intention, I made a terrible effort to free myself. I fixed myself across the door—but this man was endowed with superhuman strength. After a rapid and desperate struggle, I felt myself raised a second time from the ground, and was launched into space, while above me I heard these strange words:

"So perishes the flesh in revolt—so triumphs the immortal soul!"

And I had scarcely reached the bottom of the pit, bruised and stunned, when the heavy door was closed fifteen feet above me, intercepting from my sight the gray light from the garret.

My consternation at falling to the bottom of the pit, and feeling myself taken like a rat in a trap, was such, that I rose up without uttering a single complaint.

"Kaspar," said I to myself, with strange calmness, 'the question now is to devour the old woman or be devoured by her. Choose! As to try to escape from this den it is time lost. Wolfgang holds you under his claws and he will not let you escape—the walls are of flint and the flooring of oak as hard as stone. None of your acquaintances saw you enter the Tanner's quarter—no one knows you in this part of the city—no one will ever have an idea of searching for you here. It is all up, Kaspar, it is all up. Your last resource is this poor Catherine Wogel—or rather, you are the last resource of each other!"

All this passed through my mind like a flash of lightning. I was seized with a trembling which did not leave me for three years, and when, at the same moment, the pale face of Wolfgang, with his little lamp in his hand, appeared at the vent-hole, and when, with my hands joined together by terror, I wished to supplicate him—I perceived that I stammered in an atrocious manner—not a word issued from my trembling lips. When he saw me thus, he smiled, and I heard him murmur:

"The coward!—he prays to me!"

This was my *coup de grace*. I fell with my face against the ground, and I would have fainted—if the fear of being attacked by the old woman had not brought me to myself. Still she had not yet moved. Wolfgang's face had disappeared. I heard the maniac walk across his garret, move back the table and clear his throat with a short, dry cough. My hearing was so acute that the slightest sound reached me and made me shiver. I heard the old woman yawn, and turning round, I perceived, for the first time, her eyes glittering in the darkness. At the same time I heard Wolfgang descend the ladder; I counted the steps one by one until the sound was lost in the distance. Where had the wretch gone? But during the whole of that day and the following night he did not appear. It was only the next day, about eight o'clock in the evening, at the moment that the old woman and myself were howling loud enough to make the very walls tremble, that he returned.

I had not closed my eyes. I no longer felt fear or rage. I suffered from hunger—devouring hunger—and I knew that it would increase.

The moment I heard a slight sound in the garret I ceased my cries and raised my eyes. The vent-hole was lighted up. Wolfgang had lighted his lamp. He was, doubtless, coming to look at me. In this hope I prepared a touching speech, but the lamp was extinguished—no one came!

It was perhaps the most frightful moment of my torture. I thought to myself that Wolfgang, knowing that I was not sufficiently reduced, would not deign even to cast a glance on me, that in his eyes I was only an interesting subject, who would not be ripe for science until two or three days had elapsed, when I was between life and death. It seemed to me that I felt my hair slowly whiten on my head. And it was true—it began to turn gray from that moment. At last my terror became so great that I lost my consciousness.

Towards midnight I was awakened by the contact of a body with my own. I bounded from my place with disgust. The old woman had approached me, attracted by hunger. She had hooked her hands onto my clothes; at the same moment the cry of a cat filled the pit and froze me with fear.

I expected a terrible combat, but the poor unfortunate woman could do nothing. She had been there five days.

It was then that Wolfgang's words returned to my memory—"Once the animal soul is extinct the vegetable soul will manifest itself—the hair and the nails grow in the grave, and a green moss takes root in the interstices of the skull." I fancied the old woman reduced to this condition—her skull covered with moldy lichen and I lying beside her, our souls spreading out the humid vegetation side by side in the silence!

This picture so acted upon my mind that I no longer felt the pangs of hunger. Extended against the wall with my eyes wide open, I looked before me without seeing anything.

And while I was thus more dead than alive, a vague gleam was infiltrated through the darkness. I raised my eyes. Wolfgang's pale face appeared at the vent-hole. He did not smile; he appeared to experience neither joy, satisfaction nor remorse—he observed me.

Oh, that face made me fear! If he had smiled, if he had rejoiced over his revenge—I should have hoped to have been able to move him—but he simply observed!

We remained thus, our eyes fixed on each other. I, struck with terror; he, cold, calm, and attentive, like the face of an inert object. The insect pierced by a needle, which we observe through a microscope, if it thinks—if it comprehends the eye of man, must view it in this light.

It was necessary that I should die to satisfy the curiosity of a monster. I felt certain that prayers would be useless, so I said nothing.

After having observed me in this way, the maniac, doubtless satisfied with his observations, turned his head to look at the old woman. I followed mechanically the direction of his eyes. There are no terms that I can use that can explain what I saw—a face haggard and emaciated, limbs shrunk up and so sharp that they seemed ready to pierce the rags that covered them. Something shapeless, horrible, the head of a skeleton, the hair disheveled round the skull like dried herbs, and in the midst of all this two burning eyes and two long yellow teeth.

Fearful tiding! I could already distinguish two snails on the skeleton. When I saw this I closed my eyes with a convulsive moment, and said to myself, "In five days I shall be like that!"

When I opened my eyes again the lamp had been withdrawn.

"Wolfgang," I cried, "God is above you! God sees you! Woe to monsters!"

I passed the rest of the night in a delirium of fear.

Having dreamed again, in the delirium of fever, of the chances I had of escape and finding none, I suddenly made up my mind to die, and this resolution procured me some moments of relief. I reviewed in my mind Hasenkopf's arguments relative to the immortality of the soul, and for the first time I found that they had invincible strength.

"Yes," I cried, "the passage through this world is only a time of trial, injustice and cupidity, and baleful passions rule the heart of man. The weak are crushed by the strong, the poor by the rich. Virtue is only a word on the earth; but all is restored to order after death. God sees the injustice of which I am the victim. He gives me credit for the sufferings that I endure. He will forgive me for my ill-regulated appetites—my excessive love of good cheer. Before admitting me into His kingdom He wished to purify me by a vigorous fast. I offer my sufferings to the Lord!"

And yet I must confess that in spite of my deep contrition, my regrets for good cheer, for the society of my joyous companions, for that life which glides away in the midst of songs and good wine, made me heave many sighs. I fancied I heard soup bubbling in the pot, wine gurgling from bottles, the clinking of glasses, and my stomach groaned as if it were a living person. It seemed to be a kind of being apart from my own being, and protested against the philosophical arguments of Hasenkopf.

The greatest of my sufferings was thirst. It became so intolerable that I licked the saltpeter on the walls to give me relief.

When vague and uncertain gleams of daylight shone through the vent-hole I became furious.

"The wretch is there," I said to myself; "he has bread, a pitcher of water—he is drinking."

Then I fancied I saw him with the pitcher to his lips—I seemed to see torrents of water passing slowly down his throat. Anger, despair, and indignation took possession of me, and I ran round the pit, screaming out to the top of my voice:

"Water! water! water!"

And the old woman, reanimated, repeated after me like a maniac:

"Water! water! water!"

She crawled on her hands and knees after me. Pandemonium could have nothing more horrible.

In the midst of this scene, Wolfgang's pale face appeared for the third time at the vent-hole. It was about eight o'clock. Stopping, I exclaimed:

"Wolfgang, listen to me. Give me one drink from your pitcher, and you may leave me to die of hunger. I will not reproach you!"

And I wept.

"You are acting too barbarously towards me," I continued. "Your immortal soul will have to answer for it before God. With respect to this old woman, it is as you say judicious to experiment *in anima vili*. But I have studied, and I find your system splendid. I am worthy to understand it. I admire you! Let me only take one drink of water. What is that to you? There was never a more sublime conception than yours. It is certain that the three souls exist. Yes, I will proclaim it to the world. I will be your most firm adherent. Will you not let me take one single drink of water?"

Without making any reply, he retired.

My exasperation knew no bounds. I threw myself against the wall with the utmost violence; I apostrophized the wretch in the most bitter terms.

In the midst of this fury I suddenly perceived that the old woman had fallen senseless all her length on the ground. The idea came to me to drink her blood. Man's necessities carry him to excesses which are enough to make one tremble; it is then that the ferocious beast is awakened in him; and that all sentiments of justice and benevolence are effaced by the instinct of self-preservation.

"Of what use is her blood to her?" I said to myself. "She must soon perish. If I delay all her blood will be dried up."

Red flames passed before my eyes; fortunately when I bent over the poor old woman my strength forsook me, and I fainted away by her side with my face in her rags.

How long did I remain in this state of unconsciousness? I do not know, but I was awakened from it by a curious circumstance, the recollection of which will for ever remain imprinted on my brain. I was aroused by the plaintive howling of a dog; this howling was so feeble, so pitiable, so poignant, that it was even more touching than the lamentations of human beings, and no one could hear it without being affected by it. I rose up, my face bathed in tears, without knowing from whence came these cries, so much in harmony with my own grief. I listened attentively, and judge of my stupor, that it was I myself who groaned in this manner without being aware of it.

From this moment all recollection was effaced from my memory. It is certain, however, that I remained two days longer in the pit under the eye of the maniac, whose enthusiasm at seeing his idea triumph was so great that he did not hesitate to convoke the presence of several of our philosophers, that he might enjoy their admiration.

* * * *

Six weeks afterwards I came to consciousness in my little room in the Rue Plat d'Etaw, surrounded by my comrades, who congratulated me for having escaped from this lesson in transcendental philosophy.

It was a pathetic moment when Ludwig Bremer brought me a mirror. When I saw myself thinner than Lazarus when he was raised from the dead, I could not help shedding tears.

Poor Catherine Wogel had died in the pit.

With respect to myself I was threatened with chronic gastritis for the rest of my days; but thanks to my good constitution, and thanks especially to the care of Dr. Aloius Killian, I recovered my former good health.

It is almost needless to add that the wretch Wolfgang was brought to justice; but instead of being hung as he deserved, after a delay of six months he was brought in by the jury as insane, and was confined in the Klingenmuster, the insane asylum of Rhenish Bavaria, where visitors could hear him expatiate in a peremptory manner of the three souls. He accused humanity of injustice, and pretended that he ought to have a statue raised to his memory for his magnificent discovery.

THE DEATH WATCH

BY LUISE MUHLBACK (PSEUD. CLARA MUNDT)

TRANSLATED FROM THE GERMAN BY JOHN OXENFORD

(1847)

Count Manfred knelt, deeply affected, by the bed of his poor friend—now destined to be his death-bed. Silence and gloom were in the narrow room, which was only dimly lighted by a night-lamp. The moon shone, large and cold, through the one window, illuminating the wretched couch of the invalid. Soon loud groaning alone interrupted the melancholy stiffness. Manfred felt a chill shudder in all his limbs, a sensation of horror overcame him, and the bed of his slowly expiring friend, and he felt as if he must perforce go out among mankind, hear the breath of a living person instead of this death-rattle, and press a warm hand instead of the cold damp one of the dying man. He softly raised himself from his knees, and crept to the chimney to stir the almost extinct fire, that something bright and cheering might surround him. But the sick man raised himself up, and looked at him with fixed glassy eyes, while his heart rose higher and quicker with a breathless groaning.

The flame crackled and flew upwards, casting a harsh gleam through the room. Suddenly a coal flew out with a loud noise, and fell into the middle of the apartment upon the wooden floor. At the same time a terribly piercing cry arose from the bed, and Manfred, who looked towards it with alarm, saw that the invalid was sitting up, and with eyes widely opened and outstretched arms, was staring at the spot where the coal was lying. It was a frightful spectacle, that of the dying man, who seemed to be struggling with a deep feeling of horror; on whose features death had already imprinted its seal; and whose short nightgown was insufficient to conceal the dry and earth-gray arms and legs, which had already assumed a deathlike hue. Frightful was the loud rattle that proceeded from the heart of one who could scarcely be called alive or dead, and dull as from the grave sounded the isolated words from which he uttered, still gazing upon the coal on the floor. "Away—away with thee! why wilt thou remain there, spectre? Leave me, I say."

Manfred stood overpowered with horror, his trembling feet refused to support him, and he leaned against the wall contemplating the actions of his friend, the sight of whom created the deepest terror. The voice of the invalid became louder and more shrill. "Away with thee, I say! why dost thou cleave so fast to my heart? I say, leave me!"

Then striking out with his arms he sprung out of the bed with unnatural force, and darting to the spot where the coal was lying, stooped down, grasped it in his hand, and flung it back upon the hearth. He then burst into a loud, wild laugh, which made poor Manfred's heart quail within him, and returned back to the bed.

But the coal had burned its very dross into the floor, and had left a black mark.

The room was again quiet. Manfred now breathed freely, and calmly crept to the couch of his friend, whose quiet, regular breathing and closed eyes showed that he had fallen into a reposing sleep. Thus passed one hour, the slow progress of which Manfred observed on his friend's large watch, which lay upon the bed, and the regular ticking of which was the only interruption of the stillness of the night, except the still, quiet breathing of his friend.

The steeple clock in the vicinity announced by its striking that another hour had passed. Manfred counted the strokes—it was twelve o'clock—midnight. He involuntarily shuddered, the thoughts of the legends and tales of his childhood darted through him like lightning, and he owned to himself that he had always felt a mysterious terror at the midnight hour. At the same moment, his friend opened his eyes, and softly pronounced his name.

Manfred leant down to him. "Here I am, Karl."

"I thank you," said the sick man, in a faint voice, "for remaining by me thus faithfully. I am dying, Manfred."

"Do not speak so," replied the other, affectionately grasping the hand of his friend.

"I cease to see you," said Karl, more and more faintly and slowly; "dark clouds are before my eyes."

Suddenly he raised himself, took the watch which was lying by him, and placed it in Manfred's hand. "I thank you," he said, "for all the love you have shown me; for all your kindness and consolation. Take this watch; it is the only thing which now belongs to me. Wear it in remembrance of me. If it is permitted me, by this watch I will give you warning when I am near. Farewell!"

He sunk back—his breath stopped—he was no more.

Manfred bent over him, called his name, laid his hand upon his forehead, which was covered with perspiration; he felt it grow colder and colder. Tears of the deepest sympathy filled his eyes, and dropped upon the pale face of the dead man.

"Sleep softly," whispered Manfred, "and may the grave afford you that repose which you sought in vain upon earth!"

Once more he pressed to his bosom the hand of his deceased friend, wrapped himself in his cloak, put up the watch which Karl had bequeathed him, and retired to his residence.

The sun was already high when he awoke from an uneasy sleep. With feelings of pain he thought of the past night, and of his departed friend. In remembrance of him he drew out the watch, which pointed to the half hour, and held it to his ear. It had stopped; he tried to wind it up, but in vain—it had not run down.

"Is it possible," murmured Manfred to himself, "that there was really some spiritual connection between the deceased and this, his favorite watch, which he constantly carried?"

He sunk down upon a chair, and strange thoughts and forebodings passed through his excited mind.

"What is time?" he asked himself; "what is an hour? A machine artificially produced by human hands determines it, regulates it, and gives to life its significance, and to the mind its warnings. The awe which accompanies the midnight hour does not affect us if the hand of the watch goes wrong. The clock is the despot of man; regulating the actions both of king and beggars. Nay, it is the ruler of time, which has subjected itself to its authority. The clock determines the very thoughts as well as the actions of man; it is the propelling wheel of the human species. The maiden who reposes delighted in the arms of her lover trembles when the ruthless clock strikes the hour which tears him from her. Her grief, her entreaties are all in vain. He must away, for the clock has ordered it. The murderer trembles in the full enjoyment of his fortune, for his eye falls on the hands of the clock, and they denote the hour when the already broken eye of the man he murdered looked upon him for the last time. In vain he endeavored to smile; it is beyond his power; for the clock has spoken, and his conscience awakes when he thinks of the horror of that hour. Shuddering with the feverish chill of mental anguish, the condemned culprit looks upon the clock, the hand of which, slowly moving, brings nearer and nearer the hour of his death. It is not the rising and setting of the sun, it is not the light of day, that determines destruction; but the clock. When the hand, with cruel indifference, moves on and touches the figure of the hour which the judge has appointed for his death, the doors of the dungeon open, and he has ceased to live. As long as we live we are governed by the hour, and death alone frees us from the hour and the clock! Perhaps the whole of eternity, with its bliss, is nothing but an hour-less, clock-less existence; eternal, because without measure; blissful, because not bound to a measured time."

Manfred had once more entered the desolate residence of his deceased friend, and stood mourning by the corpse, the face of which bore, in its stiffened features, the peace which Karl had never known in life.

He thought of the life of the deceased—how poor it was in joy, and how, during the four years he had known him, he had never seen him smile. Tears came into his eyes, and he turned away from the corpse. Then his glance fell upon the black spot in the floor. The whole frightful scene of the preceding day revived in his soul, and the thought suddenly struck him, whether there might not be some connection between that particular spot and the strange excitement of Karl. Fearful suspicions crossed his mind; he thought how often conscience had unmasked he criminal, in the hour of death; he remembered the frequent mysterious gloom of his friend; he remembered the wife with whom he had long lived unhappily, from whom he had been separated, and after whose residence Manfred had often inquired. On this subject Karl had always preserved silence, and often broke out into an unusual warmth. He reflected with what obstinacy Karl remained in this room, although Manfred had often and earnestly entreated him as a friend and near relative, to go into his house. Nay, he now recollected quite clearly, that in the newspaper in which, years before, he had read the arrival of Count Karl Manfred, it was stated that he had arrived with his wife. A few weeks after he had read of his relative, Manfred had gone to him, and found him alone; and when Karl told him of his separation from his wife, had inquired no further.

All this now passed before his mind. He looked timidly back at the corpse, and it seemed to him as if this were scornfully nodding at him confirmation of his thoughts.

"I must have certainty," he cried aloud, and stooped down to the floor. He now plainly perceived that the middle boards, upon which was the burn, were looser than the others, and that the nails, which must have been there firmly, and the marks of which were still plainly to be seen, were wanting. He tried to raise the middle board, which at first resisted, but at last gave way a little. With a piece of wood he knocked the thick knife deeper into the floor; the nails became more and more unfastened, and he lifted and pulled with all the might of anxiety and curiosity. With a loud crack the board gave way entirely; he raised it, and—sight of horrors!—saw that a skeleton lay stretched out beneath. Manfred at first almost fainted; then, feeling how necessary was calmness and presence of mind, he collected himself with a strong effort, and looked hard at the skeleton. It held a paper between its teeth, which Manfred, with averted face, drew forth. Opening it, he soon recognized the handwriting of Karl. The words were as follows:

"That no innocent person may be exposed to suspicion, I hereby declare that I, Karl Manfred, am the murderer of this woman. This declaration can never injure me, as I am determined never to quit this room before my death. The small, wretched house is my own property, and as I inhabit it alone, I am secure from discovery. When I am no more the secret will be unveiled, and for the finder of these lines I add, for nearer explanation, a short portion of the history of my life.

"I am the son of a collateral branch of the rich Count Manfred. My father was tolerably rich, and loved me; but he was haughty even to excess, and quite capable of sacrificing the happiness of his child to the pride he took in his ancestors. One day I went to the shop of a clock-maker to buy a watch. The clock-maker's daughter stood at the counter in the place of her father; her beauty excited my admiration, her innocent air attracted me: I talked with her for a long time, and at last bought a valuable watch set with brilliants. I then departed, but returned in a few days, and again, and again; in short, we were enamored of each other. I told my father that I had resolved to marry the clockmaker's daughter; he cursed me and disinherited me. But I persuaded my beloved to fly with me, and one night she robbed her father of his money and jewels, and effected her escape. We went far enough to remain undiscovered, and sold our brilliants, which, with the money we had taken, was enough to afford a considerable, nay, rather abundant fortune. As for the clock, which had been the cause of my acquaintance with my beloved Ulrica, I kept that constantly by me.

"Ulrica told me that her father had made it with her own hands. One day it stopped; I tried to wind it up, but all in vain, for it would not go. I laid it aside peevishly, and when, after some hours, I again took it in hand, it went. With a feeling of foreboding, inexplicable even to myself, I observed the hour, and some days afterwards read in the paper that Ulrica's father had died a beggar. We, however, continued happy in our mutual love. Years had passed away, when, one evening, I received an invitation from one of my friends. I was on the point of going, when Ulrica asked me when I should return. I named a time; 'Leave me your watch then,' said she, 'that I may know exactly the hour at which I am to expect you, and delight myself with the prospect of your return.' I gave her the watch, and departed. When the appointed hour had arrived, I hastened back to my dwelling, entered Ulrica's chamber, and—found her in the arms of one of my friends. She screamed with fright, while I stood petrified, and consequently unable to prevent the flight of the seducer. We remained opposite to each other, perfectly silent. 'You must be more cautious,' I said at last, and tried to smile; 'you could have told by your watch when I was coming back, and when it was time to dismiss your other lover.' At these words, I took the watch, and pointed at it scornfully. 'It has stopped,' said Ulrica, turning away. The watch had indeed stopped, and had thus deceived the deceiver, and caused the discovery of her crime. With unspeakable horror, I looked upon the watch, which I still held, when the hands slowly moved, and the watch was going. I swore to be revenged on the faithless woman, but preserved a bland exterior, and, with her, quitted the city. When, after a long journey, we arrived here, I enquired, whether it would be possible to purchase a small house, in which my wife and I might dwell alone. I soon found one, and paid almost the entire remains of my ready money, and entered it with Ulrica. At night, when she was asleep, I tied a handkerchief about her mouth, that her cries might not alarm the neighborhood, and called her by her name. She awoke, and when she saw my ferocious countenance, stooping over her, knew my intention at once. She lay motionless, and I whispered into her ear: 'I have awakened you, because I would not murder you in your sleep, and because I felt compelled to tell you why I kill you: it is because you have betrayed me.' It is enough to say that I slew her. I had already turned the board from the floor, and now placed her in the cavity. I then took out the watch, as if, having betrayed the false one, it had a right to see how I revenged my wrong. It stood still, the unmoved hand pointing to the half-hour after midnight—the time when I murdered Ulrica. I laughed aloud, and sat down to write these lines. 'Tomorrow morning I shall lock up my house, and travel for a time. When I return, the body will have decayed.'

Manfred had read the manuscript, shuddering, and having finished it, looked again on the corpse of his friend. It had changed frightfully. The features which before had been so calm and clearly marked now bore an aspect of despair, and were distorted by convulsions. At this moment the mysterious watch, which Count Manfred had put into his breast pocket, began its regular sound, but so very loudly, that Manfred could hear plainly, without taking it out, that the watch was going.

An irresistible feeling of horror came over poor Manfred. He darted out of the room, and hurried into his own residence, in which he locked himself for the entire day. He had laid the watch before him, stared at it, and fearful thoughts crossed his mind. On the following day he was calm, but could not summon resolution to see the corpse again. He caused it to be quietly buried. The house he had already bought of poor Karl for the sake of contributing something towards his support. Some nights after the burial, the stillness of night was broken by an alarm of fire, and at the very house in which Count Karl had lived. At first, as the house was uninhabited, the opinion prevailed that it had been purposely set on fire, but, as it had not been insured, this opinion gained no credence. Count Manfred set out on his travels, that with the various scenes of a wanderer's life he might get rid of the gloomy mind that troubled him. The watch he took with him. He fancied that some great misfortune would befall him if he did not attend to it; he considered it as a sort of demon, always wore it, and regularly wound it up. For years it went well. Count Manfred had recovered his former cheerfulness, and indeed was happier than ever, for he loved and was loved in return. Dreaming of a happy future, he arose from his bed on the day appointed for his wedding. "I have slept long, perhaps too long," he said to himself. He caught up his watch to see how late it was, but—the watch had stopped. A loud cry of anguish arose from his heart; he hurried on his clothes, and hastened to his bride. She was well and cheerful, and Manfred laughed at himself for his foolish superstition. However, when the wedding was over, he could not refrain from looking at his watch once more. It was going. After some weeks, Count Manfred discovered that the ill-omened watch had spoken truly after all. He had been deceived in his wife, and found that she would bring him nothing but unhappiness. A melancholy gloom took possession of the poor Count. For whole days he would stare at the watch, and grinning specters seemed to rise from the dial-plate and to dance around him in derision. In the morning, when he arose from his bed, he looked trembling at his watch, always expecting that it would stop, and thus indicate some new calamity. He felt revived, and breathed again, when the hands moved on, but yet, from hour to hour, he would cast anxious glances at the watch. His wife bore him a son, and the feeling of parental joy seemed to dissipate his gloom. In an unusually cheerful mood he was seen to play with his child, sitting for half the day at the cradle, and by his own smile teaching the little one to smile also. The very watch, which had been the torment of his soul, must now serve to amuse the child, who laughed when it was held to his ear, and he could hear the soft ticking. One day, however, as Manfred approached the cradle, he found the child uncommonly pale. His heart trembled with anxiety, and, following a momentary impulse, he drew out the watch— which stood still. With a fearful cry Manfred flung it from him, so that it sounded on the ground, and, scarcely in a state of consciousness, buried his face in his hands. The child fell into convulsions, and died in a few hours. Manfred was, at first, beside himself with grief; then he became still, and walked calm and uncomplaining around the room in which the corpse lay. Having struck his fist against something, he looked down, and saw that it was his watch, which was still on the floor. He picked it up and held it to his ear—it was going. Manfred laughed aloud, til he made the silent room echo frightfully with the sound. "Good! Good!" he cried, with an insane look. "You will not leave me, devil! Stop with me then!" From this time, it was his serious conviction that the spirit of Karl the murderer, whom he had called his friend, had found no rest in the grave, but had been placed in the watch, that it might hover round him as a messenger of evil. He ceased to think of, feel, hear anything but his watch; he wound it up, trembling, every evening, and kept awake, gazing upon it. Some months afterwards his wife bore him a daughter, and died in childbed. The news made no further impression upon Manfred than that he had looked at his watch, and whispered, "It has not stopped."

When his newborn daughter was brought to him, he looked at her with indifference, and glancing at the watch said, "It will stop soon!"

His bodily strength soon gave way under this ceaseless anguish of mind. He fell into a violent fever, and, in a few weeks, was buried by the side of his son.

AN EVENING OF LUCY ASHTON'S

BY LETITIA ELIZABETH LANDON

(1833)

The autumn wind swung the branches of the old trees in the avenue heavily to and fro, and howled amid the battlements—now with a low moan, like that of deep grief; now with a shrill shriek, like that of the sufferer whose frame is wrenched in sudden agony. It was one of those dreary gales which bring thoughts of shipwrecks,—telling of the tall vessel, with her brave crew, tossed in the midnight sea, her sails riven, her guns thrown overboard, and the sailors holding a fierce revel, to shut out the presence of Death riding the black waves around them,—or of a desolate cottage on some lone sea-beach, a drifted boat on the rocks, and a bereaved widow weeping over the dead.

Lucy Ashton turned shivering from the casement. She had watched the stars one by one sink beneath the heavy cloud which, pall-like, had spread over the sky till it quenched even that last and lovely one with which, in a moment of maiden fantasy, she had linked her fate.

"For signs and for seasons are they," said the youthful watcher, as she closed the lattice. "My light will soon be hidden, my little hour soon past."

She threw herself into the arm-chair beside the hearth, and the lamp fell upon her beautiful but delicate face, from which the rose had long since departed; the blue veins were singularly distinct on the clear temples, and in the eye was that uncertain brightness which owes not its lustre to health. Her pale golden hair was drawn up in a knot at the top of her small and graceful head, and the rich mass shone as we might fancy shine the light tresses of an angel. The room was large, lofty, and comfortless, with cornices of black carved oak; in the midst stood a huge purple velvet bed, having a heavy bunch of hearse-like feathers at each corner; the walls were old; and the tapestry shook with every current of passing air, while the motion gave a mockery of life to its gaunt and faded group. The subject was mythological—the sacrifice of Niobe's children. There were the many shapes of death from the young warrior to the laughing child; but all struck by the same inexorable fate. One figure in particular caught Lucy's eye; it was a youthful female, and she thought it resembled herself: the outlines of the face certainly did, though "the gloss had dropped from the golden hair" of the picture sufferer.

"And yet," murmured Lucy, "far happier than I! The shaft which struck her in youth did its work at once; but I bear the arrow in my heart that destroys me not. Well, well, its time will come!"

The flickering light of the enormous chimney, whose hearth was piled with turf and wood, now flung its long and variable shadows round the chamber; and the figures on the tapestry seemed animated with strange and ghastly life. Lucy felt their eyes fix upon her, and the thought of death came, cold and terrible. Ay; be resigned, be hopeful, be brave as we will, death is an awful thing! The nailing down in that close black coffin—the lowering into the darksome grave—the damp mold, with its fearful dwellers, the slimy worm and the loathsome reptile, to be trampled upon you—these are the realities of dread and disgust! And then to die in youth—life unknown, un-enjoyed: no time to satiate of its pleasures, to weary of its troubles, to learn its wretchedness—to feel that you wish to live a little longer—that you could be happy!

"And," added the miserable girl, "to know that he loves me—that he will kneel in the agony of a last despair by my grave! But no, no; they say he is vowed to another—a tall, dark, stately beauty—what am I, that he should be true to me?"

She wrung her hands, but the paroxysm was transitory; and fixing her eyes on the burning log, she sat listlessly watching the dancing flames that kept struggling through the smoke.

"May I come in, Miss Ashton?" said a voice at the door; and, without waiting for an answer, an old crone entered. She approached the hearth, placed in a warm nook a tankard of mulled wine and plate of spiced apples, drew a low and cushioned settle forward, seated herself, and whispered in a subdued, yet hissing tone, "I thought you would be lonely, so I came up for half an hour's chat: it is the very night for some of your favorite stories."

Lucy started from her recumbent position, cast a frightened glance around, and seemed for the first time sensible of her companion's presence.

"Ah! is it you, Dame Addison? sooth it is but a dreary evening, and I am glad of a companion—these old rooms are so gloomy."

"You may well say so, for they have many a gloomy memory; the wife has wept for her husband, and the mother for her child; and the hand of the son has been against his father, and that of the father against his son. Why, look at yonder wainscot; see you no dark stains? In this very room—"

"Not of this room; tell me nothing of this room," half screamed the girl, as she turned from the direction in which the nurse pointed. "I sleep here: I should see it every night; tell me of something far, far away."

"Well, well, dear; it is only to amuse you. It shall not be of this room, or of this house, nor even of this country; will that please you?"

Lucy gave a slight indication of the head, and again fixed her gaze on the bright and sparkling fire; meantime the old woman took a deep draught from the tankard, disposed herself comfortably in her seat, and began her story in that harsh and hissing voice which rivets the hearing whereon yet it grates.

THE OLD WOMAN'S STORY

"Many, many years ago there was a fair peasant—so fair, that from her childhood all her friends prophesied that it would lead to no good. When she came to sixteen, the Count Ludolf thought it was a pity such beauty should be wasted, and therefore took possession of it: better that the lovely should pine in a castle than flourish in a cottage. Her mother died broken-hearted; and her father left the neighborhood, with a curse on the disobedient girl who had brought desolation to his hearth, and shame to his old age. It needs little to tell that such a passion grew cold— it were a long tale that accounted for the fancies of a young, rich, and reckless Cavalier; and, after all, nothing changes so soon as love."

"Love," murmured Lucy, in a low voice, as if unconscious of the interruption: "Love, which is our fate, like Fate must be immutable: how can the heart forget his young religion?"

"Many," pursued the sibyl, "can forget, and do and will forget. As for the Count, his heart was cruel with prosperity, and selfish with good fortune: he had never known sickness, which softens; sorrow, which brings all to its own level; poverty, which, however it may at last harden the heart, first teaches us our helplessness. What was it to him that Bertha had left the home which could never receive her again? What, that for his sake, she had submitted to the appearance of disgrace which was not in reality her?—for the peasant-girl was as proud as the Baron; and when she stepped over her father's threshold, it was as his wife.

"Well, well, he wearied, as men ever weary, of women's complaining, however bitter may be the injury which has wrung reproach from the unwilling lip. Many a sad hour did she spend weeping in the lonely tower, which had once seemed to her like a palace; for then the radiance of love was around it—and love, forsooth, is something like the fairies in our own land; for a time it can make all that is base and worthless seem most glittering and precious. Once, every night brought the ringing horn and eager step of the noble hunter; now the nights passed away too often in dreary and unbroken splendor. Yet the shining shield in the hall, and the fair current of the mountain spring, showed that her face was lovely as ever.

"One evening, he came to visit her, and his manner was soft and his voice was low, as in the days of old. Alas! of late she had been accustomed to the unkind look and the harsh word.

"'It is a lovely twilight, my Bertha,' said he; 'help me to unmoor our little bark, and we will sail down the river.'

"With a light step and yet lighter heart, she descended the rocky stairs, and reached the boat before her companion. The white sail was soon spread; they sprang in; and the slight vessel went rapidly through the stream. At first the waves were crimson, as if freighted with rubies, the last love-gifts of the dying Sun; for they were sailing on direct to the west, which was one flush, like a sea of blushing wine. Gradually the tints became paler; shades of soft pink just tinged the far-off clouds, and a delicate lilac fell on the waters. A star or two shone pure and bright in the sky, and the only shadows were flung by a few wild rose-trees that sprang from the clefts of the rocks. By degrees the drooping flowers disappeared; the stream grew narrower, and the sky became darker; a few soft clouds soon gathered into a storm: but Bertha heeded them not; she was too earnestly engaged in entreating her husband that he should acknowledge their secret marriage. She spoke of the dreary solitude to which she was condemned; of her wasted youth, worn by the fever of continual anxiety. Suddenly she stopped in fear; it was so gloomy around; the steep banks nearly closed overhead, and the boughs of the old pines which stood in some of the tempest-cleft hollows met in the air, and cast a darkness like that of night upon the rapid waters, which hurried on as if they distrusted their gloomy passage.

"At this moment Bertha's eye caught the ghastly paleness of her husband's face, terribly distinct: she thought he feared the rough torrent, and for her sake: tenderly she leant towards him—his arm grasped her waist, but not in love; he seized the wretched girl and flung her overboard, with the very name of God on her lips, and appealing, too, for his sake! Twice her bright head—Bertha had ever gloried in her sunny curls, which now fell in wild profusion upon her shoulders—twice did it emerge from the wave; her faint hands were spread abroad for help; he shrunk from the last glare of her despairing eyes; then a low moan; a few bubbles of foam rose off the stream; and all was still—but it was the stillness of death. An instant after, the thunder-clouds burst above, the peal reverberated from cliff to cliff, the lightning clave the black depths of the stream, the billows rose in tumultuous eddies; but Count Ludolf's boat cut its way through, and the vessel arrived at the open river. No trace was there of storm; the dewy wild flowers filled the air with their fragrance; and the Moon shone over them pure and clear, as if her light had no sympathy with human sorrow, and shuddered not at human crime. And why should she? We might judge her by ourselves; what care we for crime when we are not involved, and for suffering in which we have no part?

"The red wine-cup was drained deep and long in Count Ludolf's castle that night; and soon after, its master traveled afar into other lands: there was not pleasure enough for him at home. He found that bright eyes could gladden even the ruins of Rome; but Venice became his chosen city. It was as if the revelry delighted in the contrast which the dark robe, the gloomy canal, and the death-black gondola, offered to the orgies which made joyous her midnights."

"And did he feel no remorse?" asked Lucy.

"Remorse!" said the crone, with a scornful laugh; "remorse is the word for a child, or for a fool: the unpunished crime is never regretted. WE weep over the consequences, not over the fault. Count Ludolf soon found another love. This time his passion was kindled by a picture, but one of a most strange and thrilling beauty; a portrait, the only unfaded one in a deserted palace situate in the eastern lagune. Day after day he went to gaze on the exquisite face and the large black eyes, till they seemed to answer to his own. But the festival of San Marco was no time for idle fantasies; and the Count was amongst the gayest of the revelers. Amid the many masks which he followed, was one that finally riveted his attention. Her light step seemed scarcely to touch the ground, and every now and then a dark curl or two of raven softness escaped the veil; at last the mask itself slipped aside, and he saw the countenance of his beautiful incognita. He addressed her; and her answers, if brief, were at least encouraging; he followed her to a gondola, which they entered together. It stopped at the steps of the palace he had supposed deserted.

"'Will you come with me?' said she, in a voice whose melancholy was as the lute when the night-wind wakens its music; and as she stood by the sculptured lions which kept the entrance, the moonlight fell on her lovely face—lovely as if Titian had painted it.

"'Could you doubt?' said Ludolf, as he caught the extended hand; 'neither heaven nor hell should keep me from your side!'

"And here I cannot choose but laugh at the exaggerated phrases of lovers: why, a stone wall or a steel chain might have kept him away at that very moment! They passed through many a gloomy room, dimly seen in the moonshine, till they came to the picture-gallery, which was splendidly illuminated—and, strange contrast to its usual desolation, there was spread a magnificent banquet. The waxen tapers burned in their golden candlesticks, the lamps were fed with perfumed oil, and many a crystal vase was filled with rare flowers, till the atmosphere was heavy with fragrance. Piled up, in mother-of-pearl baskets, the purple grapes had yet the morning dew upon them; and the carved pine reared its emerald crest beside peaches, like topazes in a sunset. The Count and the lady seated themselves on a crimson ottoman; one white arm, leant negligently, contrasted with the warm color of the velvet; but extending the other towards the table, she took a glass; at her sign the Count filled it with wine.

"'Will you pledge with me?' said she, touching the cup with her lips, and passing it to him. He drank it—for wine and air seemed alike freighted with the odor of her sigh.

"'My beauty!' exclaimed Ludolf, detaining the ivory hand.

"'Nay, Count,' returned the stranger, in that sweet and peculiar voice, more like music than language—'I know how lightly you hold the lover's vow!'

"'I never loved till now!' exclaimed he, impatiently; 'name, rank, fortune, life, soul, are your own.'

She drew a ring from her hand, and placed it on his, leaving hers in his clasp. 'What will you give me in exchange—this?'—and she took the diamond cross of an order which he wore.

"'Ay, and by my knightly faith will I, and redeem it at your pleasure.'

"It was her hand which now grasped his; a change passed over her face; 'I thank you, my sister-in-death, for your likeness,' said she, turning to where the portrait had hung. For the first time, the Count observed that the frame was empty. Her grasp tightened upon him; it was the bony hand of a skeleton. The beauty vanished; the face grew a familiar one—it was that of Bertha! The floor became unstable, like water; he felt himself sinking rapidly; again he rose to the surface—he knew the gloomy pine-trees overhead; the grasp on his hand loosened; he saw the fair head of Bertha gasp in its death-agony amid the waters; the blue eyes met his; the stream flung her towards him; her arms closed round his neck with a deadly weight; down they sank beneath the dark river together—and to eternity."

THE HAUNTED HOMESTEAD

BY HENRY WILLIAM HERBERT

(1840)

THE MURDER

There are few wilder spots on earth, than the deep wooded gorge through which the waters of the mad Ashuelot rush southward from the pellucid lakelets, embosomed in the eastern spurs of the great Alleghany chain, whence it starts rash and rapid—meet emblem of ambitious man—upon its brief career of foam and fury. The hills—mountains, in bold abruptness, if not by actual height entitled to the name—sinking precipitous and sheer, to the bed of the chafing river, which, in the course of ages, has scarped and channelled their rude sides, and cleft the living granite a hundred fathom down, have left scant space below for a wild road, here hewn or blasted through strata of the eternal rock, there reared upon abutments of rough logs, and traversing some five times in each mile of distance, the devious torrent, as it wheels off in arrowy angles from side to side of its stern channel. Above, so perpendicularly do the cliffs ascend, that the huge pines, which shoot out from each rift and crevice of their seamed flanks, far overhang the path, dropping their scaly cones into the boiling cauldron of the stream, and almost interlacing their black boughs; so that mid-summers' noon scarce pours a wintry twilight into the damp and cavernous ravine, while a November's eve lowers darker than a starless midnight. Even now, when the hand of enterprise has dotted the whole circumjacent region with prosperous farms and thriving villages, it is a desolate and gloomy pass; but in the years immediately preceding the war of independence—when, for unnumbered miles, the land around was clothed in its primeval garniture of forest—when but two tiny hamlets, Keene and Fitzwilliam, had been late-founded on the mountain track, at that time the sole thoroughfare between the young states of New Hampshire and Vermont, with scarce a human habitation in all the dreary miles that intervened between those infant settlements, it was indeed as fearful, ay, as perilous a route as ever struck dismay into the bosom of lone traveller. Those were rude days and stern! those were days that, in truth, and in more modes than one, tried—shrewdly tried—men's souls! War had, indeed, passed over—but many of its worst attributes and adjuncts still harassed the unsettled land. Traffic had been well nigh abolished—the culture of the earth neglected—want, bitter want, pervaded the whole country—the minds of men, long used to violence and strife and rapine, slowly resumed their calm and governed tenor—disbanded soldiers, the outcasts of patriotic forces, broken and desperate characters, roamed singly or in bands, without resources or employment, through every state of the new union; nor had the Indian, undismayed by the weak government of the scarce-formed republic, ceased from his late-indulged career of massacre and havoc. Such was the period—such the nature of the times—when on a lowering and fitful evening toward the last days of October, a mounted traveller was seen to pass the sandhills, which form the jaws of the gorge on the southern side, on his way northward, to Vermont; wherein large tracts of fertile land were offered by the government for sale, at rates which tempted many to become purchasers and settlers in that romantic district. The sun had set already when he rode past the door of the one lowly tavern which then, as for the most part is the case in all new settlements, was the chief building of Fitzwilliam. A heavy mass of dark grey clouds, surging up slowly from the west, had occupied, at least, one half of the fast-darkening firmament; broad gouts of rain fell one by one at distant intervals; and the deep melancholy sough of the west wind wailed through the dismal gorge of the Ashuelot in sure foreboding of the near tempest. The landlord of that humble hostelry stood in his lowly door-way, and warned the lated wayfarer to 'light down for the night, and take the morning with him for his guide through the wild pass that lay before him; but he who was thus timely warned, shook his head only in reply, and asking, in his turn, the distance to Hartley's Hawknest tavern, learned that six miles of dangerous wild road, yet intervened between him and his destined harbor. For half a minute it seemed as though he doubted, for he drew in his rein and gazed with an inquiring glance toward the threatening heavens; at all events, his hesitation, if such it were, soon ended, he doubled the cape of his short horseman's cloak closer about his neck, touched his horse lightly with his spur, and cantered moderately onward. He was a tall and slight, though sinewy figure, with something in his air, and in the practiced grace wherewith he sat and wheeled his horse, that spoke of military service—nor did his dress, although not strictly martial, belie the supposition; the square-topped cap of otter-skin, the braided loops and frogs on his hussar-like cloak, the leathern breeches, and high boots, equipped with long brass spurs, were by no means dissimilar to the accoutrements of sundry among the regiments of continental horse, disbanded at the termination of the war, although divested of the lace and colored facings, which would have made them strictly uniform. The animal, moreover, which he rode, had evidently been subjected to the manege, for he was well upon his haunches, with the arched neck and light mouth, champing on the bit, that speak so certainly the well-trained charger—his saddle, too, equipped with holsters at the bow, and a small valise at the cantle, was covered with a handsome bear-skin; while the bridle, with its nosebag, its cavesson, and brass-scaled frontlet, had yet more certainly been decorated so for no pacific purpose. Darker, and darker yet, frowned the dim skies above him, as threading the black pass, with no guide save the chafing roar of the vexed waters, and the white glistening of their tortured spray, he hastened onwards; and now the wind, which had long sobbed and moaned among the giant pines, that lent a heavier gloom to the dark twilight road, raved out in savage gusts, whirling away the smaller branches, like straws, in their mad dalliance; the rain, at every lull, plashing upon the slippery rocks— the thunder crashing and roaring at the zenith, and the pale fires of heaven flashing in ghostly sheets across the narrow stripe of sky, which alone showed between the wood-fringed cliffs glooming on either hand, five hundred feet aloft. Yet not for rain or storm did the good charger flinch, or the bold rider curb him. With his head bowed upon his breast, his rein relaxed and free, and his foot firm in the stirrup, as confident of the high qualities of his generous steed, fleetly and fearlessly he galloped onward; turn after turn of the stern glen he doubled—bridge after bridge clattered beneath his thundering stride—mile after mile was won—and now, as he wheeled round the base of a huge rocky buttress—from which the stream, rebutted by its massy weight, swept off in a wide reach to the right hand, while on the left the hills receded somewhat from its brink, leaving a sylvan amphitheatre of a few acres circuit—the lights of the small wayside inn, known, in those days, to all who traversed the frontiers of neighbor states, as Hartley's Hawknest, glanced cheerfully upon the traveller's eyes. It was a long, low, log-built tenement, with several latticed windows looking toward the river it faced, the upper story projecting so far as to constitute a rugged sort of galleried piazza. A glorious weeping elm, that loveliest of forest trees, stood at the southern end; its drooping foliage, sere, now, and changed from its rich verdure, overshadowing many a yard of ground, and its gigantic trunk, garnished with rings and staples, whereto was fastened, as the stranger galloped up, two or three sorry-looking, ill-conditioned horses, meanly caparisoned with straw-stuffed pads and hempen halters, waiting the leisure of their masters, who were employed—as many a snatch of vulgar song, and many a burst of dissonant harsh laughter pealing into the bosom of the night, betokened—in rude debauchery within. A rudely-fashioned spout of timber discharged a stream of limpid water into a huge stone cistern, whence it leaped with a merry murmur, and ran gurgling down a pebbled channel to join the river in the bottom—and beyond this, a long range of sheds and stabling stood out at a right angle to the tavern. Pausing before the open shed, the stranger saw, with no small feeling of annoyance, that the whole length of its unplaned and sordid manger was occupied by a large drove of horses; while, by the stamp of hoofs within, and muzzling sounds as of beasts busy with their provender, he readily guessed that the stables, also, were completely crowded. Linking his panting charger, therefore, to one of the hooks in the elm-tree, and throwing his own cloak across its croupe, he stepped across the threshold into the thronged and smoky bar-room. The inn, as he had but too surely augered, was crowded to the utmost—a drove of horses, on their way southward from Vermont, had come in that same evening, their drivers having engaged every bed and pallet in the house—a dozen farmers of the neighborhood, scared from proceeding on their homeward routes by the terrific aspect of the night, had occupied the little parlor—the very bar-room was strewn with buffalo-skins and blankets, whereupon reposed a dozen sturdy forms, seemingly undisturbed by the obscene and stormy revelling of several of their comrades, who had preferred a night-long drinking bout to a hard couch and uncertain slumbers. There needed scarce a question to ascertain that not a spot remained where he could spread his cloak; nor, which weighed most with him, a shed, however lowly, wherein to stable his good horse. Nothing remained, then, but to procure a feed of oats for the worn animal, some slight refreshment for himself, and to proceed, as best he might, to Keene, still twelve miles distant, with the worst portions of the road yet to be overcome. No long space did it take the youth, for he was young and eminently handsome; and, as the lights displayed his lithe and active symmetry, set off by a close frock of forest green, edged in accordance with the fashion of the day, by a thin cord of gold, none who looked on him could fail to discover the gentleman of birth and breeding in every feature of his face, in every gesture of his active frame. And eagerly and keenly did many an eye of those who revelled around him, of those who seemed to slumber, scan his whole form, and dress, and bearing. Several gaunt, wolfish-looking men, muffled in belted blanket coats, bearded and grim and hideous, proffered him their revolting hospitality, and would fain, as it seemed, have entered into converse with him; but while offending none by anything of haughtiness or of direct avoidance, he yet withdrew himself from their company, and sat wrapped in his own meditations until the voice of the landlord summoned him to the scant meal, which he discussed in haste, and standing; this ended, he drew forth his purse to pay his reckoning; nor was it 'till he noticed the quick and fiery glances which shot from many an eye, dwelt gloatingly upon the silken network, through which gleamed many a golden coin, that he became aware of his imprudence in drawing out so large a sum, as he had thus unwittingly displayed before so doubtful an assemblage. Nor did the consequences of his error fail to stand visibly before him, when sundry of the bystanders offered to yield their places to the stranger, should he prefer to tarry; and one, a tall, dark-visaged, gloomy-looking man, wearing a long and formidable butcher-knife in his buff belt, and holding a tall rifle in his hand, announced his intention to ride some three miles on the way toward Keene, forthwith, to the spot where his own homeward path branched off from the main road, tendered his services and company, as a guide well acquainted with the pass; and even offered him a night's lodging in his own cabin. While thus addressed, the stranger was aware of a shrewd meaning look which the landlord cast toward him as he handed him his change; but seeing no mode whereby to avoid the man's society, and feeling that he should more easily be able to defend himself if assailed, against a person by his side, than against one who might, unseen, waylay him, he was contented with declining the night's lodging, and courteously accepted his assistance as a guide. The wind had quite sunk as he again mounted his recruited charger, and the storm had swept over; yet was the road as dark as a wolf's mouth through the ravine, which narrowed more and more as they proceeded farther, and was even more obscured by the precipitous hills and overhanging foliage. Slowly they journeyed on, compelled to spare their speed by the deep channels and huge stones which broke the surface of the path; and close and various were the questionings to which the traveller was subjected by his acute, although untutored, guide. Acute, however, as he was, he had met, in the stranger, his full match; for, seemingly responding to each query with perfect and accommodating frankness, he yet contrived to say no word which should give any clue to his intentions or his destination; so that when they had reached the spot where their paths separated, the countryman knew nothing more than when they had set forth, of his companion's views or business.

"Well, sir," he said, speaking in better language than might have been expected from his appearance and demeanor, "well, sir, since you will not accept my humble hospitality, I wish you a good night. We shall most likely never meet again—if so, I wish you well, sir. I, too, have been a soldier—mind, when you reach the next bridge, directly you have passed it, you take the right hand path; a little brook you'll have to ford, and it may be a thought high from this rain; but you will find it safe and a good bottom! No! no!" he added, as the traveller would have slipped a guinea into the hand he had extended—"no! no! I have done you no service; I will take no reward! Good night!"

"Good night, and thanks!" returned the other—and they parted! the traveller, in half repentant thought, blaming himself with generous self-reproach for the suspicious fears he had half entertained of his guides' good faith, and, for the moment, well nigh regretting that he had not accompanied the other to his hospitable home. But thoughts like these were soon absorbed in the necessity of looking to the guidance of his horse among the various difficulties of darkness and unknown road—and now he reached the first bridge, and the cross track by which he was directed to proceed. Yet, though he had forgot no syllable of his instructions, he hesitated; for the left hand was evidently the most trav-elled route, and that, by which he had been told to journey, seemed but a narrow and occasional by-path. He hesitated, and while he stood there, a wild whooping cry rang on his ear; a melancholy, long-protracted wail, followed by the quick flapping of wide wings. As the first sound burst on his ear, the horseman started, and half turned in his saddle, thrusting his hand, meantime, into his ready holsters—but as the final notes were followed by the heavy rush of pinions on the night wind—"Why, what a timorous fool am I," he muttered, "to be thus scared by the chance clamor of a silly fowl! Well! well! 'tis of a piece with my late doubts," and setting spurs to his reluctant horse—reluctant to turn into that by-path—he trotted forward. A few steps brought him to a small gloomy hollow—the bed of the brooklet mentioned by the farmer—now swollen by the late storm into the semblance of a wintry torrent, brawling among loose stones, and at a few yards' distance from the ford dashing a sheet of broad white foam over a rocky ridge into the fierce Ashuelot. The trees grew close down to the brink on either hand, o'ver canoping the dismal ford—the water was as black as Acheron! The traveller drew his rein, and steered his charger cautiously down the steep bank, when, as his fore feet touched the marge, a heavy blow was dealt him from behind, with a huge bludgeon, bowing him to the horse's neck. Before he could recover, a second followed, truly aimed the juncture of the spine and skull; a flash of myriad sparks streamed through his reeling eyes—his brain spun round and round—and, with a heavy sullen splash, he fell into the shallow pool—a strong hand wheeled the charger round, and a smart blow upon the quarters, sent him in full career over the self-same road he had lately traversed under the guidance of his master's hand. The fresh-ness of the water laving his forehead, lent, for a moment, a new life to the wounded traveller—he sprang to his feet, and grappled at the throat of his unseen assailant! Just at that point of time, a single sheeted flash, the last faint glimmering of the retreated storm, played for a moment on the sky—he recognized by that faint glimmer the dark visage and the gloomy scowl—he marked the glitter of the long butcher-knife, too late to parry its home thrust. One cry on God for mercy! one long, sick, thrilling gasp! one fluttering shudder of the convulsed and lifeless limbs! and his heart's blood was mingled with the turbulent stream—and he lay at the feet of his destroyer, a mere clod in the valley.

THE MYSTERY

It was now long past midnight, and—though the storm, which had so fiercely raved through the dim gorge of the Ashuelot, had spent its fury hours ago—the clouds yet hung heavy and low in grey and ghost-like wreath along the mountainsides; the stars were all unseen in their high places; the moon, hid in her vacant interlunar cave, offered no gracious rays to the belayed traveller. The lights, however, of the Hawknest, glimmering through its narrow casement, poured their long lines of yellow lustre into the bosom of the darkness, while, from within, the loud laugh of the revellers proclaimed that sleep, that night, held no uninterrupted sway over the inmates of the wayside tavern. The scene in the small bar-room was much the same as it has been described at a period some hours earlier on the same dismal night. The landlord, his avarice contending with his natural love of rest, scarce half awake, sat nodding in the bar; eight or nine men, in various postures of uneasy sleep, cumbered the unswept floor, wrapped up in blanket coats and buffalo robes; while five or six, their fellows, sat round a dirty pine table, playing at cards with a pack, the figures on which were all but invisible through the deep coat of filth and grease that covered them—and occasionally calling for some compound of the various fiery mixtures, which had already half-besotted their dull intellects. Such was the scene, and such the occupation of the casual inmates who that night filled the Hawknest tavern; when, suddenly, in the midst of a profound silence, which had endured for many minutes, unbroken, except by the fluttering sound of the cards, thrown heedlessly upon the board, the hiccough of the waking—or the heavy snore of the sleeping—drunkard!—suddenly there was heard a crash—a thundering crash, that made the walls of the low cottage reel, and the glasses positively jingle on the table—a crash, that simultaneously aroused all hands—some from their heavy slumbers, other from their engrossing game, to sudden terror and amazement! It seemed as if some ponderous weight had fallen on the floor of the room overhead. With anxious eager eyes the gazed into each other's faces, speechlessly waiting for some repetition of the sound! "What's that in the devil's name?" asked one, pot valor mingling strangely with amazement in his blank features—"What's in the chamber overhead?"

"Nothing," replied the landlord, who appeared the most thoroughly dismayed of all the company—"there's nothing in it now, nor hasn't been these ten years!"

"The chimney's fallen, then—that's it, boys! that's it, I'll be sworn, so you needn't look scart! The chimney's been shook by the wind, Jackson, and so it's jest now fell, and frightened all of us most out of our wits."

This explanation, plausible as it seemed at first sight, was eagerly admitted by the party, anxious to adopt any reasoning that might efface their fast-growing superstition—but as the speaker ceased—while two or three of the boldest were in the act of moving toward the door as if to ascertain the truth of his suggestion, a strange, wild, wailing sound was heard, as it were, of the west wind rising after a lull. There was, however, in its tone, something more thrilling and less earthly than ever was marked in the cadences of the most furious gale that ever swept over earth or ocean. Wilder it waxed and wilder—louder and louder every instant, till it was no less difficult to catch the import of words spoken in that sheltered bar-room than it had been upon a frigate's forecastle.

"God—what a hurricane!" cried one, and rushed to the door which opened directly on the road; but, as it yielded to his touch, no furious gust broke in—the air without was calm and motionless—not a twig quivered on the lofty elm, not a cloud stirred from its stance along the rocky flanks of the ravine, not a breath stirred the pendulous vane upon the gable—still that shrill, tremulous, rocking sound rang through the chambers of the tavern; and in an instant, every inmate of its walls, women and men and children, half dressed and pale, and trembling—as if ague-stricken—rushed down the creaking stairs, seeking for safety in companionship, and ere five minutes had elapsed, all were collected on the little space of greensward that sloped toward the east from the road downward to the river. Still the wild sound wailed on—and more than one of the stout woodsmen, their minds already half familiarized to that which had appalled them at the first, more from its suddenness than from any other cause, were rallying their scattered senses—when the tones rose yet shriller and more piercing, and changed, as it were, by magic, into a burst of the most fiendish and unnatural laughter; while two or three of the upper casements flew violently open, as if forced from within by some power which they could not resist. Upon the instant, actuated by some strange impulse which he could not have himself well explained, he who had been, from the first, the boldest of the party, levelled his rifle at the central window, and drew the trigger without uttering a word—the powder flashed in the pan, vivid and keen the stream of living flame burst from the muzzle, but the report, if such there were, was drowned in a yell that pealed from the same window, so horribly sustained, so long, so agonized, that the blood curdled in the stoutest hearts, while several of the women swooned outright, or fell into hysterics; and the continued outcries of the terrified children lasted long after the sounds, which had excited them, subsided into total silence—for with that awful and heart-rending shriek, the terrible disturbance ended. Some time elapsed without the utterance of a word—the distant lightning flickered across the dark horizon—the bat came flitting on his leathern wings around the eaves and angles of the low inn—the whip-poor-will was heard chanting his oft-repeated melancholy chant down in the thickets by the waterside, and the far rushing of the turbulent Ashuelot rose with a soothing murmur upon the silent night. By slow degrees the pallid and awe-stricken group recovered from their deep dismay—Dirk Ericson, the woodsman, who had discharged his rifle as fearlessly against the powers of air as though it had been against the breast of mortal foe—Dirk was a sturdy borderer from the frontiers of New York, whop had learned soldiership and woodcraft under the kindred guidance of Mad Anthony—Dirk Ericson was the first to enter the walls of the haunted dwelling, for such all now believed, closely escorted, however, by two sturdy brothers, Asa and Enoch Allen, sons of the soil, and natives of the wild gorge, through which they had so often chased the red-deer, or tapped the savage catamount. They entered, slowly, indeed, and guardedly—and with the muzzles of their true rifles lowered, and their knives loosened in the sheath as if to meet the onset of beings like themselves—but well-nigh fearlessly—for theirs were mountain-bred, tough hearts, which—the first sudden start passed over—feared neither man nor devil. They entered, but no sign or sight was there that showed of peril—lights stood there unsnuffed, capped with large, fiery fungusses, but burning quietly away—the glasses were untouched upon the board as when the revellers left them—the blankets of the sleepers lay undisturbed upon the dusty boards.

"Nothing here, boys," said the undaunted Dirk. "Let's see if the devil's upstairs yet! I a'n't afeared on him, boys, so how!" and snatching up a light, he rushed with a quick step, as though half doubtful of his own resolution, up the frail, clattering staircase. There, the large open space immediately above the bar-room, from which the other chambers opened, was, indeed, absolutely empty—there was no particle of furniture which could have fallen! no! not a billet of a wood, nor a stray brick! nor, in short, any symptom of the by-gone disturbance, except a few chips of plaster, which had been broken from the wall by Dirk's unerring bullet, and now lay scattered on the floor. They searched the house from the garret to the cellar, and found no living thing, and heard no sound, but of their own making. They joined the group upon the green, and as they told of their fruitless search, the courage of all present rose! And soon it was agreed that no one had been in the least degree alarmed; and it was almost doubted by some among the number, whether there had, indeed, been any sounds, but what might be accounted for on natural causes. While they were yet in anxious conversation, another sound came from a distance on their ears, but this time, it was one to which all there were well accustomed—the hard tramp of a horse, apparently at a full gallop down the pass from the northward.

"Here comes a late traveller," cried mine host. "Bustle, lads, bustle— best not be caught out hereaways, like a lot of scart chickens—jump, there, you Peleg Young, and fetch the lanthorn."

Some of the party, as he spoke, turned inward, and betook themselves to a renewal of their potations as to some solace for the troubles they had undergone; while others, Ericson and his confederate hunters among the number, lingered to greet or gaze at the new comer. Nearer and nearer came the hard clanging tramp—and now Dirk shook his head.

"There is no bridle on that beast," he said—"leastwise if there be a bridle, there a'n't no hand to steer it. Hark! how wildlike it clatters down yon stony pitch—now it has started off the road upon the turf—and now—its a shodden hoof, too—see how it strike the fire on the hill-side! There a'n't no rider there, or else my name's not Dirk."

Even as he spoke—bridled and saddled, but with his bridle flying loose, embossed with foam, reeking with sweat, and splashed with soil and clay of every hue and texture, a noble horse dashed at full speed into the very centre of the group, and stopping short with a couple of small, sudden plunges, and a wild whinny, stood perfectly quiet, and suffered Dirk to catch him by the bridle without any attempt at fight or resistance.

"Why, it's the traveller's horse," he cried, almost upon the instant— "the stranger gentleman's—that stopped in jest to supper, and rode on with black Cornelius Heyer. Here's a queer go, now! something's gone wrong, I reckon—show a light here!"

"The horse has come down, Dick, in the rough road; and the travel-ler's pitched off, I guess; we'll have him here to-rights," said Asa Allen.

"You're out this time, boy," answered the woodman; "this beast harnt been down this night, anyways," as he examined his knees by the light of the winking lanthorn, "and the stranger warn't the last to pitch off, if he had. That chap was an old Dragooner, and a Virginian too, I reckon. This bridle's broke, too—and see here, this long, thick wheal upon his flank— the traveller hadn't no whip with him—and the blow what made this, was struck from behind, by a man on foot—see, it slants downward, forward and downward, tapering off to the front end! There's been foul play here, anywise! Take hold of his head, Asa—and give me the light, you Peleg, till I look over his accoutrements. Pistols both in the holsters—that looks cur'ous, and—this here cover's been pulled open, though, and in a hurry, too, for the loop's broke—both loaded! Ha! here's a drop of blood—jest one drop on the pummel. The traveller's had foul play, boys—he has, no question of it!"

"And what we heerd, was sent to tell us on't!" replied another.

"Past doubt it was," said Dirk, "and we'll hear more of it, if we don't stir ourselves, and search out this unnat'ral murder. The task's fell upon us, boys; and have got jest to keep mighty straight, and obey orders! Who'll go along with me—you, Asa, and you, Enoch, I count upon— you'll stick to old Dirk's tracks, I know—who else?"

"I will,"—"and I,"—"and I," responded several voices of the rough borderers, who had again assembled at this new cause of excitement, and who were, perhaps, less alarmed at the prospect of a tramp through the woods, and even a skirmish with mortal enemies, than of passing the remainder of the night in that haunted homestead. Rifles were hunted up and loaded; pouches and horns and wood-knives slung or belted; horses were saddled; and in less than half an hour, eight hardy woodmen were in their stirrups, ready to follow old Dirk Ericson, wherever he might guide them.

"Well, Dirk, what's the fix now? how'll we set to, to find him?"

"Why, he set out from here, you see, with black Cornelius," answered the veteran, "and no one else has travelled up since they two quit, so we can take their track to where they parted; and so see, if it be, as Cornelius quit at his own turn; and if he did, two on us can jest ride up and see if he's in bed, and tell him how it's chanced; and the rest on us follow up the stranger's track to where the mischief has fell out. We'll hunt it out, I reckon—leastwise, if I lose the trail on't, there must be e'en a most plaguy snarl in't."

No more was said—the plan was evidently good—two or three lanthorns were provided; and having ascertained the tracks of the two horses—the noble charger of the stranger, and the mean gasson of the farmer—easily visible in the deep mud which lay in every hollow of the route, the little band got under way in silence. Their progress, was, of course, slow and guarded, for it was absolutely necessary to pause from time to time, and survey the ground; so to make sure that they had not o'errun the scent—but still at every halt, their caution was rewarded, for, in each muddy spot, the double trail was clearly visible. They reached the well-known turning, and, much to the relief of all concerned, in the night search, the farmer's hoof-track diverged from that of his companion, wheeling directly homeward; they could even see where the horses of the two had pawed and poached the ground, while they had held brief parley ere they parted.

"Now, then," said Dirk, 'so far, our course is clear! but now comes all the snarl on't. Well ,we must see to't how e can best. Asa and Enoch, hear to me, boys—follow up Heyer's track clear to the end on't—and take note of every stop and turn on't; and if he has gone home, creep up quiet to the windows, and see if he's in bed, or how. But don't you rouse him, no how—and when he's fairly lodged, the one on you set right down where you can watch the door, and let t'other come down to the road by the back track, past Lupton's branch, and so keep up the main road till he overtakes us. Take a light with you, boys, and keep a bright look out! The rest come on with me."

So perfect was the confidence of the whole party in the old hunter's sagacity that not a question was asked, much less an opinion given in opposition to his orders. Away rode the detachment, and on moved the main body—their work becoming, at every step, more difficult and intricate, since, having now no clue at all, they were compelled to ascertain the trail, foot by foot. Much time had been spent, therefore, before they reached the second turning of the road close to the bridge, under which Lupton's branch fell into the main river. Here, as we know already, the hapless rider had quitted the true path; and here our company, for the first time, overshot the scent—for, nothing doubting that the trail lay onward from the road, from the fork upward to the bridge, being so hard, and of a soil so rocky as to give no note of any footmarks—they galloped forward to the next muddy bottom, when, pausing to look for the guiding track, they found, at once, that it had not passed further.

"Here's the snarl, boys! here's the snarl," shouted Dirk. "Down, every one of you; we must e'en hunt it out by inches. You, Audrey Hewson, hold all the horses—Spencer and Young get forward with all the lights, and hold them low down to the earth, I tell you!"

His orders were obeyed implicitly; and in a short time the result was the discovery of the horse-track turning away from the other side of the bridge, into the blind and unused bye-path.

"There's deviltry in this," muttered the crafty veteran. "Dark as it was, there still was light enough to show the main track—and neither horse nor man would turn off into this devil's hole unless they had been told to. It's no use mounting, boys, I tell you—the trouble's hard by here, now I tell you!"

They made the trail good to the branch, the last tracks being of the hind feet on the very marge of the turbulent stream—they crossed it, but no footprint had deranged one pebble on the verge! "Try back, once more," cried Dirk, "try back—this is the very spot!" and in a few more moments the sod spurned up, where the startled charger had wheeled round in terror as his master fell, revealed another secret of the dark mystery. Every stone was now turned, every leaf or branch removed that might have been disposed to cover the assassin's tracks, but all in vain! A little dam of stones was now run out into the stream, under old Ericson's direction, so as to turn the waters into a channel somewhat different from their wonted course; a narrow stripe of mud was thus exposed to sight, which had, of late, been covered by the foamy ripples, and there, the very spot whereon the traveller's corpse had fallen, with a large foot-print by the side of it, was rendered clear to every eye! Beyond this, and one splash of blood close to the water's edge, all clue was lost. The morning dawned while they were yet busy with the search, and the broad sun came out, banishing every shadow, and revealing every secret of sweet nature, but no light does his radiance cast on this dread mystery. The woods were searched for miles around—the waters of the wild Ashuelot were dragged for leagues of distance—all to no purpose! No spot of soil had been disturbed—the pools and shallows gave up no dead.

While they were yet employed about the ford, one of the young allies returned with the tidings that Heyer's trail ran straight home—that his horse had been turned out into its wonted pasture—that the door was unlocked, and a light burning in the chamber, which showed the man calmly reclining on his bed in the undisturbed slumbers of apparent innocence.

With this all clue was lost; and, save that night after night the same hellish disturbances resounded through the chambers of the tavern, till the inhabitants, fairly unable to endure the terrors of this nightly uproar, abandoned it to solitude and ruin, the very story of the hapless traveller might well have been forgotten even on the very scene of his murder.

THE REVELATION

Days, weeks, and months rolled on—and still, as we have said, night after night the fearful din, the crash succeeded by those fiendish yells and that appalling laughter, rang through the chambers of the Hawknest Tavern. For a brief space the inmates strove to maintain their dwelling despite these awful visitations—but brief indeed was that space! For guest by guest, the old familiar customers fell off, deserting their accustomed stations by the glowing hearth in winter, or on the cool and shadowy stoop in the warm summer evenings. So widely did the terrors spread of the mysterious and unearthly sounds, which now clothed with a novel-horror the dark pass of the Ashuelot, that travellers began to shun the route entirely, preferring a circuitous and more fatiguing road to one whereon the Spirits of the Dead held, as it was almost universally believed, nocturnally their hellish orgies. The few and humble wayfarers who still held to the wonted path, hurried along, as the Spanish tourist has it, with beard on shoulder, stealing at every turn a fearful glance around them, making no halt nor tarrying on their journey, and shunning the pass altogether, save when the sun rode high in heaven.

The consequences of this change were sad in the extreme to Hartley—his occupation gone, his customers departed, his old friends gazing on him with doubtful and suspicious eyes, poverty staring him in his face, driven forth from his home at last by the overwhelming awe of those dread noises—he and his family were suddenly reduced from moderate affluence and comfort to the extremity of sordid want. A little cabin framed of rude lofs received them, a miserable hut, which had been raised for temporary occupation only, within a gunshot of the fatal bridge whereby the hapless traveller had fallen, involving in his ruin the innocent family of him who warned and would have succored him.

Game at this time abounded in the wild woods around, and by his rifle only did the unhappy landlord now support his once rich and respected household.

It is the way of the world to judge by result—and before long men who had known him from his cradle, and known his probity and worth, began to shrink from him, as one on whom the judgement of an offended Providence had weighed too visibly—whom punishment divine had marked out as a sinner of no small degree! They shrank from him at market, they drew aside from his contaminating touch even in the house of prayer—all shunned him, all with the exception of one man believed him guilty—guilty of that, too, which by no possibility, he could have committed—the murder of that youth who died at two miles distance, while Hartley was employed before the eyes of many in his own crowded bar-room. The man—the only man who drew yet closer to his side, who to the limit of his own scanty means assisted him, was Dirk, the hunter, while he who spoke the loudest in suspicious hints, and dark insinuations—who was he but the murderer?

Two years had passed, and now inseparable friends, Hartley and Dirk roved over the rude mountains side by side—there was no rock-ribbed summit which their adventurous feet had not mounted; no glen so deep but had resounded to the crack of their true rifles. Not a beast of the hills, nor a fowl of the air, but ministered to their support; and, though avoided by the neighbors as a spot, guilt-stricken and accursed, the little hut of Hartley was once again the scene of humble comfort, and of content at least, if not of happiness. The peltry, conveyed by old Dirk to the nearest market, sold or exchanged, yielded the foreign luxuries of clothing, groceries and liquor—the flesh of the deer, the hare, or the ruffled grouse simmered as temptingly on gridiron or stewpan, and tasted full as well, as veal or mutton. The little garden plot tended by Hartley's eldest, a fine lad now rising toward manhood, was rich with many a succulent root and savory herb. All prospered—poorly indeed, but hopefully and humbly!—all prospered save the man! No soothing of his anxious wife, no sparkling merriment of his loved children, no consolation cheery and bold of his bluff fellow could chase the now habitual gloom from Hartley's honest brow. To be suspected had sank, like the iron of the psalmist, into his very soul. To be condemned of men, no error ever proved against him—to be shunned like the haggard wolf—pointed by every finger in execration and contempt.

Two years had passed—and the same time, which had cast down the innocent from the good will of men, from the communion of his fellows, from wealth and happiness and comfort, had raised the real murderer to affluence and respect and honor. For many months after the perpetuation of his crime, he had pursued his ordinary avocations of the hard-working occupant of a small mountain farm; but when he found that suspicion had cast glimpse toward him but had on the contrary fixed steadfastly upon another, he gave out that a rich uncle had died suddenly in far-off Massachusetts, had journeyed thitherward, been absent several weeks, and returned rich in cattle, moveables and money, his wealthy kinsman's heir. The mountain farm, which had been heavily mortgaged, was cleared from all encumbrance. A new and handsome dwelling-house erected on a knoll o'erlooking proudly what was now called the Bridge of Blood, and Hartley's low-browed cabin. Gardens stretched down in pretty terraced slopes to the brink of the arrowy stream; orchards were planted in the rear; fine barns and out-houses were erected, among which stood now desolate and fast decaying the former homestead—the very hovel through the unshuttered lattices of which the Allens' had looked for and witnessed the feigned slumbers of the foul assassin.

Two years, as has been said, had passed; when one tempestuous evening old Dirk who still, as he would boast at times, feared neither man nor devil—set forth on his return from Fitzwilliam, wither he had come in the morning with a large pack of beaver. In driving a hard bargain with a peddler for his peltry, hour of daylight after hour had slipped away unheeded, and supper was announced, before the terms of sale were finally concluded—despite his wish to get home early, the veteran hunter could not refuse the invitation to "*sit* by," and it was eight o'clock before he started homeward—his pack supplied him with broadcloth and fifty things beside, in lieu of its furred peltry, his trusty rifle balanced on his shoulder, and his heart fortified, had that been needful, by a good stirrup cup of right Jamaica. Then as will often happen when men are in haste, accident after accident befell him; none indeed very serious, or even troublesome, but still sufficient to delay him on his route, so that his practiced eye read clearly from the position of the stars which blinked forth now and then from their dim canopy of storm that midnight was at hand ere he reached the old Hawknest.

"Well, well," he muttered to himself as he approached its lonely and decaying walls—"well! well, I've heern it afore now, and I guess it won't be the death of me, if I should hear it once again!"

Just then the winds rose high and swept the storm-clouds clear athwart the skies, and left them bright and sparkling with their ten thousand lamps of living fire. "Ha!" he exclaimed as he looked up—"I reckon its full time for't now," and as he spoke he stood and gazed with a strange sense of curiosity and wonder not altogether mixed, it is true, with a sort of half-pleasing apprehension. The windows, where the glass was yet entire, reflected back the quiet radiance of the moon—the door-way, wide open—for the door fallen inwards hung by one rusted hinge—showed cavernous and dark in the calm gleamy night—a bright wind whispered in the branches of the huge cluster, and a small thread of water from the horse-trough gurgled along its pebbly channel with a sweet peaceful murmur. The hunter's wonderment increased as he stood gazing at the tranquil scene, and he determined after a little hesitation to sit down by the streamlet's edge and wait to satisfy himself whether the fearful sounds still haunted the old tavern, or whether they indeed as he now half surmised had ceased for ever. No sooner was his resolution taken than he began to act on it—a moment's search sufficed to find a moss-grown seat of rock, another and his huge limbs were outstretched by the marge of the tinkling runnel, while with an eye as tranquil and as serene a brow, as though he were anticipating some long promised pleasure, he waited the repetition of the mysterious sounds which had so long driven from those mouldering walls all human occupants. In vain however did he wait, for the moon set, and the stars twinkled and went out, and amber clouds clothed the eastern firmament and day burst forth in its glory and no more fearful noise than the air murmuring in the branches, and the rill gurgling down to meet the noisier river, and the shrill accent of the katydid and cricket, the melancholy wailing of the whip-poor-will, or the far whooping of the answered owl fell on the hunter's ear. Cheery of heart he started up as the day dawned and hurried homeward with glad tidings—the Hawknest was no longer haunted!

On the next night at about nine o'clock a light was shining from the casement of the old bar-room, whence no light had flashed gladness on the traveller's eyes for many a weary month. Two men sat by the old round table on which lay, ready to each hand, two ponderous rifles, a watch, some food and liquor, and last not least a copy of the Testament! They were old Dirk, the hunter, and his comrade Hartley, who had returned to pass the night in that spot, and satisfy themselves fully that the disturbance was at rest for ever. It needs not to rehearse what passed that night—suffice it that no sound nor sight occurred, save the accustomed rural noises of the neighborhood; and that some two hours before daylight, they left the place convinced and joyfully on their route homeward.

Homeward they walked in glad and joyous converse, 'till on a sudden as they reached a little height commanding from a distance a view of ——'s new house and farm buildings, their eyes were suddenly attracted by an appearance of bright dancing lights—as of the aurora borealis—flashing and streaming heavenward from a focus situated as it seemed in the rear of the new-planted orchards. Strange were the sights indeed, flashes of vivid flame upleaping suddenly from earth and then a long dark interval and then a glimmering glow pervading the whole circuit of the homestead. Believing that a fire had burst out suddenly among the out buildings the veterans dashed forward with the wind and nerve that hunters alone can possess. They scaled the rocky height, dashed through the muddy hollow, reached the spot and there from the old house, now desolate and quite deserted, they saw these fearful flashes bursting at every instant. Through every chink and cranny of the door, the walls, the shutters, streamed the deep crimson glare, along the roof tree danced meteoric balls, of an unearthly pallid lustre on either gable that permanently fixed a globe or lurid fire.

"Fire! fire!" shouted Dirk—"Fire! halloa! halloa! Hans! the old house is on fire!" And with the words he rushed against the door and striking it with the sole of his foot broke every bar and fastening and drove it inwards, but within all was dark!—deep—solid—pitchy blackness.

Hartley and Dirk stared for a moment blankly each in the other's face, but the next they were met by ——, asking them with a volley of fierce imprecations what they intended by waking up his household thus with a false alarm.

"False alarm!" answered Dirk; "why had you seen it, I guess you'd not ha' thought it so false anyhow, why man, the whole air was alight with it."

"Pshaw! you're drunk both on you," returned the other. "You've brought your gammon to the wrong place, my men. Don't you see all's dark and quiet here, as honest men's homes ought to be. What are you arter I'd pleased be to know this time o'night!"

"That's neither here nor there," responded Dirk, "we saw a fire here-a-ways and we come neighbor-like to tell you on't."

"Well! where's the fire now, I'd like to be showed, then I'll think as how you meant honestly, and that's more too I tell you than all would, leastwise all men as knowed you, Hartley."

While these words had been passing, the party had been moving rapidly from the out-buildings, all walking fast under considerable excitement of their feelings toward the house, when suddenly Dirk turned about and instantly pointed toward the old homestead replied *"There 'tis!"*—and sure enough there the self-same appearances were visible! The red flame glaring out from every crack and cranny, the lurid flashes streaming high into the air above the roof tree—the incandescent globes sitting on either gable. *"There 'tis!*—what d'ye say now?"

"Pshaw! stuff," replied the other, "is that all?" and entered the house instantly, slamming the door violently after him.

"Is that all?—then he's used to it," muttered the other—"come aways, Hartley, come aways now I tell ye!—*Blood will out!*—Blood will out, man, and here I'm on the track on't now I tell you!"

Home they returned that night, and laid their plans in secret—the seventh day afterward—during the nights of all that seven, Hartley and Dirk watched undisturbed in the tavern, while the two Allens' lay in wait around the murderer's homestead, and every night beheld those wild and ominous flashes—the seventh day afterward a busy crowd were hard at work, masons and carpenters, about the ruined Hawknest. Hammers were clanging, saws were whistling and grating, and above all the merry hum of light, free-hearted labor rose on the morning air. On the tenth day the family returned to take possession, the old sign was hung out, the old bar was replenished with its accustomed bottles, and all things fell again into their ordinary course. Meanwhile night fell again into their ordinary course. Meanwhile night after night, the Allens' and old Dirk hung round —— buildings, and still the hellish lights were seen glancing and flashing bright and clearly visible for many a mile around, and still no note was taken by —— or any of the household. The autumn passed away—winter came on cold, cheerless, and severe; and the old Hawknest tavern once again re-established with all its pristine comforts, travellers once more turned their steps along the wonted road; old friends too, as prosperity returned, returned with many a greeting—men wondered how they could have doubted or for a moment thought ill of kind, good neighbor Hartley. As these events took place, rumor, and public talk were busy with ——! With the descent of Hartley's star, to borrow the Astronomer's jargon, his had risen gloriously—now Hartley was again in the ascendant; and his correspondingly declined! No fear however—no dark anticipation appeared to cloud his days—his nights, despite those fearful sights, were seemingly all fearless. Still the spies lay around him, they listened at his fastened doors, they peeped in through his guarded casements, and ere long murmurs went through the mouths how —— and his wife strove fiercely, how no peace was in that household, how no prosperity had followed those ill-gotten gains.

One night old Dirk, with his two comrades, lay there as was their wont, marking their destined prey, that night more terribly than ever the furious flames arose, and sounds unheard before—the same wild yells and bursts of fiendish laughter which had driven Hartley from his Hawk-nest, rang round the gleaming buildings! That night more bitterly than ever rose from within the dwelling house the voices of contention and strife. The shrill notes of the terrified and angry wife, pealed piercingly into the ears, while the deep imprecations of the man, answered like muttering thunder. At length the door burst open—lantern in hand —— rushed forth. "By God," he cried, "this night shall finish it, or finish me!" *And it did both!*

Straight he rushed to the desolate building, entered it, and again after brief stay rushed forth as if beneath the goad of Orestes' furies—dashed back into his own dwelling—and within ten minutes' time, a volume of fierce *real* flame burst out of every crack and cranny—the shingled walls blazed out, the thatch flared torch-like heavenward—the rafters smouldered and cracked, and leaped out into living flame, and all glowed like a tenfold furnace, and rushed earthward and was dark. The Haunted Homestead was no more upon the earth!

With that night ceased all sights or sounds unearthly, but still suspicion ceased not. Ceased not—nay it waxed ten times wilder, more rife, more stirring than before! Men muttered secretly no longer, but spoke aloud their doubts—almost their certainty. Meantime winter wore onward—Christmas was passed, and February's snows had covered the whole face of nature. It was a dark and starless night—the wonted party were assembled in the old bar room, when there arrived a stranger, a tall, dark, handsome, military-looking man, on whom scarce had Dirk's eyes and Hartley's fallen ere a quick meaning glance was interchanged between them. The likeness struck both on the instant, strange likeness to the murdered traveller.

With his accustomed depth of wild sagacity, the veteran hunter turned, without noticing apparently the stranger, on the occurrences which had so strangely agitated the inmates of that house and valley. Ere long the stranger's face gave token of anxiety and wonder, and one word led to others, and questions answered brought but fresh questions, until it came out that the man before them had at a period corresponding to that of the commencement of our tale lost his only brother—one whose demeanor and appearance agreed in all particulars with the description given by the woodsmen of the unhappy traveller, who had fallen.

It was resolved on the next morning to probe the mystery to the utmost. An appointment was made instantly for an early hour on the following day, when the two Allens, Dirk, and Hartley, professed their readiness to guide their new friend to the scene of the murder. But as the woodsmen departed one or two noticed that the night had changed—that it was mild and soft, and the snow sloppy under foot, and all predicted confidently that the slight snow would be gone on the morrow.

And so in truth it was, morn came, and the whole earth was bare, and the soft western wind swept with a mild low sigh over the woody hills. Scarce had the morning dawned, ere they were on the ground—and lo! wonders of wonders—on one spot, exactly on the site of the burnt building a little space of snow lay still—there was none else for miles around—precisely in the form of a man's body.

"He's there," cried Dirk exultingly, "he's there!—when there's a ground thaw the snow always lies over a buried log or any thing that checks the rising best—he's there. Get axes, boys, and you'll see as I tell's true!"

Axes and crows were brought, the earth was upturned, and there! there! under the very spot whereon the murderers bed had stood the night before he slept so calmly—there lay a human skeleton—a few shreds of green cloth, bordered with narrow cords of gold, a pair of horseman's pistols, rusted and green with mold. The stranger seized them. "Oh God!" he cried, "my brother's—oh! my brother's!"

The tale is told—for it boots not to dwell upon the murderer's seizure—his agony—his confession and despair. Enough the Hawknest Tavern still invites the weary travellers to enter its portal—and Hartley's name in this, third generation, is blazoned on the time-worn sign post, while near the Bridge of Blood a heap of shattered ruins are still pointed out, where stood the *Haunted Homestead.*

THE WITHERED MAN

BY WILLIAM LEETE STONE

(1834)

"It is impossible to sail while the wind tears at this rate—it's a fearful night, sir," said an elderly, weather-beaten man, addressing himself to one who appeared to be in the prime of life, and who by his impatience showed that he had been unaccustomed to having his wishes thwarted.

"Try it, Hazard," he replied, casting an anxious look at the troubled sky, and pacing backward and forward on the beach, alternately gazing on the broad Hudson, tossed by the hurricane which now roared along its surface, and then on his faithful attendant, who by his looks evinced that he thought it a desperate undertaking. "Try it, man," he repeated, "we may as well drown as—"

"Try a fool's errand and be drowned for your pains," exclaimed a rough voice, in a jeering tone, and at the same moment a man, evidently in a state of partial intoxication, emerged from the wood which stretches itself to the very brink of the river.

"You think it unsafe, then," said the stranger, in a conciliatory tone.

"Think it unsafe!" retorted the man, with a sneer; "I guess I do. But if you have a fancy for a dip in the Hudson tonight, I'm not the man that's going to say nay to it;" and bursting into a fit of obstreperous laughter, he reeled back to his companions, whose revelry was now heard by the visitants in the distance.

The gusts of wind became more and more frequent, sweeping up through the Horse Race, and howling over the mountains with indescribable fury, while the rain, which had been some time gathering in dark clouds overhead, poured down in torrents. "There is no remedy," said the stranger to his companion, who waited with considerable anxiety for his orders. "It would be madness to attempt a departure. Pull up the boat into yonder cove, and fasten her where she will be sheltered from the storm, and let us see what kind of a reception we shall meet with from those fellows." So saying, he turned towards the wood which covered a wild, rocky glen, and soon discovered by the light of a blazing fire the solitary cottage in which these revelers were carousing. As he approached, the din of human voices rung in his ear, until some kind of silence being obtained, one of the parties commenced a bacchanalian song. The location of the hut, and the appearance of the company within, had both a suspicious aspect. And as the stranger had approached unperceived, availing himself of the partial shelter from the tempest afforded by the rock which formed one side of the rural habitation, and against which rested the ends of the un-hewn timbers of which the front was constructed, he stood for a few moments to reconnoiter, and overheard the following song:

"I'll sing you a song that you'll wonder to hear,
Of a freebooter lucky and bold,
Of old Captain Kid—of the man without fear—
How himself to the devil he sold.

His ship was a trim one as ever did swim,
His comrades were hearty and brave—
Twelve pistols he carried, that freebooter grim,
And he fearlessly ploughed the wild wave.

He ploughed for rich harvests, for silver and gold,
He gathered them all in the deep;
And he hollowed his granaries far in the mould,
Where they lay for the devil to keep.

Yet never was rover more open of hand
To the woodsmen so merry and free;
For he scattered his coin 'mong the sons of the land,
Whene'er he returned from the sea.

Yet pay-day at last, though unwished and unbid,
Comes alike to the rude and the civil;
And bold Captain Kid, for the things that he did,
Was sent by Jack Ketch to the devil."

"Avast there!" exclaimed an old weather-beaten man, with curled gray hair, and a thick beard which had not met a razor for weeks. "Robert Kidd was no more hanged than I was, but spun out his yarn, like a gentleman as he was, and died of old age and for want of breath, as an honest man should."

"Nay, Wilfrid, blast my eyes if he wa'nt hanged at Execution Dock; for don't the song say so, that the boys are singing, 'When I sailed, when I sailed,' and so on?"

"No, Rollin," replied the other; "I tell you he was no more hanged than I am hanged, and what's more, they dar'nt hang him, although parliament folks raised such a breeze about it, when old Bellmont nabbed Rann there away in Boston."

"That's a likely story, Wilfred," exclaimed, with an oath, a dark, brawny-looking fellow, with bushy hair and black shaggy whiskers. "How do you know anything about it?"

"Know! Why I know all about it. Didn't I live at Governor Fletcher's, seeing as how I was born without any parents? And didn't the governor ship me as a cabin boy for Kidd? And didn't I sail from New York to the Bahamas with him, and from the Bahamas to Madagascar, and a place which I could never see, called El Dorado? And a fine time we'd had on't for one cruise—though we took a fine haul of doubloons from the Dons for all that—if that New Englander, Phipps, with the Algier-Rose, armed, they said, by the Duke of Albemarle, hadn't got the start of us, and fished up the old sows of silver from the Spanish wreck down by Hispaniola there. And didn't I see the Captain at Wapping once, long after the land-pirates said he was hanged at Execution Dock?"

"And so he was hanged," said another, "or I'll make my supper of snakes and milk."

"'Tis no such thing," replied Wilfrid; "for though I was a boy then, I've got everything logged in my memory as though 'twas but yesterday. I overheard some of the secrets one day in Fletcher's cellar, and if it hadn't been for Kidd, I guess some folks would have had less manors up along the river there. I guess, too, he'd have made some of their dry bones rattle if he'd told half he knew about Fletcher, and Bellmont, and old Somers, and the Duke of Shrewsbury, and some other big wigs that I could mention. No, you have Jack Wilfred's word for it, that the king himself would not have dared to hurt a hair of the bold rover's head, without stopping his mouth first."

"Well, whether he was twitched up by the neck or not," croaked out another hoarse voice, "I think we've his match cruising about the coast now, in old Vandrick."

"That I'll swear you have," replied Wilfred, "and you may throw in the devil to boot, for that matter. But—"

At this moment the conversation was arrested by the entrance of the stranger, who chose no longer to abide the pelting of the storm. In an instant all was hushed, and every eye fixed on him with that rude stare, with which vulgar people generally receive new faces. The stranger moved towards the fire without seeming disconcerted by his reception, and merely remarking that the night was very tempestuous, seated himself in a retired part of the room. One of the company, who seemed more inebriated than his companions, with a vacant grin between a smile and a laugh, staggered towards him with a cup of spirits, probably intending it as a mark of hospitality, and told him to drink. The offer was declined, upon which the fellow's brow darkened and, raising his arm with an air of menace, he swore a deep oath that he should fill the cup instantly, or—

At this moment the drunkard was appealed to by several voices at once, on a subject which seemed to be exciting considerable contention among the party, and the intruder, left unmolested, was now enabled to survey the strange society into which he had been so unexpectedly and unwillingly thrown. The company consisted of about twenty men, mostly in the prime of life, inhabiting the Highlands, just above the confined channel now called the Horse Race, and in the neighborhood of what was afterwards the site of Fort Montgomery. Their professed occupation was that of woodsmen; but their most profitable employment was that of assisting in the secretion of goods and valuable property brought to this retired spot by freebooters, who levied contributions at sea under the black flag and pennant. The neighboring country was exactly suited to purposes of this kind, abounding in places of concealment, where many a deed of blood had been executed without fear of detection, and many a treasure secreted without danger of discovery.

It may seem strange that mingling with desperadoes of this kind, the inhabitants should not have participated more in that ferocity of disposition which distinguishes such wretches. But this was not the case. While they assisted the pirates, they feared and hated them; and while they concealed their atrocities, never partook in them. They were bound together only by the ties of interest. Each party had become necessary to the other. The pirates having once confided in them, felt the danger of seeming to distrust them; and the Highlanders, although frequently disgusted with their visitors, did not think it safe to betray them, because they knew that the law might reckon with them for offences long past, while they would be perpetually exposed to the piratical vengeance of any who should escape. Under these feelings they drowned disagreeable reflections in revelry, and, during the absence of the freebooters, squandered away the share of spoil they received as a recompense of their silence.

Such were the people among whom the stranger now found himself, and it may easily be supposed that his sensations were not of the most agreeable kind. But he wisely judged that his best way would be to affect unconcern; and throwing out his legs before the fire, and breathing hard, as if, overcome with fatigue, he had fallen asleep, he listened to the conversation which was carried on, in an undertone of voice, by two or three of the party, who, having drunk less freely than the others, had not yielded to the same soporific influences.

"I tell you, Tom, I heard it and saw it all," said a young man, who seemed less schooled in debauchery than the rest, to an aged sailor who appeared to listen with surprise, and occasionally shuddered with horror;

"I tell you, Tom, I saw it and heard it all; and since that moment it has never been out of my sight, night or day. And it's only last night I went by that very spot, and heard a groan which I shall never forget."

"Curse him," replied the old man, "and cursed be the day I ever entered into his villainous secrets. So long as he chooses to hide his gold here, it's not for me to ask anything about how he came by it. But murder in cold blood's another thing, and Tom Cleveland's not the man to help in such work."

"Hush," replied his comrade—for the old man's voice had been unconsciously raised, as his spirit boiled at the idea of being connected with the murderer—"hush, Tom, and don't plague yourself now about the difference between hiding blood and helping to spill it. In my mind both's bad enough. But let's see what's to be done, for Vandrick will be sure to be here again in a week."

"I'll leave," said the old man, "if it costs me my life."

"And so will I," said the younger one, "for no man can prosper with blood-spots on him. But let's turn out now; the rain's almost over, and all these fellows are asleep."

"A good thing if they slept their last," muttered his companion. "Some of them know more than I thought they did, or I'd never have been here now. But come along, and let's have this tale of yours fairly out. It makes me feel as if hot water was trickling down my back to think on't."

So saying they crossed the threshold, and disappeared into the gloom. The stranger's curiosity had been strongly excited, and, rising, after they gone out, he watched the direction they took, and then striding across two or three of the revelers, who lay snoring on the floor, he silently took the same path, and, guided by their voices, was easily enabled to fix himself in a situation where he could hear all that was said without being observed.

"After I had shown him this spot," said the one who had commenced the conversation, "to which he could bring his boat in the dark narrow channel of the creek, he bade me begone, with a look that seemed to say, 'Stay at your peril.' So I thought, 'sure enough there's something he wants to keep secret, is there? But if I know half, I'll know it all.' So, after turning round the little clump of cedars, I easily crawled up and hid myself among yon pile of rocks—a place he knows nothing of—and saw as well as heard all that passed. After he and his men had dug the hole, they went back to the schooner, and never shall I forget the sight I then saw. They all came back together, and who should they have with 'em but an old man, trembling with age, who seemed as if his whole heart was fixed on the gold they had in the pot.

" 'What! Will ye not leave a poor old man sixpence, ye wretches, but bring him here to see you bury it? Many a weary night's calculations has it cost me, and many a tempest I have encountered, in earning it, ye thieves,' said the old man, looking wistfully at the gold. 'Many's the time it's been through my fingers; and am I come to this, after all my toil, to see it wasted here, when a good nine per cent might be made of any doubloon of it? Twenty thousand pounds sterling at nine PER CENT for only six years, would be—'

" 'Hold your prating, you old fool,' cried Vandrick, as he went on muttering his calculations of usury. 'You have had pleasure enough in gathering up your gold, and I hope to have the pleasure of spending it. 'Thieves' and 'wretches' call you us? And did it never occur to you, during the long years that you have been employed in stealing people in Africa as good as yourself, to sell them in Hispaniola, to look into your mirror, and see what sort of man you are yourself? For these ten years I have kept my eye on you, old boy, resolved to pick you up, whenever you might leave your El Dorado for the old country, and I've overhauled you at last. I have caught you, as you have caught thousands in Africa, and thus far I am a thousand times the better man. You never loved anything else but your gold, and cheer up, old man! you shan't be parted from it. Harkee, old fellow! will you do a message for me to the devil?'

" 'You are the devil yourself, I think,' said the old man, 'or you'd never be so wasteful of money, which cost—'

" 'How many negroes, my old Croesus?' demanded Vandrick, with a sneer.

" 'So much labor to get it,' continued the old man, without regarding the interruption, 'and might be let out, on good security, for nine *per cent*, which, on twenty thousand pounds, would yield—'

" 'Just eighteen hundred pounds a year, old Gripus,' retorted Vandrick. 'You shall go and see what the devil will give you for it. Come along,' continued the pirate captain to the men who now deposited the pot of gold in the hole which had been prepared for its reception; 'I'll be parson.' Then taking the old man by the collar, who looking wildly about him, seemed quite unconscious of their purpose, he walked three times round the pit, and turned and advanced directly to its brink. With the quickness of a flash he drew a knife from his leathern girdle, from which hung a number of pistols, and plunged it to the hilt in the bosom of the prisoner. A deep groan was the only sound he uttered, as a few drops of blood trickled from the wound, and, falling forward into the pit, he expired. The pirates then joined hands, forming a circle round the hole, while the captain repeated some strange mummery, which I cannot recollect.

"'After all this was over, they hastily covered up the hole, took such observations, and made such memoranda as would enable them to find the spot again, and returned to their vessel. But the last groan of that poor old man I cannot forget; and it's only last night, as I was walking by that spot, I heard it as plain as I did the very moment Vandrick stabbed him.'"

"It's a horrible story, indeed," responded Cleveland. "Mercy on us sinful men! To have any dealings with Vandrick and his crew! But I'll never believe the devil cares for him or his money, and I know what I'll do—"

"Not touch the gold?" said his companion, trembling at the thought.

"Never," responded his companion; "I am not going to touch what has been blasted by the black mummery of Vandrick. Preserve me from connection with the devil or his crew! But meet me here tomorrow night—" The rest was spoken so low as to be inaudible. But they agreed to meet again, and parted.

The stranger, who had heard all that passed, now left the retreat, and bent his way back to the cottage, or rude cabin rather, which was by this time cleared of its visitants. The gray tints of the morning were beginning to appear, and the sots, one by one, had strolled away from the scene of their recent and frequent carousals. He immediately walked towards the shore, where he found his attendant anxiously awaiting him, and glided down the Hudson. For reasons which are altogether unknown, he never allowed what he had heard or seen to pass his lips, and his account of it in manuscript was not discovered until many years after his death.

In the mean time the Revolutionary War had broken out, and various fortifications were planted among the fastnesses of the Highlands. Fort Montgomery had been erected on a little plain immediately north of the deep, narrow creek of which we have already had occasion to speak, and picquets of observation were posted in various directions. Among other stations the one we have just described was selected, and a sentinel paced every night fifty yards of the spot where Vandrick had concealed his treasure. On the first night of duty at this point, during the middle watch, the sentinel heard the noise of approaching footsteps among the bushes skirting the margin of the creek, with low, sepulchral voices, mingled with harsh, shrill, and unearthly sounds, as of people in half-suppressed conversation. Having hailed without answer, he fired his piece, and retreated instantly to the guardhouse. A sergeant with a squadron of men was dispatched to the spot, but no enemy could be discovered, although the sentinel stoutly persisted that he heard noises which were ample cause of alarm. The second night a similar alarm was given by another sentinel when upon the middle watch, with the additional assurance that he had seen a mysterious shadow, like a boat with persons therein, skimming along under the deep shade cast upon the water by the opposite mountain, until it came over against the mouth of the creek, when it shot across the river in a twinkling, and disappeared amid the foliage which overhung the cove. Presently afterwards he heard the noise; but it was not until he had actually seen figures moving among the trees, that he discharged his piece. These alarms were repeated several times, and always with the same unsatisfactory results. At length a resolute fellow by the name of Bishop, of the Connecticut line, volunteered to mount guard upon this startling post during the hours of alarm, vowing with many bitter oaths, that he would not yield an inch until he encountered some overpowering force, and given them three rounds of lead and twelve inches of cold iron.

He was a man of great personal bravery, and was resolved not to be trifled with; and his comrades well knew that what he said was no idle boasting. They knew that whether encountered by "a spirit of health or goblin damned," bringing with it "airs from heaven or blasts from hell," it would be all the same to Thal Bishop; he would "speak to it," and have a brush with it, too, if he could. Bishop had no superstition about him; but still he had heard of the utility of silver bullets in certain exigencies, and he thought it was no harm to cut a few Spanish dollars into pieces to be used as slugs with his balls; and his cartridges had accordingly been made up with a leaden bullet and three silver slugs each. Thus provided, with a heart that never quailed, and limbs that never shook, he repaired to his station.

It was a clear night, and the moon rose so late in the evening, that the lofty mountains on the east side of the river, now called Anthony's Nose, cast its dark shadow far across the water. Bishop had not occupied his post until midnight, before his vigilant eye discovered what seemed to be the shadow of a boat, with a sail set, issuing from a little cove at the foot of the mountain before mentioned, some three-quarters of a mile down the stream. The shadow seemed to glide along near the bold shore on that side of the river, until opposite the mouth of the creek, when it darted across and disappeared in its estuary. Bishop soon heard a rustling among the trees. He cocked and pointed his piece, and stood firm. Very soon he saw figures gliding among the bushes, and presenting his musket in that direction, he commanded them to "Stand." No attention being given to the caution, he fired and immediately reloaded. While he was thus occupied, a figure considerably below the common size, wrinkled and deformed, made its appearance, and approached him. He immediately fired with a precision that he judged would have winged a duck at a hundred yards. But regardless alike of lead and silver, the figure, unmoved, kept his way. As he approached, and came crowding steadily on, Bishop involuntarily retreated, but not without loading and firing at every step. Still the strange figure pressed on. At one moment by the light of the moon he caught a full view of this mysterious visitant, but could distinguish nothing about him peculiar, excepting the piercing keenness of his sunken eye, and the air of magisterial authority with which the little withered semblance of humanity waved him to retire. On the first report of Bishop's musket, the guard, which was to a man upon the "qui vive," was mustered, and marched, or rather ran towards the spot. Their curiosity, however, was not satisfied; for after he had passed a certain boundary, the figure always disappeared, and the foremost only of the guard now arrived in season to catch a glimpse of him as he vanished into thin air.

These circumstances soon became noised abroad, the tale, as usual, losing nothing in its progress; and the officers of the garrison, becoming satisfied that no sentinel could be kept upon the post, after due consultation abandoned it. Every inquiry was of course made about this unaccountable appearance; but nothing satisfactory could be obtained. All the inhabitants from Haverstraw and the shores of the Tappen Sea to Buttermilk Falls had a dread of that spot. An old man, who kept the ferry at the entrance of the Horse Race, and who was the patriarch of that region, was the only being able to give any account of it. He said that groans had been heard there, and figures seen about it, for fifty years; and that when he was a child, the inhabitants were greatly alarmed by the appearance of a mysterious bark, which, gliding down the river, shot into the cove formed by the mouth of the creek with the swiftness of an arrow. No human being could be seen in it excepting the helmsman, who was a little deformed man with withered cheek and sunken blue eye. He never left the helm, and wherever he turned the vessel, blow the wind as it would, or not at all, she darted forward with the swiftness of lightning. Her sails were black, and her sides were painted of the same color; and a black flag with a death's head and cross-bones, floated from the top of her mast. After remaining there about an hour, when last seen by the inhabitants, she departed, and had not been heard of since. A few hours after her last visit, there was found at the head of the cove a freshly dug pit, in the bottom of which the shape of a large pot was distinctly defined in the earth, and a skull, with a few human bones, were scattered about the ground. Groans are still said to issue from the wood, at the hour of midnight, and a figure similar to that which has been described, is reported to flit restlessly through the glade. Certain it is, that old and young alike are careful to avoid getting benighted near the Haunt of The Withered Man.

LA MALROCHE

BY LOUISA STUART COSTELLO

(1833)

When the wanderer in the Montre-Dores has reached the basaltic mass, on which stand frowning in ruin the remains of the castle of Murat-le-Quaire, he looks round on a vast forest of pines of gigantic dimensions, and his eye follows the course of the Dordogne as the mysterious river winds along between the granite rocks which bound it, and as it emerges in light amongst the emerald meadows, whose freshness soothes the sight; here and there remnants of antique forests of beech are scattered along the banks, and numerous villages start up close to their embowering shades.

Amongst them is the secluded hamlet of Escures, placed at the foot of a dark and rugged mountain, separated from it by a broad plateau of basaltic formation, wild, barren, and desolate. The mountain is called La Malroche, and has a very bad reputation in the neighborhood; indeed, the village of Escures is seldom visited by any of the peasants, unless some particular business obliges them to seek it. The inhabitants of Quaire, La Bourbole, Prenioux, and Saint Sauves, are all unwilling to pass through Escures, and frequently go out of their way to avoid it.

There are not many people residing there now; and one of the reasons assigned is its vicinity to La Malroche, where it is well known that the witches keep their Sabbath, and send down their evil influence.

No one cares to live at Escures but very poor persons, or those whom long habit has rendered callous to its bad name. Amongst these was an old woman, called La Bonne Femme, not because she was possessed of any particular virtue or amiability, but from the circumstance of her following the calling of an attendant on lying-in women. She certainly had no right whatever to be called *good*, for she was malignant, cross, ill-looking, and dangerous; but though she inspired fear in general intercourse, all felt confidence in her skill. No one was more active or useful when called upon; and in all case, particularly those of danger, La Bonne Femme was eagerly sought after, and rewarded liberally.

It had, however, more than once happened that accidents had occurred to her patients and their infants who have on a former occasion offended her; indeed, she seemed to be endowed with a memory peculiarly retentive of injuries, and had been known to revenge herself on several generations, for she was of great age; so old that no one was who was her contemporary, or could relate anything of her early life.

These facts being known, it was with some degree of trepidation that Cyprien, the young *vacher* of Quaire, whose pretty little wife, Ursule, had just been taken ill, bent his steps in the direction of Escures, and on arriving inquired for the cottage of La Bonne Femme.

She was not at home, but he was told by her next door neighbor that he might open her door and go in, as she would soon return. "She is gone up to Malroche to gather herbs," was the remark, "as she knew she would be required today, and will come back prepared with the remedies."

Cyprien went into the hut of the useful but dreaded personage, whose assistance he sought, and sat down near the open door to watch for her coming.

He felt a sort of tremor creeping over him as he glanced around the dim apartment, in which he observed heaps of stones of various colors, piled along the wall, pans filled with dark liquids, and vials of singular shapes.

He dared not approach the hearth where, in the midst of the smoldering ashes, simmered a huge, black, earthen pot, at whose contents he did not venture to guess. He sat and looked towards the mountain, which was purple, and almost transparent, and saw plainly by this appearance and that of the sky that a heavy shower was about to fall; for the clouds rested immovably on the peaks of strangely shaped rocks, while a dark canopy hung suspended over La Malroche, which became very moment denser and thicker, until it appeared to close in the summit altogether.

Cyprien began to grow uneasy, for the day was shortening; it was some distance to Quaire, and he feared that the old woman would be displeased at having to accompany him back to Ursule, whose situation caused him also extreme anxiety. At length, he beheld La Bonne Femme slowly descending the steep path above, and with a spring he hurried to meet and offer her his support.

"Who are you that ask my aid?" she inquired, when he had told his business.

"I am the *vacher* of Quaire," he answered, "and live in the cottage by the Dry Lake."

"Oh!" said she, "you married Ursule Bilot, about a year ago—the daughter of Simon Bilot, an old friend of mine?"

"The same," replied Cyprien; "she requires your speedy help, good mother; for I left her suffering much."

The old woman, without further remark, bustled about, collecting various articles of her trade, and in a very short time was ready to attend the young husband, who expected soon to become a father. The rain by this time had begun—fine, and piercing, and steady—but the old woman expressed no annoyance at being obliged to go through it, and cheerfully accepted the arm of Cyprien, who led her over the stony way which conducts between the hills to the village to the village where he lived.

The spot called Dry Lake is a wide space which extends beneath the mountain of Murat; all the appearances around prove it to have been formerly a sheet of water, dried up, probably, at the period of a sudden eruption of one of the volcanoes in its vicinity; shells and sand are to be found in the ravines which occur on its surface, and its rounded form shows what was its former nature. There is some pasture here for cattle, which is taken advantage of by the *vachers*; and here Cyprien had erected his simple cottage, the retreat of himself and his wife—the beauty of the village, with whom all the swains had been in love, and whom his long affection had been fortunate enough to gain; for Ursule was as good as she was beautiful, and repaid his love with a devotedness of which he was deserving.

They gained a tolerable living; for Cyprien, during the long months of winter, when the cattle could no longer be driven to the mountains, used to employ himself in various ways. Amongst other things, he was famous for making the musical instrument to which the peasants of Auverge dance their bourees. This instrument is called *la tsabretta*, because it is made of goat-skin, and those fabricated by the hand of Cyprien were much sought after.

The young husband and his companion reached the door of the cottage quite late, drenched with wet, and chilled with cold. They, however, found a warm fire; and La Bonne Femme was welcomed with great cordiality by the aunt of Ursule, who attended on her.

That night a son was born to Cyprien, who hailed with delight a fine healthy child, so large as to be quite remarkable; his strength was astonishing, and his whole appearance denoted a robust constitution. After a few days, La Bonne Femme departed, leaving Ursule nursing her child, and quite well and happy. No sooner, however, had she left the cottage, than the infant began to cry so violently that everyone was alarmed: he clamored and struggled so that he could hardly be held, and stretched out his arms towards the door, as if he asked for the old woman. Cyprien, finding there was no peace to be obtained, ran after her as fast as he could, and at length overtaking her, entreated her to return and pacify the child.

"What!" cried she, with a sinister smile, "does it work already?"

She followed the father, and on her entering the cottage, the child ceased crying, and was seized with trembling.

She took it, whispered something in its ear, and giving it back to Ursule, it became perfectly quiet, and fell asleep. She then departed, and took her way home. Nine days after this, about the same hour as before—just at dusk—the infant began to cry in the same manner, and stretch its arms towards the door, trying apparently to get out. The father, mother, and nurse knew not what to do to restrain it, for it was so strong that they had great difficulty in keeping it in bed. All of a sudden, there seemed to come a blast of air into the chamber, the cottage door banged violently, and the child fell into a profound sleep, from which no efforts could wake it for nine days longer, when it roused itself at the same hour, and the same scene took place.

The parents now became very uneasy and harassed with continual watching and care. The child grew in a surprising manner, notwithstanding its lethargic existence, broken only in this strange way; but there was something about it unnaturally large, strong and cunning-looking. At the end of six months, it could walk and run, and at this period its long slumbers ceased, and a singularity of another kind appeared respecting it. It now never slept at all, but its whole delight was in playing the *tsabretta*, and making so great a noise that no one in the adjoining cottages had any peace.

Night and day the din continued, until everyone was worn out; and at length it became generally considered that the child had been bewitched, and some measures ought to be taken to remove it from such a visitation.

Cyprien, therefore, set forth one morning to the neighboring village of Saint Sauves, in order to consult with the cure of that parish—a man both learned and pious, and who had, on more occasions than one, relieved families laboring under afflictions sent by the fairies and witches. No one doubted that La Bonne Femme had cast a spell over Ursule and her child; and it was well remembered by some of the old people, that when Ursule herself was born the same old woman had attended her mother, who had an aversion to her, and had inadvertently remarked to her husband—"Why did you bring me this old witch?" This La Bonne Femme had overheard, and had revenged herself at the time, for the mother of Ursule never afterwards rose from her bed; her vengeance was not, however, it appeared, complete, for she had wreaked it on her grandchild.

The cure of St. Sauves was much shocked at the communication of Cyprien, and taking with him his crucifix and a vial of holy water, they set out together to the cottage of Le Bonne Femme. The moon had risen brightly over La Malroche, as they approached its vicinity, and just as they turned an angle of a rock, a peculiar sound made them start; they paused a moment to listen, and were soon aware of the howling of wolves. Presently, to their dismay, they saw a troop of those animals scouring along the plain below, and apparently mounting the elevated part where they stood. They crept into a fissure, and held their breath as the grisly party came nearer; and what was their horror to observe, as they approached, that each of the wolves had human faces, and the two foremost wore those of La Bonne Femme and Cyprien's little son!

The cure, though at first startled, recovered his presence of mind, and rushing forward, cast the holy water over the child thus transformed, when a loud howl burst forth from all the band, a thick cloud suddenly enveloped them, and when it cleared away they saw at their feet what seemed the lifeless form of the infant, in its natural shape.

They raised it up, bound the crucifix to its breast, and carried it with care to the cure's dwelling. There, by his desire, Cyprien left it, and returned home to his wife. He found all the family in tribulation at the loss of the child; for it appears that soon after the father left the cottage on his mission, La Bonne Femme had looked in at the window, at sight of which the infant, who was, as usual, playing on the *tsabretta*, cast it down, and rushed out of the door, when both fled away with fearful speed across the Dry Lake, and were seen no more.

The cure devoted himself with prayer and fasting to the preservation of the child, and it at length recovered, but was now a changed being. Precocious as before, it appeared endowed with extraordinary intelligence, and showed such evident signs of an early advocate to the church that it was agreed to place it in the convent of St. Sauves, there to be educated and watched over, in order that the evil one might never resume his dominion over it.

Cyprien made a vow never more to make *tsabrettas*, as they led to ill, inasmuch as they encouraged profane pastime, and were usually the accompaniment to the dance of the country, called *la goignade*—looked upon as so improper by the Bishop of Aleth, that he had excommunicated those in his diocese who ventured to perform the dance.

A procession was made to La Malroche by the monks of the convent, and many ceremonies of exorcism took place. La Bonne Femme was found dead in her cottage soon after, burnt almost to a cinder, lying beside a pile of flame-stained stones, of which it was generally believed that she made her fire, for no wood was ever seen in her domicile. She was buried on the summit of La Malroche, and her restless spirit is said still to be seen at times scouring over the plateau in the form of a wolf, when it howls fearfully at the moon. Whenever this is heard the inhabitants of the villages round cross themselves devoutly, and utter a prayer to their patron saint to preserve their children from her evil influence.

THE THREE VISITS

BY AUGUSTE VITU

(1850)

In the month of August, 1845, a column of French soldiers, composed of Chasseurs d' Afrique, of Spahis, and several battalions of the line, were crossing the beautiful valley of orange-trees and aloes, at the base of Djebel-Ammer, one of the principal spurs of Atlas.

It was nine o'clock at night, and the atmosphere was calm and clear. A few light and fleecy clouds yet treasured up the melancholy reflection of the sun's last beams, which, in copper bands, were radiated across the horizon.

The march was rapid, for it was necessary to catch up with the advance guard, which had been pushed forward to make a razzia, the object of which was to bring into subjection one or two mutinous tribes.

The Marechal de Camp who commanded this advanced party had halted with a field-officer, to observe this party defile into its place with the rear guard.

The day had been very warm, and luminous masses of vapor from time to time rose from the surface of the ground, like white apparitions in the midst of sombre space.

"Look, Corporal Gobin, look there," said a soldier; "I saw something like a white sheet. Think you it can be a Bedouin?"

"Fool," said the corporal, "it is a cactus-leaf, lit up by the moon."

"Bah! that I can see distinctly, but I had reference to something else, of an elongated form. It is now out of sight. Look! there is another."

"They are nothing but heat-balls, my child," said the corporal.

"That may be, Corporal, but in this country I do not feel safe."

Just at that moment the soldier who was speaking to the corporal passed by the General.

"What," said Gobin, "annoys you?"

"Nothing of any great importance; but out of all these alleys things dance the air. Those immense plants, the edges of the leaves of which cut like those of sabres. There are other green machines which look like stitching-needles. They do not seem natural to me. The night, too, is haunted by evil spirits."

"Will you hold your tongue, Conscript?" said the corporal, with vivacity. "You are not going to give us a ghost story?"

"Why should I not? I am not afraid of ghosts, though you and the rest are. The ghost of an Arab must be a funny affair."

Gobin said, very sententiously, "A man, my lad, must come precisely from your village to be so utterly without tact—I may almost say, without sentiment. Do you not know one should never talk of such matters before the General?"

"Bah! you do not mean to say General Vergamier is afraid?"

"Vergamier afraid! He who won every step on the battle-field—who is a Commander of the Legion of Honor, and has every seam of his coat covered with other orders! I tell you what, Gabet, you will never become Minister of War."

"Then, if the General is so brave, why should not one speak of ghosts before him?"

"That is a whim of his. He says such stories always do harm, especially after night. It is a weakness, Conscript, I know, unworthy of such a brave man, and therefore is it that he so carefully conceals it."

"Then how, Corporal, do you know anything about it?"

"I have an old friend named Rabugeot, a sapper of the 22nd, who was a servant of the General, and who, one night when he was drunk, under the pledge of secrecy, told me the whole affair."

"Well, you take fine care of the secret. Did I ask you if the General—"

"Silence! Gabet: I think the General suspects we are talking of him."

The fact was, the General had heard every word the two soldiers had said, and their conversation had produced a truly painful impression on him. So much so that his friend the Surgeon-Major, Edouard Banis, asked him, with surprise, what was the matter.

"Do you believe in ghosts?" asked the General.

The major blushed.

"Why not?"

"Then, when the body dies, the soul survives?"

"Thus expressed, the subject-matter disappears."

"Give me your opinion on the matter."

"What do I know of the matter, General? If life be the manifestation, or rather the emanation, of a general and eternal principle, under a finite form, as the disciples of Swedenborg and other mystics think, spiritual apparitions are not only possible but natural."

"Your own opinion, Doctor?"

"Frankly, I do not know what to say. I have never seen a ghost, and consequently have a right to doubt their existence. Such phenomena do not seem to me contrary to the general laws of nature, and are rather to be admitted on scientific principles—since, if they exist, from their very nature they escape the material control of the senses; and if the soul be in contact with another soul, it alone can establish the presence of the apparition. The body feels, sees, and hears nothing. At Weinsburg, in Germany, I saw Doctor Justinius Korner and Albertus Trintzius, his disciple. These men told me terrible things. I have, however, the faith of Saint Thomas, and wish to see and touch."

"But, Edouard," said the General, "I have myself seen."

The gallant officer who made this strange confession to M. Banis was a man still young, for he was scarcely thirty-eight. His fine and noble figure, rather full than otherwise, received a kind of melancholy grace from the sad melancholy of his mild blue eyes, which softened the rudeness of his hale complexion, and the full white moustache which covered his whole upper lip. His hair was short and silky, his ear was small, and his teeth regular. His broad brow, expressive of thought, announced him a dreamer. General Etienne Vergamier, with his tall stature, his broad shoulders, his physical power, his mild expression, and his sweet and charming smile, might have served as a model for one of those northern heroes, sons of Ossian and Fingal, who as they fought sang heroic rhymes.

The Doctor was a cold methodical man. He was however intelligent and deeply learned, and heard the confession of the General with the greatest astonishment and curiosity. Let one, however, be ever so great a physician and naturalist, the passion for the supernatural yet exerts its painful influence.

Vergamier pushed his horse to a trot, and was silent for some time. The Doctor respected his reverie, but finally gave vent to his curiosity, fully as his intimacy with the General permitted.

"We have a long route before us. The road is becoming bad, and we must perforce slacken our pace. Tell me, General, the event to which you referred just now. This is a proper time to talk of ghosts."

"Why should I, Doctor? You would not believe me."

"I believe in sensations, of all kinds. You will however permit me to discuss the principles of yours?"

"Ah! You wish to insert your physiological scalpel into the secret of secrets of my heart. I beseech you, however, not to laugh. I tell you an absolute fact."

The time was well-chosen for such a story. As the column approached Djebel-Ammer, the soil, which had hitherto been grassy and fertile, became barren and desolate. The orange-trees gave place to mastich-wood and the most horrible cactus. The arbuti lifted directly to heaven their blood-red trunks and regular branches, on which the leaves were so glittering that rays of the moon made them splendid as the scanthi of candelabra. On the right side and on the left arose layers of black and blue rocks, like vast Japanese vases, from which arose great cactus, with leaves dentelated as the claws of a gigantic crab. Fine and dry briars rattled as they quivered in the breeze, and the pale light of the rising stars made gigantic silhouettes of the shadows of the horses and men. The wolves howled in the distance, and large birds hovered in the air, uttering the most melancholy cries while they were on the wing. The tramp of the horses on the dry ground sounded most sadly. Every now and then the sharp clang of a carbine was heard, as some soldier fired at any bush which waved or any stone which fell down the overhanging rocks. In Africa, behind every waving bush, above every rolling stone, there is an enemy.

"When I was twenty years old," said the General, "I left Saint-Cyr, with my best friend Charles de Mancel, a fine young fellow, blond, pale, delicate-looking—dreamy as a poet, yet strong as a Kabyle and brave as a lion. We had from our very childhood been intimate, and in the various quarrels of our school-boy life, time and again we had fought for each other. We were devoted to each other, and were distressed at the idea of our separation, consequent we thought on our entry into service.

"More lucky than we had expected to be, we met at the capture of Fort de l'Empereur, as second lieutenants.

"A few days after, Algiers was stormed, and George was among the first who entered the city. I saw him fall from a gun-shot wound in the left side.

"I bore him on my shoulders to a house which had been deserted by the inhabitants at the commencement of the cannonade. I placed him in the calm, voluptuous, perfumed room of a woman. The bed was out of order, and in it I placed George, and as well as I could, stanched the blood. He was so debilitated that he could scarcely look steadily. He clasped, however, one of my hands in his, and pressed it convulsively whenever the pain became insupportable.

"He was however calm for a short time.

"'Etienne,' said he, 'I die young, and regret the loss of life. We are about to separate, but who knows if it will be for an eternity? No one knows what passes beyond the tomb: perhaps there are other sufferings, perhaps pleasure, or it may be annihilation. If, however, my soul be immortal; if in unknown regions it preserves its affections and memories, thank God! If it be true that we may see those we have fondly loved, be sure, dear Etienne, that I will return some calm spring evening. I feel that I can die more easily, yet I suffer. When my mother died, she told me she would return, and kept her word. Last night she smiled on me. I see her now, Etienne, weeping.'

"He died."

The General was silent for a few moments, and with a suppressed voice continued, "I will not describe to you my horrible sufferings. George was buried amid the beating of drums and shouts of victory. I shed bitter tears, for I knew my youth was buried with my friend. The adieu of George made a deep impression on me, and I suffered on that night with awful dreams. For six months I was nervous as a woman. I tell you, doctor, I was afraid to be alone in the dark. One or two years, however, passed by, and the recollection of my friend, though profoundly engraved in my heart, yielded to the exigencies of my profession and to care for the future. My puerile fear, which was a disease, became cured. Yes, the more I think of it, the more satisfied I am, that I was entirely cured, and that my mind was sane and healthy. Just then, however, a circumstance I am about to relate struck me with amazement.

"I had just been made second captain. After several severe, and, I venture to say, honorable campaigns, I returned to Algiers, with my senses yet ardent and almost virgin, and with all my prize-money in my possession. I plunged madly into all the dissipation of a garrison town, making one endless orgy of both day and night. I gambled with that madness which characterizes the conduct of him who yields for the first time to this vice. At first I won, then my luck was bad. One night at a cafe of the street Bab-Azoun, I lost 14,000 francs, the remnant of my fortune. The sum was large and created much conversation in Algiers.

"About ten o'clock an orderly delivered me a message that the Colonel wished to speak to me. Pale and uneasy, though I knew not why, I obeyed the order.

"I found my good Colonel more pale and uneasy than I was.

"'Captain,' said he, gasping as if in despair, 'the military chest of my regiment was broken open this morning and there were taken from it *fourteen thousand francs*. Do you understand? *Fourteen thousand francs.*'

"The old officer advanced toward me, with his arms folded on his chest, and a stern and menacing eye.

"I felt the pulses of my temples bound and my very brain seemed ready to burst. I drew back with indignation.

"'This handkerchief was lost by the robber, and found under the chair of the treasurer. See, sir, it bears your ciphers, E.V.'

"I took the handkerchief mechanically; it was indeed mine. My knees quivered, my eyes became filled with tears, and I could not articulate.

"'Now, sir,' said the Colonel, 'go and blow your brains out.'

"I left the room without uttering a word, completely overwhelmed at being called a criminal and a robber. It did not enter into my mind to declare my innocence, or to demand any inquiry. No, I returned to my quarters and took from the arm-rack a loaded pistol.

"I paused and began to sob. Rapidly I recalled the happiness of my childhood, my first campaign, my mother and George, especially the latter.

"'To die. To die disgraced!' murmured I.

"'You shall not die,' said a clear, vibrating voice, at once metallic and deep, but which seemed to proceed from no human organs.

"The pistol fell from my hand. George stood before me. His eye was fixed, but, brilliant as a star, illumined his pale and diaphanous complexion.

"Explain this to me, doctor. As I detail this horrible affair, I feel my hair grow erect, my teeth chatter, and my voice to quiver. In the presence of George, however, I experienced a serene joy, an ideal and unmingled happiness. My youth, my dreams of love, appeared again to cheer me. But a moment before I had seemed oppressed beneath an unaccountable fatality, but now knew myself watched over by an almost divine power. I will even say, that the apparition of George did not astonish me. It seemed to me a fact simple and natural. We spoke to each other as brothers, who had been long separated.

"'Etienne, what were you about to do?' said he to me sadly. 'I have come to save you. Your servant is guilty; he robbed the chest of fourteen thousand francs, as he robbed you of the handkerchief. You confided in that man, and thought him honest. So he was, but he has a Moorish mistress who makes him purchase her favors dearly. Two thousand francs will be found in his bed, and twelve hundred in her house. Go directly to the Colonel. I have no more to say.'

"I was alone. A sentiment of reality returned to me, and I dashed open the blinds of my window.

"In the shade of the white walls of the barrack yard, beneath the dark blue of the torrid sky, the soldiers were idly smoking, wrapped in their 'bournous.' A negro boy was feeding a flock of Numidian fowls, the green plumage of which reflected every tint of the rainbow. Above all towered the white parapets of the Casbah, while calm and silent the waves of the Mediterranean were seen in the distance. I was alive. I did not dream. This impossible hallucination, this phantasmagoria was the truth. Terror seized on me. Icy chills passed from my brain to my feet. My nerves became contracted, and from that moment I began to grow gray."

Here the General paused and ordered a halt. The column had left the rocks, and before it lay a rolling plain through which a river wound its way. At the other side of the plain rose the black and threatening walls of the Djebel-Ammer, or mountain of Ammer.

General Vergamier dismounted, and leaning on the doctor's arm, continued:

"Subsequent events proved all the spectre had said to be true. The servant confessed the crime, and the money was found. The good old Colonel, distressed at what he had said, would willingly have shot himself. All my brother officers came to see me. A few days after, at the instance of the Colonel, I was made a Chevalier of the Legion of Honor. The reparation was complete."

The doctor was silent.

"You do not believe me," said the General. "Well, I scarcely would believe another, myself, on such evidence. I saw George, I am sure, but I can scarcely realize the fact. The thing however took place, Doctor, or I am a madman."

"Did you ever see the apparition again?" asked the Doctor, who had been much amazed by the story.

"I did," replied General Vergamier, in a melancholy tone. "I saw him the evening before my duel with Major Berkard de Ris. I had just come from drill, fatigued and melancholy, and had gone into my room in which there was no light, but a fire of dry branches. George sat in my chair, sad and moody. As I entered, he arose, and said 'I was waiting for you. Tomorrow you will fight with de Ris, who is a swordsman. You do not fence enough.' George leaned against the wall, and I saw that he had a sword in his hand. I took down a foil and put myself *en garde*. 'Pay attention,' said George, 'I am about to give you a lesson. See this pass. Engage him thus, and then thus. Very well, you did not thrust far enough through.'"

"'I dared not,' said I, and the cold sweat stood on my brow.

"A languid smile played on his lips. We fenced again and with such violence that my sword broke on the wall. I ran George through and through. Strange, however, to say, my sword met with no resistance."

"'Very well,' said George. 'With a quick eye, coolness, and a steady hand, you will do well.'

"'George,' said I, with a reproachful voice, 'why do you leave me? Is there anything above which retains you?'

"George shook his head sadly.

"I said 'Will you return?'

"'Once more,' replied he, 'but thenceforth we will not be separated.'

"The vision disappeared.

"I am in my senses," continued the General, "and am sure of all I say. I, General Vergamier, took a fencing lesson from a ghost. You know the result of the duel. Doctor, that was long ago, and now I expect the third visit."

The Doctor could not suppress a feeling of uneasiness, he was so much disturbed by the feverish state of the General.

"To horse," said he, assuming the command. "Control yourself. You have told me only what you have dreamed. Do not think of the matter. Be calm and composed. It is almost day."

"Doctor, I have not seen George for a long time."

The column soon turned to the left to follow the torrent of the Oued along the plain. General Vergamier, wrapped up in his cloak, did not speak, except to give an order from time to time. At dawn, fires were seen on the declivities of the Djebel-Ammer. They were the bivouacs of the first column, with which Vergamier had orders to unite his own command. This was soon done.

The little army was encamped on the side of the army and saw at its feet a vast plain covered with a plentiful harvest and intersected by a network of canals fed with water from the Oued. On the other side of the mountain was a large Arab village, the irregularly-built houses of which seemed ready to fall into the valley. Vast rocks of trachytic porphyry were piled above it, and all was in the midst of a gigantic forest of cyprus, fig and pine trees.

At the command "Break ranks," given by the General and repeated by all the officers, the soldiers scattered over the plain laughing and shouting.

"Here, Conscript," said Corporal Gobin to Gabet, at the same time throwing him a box of matches, "go make your first fire."

"One sous a packet, two sous a box," said an old gamin of Paris, from the neighborhood of the Temple.

The plain was soon in a blaze, and the soldiers were forced to retreat before it. A light crackling of the grass was heard, then a whirlpool of blaze seemed to be formed in the midst of an immense mass of smoke. The matches, insignificant as they usually seem, in a country like Africa become terrible weapons, were seen everywhere busy in effecting the razzia. When the whole field was on fire, the column united again, to ascend the mountain; it crossed the ravines and valleys, and in the gorge of an immense pass, descended with loud hurrahs toward Djebel. Everywhere the greenish blaze of the match was visible, and the burning junipers made all the atmosphere fragrant.

The slope of the mountain was scarcely descended, when the village was in a blaze as if it had been built of straw. A few Arabs hurrying from the houses exchanged shots with a handful of Spahis without much injury to either side. There were, however, two or three men wounded, and the doctor had taken care of them, when the column reached the base of the mountain. The conflagration had so closely followed the column that it seemed in pursuit of it. The fire wound round them like a serpent, until both man and the element paused on the banks of the Oued. The fire went out about dawn.

The plain, the village, and the river were confounded in one sea of fire, the waves of which reached the mosses of the forests, hung on the side of the mountain. The Djebel was soon covered with a diadem of flames. The rays of the sun with difficulty pierced the smoky atmosphere of this vast furnace, giving it the appearance of molten copper.

General Vergamier had left his escort. At the commencement of the razzia he had dismounted, and after he had given his horse to a chasseur, attempted to ascend the mountain by a winding path which required both a quick eye and active foot.

Buried in thought, Vergamier did not observe that on his right hand rose impassable rocks, which stood like a wall between himself and his men. He, however, heard the firing distinctly, repeated by a thousand echoes, and even the roaring of the flame. Leaning on his saber he continued to ascend.

Soon he ceased to hear these sounds, and a winding of the path led him away from the ravine through which the column defiled. The whole mountain was silent as the tomb.

The General reached a kind of fertile plateau, where the table forest of Ammer began. Nothing could be more melancholy than the deep recesses of the cypress. Vergamier rapidly walked amid them. The soil was strewn with fragments of feldspar, sharp and pointed, which had been broken from the rocks by some tempest. They wounded his feet as if they had been razors. Vergamier, however, did not heed it. He paused at a torrent which fell over a prodigious rock, and drank a mouthful of water from the hollow of his hand. He then sat down on a mossy rock and became wrapped in meditation.

He passed in review his career. He saw himself again in the white plains of his native Champagne, in the silent halls of Saint Cyr, at Sidi-Ferruch and his first fight, amid the blue mists of Paris, the gigantic and glorious. He saw himself at the Tuileries, where his valor had been rewarded, and Palais-Bourbon, where he had been received with acclamations: He saw himself at the little drawing-room of the poet Nanteuil, with his kind heart and artistic luxury. He saw all whom he had loved.... George. He looked around.

Above him was the stern rock with the black spiral trees which crowned it, shutting out the light. Behind him, near a cypress tree was a man.

"George!" said he.

He covered his face with his hands....

At eight o'clock, Doctor Banis, uneasy at the long absence of the General, had the mountain searched by a party of Spahis. About noon they found the body of General Vergamier at the foot of a deep ravine, completely crushed by his horrible fall. The soldiers thought that their General had been pushed over by some Arab, who had laid in the ambuscade amid the underwood. Doctor Banis, however, knew that he had received the last visit of George.

LIEUTENANT CASTENAC

BY ERCKMAN-CHATRIAN

(1866)

In 1845 I was attached as surgeon-major to the military hospital of Constantine. This hospital rises in the interior of the Casbah, over a precipice of from three to four hundred feet in height. It commands at once the city, the governor's palace, and the vast plain beyond, as far as the eye can reach. It is at once a comprehensive and savage scene. From my window, left open to inspire the fresh breezes of the evening, I could see the vultures and ravens soaring around the inaccessible cliffs before withdrawing for the night into their fissures and crevices. I could easily throw my cigar into the Rummel, which flows along the foot of the giant wall. Not a sound, not a murmur came to trouble the calm of my studies, till the evening bugle and drums, repeated by the echoes of the fortress, called the men to their quarters.

Garrison life had never any charms for me; I never could accustom myself to absinthe and rum, or to the *petit verre de cognac*. At the time I am now speaking about that was called wanted in *esprit de corps*, but my gastric faculties did not permit my having that kind of *esprit*. I occupied myself there with visiting my patients, prescribing and dressing, and then I retired to my room to make notes of the cases, to read a book, or sit at the window contemplating the gloomy, savage scene before me.

Every one got accustomed to, and put up with, my retiring habits, save a certain lieutenant of Voltigeurs, Castagnac by name, whom I must introduce to you *in propria persona*.

On my first arrival at Constantine, getting down from the carriage, a voice shouted out behind me:

"*Tiens*! I'll lay a bet that is our surgeon-major."

I turned round and found myself in the presence of an infantry officer, tall, thin, bony, with a red nose and gray moustache, his kepi over his ear, its peak stabbing the sky, his sword between his legs; it was Lieutenant Castegnac, and who has not seen the same military type?

While I was familiarizing my eyes with this strange physiognomy, the lieutenant had seized my hand.

"Welcome, Doctor! Delighted to make your acquaintance. You are tired, I am sure. Come in—I will introduce you to the *Cercle*."

The *Cercle* at Constantine was the restaurant and bar of the officers united. We went in. How was it possible to resist the sympathetic enthusiasm of such a man! And yet I had read Gil Blas!

"Garçon, two glasses. What do you take, doctor—cognac or rum?"

"Neither. Curacoa, if you please."

"Curacoa! Why not say *parfait amour* at once? Ah, ah, ah! You have a strange taste. Garcon, a glass of absinthe for me, full to the brim; be attentive. Your health, doctor!"

"Yours, Lieutenant!"

And so I was forthwith in the good graces of this strange man. But it is needless to tell you that the intimacy did not last long.

Castagnac had habits that were especially antagonistic to my own. But I made the acquaintance of other officers, who joined me in laughing at the originality of his character.

Among them was a young man of merit, Raymond Dutertre, who said that he has likewise been obliged to drop his acquaintance, but that Castagnac having taken it up as a personal affront, they had gone outside the walls, and he, Dutertre, had administered to him a severe chastisement, which chagrined him all the more, as he had previously bullied with impunity, on the faith of one or two successful duels.

Things were in this condition, when about the middle of June, a malignant fever broke out in Constantine, and among the hospital patients were both Castagnac and Dutertre; but Castagnac was not there for fever; he was invalided by that strange nervous affliction called delirium tremens (and in our bashful army D.T.), and which is especially common among those who, in Algeria, are given to the frequent imbibation of absinthe.

Poor Castagnac used to get out of his bed during the attacks and run along the floor on all fours, as if he were catching rats. He also mewed like a cat, but the only words that he uttered were, "Fatima! oh Fatima!"—a circumstance that induced me to suppose that the poor fellow had experienced some disappointment in love, for which he sought consolation in the abuse of spirituous liquors.

When he recovered from his fits he would invariably ask the same question:

"What did I say, doctor? Did I say anything?"

I naturally replied that he had said nothing of importance, and bade him quiet himself.

But he was not satisfied, and after trying to search my inner thoughts with his fierce eyes, he would give up the attempt and resign himself to his couch, with the equally invariable observation:

"A glass of absinthe would do me a great deal of good."

One morning, as I was entering into Castagnac's room I saw Dutertre, who was nearly convalescent, hastening after me along the passage.

"Doctor," he said, taking me by the hand, "I have come to ask you a favor. Will you give me permission to go out for a day?"

"Anything, my dear friend, but that. The fever is still raging in the town, and I cannot expose you to a relapse."

"Well, give me then two hours—the time to go and come back."

"It is impossible, my good friend. In another week, if you go on well, we will see what can be done."

He withdrew, evidently deeply chagrined. I was sorry, but could not help it, but on turning around was surprised at seeing Castagnac following the retiring suitor with a strange look.

"What was Raymond asking for?" he inquired.

"Oh, nothing! He wanted to go out, but I could not sanction it."

"You refused him permission, then?" persevered the sick man.

"It was my duty to do so."

Castagnac said no more, but resumed his recumbent position with a grim smile, I was almost about to say a diabolical expression of countenance, which I could not account for, but which filled me with strange apprehensions.

That same evening my duties called me to the amphitheatre, where an autopsy claimed my attention. The so-called amphitheatre was in reality a vaulted dungeon fifteen feet long by twenty feet wide, with two windows opening upon the precipice and looking in the direction of the high road to Phillipville. The body lay upon a table slightly inclined, my lamp was placed upon a stone that advanced out of the wall, and I remained engaged in my examination till near eleven o'clock.

On leaving off at length, I was horrified at seeing the window blocked up by innumerable owls, small and gray-colored, with their feathers all erect, their green eyes sparkling through the semi-obscurity. They were waiting till I had done.

I rushed horrified to the window and drove the rapacious birds away, like so many great dead leaves carried off by the night wind. But, at the very moment, I heard a noise—a strange sound, almost imperceptible in the depths of the abyss. I stopped, and putting my head out of the window, held my breath so as to be able to catch the sounds more distinctly.

Castagnac's room was immediately over the amphitheatre; and below, between the precipice and the wall of the hospital, was a space, not above a foot in width, covered with broken pottery and bottles, the refuse of the infirmary. In the stillness that reigned around, I could distinctly hear a man groping his way along this dangerous shelf.

"Heaven grant!" I said to myself, "that the sentinel does not see him. A single false step, and he is a lost man!"

I had barely had time to make this reflection to myself, when I heard the hoarse voice of Castagnac calling from above:

"Raymond, where are you going?"

It was a condemnation to death. At the very instant I heard some of the broken pottery slipping down the incline, followed by the fall of a heavy body. I heard the sighs of a man struggling as if to hold for his life—a groan that went to the very marrow of my bones and bedewed my forehead with a cold, clammy perspiration, and then all was over! Not exactly all, for I heard a diabolical burst of laughter above, and then a window closed with such impetuosity that it was followed by the sound of broken glass. And then the deep silence of night spread its shroud over this frightful drama.

After I had somewhat recovered from the state of inexpressible horror in which I had been thrown, I went to bed. To sleep, however, was out of the question; all night long I was haunted by those lamentable sighs and by that demoniac laugh.

The next morning a feeling of horror came over me, which prevented me verifying my impressions till I had visited my patients.

It was not till that was accomplished that I directed my steps to Dutertre's room.

I knocked; there was no answer. I entered; there was no one there. I inquired of the hospital attendants; no one had seen him go out. Summoning all my courage, I went next to Castagnac's room. A glance at the window satisfied me that two panes were broken.

"It blew hard, lieutenant, last night," I remarked.

Castagnac lifted up his head, till then buried in his bony hands as if in the act of reading. "*Parbleu!*" he said; "two windows broken, only that!"

"Your room, lieutenant, appears to be more exposed than others, or, perchance, you left your window open?"

An almost imperceptible muscular contraction furrowed the cheeks of the old miscreant, and he at the same time fixed so inquiring a look at me, that I felt glad of a pretense to withdraw.

Just as I was going out, I turned back suddenly, as if I had forgotten to ask a question:

"By-the-by, lieutenant, has Dutertre been to see you?"

A shudder passed through his gray hairs.

"Duterte!"

"Yes, he is gone out, and no one knows where. I thought, perhaps—"

"No one has been to see me," he interrupted, abruptly; "no one whatsoever."

I went out, convinced of his guilt, but I had no proofs. I determined to wait and watch, and in the meantime contented myself with reporting the disappearance of Lieutenant Raymond Dutertre to the *commandant de place.*

Next day some Arabs, coming with vegetables to the market of Constantine, made known that they had seen from the road to Phillipeville a uniform dangling in the air on the face of the rocks of the Casbah, and that birds of prey were flying around in hundreds.

These were the remains of Raymond, and it was with the greatest possible trouble that they were recovered by letting down men by means of ropes.

The catastrophe furnished subject of conversation to the officers of the garrison for tow or three days, and was then forgotten. Men exposed to perils every day do not dwell upon unpleasant topics. Jacques dies, Pierre takes his place. The regiment is alone immortal.

My position with regard to Castagnac grew, in the meantime, more painful every day. My actions were constrained in his presence—the very sight of him was repulsive.

He soon detected it, and suspicion was awakened on his side.

"He doubts that I suspect him," I said to myself; 'if he was sure of it I should be a lost man—that villain stops at nothing!'"

Providence came to my aid. One afternoon I was leaving the Casbah for a stroll in the town, when one of the hospital assistants brought me a paper, which, he said, had been found in Raymond's tunic.

"It is the letter," he said, "of a *particuliere*, Fatima by name. I thought, sir, it might interest you."

The perusal of this letter filled me with surprise. It was brief, merely making an appointment, but what revelations in the name!

"What, then, those exclamations of Castegnac's in his fits," I said to myself, "had reference to a woman, and Dutertre had also relations with her. It was to keep this appointment that he had asked my leave to go out! Yes, the note is dated the 3rd of July. The very day. Poor fellow, not being able to get out in the day, he ventured forth by night by that frightful road, and Castagnac was awaiting him!"

As I was thus reflecting, I had arrived in front of a vaulted building or archway, open as usual to the wind, and where an old patient of mine, Sidi Humayun by name, distributed coffee to a few scanty customers.

I determined at once to consult this *kawafi*, so I took my place on the matting by the side of half a dozen natives in their red fezzes with blue silk tassels, and their long chibuks in their lips.

The *kawafi*, pretending not to know me, brought me my pipe and cup of coffee in silence.

Presently the muezzin was heard calling to prayers; the faithful rose up, stroked their beards, and departed slowly for the mosque. I was alone.

Sidi Humayun, looking around him to see that we were really so, then approached me, and, kissing my hand, "Lord Taleb," he said, "what brings you to my humble abode? What can I do in your service?"

"I want you to tell me who Fatima is."

"Lord Taleb, in the name of your mother, do *not see* that woman."

"Why so?"

She is perdition to the faithful and to the infidel. She possesses a charm that kills. Do not see her!"

"Sidi Humayun, my resolve is made. She possesses a charm; well! I possess a greater. Hers entails death, mine gives life, grace and beauty! Tell her that Sidi; tell her that the wrinkles of age disappear before my charm. I must see her."

"Well, then, since such is your will, Lord Taleb, come back tomorrow at the same hour. But remember what I said to you: Fatima makes an evil use of her beauty."

You may imagine if I awaited the appointed time with impatience. I thought the muezzin would never summon the faithful to prayer again.

At last his low, plaintive, monotonous voice made itself heard from the top of the minaret, and was taken up from one to another, till it seemed as if soaring over the indolent city.

I slowly paced my way to the coffee-house, so as to give time to the guests to retire. Sidi was already shutting up his shop.

"Well!" I said to him, breathless with anxiety.

"Fatima awaits you, Taleb."

He affixed the bar, and, without further explanation, led the way.

Leaving the main street, he entered the Suma, a passage so narrow that two could not walk abreast—a mere cloaca, yet crowded with industrious persons of many nations—Moors, Berbers, Jews, Copts and Arabs.

Suddenly Sidi Humayun stopped at a low doorway and knocked.

"Follow me," I said; "you will act as interpreter."

"Fatima can speak French," he replied, without turning his head.

The door was opened by a Nubian slave, who, letting me in, as quickly shut it against the *kawafi*.

She then led the way to an interior court paved with mosaic-work, and upon which several doors opened.

The slave pointed to one, by which I entered a room with open windows shaded by silken curtains with Moorish designs. An amber-colored mat covered the floor, while cushions of violet-colored Persian shawls lined the divan, at the extremity of which sat Fatima herself, her eyes veiled by long, dark lashes, straight and small nose, pouting lips and beautiful little feet.

"Come in, Lord Taleb," she said; "Sidi Humayun has told me of your visit. You are good enough to interest yourself in the fate of poor Fatima, who is getting aged—yes, she will soon be seventeen—seventeen! the age of regrets and wrinkles. Ah! Lord Taleb, sit down, you are welcome!"

I scarcely knew how to reply, but, recovering myself, I said:

"You scoff with infinite grace, Fatima. I have heard your wit spoken of no less than your beauty, and I see that I have heard the truth."

"Ah!" she exclaimed. "By whom, then?"

"By Dutertre."

"Dutertre?"

"Yes, Raymond Dutertre, the young officer who fell over the precipice of the Casbah. He whom you loved, Fatima."

She opened her great eyes in surprise.

"Who told you that I loved him?" she inquired, looking at me with a strange expression. "It is false! Did he tell you so?"

"No. But I know it. This letter proves it to me—this letter, which you wrote, and which was the cause of his death, for it was to get to you that he risked himself at night upon the rocks of the Casbah."

Scarcely had I uttered the words than the young Oriental rose up abruptly, her eyes lit up with a gloomy passion.

"I was sure of it!" she exclaimed. "Yes, when my Nubian brought me word of the accident, I said to her, 'Alissa, it is he who has done it. The wretch!'"

"Whom do you mean, Fatima?" I said, astonished at her anger. "I do not understand you."

"Of whom? Of Castagnac! You are the Taleb at the hospital. Well, give him poison. He is a wretch. He made me write to the officer to tell him to come here. I refused to do it. Yet this young man has sought my acquaintance for a long time, but I knew that Castagnac owed him a grudge. When I refused, he declared he would come out of the hospital to beat me if I did not, so I wrote. Here is his letter."

I went forth from Fatima's with a heavy heart, but my resolution was soon made.

Without losing a minute on the way, I ascended to the Casbah, entered the hospital, and knocked at Castegnac's door.

"Come in! What, is it you!" he said, forcing a smile. "I did not expect you."

For an answer I showed him the letter that he had written to Fatima.

He turned pale, and, having looked at it for a second, made a movement as if to throw himself upon me.

"If you make a step toward me," I said, placing my hand upon the hilt of my sword, "I will kill you like a dog. You are a wretch. You have assassinated Dutertre. I was at the amphitheatre; heard all. Do not deny it! Your conduct toward that woman is infamous; a French officer to lower himself to such a degree of infamy! Listen! I ought to deliver you over to justice, but your dishonor would defile us all. If an atom of heart remains within you, kill yourself! I grant you till tomorrow. Tomorrow by seven, if I find you still living, I will myself take before the *commandant de place.*"

Having said this, I withdrew without waiting for his reply, and went at once to give the strictest orders that Lieutenant Castagnac should not be permitted to leave the hospital under any pretext whatsoever.

Since Castagnac's guilt had been rendered evident to me I had become pitiless. I felt that I must avenge Raymond.

Having procured a torch, such as our *spahis* use in their night carousals, I shut myself up in the amphitheatre, closing its strong doors with double bars. I took up my position at the window, inhaling the fresh breeze of the evening, and thinking over the horrible drama in which I was called to play so prominent a part, till night came on.

Some hours had passed thus, and all was buried in the deepest silence, when I heard stealthy steps descending the staircase. They were followed by a knock at the door. No answer. A febrile hand then sought for the keyhole.

"It is Castegnac," I said to myself.

"Open!" exclaimed a voice from without. I was not deceived; it was him.

A stout shoulder made an effort to shake the door from its hinges. I moved not, scarcely breathed. Another and a more vigorous effort was then made, but with the same want of success. Something then fell on the ground, and the footsteps receded.

I had escaped assassination.

But what would become of him?

Once more, as if by instinct, I took up my position at the window. I had not waited long before I saw the shadow of Castagnac advancing along the foot of the wall. The hardened criminal stopped some time to look up at my window, and seeing nothing, moved on slowly with his back to the rampart. He had got over half the distance, when I cast the shout of death at him, "Raymond, where are you going?"

But whether he was prepared for whatever happened, or that he had more hardihood than his victim, he did not move, but answered me with ironic laughter.

"Ah, ah! you are there, doctor; I thought so. Stop a moment, I will come back; we have a little matter to arrange together."

Then lighting my torch, and raising it over the precipice, "It is too late," I said; "look, wretch, there is your grave!"

And the vast steps of the abyss, with their black shining rocks, were illuminated down to the depths of the valley. It was so terrible a vision that I involuntarily drew back myself with horror at the scene.

What must it have been to him who was only separated from it by the width of a brick? His knees began to tremble, his hands sought to cling to something of the face of the wall.

"Mercy!" exclaimed the assassin, in a hoarse voice; "have mercy on me!"

I had no heart to prolong his punishment. I cast the torch forth into space. It went down slowly, balancing its flame to and fro in the darkness, lighting up rock and shrub on its way, and casting sparks on the void around. It had already become but as a luminous point in the abyss, when a shadow passed by it with the rapidity of lightning.

I then knew that justice had been done.

As I reascended to my own room, my foot struck against something. I picked it up; it was my sword. Castegnac, with characteristic perfidy, had resolved to kill me with my own sword, so as to leave an opening for belief in suicide. I found, as I had anticipated, my room in utter disorder; the door had been broken open, my books and papers ransacked, he had left nothing untouched. Such an act completely dissipated whatever involuntary pity I might have felt for the fate of such a wretch.

TORTURE BY HOPE

BY VILLIERS DE L'ISLE-ADAMS

(1883)

Below the vaults of the *Official* of Saragossa one nightfall long ago, the venerable Pedro Arbuez d'Espila, sixth prior of the Dominicans of Segovia, third Grand Inquisitor of Spain—followed by a *fra redemptor* (master torturer), and preceded by two familiars of the Holy Office holding lanterns—descended towards a secret dungeon. The lock of a massive door creaked; they entered a stifling *in pace*, where the little light that came from above revealed an instrument of torture blackened with blood, a chafing-dish, and a pitcher. Fastened to the wall by heavy iron rings, on a mass of filthy straw, secured by fetters, an iron circlet about his neck, sat a man in rags: it was impossible to guess at his age.

This prisoner was no other than Rabbi Aser Abarbanel, a Jew of Aragon, who, on an accusation of usury and pitiless contempt of the poor, had for more than a year undergone daily torture. In spite of all, his blind obstinacy being as tough as his skin, he had refused to abjure.

Proud of his descent and his ancestors—for all Jews worthy of the name are jealous of their race—he was descended, according to the Talmud, from Othoniel, and consequently from Ipsiboe, wife of this last Judge of Israel, a circumstance which sustained his courage under the severest of the incessant tortures.

It was, then, with tears in his eyes at the thought that so steadfast a soul was excluded from salvation, that the venerable Pedro Arbuez d'Espila, approaching the quivering Rabbi, pronounced the following words:—

"My son, be of good cheer; your trials here below are about to cease, If, in presence of such obstinacy, I have had to permit, though with sighs, the employment of severe measures, my task of paternal correction has its limits. You are the barren fig-tree, that, found so oft without fruit, incurs the danger of being dried up by the roots...but it is for God alone to decree concerning your soul. Perhaps the Infinite Mercy will shine upon you at the last moment! Let us hope so. There *are* instances. May it be so! Sleep, then, this evening in peace. Tomorrow you will take part in the *auto de fe*, that is to say, you will be exposed to the *quemadero*, the brazier premonitory of the eternal flame. It burns, you are aware, at a certain distance, my son; and death takes, in coming, two hours at least, often three, thanks to the moistened and frozen clothes with which we take care to preserve the forehead and the heart of the holocausts. You will be only forty-three. Consider, then, that, placed in the last rank, you will have the time needful to invoke God, to offer unto Him that baptism of fire which is of the Holy Spirit. Hope, then, in the Light, and sleep!"

As he ended this discourse, Dom Arbuez—who had motioned the wretched man's fetters to be removed—embraced him tenderly. Then came the turn of the *fra redemptor*, who, in a low voice, prayed the Jew to pardon what he had made him endure in the effort to redeem him; then the two familiars clasped him in their arms: their kiss, through their cowls, was unheard. The ceremony at an end, the captive was left alone in the darkness.

Rabbi Aser Abarbanel, his lips parched, his face stupefied by suffering, stared, without any particular attention, at the closed door. Closed? The word, half unknown to himself, awoke a strange delusion in his confused thoughts. He fancied he had seen, for one second, the light of the lanterns through the fissure between the sides of this door. A morbid idea of hope, due to the enfeeblement of his brain, took hold on him. He dragged himself towards this strange thing he had seen; and, slowly inserting a finger, with infinite precautions, into the crack, he pulled the door towards him. Wonder of wonders! By some extraordinary chance the familiar who had closed it had turned the great key a little before it has closed upon its jambs of stone. So, the rusty bolt not having entered its socket, the door rolled back into the cell.

The Rabbi ventured to look out.

By means of a livid obscurity he distinguished, first of all, a half-circle of earthy walls, pierced by spiral stairways, and, opposite to him, five or six stone steps, dominated by a sort of black porch, giving access to a vast corridor, of which he could only see, from below, the nearest arches.

Stretching himself along, he crawled to the level of this threshold. Yes, it was indeed a corridor, but of boundless length. A faint light—a sort of dream-light—was cast over it; lamps suspended to the arched roof, turned, by intervals, the wan air blue; the far distance was lost in shadow. Not a door visible along all this length! On one side only, to the left, small holes, covered with a network of bars, let a feeble twilight through the depths of the wall—the light of sunset apparently, for red gleams fell at long intervals on the flagstones. And how fearful a silence!. . . Yet there—there in the depths of the dim distance—the way might lead to liberty! The wavering hope of the Jew was dogged, for it was the last.

Without hesitation he ventured forth, keeping close to the side of the light-holes, hoping to render himself indistinguishable from the darksome color of the long walls. He advanced slowly, dragging himself along the ground, forcing himself not to cry out when one of his wounds, recently opened, sent a sharp pang through him.

All of a sudden, the beat of a sandal, coming in his direction, echoed along the stone passage. A trembling fit seized him, he choked with anguish, his sight grew dim. So this, no doubt, was to be the end! He squeezed himself, doubled up on his hands and knees, into a recess, and, half dead with terror, waited.

It was a familiar, hurrying along. He passed rapidly, carrying an instrument for tearing out the muscles, his cowl lowered; he disappeared. The violent shock which the Rabbi had received had half suspended the functions of life; he remained for nearly an hour unable to make a single movement. In the fear of an increase of torments if he were caught, the idea came to him of returning to his cell. But the old hope chirped in his soul—the divine "Perhaps," the comforter in the worst of distresses. A miracle had taken place! There was no more room for doubt. He began again to crawl towards the possible escape. Worn out with suffering and with hunger, trembling with anguish, he advanced. And he, never ceasing his slow advance, gazed forward through the darkness, on, on, where there *must* be an outlet that would save him.

But, oh! steps sounding again; steps, this time, slower, more sombre. The forms of two Inquisitors, robed in black and white, and wearing their large hats with rounded brims, emerged into the faint light. They talked in low voices, and seemed to be in controversy on some important point, for their hands gesticulated.

At this sight Rabbi Aser Abarbanel closed his eyes, his heart beat as if it would kill him, his rags were drenched with the cold sweat of agony; motionless, gasping, he lay stretched along the wall, under the light of one of the lamps—motionless, imploring the God of David.

As they came opposite to him the two Inquisitors stopped under the light of the lamp, through a mere chance, no doubt, in their discussion. One of them, listening to his interlocutor, looked straight at the Rabbi. Under this gaze—of which he did not at first notice the vacant expression—the wretched man seemed to feel the hot pincers biting into his poor flesh; so he was again to become a living wound, a living woe! Fainting, scarce able to breathe, his eyelids quivering, he shuddered as the robe grazed him. But—strange at once and natural—the eyes of the Inquisitor were evidently the eyes of a man profoundly preoccupied with what he was going to say in reply, absorbed by what he was listening to; they were fixed, and seemed to be looking at the Jew *without seeing him*.

And indeed, in a few minutes, the two sinister talkers went on their way, slowly, still speaking in low voices, in the direction from which the prisoner had come. They had not seen him! And it was so, that, in the horrible disarray of his sensations, his brain was traversed by this thought: "Am I already dead, so that no one sees me?" A hideous impression drew him from his lethargy. On gazing at the wall, exactly opposite to his face, he fancied he saw, over against his, two ferocious eyes observing him! He flung back his head in a blind and sudden terror; the hair started upright upon his head. But no, no. He put out his hand, and felt along the stones. What he saw was the *reflection* of the eyes of the Inquisitor still left upon his pupils, and which he had refracted upon two spots of the wall.

Forward! He must hasten towards that end that he imagined (fondly no doubt) to mean deliverance; towards those shadows from which he was no more than thirty paces, or so, distant. He started once more—crawling on hands and knees and stomach—upon his dolorous way, and he was soon within the dark part of the fearful corridor.

All at once the wretched man felt the sensation of cold *upon* his hands that he placed on the flagstones; it was a strong current which came from under a little door at the end of the passage. O God, if this door opened on the outer world! The whole being of the poor prisoner was overcome by a sort of vertigo of hope. He examined the door from top to bottom without being able to distinguish it completely on account of the dimness around him. He felt over it. No lock, not a bolt! A latch! He rose to his feet: the latch yielded beneath his finger; the silent door opened before him.

"Hallelujah!" murmured the Rabbi, in an immense sigh, as he gazed at what stood revealed to him from the threshold.

The door opened upon gardens, under a night of stars—upon spring, liberty, life! The gardens gave access to the neighboring country that stretched away to the sierras, whose sinuous white lines stood out in profile on the horizon. There lay liberty! Oh, to fly! He would run all night under those woods of citrons, whose perfume intoxicated him. Once among the mountains, he would be saved. He breathed the dear, holy air; the wind reanimated him, his lungs found free play. He heard, in his expanding heart, the "Lazarus, come forth!" And, to give thanks to God, who had granted him this mercy, he stretched forth his arms before him, lifting his eyes to the firmament in an ecstasy.

And then he seemed to see the shadow of his arms returning upon himself; he seemed to feel those shadow-arms surround, enlace him, and himself pressed tenderly against some breast. A tall figure, indeed, was opposite to him. Confidently he lowered his eyes upon this figure, and remained gasping, stupefied, with staring eyes and mouth driveling with fright.

Horror! He was in the arms of the Grand Inquisitor himself, the venerable Pedro Arbuez d'Espila, who gazed at him with eyes full of tears, like a good shepherd who has found the lost sheep.

The sombre priest clasped the wretched Jew against his heart with so fervent a transport of charity that the points of the monacol hair-cloth rasped against the chest of the Dominican. And, while the Rabbi Aser Abarbanel, his eyes convulsed beneath his eyelids, choked with anguish between the arms of the ascetic Dom Arbuez, realizing confusedly *that all the phases of the false evening had only been a calculated torture, that of Hope*! the Grand Inquisitor, with a look of distress, an accent of poignant reproach, murmured in his ear, with the burning breath of much fasting:—"What! my child! on the eve, perhaps, of salvation. . . you would then leave us?"

THE BLACK CUPID

BY LAFCADIO HEARN

(1880)

There was a small picture hanging in the room; and I took the light to examine it. I do not know why I could not sleep. Perhaps it was the excitement of travel.

The gilded frame, massive and richly molded, enclosed one of the strangest paintings I had ever seen, a woman's head lying on a velvet pillow, one arm raised and one bare shoulder with part of a beautiful bosom relieved against a dark background. As I said, the painting was small. The young woman was evidently reclining upon her right side; but only her head, elevated upon the velvet pillow, her white throat, one beautiful arm and part of the bosom was visible.

With consummate art the painter had contrived that the spectator feel as though leaning over the edge of the couch—not visible in the picture—so as to bring his face close to the beautiful face on the pillow. It was one of the most charming heads a human being ever dreamed;—such a delicate bloom on the cheeks;—such a soft, humid light in the half-closed eyes;—such sun-bright hair;—such carnation lips;—such an oval outline! And all this relieved against a deep black background. In the lobe of the left ear I noticed a curious earring—a tiny Cupid wrought in black jet, suspending itself by his bow, which he held by each end, as if trying to pull it away from the tiny gold chain which fettered it to the beautiful ear, delicate and faintly rosy as a seashell. What a strange earring it was! I wondered if the black Cupid presided over unlawful loves, unblest amours!

But the most curious thing about the picture was the attitude and aspect of the beautiful woman. Her head, partly thrown back, with half-closed eyes and tender smile, seemed to be asking a kiss. The lips pouted expectantly. I almost fancied I could feel her perfumed breath. Under the rounded arm I noticed a silky floss of bright hair in tiny curls. The arm was raised as if to be flung about the neck of the person from whom the kiss was expected. I was astonished by the art of the painter. No photograph could have rendered such effects, however delicately colored; no photograph could have reproduced the gloss of the smooth shoulder, the veins, the smallest details! But the picture had a curious fascination.

It produced an effect upon me as if I were looking at a living beauty, a rosy and palpitating reality. Under the unsteady light of the lamp I once fancied that I saw the lips move, the eyes glisten! The head seemed to advance itself out of the canvas as though to be kissed. Perhaps it was very foolish; but I could not help kissing it—not once but a hundred times; and then I suddenly became frightened. Stories of bleeding statues and mysterious pictures and haunted tapestry came to my mind; and alone in a strange house and a strange city I felt oddly nervous. I placed the light on the table and went to bed.

But it was impossible to sleep. Whenever I began to doze a little, I saw the beautiful head on the pillow close beside me,—the same smile, the same lips, the golden hair, the silky floss under the caressing arm. I rose, dressed myself, lit a pipe, blew out the light, and smoked in the dark, until the faint blue tints of day stole in through the windows. Afar off I saw the white teeth of the Sierra flush rosily, and heard the rumbling of awakening traffic.

"Las cinco menos quarto, senor," cried the servant as he knocked upon my door,—"tiempo para levantarse."

* * * *

Before leaving I asked the landlord about the picture.

He answered with a smile, "It was painted by a madman, senor."

"But who?" I asked. "Mad or not, he was a master genius."

"I do not remember his name. He is dead. They allowed him to paint in the madhouse. It kept his mind tranquil. I obtained the painting from his family after his death. They refused to accept money for it, saying they were glad to give it away."

* * * *

I had forgotten all about the painting when some five years after I happened to be passing through a little street in Mexico City. My attention was suddenly attracted by some articles I saw in the window of a dingy shop, kept by a Spanish Jew. A pair of earrings—two little Cupids, wrought in jet black, holding their bows above their heads, the bows being attached by slender gold chains to the hooks of the earrings!

I remembered the picture in a moment! And that night!

"I do not really care to sell them, senor," said the swarthy jeweler, 'unless I get my price. You cannot get another pair like them. I know who made them! They were made for an artist who came here expressly with the design. He wished to make a present to a certain woman."

"Una Mejicana?"

"No, Americana."

"Fair, with dark eyes—about twenty, perhaps, at that time—a little rosy?"

"Why, did you know her? They used to call her Josefita. You know he killed her? Jealousy. They found her still smiling, as if she had been struck while asleep. A 'punal.' I got the earrings back at a sale."

"And the artist?"

"Died at P——, mad! Some say he was mad when he killed her. If you really want the earrings, I will let you have them for sixty pesos. They cost a hundred and fifty."

THE BUNDLE OF LETTERS

BY MORITZ JOKAI

(1891)

One of the celebrated medical practitioners of Pesth, Dr. K—, was one morning, at an early hour, obliged to receive a very pressing visitor. The man, who was waiting in the anteroom, sent in word by the footman that all delay would be dangerous to him; he had, therefore, to be received immediately.

The doctor hastily wrapped a dressing-gown about him, and directed the patient to be admitted to him.

He found himself in the presence of a man who was a complete stranger to him, but who appeared to belong to the best society, judging from his manners. On his pale face could discerned traces of great physical and moral sufferings. He carried his right hand in a sling, and, though he tried to restrain himself, he now and then could not prevent a stifled sigh escaping from his lips.

"You are Dr. K—?" he asked in a low and feeble tone of voice.

"That is my name, sir."

"Living in the country, I have not the honor of knowing you, except by reputation. But I cannot say that I am delighted to make your acquaintance, because my visit to you is not a very agreeable one."

Seeing that the sufferer's legs were hardly able to sustain him, the doctor invited him to be seated.

"I am fatigued. It is a week since I had any sleep. Something is the matter with my right hand; I don't know what it is—whether it is a carbuncle, or cancer. At first the pain was slight, but now it is a continuous horrible burning, increasing from day to day. I could bear it no longer, so threw myself into my carriage, and came to you, to beg you to cut out the affected spot, for an hour more of this torture will drive me mad."

The doctor tried to reassure him, by saying that he might be able to cure the pain with dissolvents and ointments, without resorting to the use of the bistory.

"No, no, sir!" cried the patient; "no plaisters or ointments can give me any relief. I must have the knife. I have come to you to cut out the place which causes me so much suffering."

The doctor asked to see the hand, which the patient held out to him, grinding his teeth, so insufferable appeared to be the pain he was enduring, and with all imaginable precaution he unwound the bandages in which it was enveloped.

"Above all, doctor, I beg of you not to hesitate on account of anything you may see. My disorder is so strange, that you will be surprised; but do not let that weigh with you."

Doctor K— reassured the stranger. As a doctor in practice he was used to seeing everything, and there was nothing that could surprise him.

What he saw when the hand was freed from its bandages stupefied him nevertheless. Nothing abnormal was to be seen in it—neither wound nor graze; it was a hand like any other. Bewildered, he let it fall from his own.

A cry of pain escaped from the stranger, who raised the afflicted member with his right hand, showing the doctor that he had not come with the intention of mystifying him, and that he was really suffering.

"Where is the sensitive spot?"

"Here, sir," said the stranger, indicating on the back of his hand a point where two large veins crossed, his whole frame trembling when the doctor touched it with the tip of his finger.

"It is here that the burning pain makes itself felt?"

"Abominably!"

"Do you feel the pressure when I place my finger on it?"

The man made no reply, but his eyes filled with tears, so acute was his suffering.

"It is surprising! I can see nothing at that place."

"Nor can I; yet what I feel there is so terrible that at times I am almost driven to dash my head against the wall."

The doctor examined the spot with a magnifying-glass, then shook his head.

"The skin is full of life; the blood within it circulates regularly; there is neither inflammation nor cancer under it; it is as healthy at that spot as elsewhere."

"Yet I think it is a little redder there."

"Where?"

The stranger took a pencil from his pocket book and traced on his hand a ring about the size of a sixpenny-piece, and said:

"It is there."

The doctor looked in his face; he was beginning to believe that his patient's mind was unhinged.

"Remain here," he said, "and in a few days I'll cure you."

"I cannot wait. Don't think that I am a madman, a maniac; it is not in that way that you would cure me. The little circle which I have marked with my pencil causes me internal tortures, and I have come to you to cut it away."

"That I cannot do," said the doctor.

"Why?"

"Because your hand exhibits no pathological disorder. I see at the spot you have indicated nothing more amiss than on my own hand."

"You really seem to think that I have gone out of my senses, or that I have come here to mock you," said the stranger, taking from his pocket-book a banknote for a thousand florins, and laying it on the table. "Now, sir, you see that I am not playing off any childish jest and that the service I seek of you is as urgent as it is important. I beg you to remove this part of my hand."

"I repeat, sir, that for all the treasures in the world you cannot make me regard as unsound a member that is perfectly sound, and still less induce me to cut it with my instruments."

"And why not?"

"Because such an act would cast a doubt upon my medical knowledge and compromise my reputation. Everybody would say that you were mad; that I was dishonest in taking advantage of your condition, or ignorant in not perceiving it."

"Very well. I will only ask a small service of you, then. I am myself capable of making the incision. I shall do it rather clumsily with my left hand; but that does not matter. Be good enough only to bind up the wound after the operation."

It was with astonishment that the doctor saw that this strange man was speaking seriously. He stripped off his coat, turned up the wrist-bands of his shirt, and took a bistory in his left hand.

A second later, and the steel had made a deep incision in the skin.

"Stay!" cried the doctor, who feared that his patient might, through his awkwardness, sever some important organ. "Since you have determined on the operation, let me perform it."

He took the bistory, and placing in his left hand the right hand of the patient, begged him to turn away his face, the sight of blood being insupportable to many persons.

"Quite needless. On the contrary, it is I who must direct you where to cut."

In fact he watched the operation to the end with the greatest coolness, indicating the limits of the incisions. The open hand did not even quiver in that of the doctor, and when the circular piece was removed, he sighed profoundly, like a man experiencing an enormous relief.

"Nothing burns you now?"

"All has ceased," said the stranger, smiling. "The pain has completely disappeared, as if it had been carried away with the part excised. The little discomfort which the flowing of blood causes me, compared with the other pain, is like a fresh breeze after a blast from the infernal regions. It does me a real good to see my blood pouring forth: let it flow, it does me extreme good."

The stranger watched with an expression of delight the blood pouring from the wound, and the doctor was obliged to insist on binding up the hand.

During the bandaging the aspect of his face completely changed. It no longer bore a dolorous expression, but a look full of good humor was turned upon the doctor. No more contraction of the features, no more despair. A taste for life had returned; the brow was once again calmed; the color found its way back to the cheeks. The entire man exhibited a complete transformation.

As soon as his hand was laid in the sling he warmly wrung the doctor's hand with the one that remained free, and said cordially:

"Accept my sincere thanks. You have positively cured me. The trifling remuneration I offer you is not at all proportioned to the service you have rendered me: for the rest of my life I shall search for the means of repaying my debt to you."

The doctor would not listen to anything of the kind, and refused to accept the thousand florins placed on the table. On his side the stranger refused to take them back, and, observing that the doctor was losing his temper, begged him to make a present of the money to some hospital, and took his departure.

K— remained for several days at his townhouse until the wound in his patient's hand should be cicatrised. During this time the doctor was able to satisfy himself that he had to do with a man of extensive knowledge, reflective, and having very positive opinions in regard to the affairs of life. Besides being rich, he occupied an important official position. Since the taking away of his invisible pain, no trace of moral or physical malady was discoverable in him.

The cure completed, the man returned tranquilly to his residence in the country.

About three weeks had passed away when, one morning, at an hour as unduly as before, the servant again announced the strange patient.

The stranger, whom K— hastened to receive, entered the room with his right hand in a sling, his features convulsed and hardly recognisable from suffering. Without waiting to be invited to sit down, he sank into a chair, and, being unable to master the torture he was enduring, groaned, and without uttering a word, held out his hand to the doctor.

"What has happened?" asked K——, stupefied.

"We have not cut deep enough," replied the stranger, sadly, and in a fainting voice. "It burns me more cruelly than before. I am worn out by it; my arm is stiffened by it. I did not wish to trouble you a second time, and have borne it, hoping that by degrees the invisible inflammation would either mount to my head or descend to my heart, and put an end to my miserable existence; but it has not done so. The pain never goes beyond the spot, but it is indescribable! Look at my face, and you will be able to imagine what it must be!"

The color of the man's skin was that of wax, and a cold perspiration beaded his forehead. The doctor unbound the bandaged hand. The point operated on was well healed; a new skin had formed, and nothing extraordinary was to be seen. The sufferer's pulse beat quickly, without feverishness, while yet he trembled in every limb.

"This really smacks on the marvelous!" exclaimed the doctor, more and more astonished. "I have never before seen such a case."

"It is a prodigy, a horrible prodigy, doctor. Do not try to find a cause for it, but deliver me from this torment. Take your knife and cut deeper and wider: only that can relieve me."

The doctor was obliged to give in to the prayers of his patient. He performed the operation once again, cutting into the flesh more deeply; and, once more, he saw in the sufferer's face the expression of astonishing relief, the curiosity at seeing the blood flow from the wound, which he had observed on the first occasion.

When the hand was dressed, the deadly pallor passed from the face, the color returned to the cheeks; but the patient no more smiled. This time he thanked the doctor sadly.

"I thank you, doctor," he said. "The pain has once more left me. In a few days the wound will heal. Do not be astonished, however, to see me return before a month has passed."

"Oh! my dear sir, drive this idea from your mind."

The doctor mentioned this strange case to several of his colleagues, who each held a different opinion in regard to it, without any of them being able to furnish a plausible explanation of its nature.

As the end of the month approached, K—— awaited with anxiety the reappearance of this enigmatic personage. But the month passed and he did not reappear.

Several weeks more went by. At length the doctor received a letter from the sufferer's residence. It was very closely written, and by the signature he saw that it had been penned by his patient's own hand; from which he concluded that the pain had not returned, for otherwise it would have been very difficult for him to have held a pen.

These are the contents of the letter:—

"Dear doctor, I cannot leave either you or medical science in doubt in regard to the mystery of the strange malady which will shortly carry me to the grave.

"I will here tell you the origin of this terrible malady. For the past week it has returned the third time, and I will no longer struggle with it. At this moment I am only able to write by placing upon the sensitive spot a piece of burning tinder in the form of a poultice. While the tinder is burning I do not feel the other pain; and what distress it causes me is a mere trifle by comparison.

"Six months ago I was still a happy man. I lived on my income without a care. I was on good terms with everybody, and enjoyed all that is of interest to a man of five-and-thirty. I had married a year before—a young lady, handsome, with a cultivated mind and a heart as good as any heart could be, who has been a governess in the house of a countess, a neighbor of mine. She was fortuneless, and attached herself to me, not only from gratitude, but still more from real childish affection. Six months passed, during which every day appeared to be happier than the one which had gone before. If, at times, I was obliged to go to Pesth and quit my own land for a day, my wife had not a moment's rest. She would come two leagues on the way to meet me. If I was detained late, she passed a sleepless night waiting for me; and if by prayers I succeeded in inducing her to go and visit her former mistress, who had not ceased to be extremely fond of her, no power could keep her away from home for more than half a day; and by her regrets for my absence, she invariably spoiled the good-humor of others. Her tenderness for me went so far as to make her renounce dancing, so as not to be obliged to give her hand to strangers, and nothing more displeased her than gallantries addressed to her. In a word, I had for my wife an innocent girl, who thought of nothing but me, and who confessed to me her dreams as enormous crimes, if they were not of me.

"I know not what demon one day whispered in my ear: Suppose that all this were dissimulation? Men are mad enough to seek torments in the midst of their greatest happiness.

"My wife had a work-table, the drawer of which she carefully locked. I had noticed this several times. She never forgot the key, and never left the drawer open.

"That question haunted my mind. What could she be hiding there? I had become mad. I no longer believed either in the innocence of her face or the purity of her looks, nor in her caresses, nor in her kisses. What if all that were mere hypocrisy?

"One morning the countess came anew to invite her to her house, and, after much pressing, succeeded in inducing her to go and spend the day with her. Our estates were some leagues from each other, and I promised to join my wife in the course of a few hours.

"As soon as the carriage had quitted the courtyard, I collected all the keys in the house and tried them on the lock of the little drawer. One of them opened it. I felt like a man committing his first crime. I was a thief about to surprise the secrets of my poor wife. My hands trembled as I carefully pulled out the drawer, and, one by one, turned over the objects within it, so that no derangement of them might betray the fact of a strange hand having disturbed them. My bosom was oppressed; I was almost stifled. Suddenly—under some lace—I put my hand upon a packet of letters. It was as if a flash of lightning had passed through me from my head to my heart. Oh! they were the sort of letters one recognises at a glance—love letters!

"The packet was tied with a rose-colored ribbon, edged with silver.

"As I touched that ribbon this thought came into my mind: Is it conceivable?—is this the work of an honest man? To steal the secrets of his wife!—secrets belonging to the time when she was a young girl. Have I any right to exact from her a reckoning for thoughts she may have had before she belonged to me? Have I any right to be jealous of a time when I was unknown to her? Who could suspect her of a fault? Who? I am guilty for having suspected her. The demon again whispered in my ears: 'But what if these letters date from a time when you already had a right to know all her thoughts, when you might already be jealous of her dreams, when she was already yours?' I unfastened the ribbon. Nobody saw me. There was not even a mirror to make me blush for myself. I opened one letter, then another, and I read them to the end.

"Oh, it was a terrible hour for me!

"What was in these letters? The vilest treason of which a man has ever been the victim. The writer of these letters was one of my intimate friends! And the tone in which they were written!—what passion, what love, certain of being returned! How he spoke of 'keeping the secret!' And all these letters dated at a time when I was married and so happy! How can I tell you what I felt? Imagine the intoxication caused by a mortal poison. I read all those letters—every one. Then I put them up again in a packet, re-tied them with the ribbon, and, replacing them under the lace, relocked the drawer.

"I knew that if she did not see me by noon she would return in the evening from her visit to the countess—as she did. She descended from the *caleche* hurriedly, to rush towards me as I stood awaiting her on the steps. She kissed me with excessive tenderness, and appeared extremely happy to be once again with me. I allowed nothing of what was passing within me to appear in my face. We conversed, we supped together, and each retired to our bedrooms. I did not close an eye. Broad awake, I counted all the hours. When the clock struck the first quarter after midnight, I rose and entered her room. The beautiful fair head was there pressed into the white pillows—as angels are painted in the midst of snowy clouds. What a frightful lie of nature's is vice under an aspect so innocent! I was resolved, with the headlong willfulness of a madman, haunted by a fixed idea. The poison had completely corroded my soul. I resolved to kill her as she lay.

"I pass over the details of the crime. She died without offering the least resistance, as tranquilly as one goes to sleep. She was never irritated against me—even when I killed her. One single drop of blood fell on the back of my hand—you know where. I did not perceive until the next day, when it was dry.

"We buried her without anybody suspecting the truth. I lived in solitude. Who could have controlled my actions? She had neither parent nor guardian who could have addressed to me any questions on the subject, and I designedly put off sending the customary invitations to the funeral, so that my friends could not arrive in time.

"On returning from the vault I felt not the least weight upon my conscience. I had been cruel, but she had deserved it. I would not hate her—I would forget her. I scarcely thought of her. Never did a man commit an assassination with less remorse than I.

"The countess, so often mentioned, was at the chateau when I returned there. My measures had been so well taken that she also had arrived too late for the internment. On seeing me she appeared greatly agitated. Terror, sympathy, sorrow, or, I know not what, had put so much into her words that I could not understand what she was saying to console me.

"Was I even listening to her? Had I any need of consolation? I was not sad. At last she took me familiarly by the hand, and, dropping her voice, said that she was obliged to confide a secret to me, and that she relied on my honor as a gentleman not to abuse it. She had given my wife a packet of letters to mind, not having been able to keep them in her own house; and these letters she now requested me to return to her. While she was speaking, I several times felt a shudder run through my frame. With seeming coolness, however, I questioned her as to the content of the letters. At this interrogation the lady started, and replied angrily:—

"'Sir, your wife has been more generous than you! When she took charge of *my* letters, she did not demand to know what they contained.

She even gave me her promise that she would never set eyes on them, and I am convinced that she never read a line of any one of them. She had a noble heart, and would have been ashamed to forfeit the pledge she had given.'

"'Very well,' I replied. 'How shall I recognise this packet?'

"'It was tied with a rose-colored ribbon edged with silver.'

"'I will go and search for it.'

"I took my wife's keys, knowing perfectly well where I should find the packet; but I pretended to find it with much difficulty.

"'Is this it?' I asked the countess, handing it to her.

"'Yes, yes—that is it! See!—the knot I myself made has never been touched.'

"I dared not raise my eyes to her; I feared lest she should read in them that I had untied the knot of that packet, and something more.

"I took leave of her abruptly; she sprang into her carriage and drove off.

"The drop of blood had disappeared, the pain was not manifested by any external symptom; and yet the spot marked by the drop burned me as if it had been bitten by a corrosive poison. This pain grows from hour to hour. I sleep sometimes, but I never cease to be conscious of my suffering. I do not complain to anybody: nobody, indeed, would believe my story. You have seen the violence of my torment, and you know how much the two operations have relieved me; but concurrently with the healing of the wound, the pain returns. It has now attacked me for the third time, and I have no longer strength to resist it. In an hour I shall be dead. One thought consoles me; it is that she has avenged herself here below. She will perhaps forgive me above. I thank you for all you have done for me. May heaven reward you."

A few days later one might have read in the newspapers that S——, one of the richest landowners, had blown out his brains. Some attributed his suicide to sorrow caused by the death of his wife; others, better informed, to an incurable wound. Those who best knew him said that he had been attacked by monomania, that his incurable wound existed only in his imagination.

NISSA

BY ALBERT DELPIT

(1892)

Gaston lighted a cigarette, saying,
"It isn't a long story, but it is dramatic. Confound it! Whenever I think of it, a chill through every vein. You remember that two years ago I was sent on a mission to Persia to study and describe the province of Irak-Adjemi. I began by settling in Ispahan, and completed my studies in three months. But, had I returned at once, my reputation for thorough scholarship would have been lost. I was almost bored to death, when the governor was changed. The Shah sent, in place of the former one, his cousin Malcom-Khan."

"The one who has been in France?"

"Yes, and you knew one of the heroes of my story, Mehmed-Aga, who was on the staff of the prince. He has the rank of general or rather, as they call it in Persia, *sertip*."

"I remember. A man of about thirty, very elegant and clever, who sometimes supped with us?"

"You can understand my pleasure in meeting him there. There is something particularly charming about these Orientals who have become semi-Parisians. Contact with our civilization seems to refine and soften their primitive barbarism. At the end of a week the *sertip* and I were inseparable."

"And the drama?"

"You are in too great of a hurry. I haven't finished the introduction. One morning I was riding on horseback through the city, lost in reverie, and for the hundredth time enjoying its fairy-like charm. Imagine broad avenues, lined on the right and left by arcades, the whole interspersed with huge plane-trees, watered by ever-flowing rills; farther beyond—"

"A description! My dear fellow, you're not working for the ministry. You promised me a dramatic story; tell it. Above all, don't wander into descriptions."

Gaston sighed, and then continued.

"I was approaching the mosque of Tchechel-Sutoun, when at a street corner, I saw a woman in a litter. Usually Persian women in the street look like bundles. They are veiled, of course, or rather they wear on their heads a sort of curtain which covers their faces. This Persian, on the contrary, displayed a slender, graceful figure. Her eyes were large and full of fire. My horse was walking and slowly followed the litter. I fancied that the stranger looked back once or twice, but as flirtations are extremely improbable occurrences in the East, I paid little heed and had nearly forgotten the meeting when, two days later, I again encountered the litter. This time I was not alone. Mehmed Aga was with me. I recognized the veiled lady at a glance, especially her marvellous eyes, whence flashed a beam of lambent flame. As before, she looked back, but for a longer time. I glanced at the *sertip*, he pretended not to have noticed anything. We moved on in this way for about ten minutes when the litter turned abruptly toward the Djoulffa bridge, one of the finest pieces of architecture in the world. It has thirty huge arches over the Zenderud, a very changeable river. In the summer you may cross it dry-shod; in the month of November, the time when this adventure occurred, its waves were as swift and violent as a torrent leaping from Alpine glaciers. The Djoulffa bridge is a sort of meeting place for people who go out in the cool air of the evening. I hesitated, therefore, to follow my *incognita* openly, but she had no scruples. Leaning half way out of the litter she dropped her handkerchief. Oh, these Persian women are quick-witted."

"And did the *sertip* say nothing?"

"Not at the moment. He kept silent during the rest of our ride, but twisted his moustache as if his thoughts were far away. 'Come in,' he said when we reached the palace; and, after we were smoking in his private room, he added:

"'My dear fellow, I made no comment just now. But instead of keeping that dainty handkerchief pressed close to your heart, you are going to throw it into the fire.'

"'What do you mean?'

"'I mean that you are not to be strangled or stabbed, or flung into the Zenderud. I am in charge of the police in this city, and answerable to the French legation.'

"'But—'

"'Not another word. You Parisians are the most amazing fellows! You always imagine yourselves on the Boulevard des Capucines. We are in the East, my dear boy, and in the East, husbands do not jest. Your stranger is no stranger to me. Her name is Nissa.'

"'Nissa!'

"'If the name is charming the husband is not. He is a very rich merchant, famous for his violent temper and his jealousy. His mother was of English origin, but he is thoroughly Oriental in character. He'd kill you like a dog.'

"'And what is this Ispahan Bluebeard's name?'

"'Astoulla. I don't wish you to make his acquaintance. But you know where he lives. His house is just on the river brink at the end of the bridge.'

"'And Nissa, what do people say of her?'

"'Oh, true Parisian! People don't talk about women in our country, or if they do—well, they are sewed up in a sack and flung into the water.'

"'What an outrage!'

"'Oh, we are civilized now,' replied the *sertip* cooly. 'Formerly a live cat would have been put into the bag, also. Terrified by the water, the cat would tear the woman's face. This is no longer done—at least, not frequently. The result of European influence!'

"This little conversation was rather a wet blanket on my enthusiasm. Besides, Mehmed Aga had the good taste not to push the subject further. I dined with him and in the evening he sent for some musicians who played several airs for us in the fashion of the country. But my thoughts were preoccupied. I still saw the graceful figure bending from the litter, and the little hand which dropped from the handkerchief. A persistent voice murmured in my ear like the refrain of a ballad: 'Nissa!—Nissa.' All night long I suffered from nightmare, in which a huge cat named Astoulla scratched my face. I woke at eleven o'clock in the morning, completely disenchanted.

* * * *

"While sitting on the terrace that evening a hideously ugly old woman entered the low doorway of the house and asked to see me. As soon as we were alone, she said:

"'Are you a brave man?'

"I smiled with the fatuity peculiar to men who are asked that question.

"'I have a proposal to make,' she added. 'It is dark. No one will see us. You must follow me. When half way, I shall tie a bandage over your eyes, but you must swear not to try to discover where I am taking you.'

"'I promise.'

"She made a grimace, which rendered her still more frightful. I had consented off hand, urged by an irresistible impulse. Daylight had dispelled my fears, the nightmare had gradually faded from my mind, and I constantly heard the voice murmuring in my ear: 'Nissa! Nissa!' The old woman evidently came from her. I went into my room and took a small revolver. Five minutes after we were on our way. It was crazy, utterly absurd, I am perfectly aware of that. But there are some absurdities concerning which we do not reason. The unknown Nissa exerted some mysterious power over me. I had not even seen her, yet I ardently longed for her presence. Her sparkling eyes had fired my heart.

"When we reached the Djoulffa bridge the old woman stopped, and, drawing a handkerchief from her pocket, tied it firmly over my eyes. I could see nothing; then she seized my hand, and I let her lead me. By the cooler air I guessed that we were crossing the river; then I heard the sound of voices at the right and left. It never entered my mind that I might be noticed by these passing pedestrians. I was completely absorbed in my dream, thinking of the young Persian's graceful figure, delicate little hand, and glowing eyes. After a few minutes' walk the old woman turned toward the right, but we did not leave the banks of the Zenderud. I heard its tumultuous waves dashing against the arches of the bridge. At last my guide stopped; I heard the creaking of a key, and the old woman said under her breath:

"'Go up.'

"We mounted only five steps, then my feet pressed a thick, soft carpet. At the same time the bandage was snatched away. I found myself in a somewhat small room, dimly lighted by a copper lamp. Usually, in Persia, the walls are bare. Here, on the contrary, they were draped with yellow cashmere. Perfumes were burning in a brazier—the acrid Oriental perfumes which intoxicate like the fumes of old wine. Against the background of yellow cashmere on the walls hung musical instruments, the *nefir* which resembles our hautboy, timbals, two *kematches*, a sort of viol, and, here and there, weapons interspersed with necklaces. Outside was the dull, rhythmic beat of the waves of the river. Drawing aside the portiere, I saw that it washed the very walls of the house. Almost instantly I heard a slight, rustling noise, and turning saw—Nissa. I was fairly dazzled. She was probably seventeen or eighteen. Her thick black hair, falling on her neck and shoulders, reminded one of the raven locks of Regnault's Salome. Her face, somewhat creamy in tint, resembled mother of pearl, but I was especially struck by the contrast between her dazzling white teeth and very black eyes. The lashes, lids, and lips were painted. She gazed calmly at me with her sparkling eyes, then took my hand and leading me to a sofa, said:

"'My husband has gone to Teheran; we can have a little fun.'

"She spoke in English, with a marked guttural accent, then tapped with a copper ring on a small drum and coffee was served. Afterwards, she began to talk in low, rapid tones, telling me that she was terribly bored and had noticed me at once. Meanwhile her glances grew more tender, her hand gently pressed mine. Just at that moment there was a noise in the next room. She sprang up, trembling from head to foot. Her graceful advances, the caress, the sudden terror that succeeded each other so rapidly that I had not had time to analyze my own impressions. Still with the same swift, feline grace, she darted to the wall, snatched a small, sharp dagger, and slipped it up her sleeve. Then, turning to me with an energetic gesture, she whispered, 'Wait!' and vanished behind the heavy drapery.

* * * *

"A vague sense of anxiety stole over me. I remembered the *sertip's* warnings. Perhaps I had been a little imprudent. Suddenly the noise in the next room commenced again; I heard voices, a short struggle—silence followed. All at once the portiere was raised and Nissa appeared again. She was very pale, so pale that the mother of pearl tints in her complexion blended with the pearl necklace she wore. She stood half leaning against the wall, like a white statue relieved against the yellow background of the drapery. Then she advanced a few paces into the apartment, smiling: her hands and the knife were red.

"'Great Heavens! What has happened?'

"'Nothing,' she replied, flung the knife into a corner, and added quietly:

"'It was my husband. He would have killed us; I preferred to anticipate him. Come and help me throw the body into the water.'

"I stood motionless, gazing at her in horror. She looked at me, but her eyes expressed the most absolute contempt, and I shall never forget the tone in which she said:

"'Oh! how nervous these Frenchmen are!'

"Shrugging her shoulders, she called a female servant and told her to open the window. Then, as if they were doing the most everyday thing, the two lifted the corpse and flung it into the water, which swept it away. In truth, the adventure was becoming too Oriental for a Parisian. I confess that I was overwhelmed with frantic terror, and waiting for nothing more, rushed off like a madman. How did I go? I have actually no idea. At the end of ten minutes I found myself again in the city, through which I rushed at full speed as if pursued by a legion of fiends.

"On reaching home I double-locked my door, execrating Nissa and all the houris of the Oriental world.

* * * *

"What a night I spent! I did not sleep until the morning and then fell into a leaden stupor. When I awoke, the sun, already high in the heavens, was pouring floods of light into my room. I felt overwhelmed by a sort of moral paralysis. A man does not disappear without the interference of justice. Nissa did not even conceal her deed; the servant had seen and helped her. I should be implicated in the affair, and the bare thought of being mixed up with such a crime made my hair bristle with horror. Should I confide the whole matter to the French Minister? Unfortunately he had just obtained leave of absence, and the first Secretary of Legation was too young for me to apply to him. In any case my whole future was destroyed. I remained all day a prey to the keenest anxiety, not daring to leave the house. Evening came before I had formed any plan, and still there was no news of Nissa. Had she been arrested? What had become of her? I went to bed early, but could not sleep. The second day, unable to endure the situation longer, I resolved so visit the *sertip*. Anything would be preferable to the uncertainty in which I was living. I felt sure that Mehmed-Aga would not go out before breakfast, so I reached the palace at noon. I was told that he was in his office as usual and, after being announced, I entered. The *sertip* was peacefully smoking his *chibouque*.

"'Ah, is it you?' he said. 'Are you well?'

"'Very well. thank you.'

"'By the way,' he added, 'have you heard the news?'

"'The news—the news? No, I—I don't know anything.'

"'You remember the rich merchant, Astoulla?'

"'Remember As—'

"'Why yes, the husband of Nissa, of whom we were speaking.'

"I felt the blood mount to the roots of my hair. It was all over, the crime was known, and I dared not think of the end of the adventure. I stammered an almost unintelligible 'yes.'

"'Poor fellow!' continued the *sertip*. 'He has suddenly disappeared.'

"I felt a curious choking sensation in the throat but managed to answer:

"'What! he has—he has disappeared? Why! That's very—very queer.'

"'Yes, *very* queer.'

"And the *sertip* looked intently at me. I could bear his gaze no longer, and was on the point of confessing everything, when he said:

"'He was going to Teheran, and all at once he vanished. Nothing more has been heard of him.'

"For the second time the *sertip* looked intently at me. A brief silence followed. Then, puffing a cloud of smoke from his *chibouque*, he added with the most peaceful tranquility:

"'God is great!'"

THE DREAM

BY JOHN GALT

(1833)

Amidst the mountains of the "north countrie" is an extensive blue lake, on which, at noon, no shadow can be traced; the hills and uplands, by which it is surrounded, all present their brightest sides to its beautiful waters, and, for upwards of an hour, it then appears as a mirror on which the sun shines with peculiar lustre.

The streams, which rush into this crystalline basin, are clear, cool and picturesque; several, on account of their romantic features, are visited by young travelers, and persons accustomed to indulge in the reveries of imagination; but there is one sylvan rivulet more deserving of attention than them all, and which, from its quiet flow and sequestered course, is seldom noticed. From a remote rock leaps in it a south running spring, which, from that circumstance, is much frequented on Hallows-eve by the swains and maidens who dwell in the neighborhood, repairing to its banks to perform its divinations.

The effusion from this natural fountain is mineral and tepid: it sends a slight aromatic fragrance, and possesses the power of producing sleep, in which the dreams are wonderfully consistent with themselves and delightful in their incidents; but it is thought to have some intoxicating quality, and, in consequence, is but seldom tasted.

One summer's day a shepherd boy, belonging to the adjacent hills, had strayed into the glen in which this forbidden water descends. He was, in many respects, a singular stripling, and had a strange pleasure in lone places, and where, in ancient times poets would have seen nymphs and fauns pursuing their innocent gaieties. His father, a village schoolmaster, had given him the romantic name of Driades, and delighted in filling his fancy with recitals of courtly pageants and fantastical adventures. Thus, without endeavor on the boy's part, he was unlike the other lads of the village, and yet withal, more gentle, good, and simple, than any of the other boys that might have been his companions.

Driades, finding himself alone in the green hollow where the spring gushed odoriferously from the rock, sat himself down. He had never been there before, and the leaves of the birch and hazel shed into the sultry air their sweetest perfume. On all sides rocks and cliffs and feathery trees hung above him, and no sound molested the calm that breathed there but the falling waters and the occasional call of the merle to her mate. It was a warm and soft day, and all around were images of peace and rest. Confidence was vocal in the bowers, and the genius of the place whispered tranquility to the blameless and unguarded Driades.

Overpowered by his previous journey and the warmth of the day, he approached the enticing waters. He had never heard of their qualities, and, allured by their brightness, drank of them freely; surprised at tasting them tepid, and yet leaping from the rock, he renewed his draught to assure his palate that he was not mistaken. In doing this he discovered their faint and delicious odor, and tasted again and again, until he had inadvertently indulged in a more copious draught than those acquainted with the spring would have ventured to take.

In the course of a few minutes the intoxicating influence of the waters began to prevail, and he stretched himself upon the green sward and surrendered his senses to sleep. The day, the place, and the thoughtlessness of Driades were propitious to his slumber, and he continued, for several hours, in unmolested repose; but late in the afternoon, near the time that the sun was setting, a stranger, who had taken up his abode for a short time on the banks of the lake, happened to explore the untrodden margin of the rill into which the medicinal water was flowing. Seeing the entranced youth lying in defenceless sleep in the sylvan dells, he went towards him and awakened him.

Driades, in rising from his couch, stretched out his arms, and yawning with pleasure, reproached the stranger mildly for disturbing a dream, the pleasantest he had ever enjoyed.

Surprised by the look and expression of the boy, the stranger paused beside him, and enquired of what his dream had consisted. After a short explanation they seated themselves together on the embroidered turf, and Driades thus related the story of the vision which had so charmed his slumber:—

"I thought myself," said Driades, "in a grand and gorgeous metropolitan city; all around me were lofty structures and solemn temples, pinnacles crowned with gold, vast colonnades, stairs and sculptured palaces, triumphal arches and surpassing domes. I beheld objects of wealth and dominion, and on every side I heard the buzz of a great multitude, and saw chariots and horsemen and nobles in all the pomp of honors, antiquity, and power. Presently, from a stupendous portico, heralds and trumpeters issued forth, and, with a flourish, announced the great king: all the crowd of spectators knelt at the sound and in due time, I beheld, after a retinue of officers clothed in oriental splendor, the monarch, borne on a golden throne, into the midst of them. Of the ceremonies then performed, and the decrees he issued, I cannot speak, but the plaudits which his wisdom received were loud and long, and he was hailed by the vast multitude that filled the spacious courts of the palace with demonstrations of praise and joy.

"When this resplendent scene had lasted some time, the king retired into his interior halls; his attendants followed, and the crowd dispersed. All went away, and I was left alone; but at last I too moved from my situation, and began to examine more in detail the edificial grandeur of that Babylonian town: wherever I turned, my sight was perplexed with new wonders; pleasure sparkled in every visage, and methought the New Jerusalem could present no superior splendor and happiness.

"But I was alone: in all the tides of that multitude I saw no friend; I heard no congratulations, I was sad, I knew not what for; I wandered along, a lonely and destitute boy.

"For a time my disconsolate feelings were painfully awake; I desired to participate in the revels that rung around me, and I longed to share the feats and renown of those that the king delighted to honor.

"While I was standing in this state, a venerable old man addressed me; his locks were of snowy whiteness bound with a golden fillet, and his loose dark brown robes, though in form and color betokening simplicity and riches, showed that he was no common man.

"He enquired from what part of the mountains I had arrived—what I knew, and my objects in visiting the metropolis.

"I replied to his questions with humility and candor. I told how my youth had been spent, and how I had strayed into that wonderful city, nor did I conceal from him my friendlessness and the fears which weighed upon my heart.

"Pleased with my replies and interested in my forlorn situation, he invited me to follow him to his house; and promised me a refuge among his servants.

"I obeyed this benevolent old man, and followed him to his dwelling. It was a noble building, constructed of the richest materials and in a manner that showed the taste and opulence of the possessor. At the magnificent portal he committed me to the care of his steward, a person whose appearance was calculated to ensure esteem, and I was soon enrolled among the members of his household.

"Delighted to have found, so early, a patron so estimable, I strove to attract in my servitude, the notice of the steward, nor was I in this ineffectual. He saw my industry, he praised my intelligence, and my heart beat with happiness without pride.

"In the course of a short time after this fortunate overture, one of the principal servants of the establishment happened to die, and the steward, notwithstanding my youth, spoke to his venerable master in my behalf, and recommended me as a fit person to be the successor of the dead. I was accordingly promoted, and the increase of the cares of my trust made me more ardent in my desire to give satisfaction. Everything prospered with me; the steward exulted in having recommended me, our master was content with my efforts, and I was untired myself in my solicitude to merit attention.

"I had not been long in the enjoyment of this felicity when another vacancy occurred in the household by the death of a clerk who was employed in the land office of our master. It had been observed that, during the intervals of my particular vocation, I had engaged myself in arithmetical studies, which the good-natured steward had observed, and had told his master that I belonged to another class than the menial order to which I was consigned. The old man acknowledged that he had himself noticed me, and said, if the steward deemed me fit for the clerkship, he had his full consent to remove me into the office.

"This was an era in my existence: I was raised from servility to an honorable station, in which there was no limit to the elevation I might obtain; instead, therefore, of giving my leisure, like the other young men, to revelry and ease, I redoubled my industry. Every moment was precious, and every hour, when I might have been idle, was spent in the attainment of some new accomplishment. The steward deemed his duty well performed in facilitating my rise, and our master was pleased often to converse with me, and to show the preference which my assiduity had inspired. Thus, step by step, I was promoted in that household, and, perhaps, might have reached to great eminence; but it was thought my merits were so superior that my services should be devoted to the king: accordingly, one day our excellent master spoke to me on the subject, and enquired how I would like the service of the state. So great an honor I had never dreamt of; but I replied that, in whatever situation it should please heaven to place me, I would endeavor to do my duty, as the best means in my possession, to prove my gratitude to my friends.

"The old man was pleased with my answer, and procured me, in the course of the same day, employment with the ministers of the crown.

"In a few years my success surprised myself. I was not only promoted by the routine of accidents, but chosen for merit; and I rose in time to fill an office of important trust.

"In this situation, honored by the king and esteemed by his subjects, I gathered wealth and found myself in the ranks of those who wear the decorations of renown.

"At this juncture a great calamity overtook my old master—a fearful inundation ravaged his lands, his cattle perished in the deluge, and his vines, fig-trees and olives, were swept away. In the midst of this desolation I beheld the misery to which he was reduced; my heart yearned with the remembrance of his kindness, and I mourned to think that one who had been accustomed to such opulence should, in his old age, be so exposed to the stings of poverty. I called also to mind, with a softer sentiment, that he had an only child—a daughter who must share his distress; and the fortune I had made by this time was sufficient to mitigate the pangs of their unmerited loss.

"I went to him, and said that all I possessed he was welcome to, and, to prove the sincerity of my offer, I proposed to wed his daughter. He made no answer, but went into the apartment where she was sitting, and repeated what I had said; tears rushed into her eyes, and she came at once to me with outstretched hands, and became my wife.

"In the course of time the old man died, and she was the inheritrix of all his vast domains, which more propitious seasons began to renovate. With her I had many children, our daughters, good and fair, were selected for wives by the primates of the land; and our seven sons maintained the character which their father had earned with the public. All around was green and fertile; honors were at my acceptance; abundance poured her horn at my feet; and— But you awoke me at this moment."

"Ah!" said the stranger, "yours, Driades, has been a common dream: youth is beguiled by many such fancies; after a long life, such as you have described, he awakes to his real condition, and finds that all which he deemed so bright and fair was but a vision."

Excerpted from *The Stolen Child.*

Lightning Source UK Ltd.
Milton Keynes UK
UKHW010314311220
376156UK00001B/153

9 781434 441089